UnReap My Heart

KATE EVANGELISTA

OMNIFIC PUBLISHING
LOS ANGELES

Omnific Publishing
1901 Avenue of the Stars, 2nd floor
Los Angeles, CA 90067
www.omnificpublishing.com

First Omnific eBook edition, September 2013
First Omnific trade paperback edition, September 2013

Library of Congress Cataloguing-in-Publication Data

Evangelista, Kate.
  UnReap My Heart / Kate Evangelista – 1st ed.
  ISBN: 978-1-623420-49-9
  1. Love — Fantasy. 2. Paranormal — Fiction.
  3. Young Adult — Fiction. 4. Romance — Fiction. I. Title

10 9 8 7 6 5 4 3 2 1

Cover Art by Liliana Sanches
Cover Design by Micha Stone and Amy Brokaw
Interior Book Design by Coreen Montagna

Printed in the United States of America

To Dom,
my co-pilot, big little bro.
Everyone deserves a second chance.

Chapter 1

WTF

Damn, it's good to be back.

Balthazar took a breath of the dank and stagnant air. In the Underverse, the place parallel to the human world where all good things came to die, the air could never be considered fresh. Anyway, fresh always meant something other than air. Bad things.

One side of Balthazar's lips pulled up. *Yup, good to be back.*

Time to mess things up.

He'd been running nonstop for a day and a night. A barren wasteland separated his destination from the rest of the Underverse. As he neared the border of the Crossroads, the place where reaped souls were processed, he stopped, taking in the place his nemesis called home. A millennia ago, before his banishment to the Nethers—basically hell on steroids—he would have gone into the Crossroads guns a-blazin'.

He smiled at his empty hand.

Not guns.

A scythe.

Yes, he would have crashed through the entrance and marched his way into that tacky room D called an office and challenged Death for his seat at the Crossroads. He had dreamed of becoming the Master of Reapers every miserable day he spent in the Nethers. When not fighting to survive, Balthazar worked out the sequence of events.

First, he'd rip open the invisible barrier protecting the Crossroads using the Keeper's Key—he had thought its existence a myth until an enterprising demon gave him the deets to its location. It was a total bitch to retrieve. Balthazar had to fight through a horde of soul-sucking Wraiths. Nasty things, Wraiths, with their dot-sized ruby eyes, skeletal arms and clawed fingers, tattered black robes, and—the worst part—their wrinkled faces and rows of serrated teeth. One bite burned like a thousand needles injecting acid into the skin. Imagine having twenty of them chomping down on you. Not exactly a day at the spa.

The soul-sucking had actually been the least of his worries when he'd gone up against the horde. Wraiths liked to torture their food first. To keep them alive as long as possible. Not that Balthazar had much of a soul to give. He just hadn't wanted to stick around so the Wraiths could find that out about him. He winced at the memory. His left shoulder still ached some nights from a particularly nasty bite. Never again would he let his guard down against the creatures.

But totally worth it.

He returned to his to-do list as he ran the last few miles to the border of the Crossroads. He imagined releasing his scythe and fighting his way to D. He didn't care if he had to go through Tomas, D's right hand and the Reaper of California. Balthazar could take him. He could take all of them in his sleep.

The only hard part in this fool's mission involved fighting D. He'd be a tricky opponent on good days and a deadly one on the worst. He hadn't held the title of Death for countless millennia for nothing. Balthazar grudgingly respected D for it.

Ah, to be the new Death. He could taste it on his tongue already. His scowl turned into a full-blown smile. In the barren land surrounding him, nothing stirred other than the dust kicked up by his feet. In the distance, a tall wall rose. Balthazar's skin prickled. The ominous electric charge emitted by the barrier protecting Death's home said he'd arrived at the border of the Crossroads.

He stopped running a couple of feet away from the invisible barrier and knocked. It rippled under his knuckles. He pulled on his fingerless gloves and grinned. He'd have control of the place by sunup. He felt it in his gut. Even that prick Nikolas would bow down before him.

Balthazar patted down his leather overcoat then reached into his countless pockets. Nothing felt like the Keeper's Key. Where had he put the damn thing? Eventually, the dull ache in his ankle reminded him. He cursed himself as all kinds of stupid for forgetting. He took a knee and reached into his boot. He'd stuffed the key in there in case he ran into trouble on the road. He pushed back to his feet and studied the tiny black skull missing its jaw. In its eye sockets gleamed with a pair of blood red diamonds.

"All that trouble for this ugly thing," he said and huffed a laugh.

Well, the key did have the power to open any door in existence, so of course it would be guarded within an inch of its life. And, yes, it lived. Balthazar felt its life force pulse against his fingertips. In the Underverse, powerful beings could infuse their life force into inanimate objects and bring them to life. Some used the objects for protection, like his scythe and Death's cloak, while others created artifacts like the key.

With his other hand, he summoned his scythe—a black staff, with an obsidian stud on one end and a gleaming black blade on the other. Simple. Black on black. Balthazar admired it like he would a lover. It was the only weapon he trusted with his life, and it had saved him enough times to merit that exception. On principle, Balthazar trusted no one, not even his mother—and she'd died long ago.

Shaking off memories of her, he affixed the skull to the base of his scythe's blade. Energy sparked at the first contact, almost causing Balthazar to drop the key. It hurt like a bad migraine. His whole arm went numb from the pain. Electric shocks danced over his skin. His silver hair stuck out in every direction. At one point, Balthazar thought he would have preferred being struck by lightning.

He bit down hard until his jaw locked and tried again. The resulting electric shock rippled out of him like a bomb detonating. The burn began to stretch all the way to his legs, the numbness spreading fast, but he didn't stop. He pushed the key into his scythe until it was embedded halfway.

Once the key was attached, he leaned on his scythe's staff for support. Breathing hard, he healed himself with every inhalation. He cursed the demon seven ways till Sunday for not telling him about the effects of melding the key with the scythe. He needed all the strength he could spare for the fight of his life. A small voice in his head begged him to rest before entering the Crossroads.

Balthazar pushed away his annoying conscience. He never listened to it. Why it bothered to keep warning him against anything escaped his understanding. He shook away the last of the excess energy zinging through his body and twirled his scythe like a baton.

He touched the tip of the blade against the barrier. It tore through it like gel. Laughing like a maniac, he created a rip big enough to pass through. The key worked. Barely surviving the great Wraith massacre had actually paid off.

"Oh, D!" he called when he stepped into the Crossroads. "I'm home."

Not waiting for a response, Balthazar took off into a flat out run, balancing his scythe behind his back with both hands. He couldn't wipe away the smile on his face no matter how hard he tried. Today he would become all powerful. A smile wouldn't hurt. Sure it made him look like a crazed psychopath—and maybe he'd become one in many ways—but he didn't care. He reserved the right to be the bad guy in this story.

The high walls of the sprawling compound grew taller the closer he got to it. He didn't slow down. His eyes darted along the perimeter. No sentries. The clenched fist of suspicion in his gut almost stopped his progress. There should have been shadow guards posted along the walkway.

Balthazar sprinted up the wall, his back parallel to the ground. At the top he stared down at the compound. The seven buildings within swarmed with movement. Instead of the usual calm and order, the Reapers' minions—in all shapes and sizes, some humanoid, some creatures made to scare children at night—ran in all directions around the two-story main brick building at the center. The shadow guards scrambled in the yard beside the barracks like they'd been given conflicting orders. There was not a Reaper in sight near the processing warehouse at the back. And the souls. Where had they gone? The four buildings that usually housed them looked dark and empty.

Interesting.

Balthazar planted his scythe beside him and crossed his arms, trying to make sense of the chaos. What could have disrupted the order of the Crossroads? D maintained the place like a well-oiled machine. He liked everything in its place and on time. He stuck to a strict schedule. Judging from the chaos below, something must have broken his OCD tendencies.

Balthazar didn't like it one bit. On the day of his homecoming, he was standing at the wall trying to figure out answers to way too many questions instead of hacking his way to D.

Seeing no way around the situation, Balthazar set aside his siege plans, determined to get to the bottom of this mess. If he challenged D for his seat, he'd do it when it didn't seem so damn easy. He pulled his scythe off the walkway and jumped off the wall. He landed on light feet and made his way to the main building at the center of the compound. Its two-story brick was just an illusion, like many things in the Crossroads. Inside, a whole other dimension existed, easy to get lost in if you didn't know how to navigate the halls. D had designed the main building like a labyrinth to keep intruders confused. The bastard.

At the entrance, Balthazar froze. The souls of the unborn quivered in the hallway. Usually the whisps had tasks that kept them in constant motion. Right now, they just floated in the hall, shaking. Their whimpering grated in his ears. He picked up the closest whisp and stared it down until it stopped and stared back.

"What's going on here?"

Mistake. The question rattled the whisp even worse. Instead of just whimpering, it wailed. Balthazar rolled his eyes to the ceiling and flicked the thing away. It bounced off a wall, and when the whisp landed, it shook its head dazedly before it joined the chorus of whimpers again.

Unable to stand their pathetic cries, Balthazar shoved his way through the whisps. The ones that didn't get out of the way fast enough he trampled beneath his boots.

At the end of the first hallway, he paused to get his bearings. The hall branched out into eight corridors. As a security precaution, D changed the path to his office daily. As if the guy hadn't been busy enough. Balthazar lifted his free hand to his lips and blew on his palm. Smoke from his breath pointed him in the right direction. He took the seventh path to the left.

"Balty, that you?" someone with a thick Texan accent asked from behind him.

Balthazar winced at the affectation. He turned on his heel and faced the Reaper who was clad in jeans, cowboy boots, a button down shirt, and a ten gallon hat. "How many times do I have to tell you to stop calling me that, Tex? I'd hug you, but I'm not feeling it."

The Reaper of Texas stared at him like he couldn't believe he stood there. His next question pretty much confirmed it. "How'd you get in here?"

"Oh come on, Travis. Like it's that hard."

"But we're on lockdown. No one gets in or out."

He snorted. "Bullshit."

Lockdown—a precaution D had put up against something happening to him—kept Reapers outside the Crossroads safe from any danger inside. It also kept anything stupid enough to attack D trapped until the Reapers left in the Crossroads handled the situation. If anything, the lockdown had come too early because Balthazar hadn't done anything yet.

"Doesn't this look like a lockdown to you?" Travis gestured toward the space above his head.

"I actually don't know what a lockdown looks like. Do you?"

"I can't leave the Crossroads, nor can the other Reapers, so yeah, it's a lockdown."

"I got in."

"That's the billion soul question, now isn't it?"

Balthazar pointed at the skull on his scythe. "Keeper's Key."

Travis's eyebrows disappeared into his hat. "Thought that was a myth."

"Hiding in the Nethers all this time."

"Huh. Well, will you look at that."

"Don't sound so excited."

Travis stuffed his hands into the front pockets of his jeans and shrugged. "As much as I want to catch up with you, I have other things to worry about. We're not up to snuff right now. If you're not going to help, come back another day, Balty."

He disappeared.

Balthazar paid no attention to the urge to follow the Reaper of Texas to wherever he decided to go and beat the crap out of him. There'd be time for that later. First, he had to find out what the hell had happened at the Crossroads. He turned back around and continued toward D's office.

With every corner he rounded, the halls got darker and darker. He fished out a Zippo from the side pocket of his overcoat. He flicked the lid and used his thumbnail to light it. The flame danced before it settled into a steady burn. Balthazar followed the darkness until he reached D's doors and realized the shadows undulated like waves around him. D's cloak was leaking out of his office. Balthazar let go of the lighter, and it floated beside his head. He reached out and a section of the cloak hissed at him.

"Hey!" Balthazar barked. The cloak lived and acted like a guard dog. If he didn't establish his dominance over it, the bite would hurt more than necessary. He pushed out some of his aura like his own shadow stretched by the sun until it touched the cloak. It whined like a hurt puppy and pulled back. Balthazar reached out again and instead of being attacked, the cloak actually clung to his hand like it asked for a rub behind the ears. He smiled at the submission of the thing.

"Open the doors," he said in a soft, deadly voice. "Let me in."

The robe receded into the office. The natural light of the hallway returned, casting the polar bear skin rug and zebra skin upholstered couch in bright white. Balthazar squinted, but not from D's ugly taste in furniture. The couch and rug would be the first to go when he took his rightful place as the new Death.

All in good time. He grinned at the truth of his thought. Yes. He'd get his chance to change things as soon as he settled this nonsense with the lockdown.

The doors opened inward with a loud creak, like the hinges hadn't been oiled in years. Feeling good about himself, Balthazar walked into D's office then stopped in shock.

"Son of a b—"

Chapter 2

FYI

Arianne sat and traced the letters carved on the headstone. The marble played between cold and warm. Blades of grass tickled her calves.

"It's weird, really," Arianne said. "I wish I'd gone to talk to you sooner." She paused. "I wish things had turned out differently. Maybe it's my fault."

A breeze ruffled her hair, teasing strands out of the loose bun she'd twisted them into. She'd removed her wide-brimmed hat a while back and cradled it now on her lap.

"There are so many things I wish I hadn't done," she continued. "I think we all feel that way." A deep sigh came from a sad place in her heart.

A brown thrasher burst into song.

"I visited Ben before you." She chuckled. "I know, I know, I should have come to you first, but you're a talker. He, at least, just listens. I'm still mad at him. He's so selfish sometimes. But we'll figure things out. He loved you so much. I wish I could find someone who'd love me like that." Her shoulders dropped a degree. "I miss you both so much." A sniff turned into a whimper. Arianne fished out a tissue from her dress pocket and blew her nose. "I know I promised not to cry."

Arianne breathed in, tilting her head to receive a kiss from the sun she couldn't see. "Niko asked me out last night," she said. "I'm not sure what to say. Dad says we dated. Even if I can't see him, I get the feeling he stares at me a lot. And the way he follows me every-where…it freaks me out a little. I let him come to the house because he says he wants to help me." Arianne played with the wadded ball of tissue in her hands. "It's either talk to him or go to therapy. He's sweet and he really does help."

Blades of grass rubbed against each other in the breeze, creating a hushed *shhh*.

"I know." Arianne nodded once. "I should give him a chance."

Arianne gasped awake. What just happened? She'd been talking to Carrie's grave. She couldn't remember Niko. And she couldn't see. Because her sister had died and Niko had refused to reap Arianne's soul, Arianne made a deal with Death. For Niko's humanity, she would lose her sight and her memory of him.

A dream?

Whoa. Totally unreal. Freaky to the tenth power.

She sat up in an unfamiliar bed made of sun-bleached animal bones. At least she thought they were animal bones. The alternative only added to the freak factor of the room. The cushion felt feathery soft beneath her and the white sheets looked harmless enough. She pushed back messy strands of her red hair and stared at her hands. Death's melodic voice asking for her eyesight still rang in her ears. Since she could still clearly see, what could have happened?

Niko, the boy she loved, had a secret. Outside of high school he reaped souls as the Reaper of Georgia, and in order to save his life from Death's clutches, Arianne had been ready to sacrifice everything for him. Now she sat on a bed with white sheets in a room with a blood red rug on the floor, a painting on the wall she recognized as *The Scream* by Edvard Munch, and a gilt frame mirror. No chairs. No tables. No closets.

She untangled her limbs from the sheets and swung her legs over the side of the bed. The second her feet hit the cold floor, she squeaked and hopped to the rug. Its rough fiber tickled the pads of her feet. She looked down and curled her toes, then she picked at the black robe she still wore, the one that Tomas had given her to wear after he'd pulled her soul out of her body so she could enter the Crossroads. She turned in a tight circle and saw the red thread that connected her soul to her body. It meant her heart still kept her alive. She breathed a sigh of relief, but her relief didn't last long. If she could still see and she could still remember her feelings for Niko, where could he be?

Arianne scanned the walls for a door. The worry bubbling in her chest turned into a tight band of panic. She stepped off the warm rug, wincing at the coldness of the floor, and hurried to one wall. She ran her hand along it. No door. Then she stopped at the painting. Its screaming alien face stared back at her. The orange swirling sky reminded her of pulled taffy. Weird, but at the same time, comforting.

She turned on her heel and faced the mirror opposite the painting. Her eyes widened. She looked so pale in the room's light—wherever it came from. No lamps or ceiling lights. She took several tentative steps forward until she reached her reflection and touched the cold glass, meeting her reflection's fingertips. She looked thinner than she remembered. The beginnings of purple smudges stood out beneath her pale blue eyes. She touched her cheeks the way the alien in the painting did. She almost didn't recognize herself. Something had gone wrong. What had happened after she closed her eyes to wait for Death to do his thing?

"Ari," said a smooth older voice.

With a flood of relief rushing through her, Arianne turned to face Tomas, the Reaper of California—her guide into the Crossroads. He still wore the expensive three piece suit that, along with the salt and pepper color of his hair, made him look distinguished. Niko had told her once that Tomas raised him as a mentor would have, but Arianne had a feeling they meant more to each other than just that. That Niko thought of Tomas as a father figure. If he hadn't loved Niko like a son, the older Reaper wouldn't have bothered going through all the trouble of taking Arianne and her best friend, Ben, to the Crossroads so she could save him.

The thought of Ben brought an ache to Arianne's chest. Since she'd had a Death Certificate out on her, Ben had sacrificed himself so she could live. She still hadn't properly mourned his death. Too soon. From the serious expression on Tomas's face now, breaking down would be so uncool. She pushed aside the pain until she had some time alone to process everything and gave all her attention to the Reaper of California.

"How'd you get in here? No doors," she said. "Stick me in your freakiest room, why don't you?"

Tomas scratched along the line of his eyebrow. "There's a door. I'm just not showing it to you. I can't risk having you roam around the Crossroads unprotected. Especially now. And what's freaky about this room?"

"Duh!" Arianne turned in a small circle. Then she stopped, staring at her hands again. "Tomas, I feel…weird." She could feel her heartbeat. Her lungs expanded with every inhalation. Strange. She followed the lines on her palms before making a fist. Her hands felt the same. Almost normal, but still weird.

"Since your soul is still attached to your body, you can still feel things like your heartbeat. You're still alive, but since we left your body at Niko's house, you don't have to worry about eating or drinking."

Arianne met his gaze and dropped her hands to her sides. "Won't my body need to eat?"

"I left it in a state of suspended animation. Until you return, nothing will happen with your body. It's almost like you're in a coma."

Was that supposed to comfort her? The thin line his lips became worried Arianne. "What happened? I thought I made a bargain with Death?"

"Too many questions, each with answers more complicated than the next." Tomas stuffed his hands into the pockets of his pants. "I just came here to check on you. Now that you look fine—"

"You can't leave me here without telling me anything," Arianne interrupted. "Shouldn't I be back in my body by now?" She left out the blind part. She couldn't imagine how that would be—not being able to see. It scared her.

Tomas shook his head. "I don't know all the details yet, so it won't be easy to answer you."

"Try."

"Ari, something happened while my Master was preparing to take your sight and memories."

"What about Niko? Where is he?"

Tomas snapped his fingers, and they stood in a room with a glowing floor and rows of crystal coffins lining the entire space. Arianne blinked away the nausea of suddenly being transported somewhere else, then her eyes landed on the nearest coffin. Inside milky liquid floated the boy she'd risked everything for. She ran to the coffin and splayed her hands over the top. His black hair spread out like a wild halo, his handsome face young and peaceful. It looked like he simply slept. Arianne swallowed against the sudden prickly lump in her throat.

"Niko." His name seemed to echo inside the room.

Tomas stood beside her and placed his hand on top of the coffin too. "Death put him here so he could begin his change from Reaper to human before—"

The panic that had been slowly receding returned, constricting her attempts at breathing normally. "What happened, Tomas?"

"Death couldn't finish what he started with you and Niko because someone betrayed us. Someone hurt the Master enough to disrupt the order in the Crossroads. We can't leave and no one can come in unless we find who's done this."

Arianne shivered at the quiet calm in Tomas's voice. He sounded so serious. Niko got that way sometimes, too. She returned her gaze to his sleeping face.

"What will happen to him?"

"Niko can stay here for a while and no harm will come to him. But if we don't figure out how to save Death, I'm afraid of what will happen to Niko…to all of us."

Arianne's breath hitched. "You said 'we.'"

Tomas snapped his fingers again, and they were back in the room Arianne woke up in. Her heart dropped. She didn't want to leave Niko's side.

"Take me back there," she said.

Tomas shook his head. "And what will you do? Standing in that room won't help him, Ari. I know you're worried. I'm worried too. But if I don't restore order to the Crossroads, I'm afraid saving Niko will be the least of our concerns."

"So we find the traitor." It sounded simple enough.

Tomas stared at her, his gray eyes turning cold. She knew she sounded like a kid trying to talk like an adult. She swallowed down the urge to argue. The angrier she got the more Tomas would think of her as immature. Yes, he'd lived longer compared to a seventeen-year-old, but she'd been through more than anyone should have to go through. She'd given her dying sister a chance at life by donating a kidney and almost died on the operating table, so now she had the curse of seeing the souls of dead people. Then she'd learned the guy she'd had a crush on since she started high school reaped souls for a living. There was also the torture she'd suffered on a daily basis in school because of Darla's misguided feelings. She couldn't just sit around waiting for Tomas to solve the problems at the Crossroads. She had to do something.

Arianne breathed in and out slowly. "Tomas, you said we. I'm already here. You might as well let me help you."

The old Reaper sighed like he needed a good night's sleep. "I don't know if you *can* help. The lockdown doesn't allow us to do much."

"Lockdown?"

"The Crossroads is connected to Death. When Death is under attack, he shuts down everything."

"Oh. Like a base going into a lockdown." All those videogames Ben made her play helped her visualize it. And from the way Tomas nodded, she'd gotten it right.

"Since we can't leave and no one can come in, we're pretty much on our own. For what I need you to do, you need to get out of the Crossroads."

"That's it?" Arianne's voice climbed an octave. "You're giving up? There has to be another way."

Tomas froze. He closed his eyes and stood absolutely still. Arianne didn't dare breathe. She wanted to ask him what had happened, but from the way his eyebrows came together, he didn't need her disturbing him. Who could be powerful enough to attack Death? He had the power to freakin' end people's lives. If Death could get hurt, then the person doing the hurting must be really badass. Arianne didn't want to think who could possibly be more powerful than Death and how they could possibly stop him or her.

Tomas opened his eyes and breathed in deeply. "Someone's managed to get into the Crossroads."

Hope blossomed in her chest, easing her breathing. "That's a good thing, right?"

Tomas's frown deflated her hope almost immediately. "Not necessarily. Like I said, no one should be able to get in or out. Whoever caused the lockdown is powerful enough to incapacitate Death, but the lockdown is absolute. Not even the traitor can escape. So anyone who could enter the Crossroads now…"

"Is even scarier than the traitor," Arianne finished for him.

"There aren't many beings out there scarier than the Master," he agreed. "In fact, I can count them on one hand. But a majority wouldn't even bother to come to the Crossroads. I'm pretty sure the traitor is someone Death knows, because how else could he or she get close enough to hurt him without alarming the Master first?"

That made sense. All those crime procedurals she watched with her father were paying off. Death wouldn't have his guard up with someone he knew. Whoever caused the lockdown knew Death and vice versa.

"But wait," she said. "If Death was with us while I was bargaining with him, how could someone hurt him? I mean, we were the only ones in that torture room, right?"

Tomas nodded once. "Death can exist in many planes within the Crossroads. What you saw at the torture room was a reflection of his real self."

"So…"

"His real self is always in his office signing Death Certificates," Tomas said. "He has some omnipresence, but only within the Crossroads. He goes where he is needed without sacrificing time in the office. But sometimes he leaves the office to 'get some fresh air.' His words, not mine."

"He was attacked in his office?"

"I think so. That's why his reflection disappeared before he could finish your bargain."

Lucky. Arianne didn't want to seem grateful to whoever had hurt Death, but if that person had been a second later, she'd be blind right now. She remembered her dream and shuddered. Maybe if she helped save Death he would call it even, disregard the bargain, and still give Niko his humanity.

"Who do you think got into the Crossroads if we're in a lockdown?"

Tomas's face turned grim. "I'm going to hate to find out."

Chapter 3

DIY

Balthazar hurried to the center of the room where D sat slumped over in his skeleton chair. A thick pool of D's blood spread like an amoeba from the chair's legs outward. The rest of D's crap inside the office seemed untouched, which ruled out a struggle. D must have been in his chair when the large curved dagger sticking out from the center of his chest went in.

Balthazar touched the dagger's ornately carved handle. Explosive electricity shot through his body for the second time that day. Dammit! This one — more powerful than the first — threw him across the room. D's robes quivered and expanded like a peacock's tail behind its master. Balthazar slammed against the far wall outside D's office and bounced off, face-planting on the hallway floor. Losing his dignity hurt more than the actual impact. He should have checked before reaching for the dagger. D would have removed it himself if he could. Obviously, some sort of energy field protected it. Balthazar cursed himself for being stupid. His scythe — floating beside D's chair — laughed at him.

"Shut up," he said through his teeth as he picked himself up. He dusted off his overcoat and marched back into the office, moving along the perimeter of the blood pool to assess the situation. Normally, the sight of his nemesis in pain would have given Balthazar some pleasure. Since he had nothing to do with that pain, he felt cheated.

"Whoever did this had stones of steel," he said to his scythe. It finally stopped laughing and floated to Balthazar's side. "Oh, don't you make up with me now. I'm still pissed at you."

Like a cat, his scythe rubbed itself against Balthazar's side and purred. He rolled his eyes to the ceiling and opened his hand. The scythe came to his palm. Once he wrapped his fingers around its staff, it sighed in contentment and disappeared. He wouldn't admit it aloud, but he was powerless against the thing. During his banishment, his scythe became his only company and—dare he even think it—his friend. It kept watch while he slept. It helped him hunt. And most importantly, it had saved his life more times than he cared to count. He owed it. A lot.

Balthazar returned his attention to D. "Who did this to you, bro?"

As if in answer to his question, D groaned. Balthazar leaned closer so he could hear what D mumbled. At least he assumed actual words were coming from D's lips and not incoherent babble caused by the blood loss. Then, like a flash of lightning, D's hand shot up and pulled Balthazar by the hair until D forced him to kneel beside the chair.

"I usually ask for dinner first," Balthazar grumbled. He didn't struggle against D's hold, giving the other being a chance to lift his head and stare into his eyes. He fought against the initial pull of D's androgynous beauty. Lesser beings would be struck dumb by the sight of him, but Balthazar knew how to negate the force of D's attraction.

D's eyes, not one color specifically but more like a refraction of light, focused on Balthazar. Blood dripped from the corner of his lips to his chin when he smiled.

"What are you doing here, Balthazar?"

He sounded so feral. So unlike the genteel, almost urbane Death Balthazar knew. Only once before had D sounded like this. A thousand years ago, on the day Balthazar first challenged him for his seat. Before D banished him to the Nethers. Balthazar knew that day well. He'd replayed it in his head over and over since. D must be really hurting to revert to his more primal nature.

"Honey, I'm home." Balthazar puckered his lips as if to kiss D. He couldn't help but goad the Master of the Crossroads, since he was obviously in pain.

D pushed him away and grunted. "Now's not a good time, Balthazar."

Since Balthazar's head only tilted when D pushed at him, it spoke volumes of how weak D had become. His shallow breaths and ashen pallor proved Balthazar's suspicions. He wasn't weak from the blood loss. Bleeding out wouldn't kill Death. The dagger must have done more damage than seen on first inspection. Balthazar pushed up to his feet, ignoring the blood clinging to his pants, and crossed his arms. He watched D carefully.

"Are you going to tell me what happened here or should I pry it out of your head?" Balthazar asked like he didn't relish the task of rummaging through D's head, but actually, he'd have a lot of fun scrambling some stuff while there. He didn't have to wait long for D to respond.

"As you can see, I've been stabbed."

"Duh, Sherlock. How could I have missed that?" Balthazar grimaced. "Damn thing threw me across the room."

"Had to pick your ass up off the floor, didn't you?" D barked a laugh then groaned. He rested his hands on the armrests of his chair instead of grabbing for his chest, which Balthazar suspected he wanted to do. Since any contact with the dagger meant an electric shock that felt equivalent to sitting on a million electric chairs at full power, he didn't know what it would do if D attempted to remove it. Probably why he kept his hands out of the way.

"So, are you going to tell me who did this?"

The tic in D's jaw said more than a lie ever would. Balthazar had known the guy long enough to pick up on his nonverbal cues. He wouldn't budge on the information. But why?

"Okay, you're obviously in stubborn mode. I might as well pry it out of you." He closed his eyes and spread his consciousness to D's mind. Like the electric shock that threw him out of the room, an unseen force pushed his consciousness back into his own head. Not only that, it used enough force to actually bring Balthazar to his knees, clutching at his head.

Despite the pain, D chuckled.

"A little warning would have been nice," Balthazar grunted out. "You're such a prick sometimes. No, scratch that. You're a prick all the time." He got up and stared at D. He had the urge to hit something — mostly D — but he didn't know what that would do to him, so he settled on pumping his hands to dissipate some of his frustration.

"I would have told you not to enter my mind, but you always loved jumping the gun, didn't you, Balthazar?"

He hated the way D said his name. It always sounded like he had affection for Balthazar, like a disappointed father would for a child who disobeyed him. The pretentious tone always pissed him off. He suspected D did it for that reason alone.

"Can the 'tude, D. I came here to challenge you for your seat, but it looks like someone beat me to it. Now, tell me who this bastard is so I can hunt him down, make him pay for stealing my chance at kicking your ass, and restore some order here. The whisps get annoying when they don't have someone ordering them around. Plus, the shadow guards are getting antsy. You know how they are when you're not in control."

"I'm surprised you don't recognize the dagger." D pointed at the inch of the blade still sticking out of his chest.

Balthazar leaned in and studied the partial inscription. He didn't need to read the whole thing to know what it said. The script alone showed enough. He straightened and shook his head.

"You really know the best people to piss off, huh?"

D snorted. "Last I heard only you knew the location of this dagger. Did you get chatty during your banishment?"

Balthazar flipped D off. "Unlike some of your pansy ass Reapers, I can keep my trap shut. No matter how much I hate your guts and everything you stand for, I still honor my word. Something you obviously don't, judging from the dagger sticking out of your chest. I'm surprised whoever stabbed you didn't go in from behind. You really aren't going to tell me?"

D shook his head once. "I will take care of the traitor myself. I just need to get the dagger out first."

"And how do you propose to do that? That's Brianne's Bitterness, the only thing in this world that could hold a being as powerful as you down. Worse, whoever stabbed you is currently sucking out your power. Didn't I tell you pissing off my mother would bite you in the ass one day? I guess dying didn't stop her from getting her revenge."

D got really quiet all of a sudden. For a second Balthazar thought he'd died. Impossible since Death couldn't really *die*. Not in the traditional "dying" sense anyway. If someone wanted D dead, he or she had to challenge him for his seat. Once defeated, which would be a long shot, D would fade away into nothingness, thus transferring his power to the victor. Balthazar knew better than most that it took a lot to defeat Death, and Brianne's Bitterness, born from the soul of a really powerful Heavenly Host — in this case, his mother — slighted eons ago, didn't have that kind of power. Using his mother's dagger meant someone had cheated. The blade merely kept the stabbee in place for the stabber to siphon all the creature's energy. D wouldn't die from that. But Death not having any power meant he'd lose control of the Crossroads. If that happened, well…it would make the Nethers look like a theme park. Balthazar didn't even count that as the worst part.

"If you lose control, the chaos would spill into the human world and the rest of the Underverse," Balthazar said. "I'm pretty sure that's going to piss off a whole lot of powerful forces who could bring down a ton of hurt here."

"We can't allow that," D whispered so softly Balthazar had to remind himself he actually heard the words.

"*We?*" He tilted his head. "Where did that 'we' come from?"

D shot him a pointed glare. Balthazar had to admit, from D's seated position while bleeding out, the stare looked pretty intimidating. But not intimidating enough. His eyebrow twitched.

"You seriously think staring me to death will work? I'm not helping you."

"You said it yourself." D's breathing turned labored and really raspy, like he'd been smoking three packs a day for twenty years. "If you want to get a chance to challenge me for my seat, I need to get my house in order. For me to do that I need the dagger out and the traitor dealt with. You see, I would love to beat your ass into the ground again for your impertinence, but I can't exactly do that with this damn dagger in my chest."

Balthazar threw back his head and laughed. The sound bounced off the walls. Then he doubled over and hugged himself, the force of his laughter shaking his entire body. Once he managed to pull himself together, he breathed in deeply and wiped away a stray tear from the corner of his eye. He sighed, a huge smile on his face.

"Precious!" He slapped his thigh, another round of chuckles escaping. When he could speak again, he continued. "Are you seriously trying to use my hatred for you and my desire for your position to con me into helping you?"

D gave him a half grin. "Is it working?"

"Damn if it's not."

Balthazar slapped D on the shoulder. Before his hand could make contact, the invisible force threw him to the back of the room. He knocked D's desk over, spilling piles of Death Certificates everywhere. This time, it was D who laughed.

In the rain of parchment with the names of people supposed to die, Balthazar cursed like a sailor. He picked himself up off the ground, suppressing his groan by spitting out the nastiest words he could think of.

"Oh, that one's new," D said from his seat. "Where'd you pick up that particularly colorful description of someone's mother? It's really creative."

Balthazar snorted. "Demons know their stuff. Why do you think the possessed have the most colorful vocabulary?" The movie *The Exorcist* hadn't messed up that part. Demons, especially those trapped in the Nethers, had the foulest language in all the Underverse.

"I take it your stay in the Nethers did you some good?"

"If you think having to survive on a daily basis and having to kill my way through the nastiest things this world we live in could create as having done me some good, then yes. And to that I say, up yours."

"Put your finger down, Balthazar. There's no need to be vulgar with me."

He dropped his hand to his side and frowned. "Do you really believe pissing me off is in your best interest right now?"

"You're right," D said.

"What?" Balthazar cupped his ear and turned it toward D. "Can you say that again? I don't think I heard you properly."

"Unlike you—" D sighed "—I'm not afraid to admit when I'm wrong. You're right. I shouldn't antagonize you more than I already have. My apologies."

Damn if that didn't make Balthazar feel superior. Getting the tough guy to admit he'd been wrong felt better than slicing through a banshee just to get it to shut up. Then he asked the question that had popped up the second D asked for his help.

"What makes you think I'm your guy for this? I could just as easily stab you in the back. Well—" he pointed at the dagger "—not that you don't already know how that feels."

D snapped his fingers, and Balthazar's scythe manifested without Balthazar summoning it. Another thing he hated. Since he'd chosen a scythe, it meant D had some power over it. Balthazar had worked hard for centuries to wean his weapon from D's influence. It seemed he had more work to do. He slanted his gaze at the scythe and mouthed the word "traitor" at it. The thing quivered.

"You have the Keeper's Key."

"What about it?" He didn't like the turn this conversation was taking.

"You're the only one who can get in and out of the Crossroads right now."

"And?"

"You're taking Arianne with you," said someone from the entrance to D's office.

Chapter 4

OMG

The letters W-H-A-T and a giant question mark danced around in Arianne's head. What Tomas said distracted her enough from the grisly scene in Death's office, forcing her to look up at the old Reaper.

"What?" It had to be asked. The word already floated around anyway. "Hold on a sec. What do you mean I'm going with him?" She pointed at the guy standing beside a clearly bleeding-out Death. Like way too much to be a good thing.

Tomas glanced down at Arianne and gave her a smile that said *sorry* and *please* at the same time. "Remember when I said we'll need your help? Now's that time."

His words flew over Arianne's head. She stood there slack-jawed like she'd been smacked. Sure she'd help out, but to have them pass her off to…to…she looked back at the guy dressed in all black.

Besides his floor-length coat and boots, buckles covered almost every part of him over his leather pants and shirt, jingling when he crossed his arms. Her wondering gaze landed on his face. He looked too young to have that silver hair, and in the right light or when he titled his head like he did just that second, it looked like the strands had white highlights. Not possible. But since she found herself in a place called the Crossroads where they processed the souls of the dead, nothing seemed all that impossible. Weird, for sure, but not impossible.

His hair fell like needles over his forehead, stopping just above his eyes. And what awesome eyes they were — all black with a white center. They reminded her of a bull's eye but without the red in the middle. Those eyes looked at her now, and she shivered. He seemed to see straight into the place where she hid all her secrets.

He had a face made for magazine covers. Could someone say *GQ* model? That razor sharp jaw and those angular features caught the light prefectly. If she'd had a camera she wouldn't mind snapping a few pictures. And those lips…she stopped. She didn't know him, and something told her she *shouldn't* get to know him.

She reminded herself to focus on Niko. He slept in that coffin, and if she didn't say yes to whatever Tomas and Death had planned, God only knew what would happen to him. Tomas had said Niko couldn't stay in the coffin for long. If she resisted or wasted more time, she had no idea how it would affect him. She wanted him back alive and healthy, with all his parts intact. She hadn't come to the Crossroads to save him only to lose him in the end because she didn't help out. She could do this. She repeated the words in her head like a mantra. She couldn't consider the alternative if she failed.

She tore her gaze from the creepy, staring *GQ*-model guy and settled it on Death, finally seeing what kept him in the chair.

"Why doesn't anyone just remove the knife?" Her voice climbed an octave when she said knife. Even if she'd made up her mind to help, it didn't mean she was a hundred percent okay with it.

The guy beside Death snorted. "You'd think we would have thought to do that by now."

She didn't like his tone, which translated to her not liking him at all. Yes, that made things *so* much easier.

"Balthazar," Tomas said. He made the guy's name sound like an exasperated sigh. "I should have known you would be the one who could break into a lockdown."

"I'll take that as a compliment, old man." Balthazar grinned.

Arianne crossed her arms and scowled. She decided she didn't like that grin either. Did they really expect her to go anywhere with this guy? Oh, she could already feel the aggravation he'd cause her. Arrogant types like him were hell to work with.

"He found the Keeper's Key." Death finally spoke, but his voice sounded really weak.

For the first time since she'd met him—even though he'd just tortured Niko into returning to his post as Reaper of Georgia—Arianne felt sorry for Death. Even if he wanted to take away her eyesight and memories of Niko in exchange for Niko's humanity, no one deserved to be stabbed in the chest. She winced. The knife must be really hurting him for him to sound like he stood outside Death's door. Ironic, really. Maybe, in the back of her mind somewhere, she did think he deserved it. A little.

Tomas's voice pulled her back into the conversation. "Impressive. Took him long enough."

"Whoa! Back that truck up." Balthazar raised both his hands. His face contorted in confusion. "This has to be some kind of massive joke. Are you saying you sent me to that godforsaken hellhole just so I could come back with the damn key?"

His voice ended in a snarl, and Arianne backed up a step and put Tomas between herself and the increasingly pissed off guy. Or was he some sort of creature? Maybe one of the Reapers? Whatever. She couldn't be sure until the people in the room started explaining.

"Shouldn't we start figuring out what we need to do next?" she said from behind Tomas.

"Shut up, little girl!"

Balthazar's acidic tone forced her out of hiding. "Excuse me? What did you just call me?"

Mischief glinted in Balthazar's eyes. "Trust me, that's the tamest thing I'll call you. But don't tempt me."

Arianne returned behind Tomas's protection. "Jerk."

A corner of Tomas's lips quirked up. "Balthazar has that effect on people. Don't mind him, Arianne."

Balthazar cleared his throat. "Don't talk about me like I'm not here, old man."

"Yes, Balthazar," Tomas said like the conversation was over. "I think you're forgetting that our Master—"

"He's not *my* master," Balthazar barked.

"—has foresight," Tomas continued like Balthazar hadn't interrupted him, all the while still turning to face Arianne. "He doesn't do anything without reason. You should know that more than anyone in this room."

"I'd like for us to keep chatting," Death said, "but as you can see, I am more than incapacitated. I would like to get this dagger out as soon as possible. There's only so much time left and I don't think I can hold on for long."

Stepping out of Tomas's protective space, Arianne moved directly in front of Death just outside the pool his blood made. Barefooted or not, she wouldn't be caught dead standing in blood. Gross. She shook away the need to shiver and focused on Death.

"Who did this to you?" she asked.

"Good luck getting that out of him," Balthazar answered.

She scowled at him. "I wasn't asking you."

Balthazar's eyebrows disappeared into the fringe of his hair. Point to her, but she didn't let herself get smug. She faced Death again and waited.

The beautifully handsome man sitting surrounded by a pool of his blood heaved a weighty sigh. "Niko will not last long if I don't get out of here."

Her breath caught in her chest.

"Playing dirty already, D?"

"Balthazar," Tomas warned. "Shut your mouth before I shut it for you."

Arianne couldn't be sure, but in her periphery it looked like the guy wearing way too many buckles gave the Reaper of California the finger. Far too much testosterone in one room — it made her head spin. Something told her punches would fly if she didn't get this over with, and she was not getting in the middle of that. Not when Death seemed like he was bleeding to death. She hated the pun, but she couldn't think of anything better.

To hurry things along, she asked, "How can I help?"

"You must find the Redeemer."

Balthazar's hiss caused her insides to quiver. She looked at him, but his face had gone completely blank. She glanced over her shoulder at Tomas, but his expression had turned unreadable too.

"You know what I hate most?" she said to no one in particular. "Secrets. Way too many and it just gets really hard to find the truth under all the bullcrap."

"It's bullshit, not bullcrap. If you're going to curse, you might as well say it right."

"Shut up, Balthazar," Tomas spat.

"I'm telling you what you need to know and nothing more," Death said, some strength returning to his voice. Arianne suspected he faked it.

"Okay, so why me?"

Balthazar, ignoring Tomas's order, answered. "Only a being still tethered to the human world can identify the Redeemer. And from the looks of that red thread, you're human. I don't even want to know why you're here."

Arianne raised an eyebrow at him before she looked back at Death. "What do we do when we find the Redeemer?"

"The Redeemer is the only one capable of pulling out the dagger," Tomas said grimly from behind her.

"Okay." She ignored the fact that too many people were answering her questions. So long as their answers helped her understand the situation and what they needed from her, she didn't care where they came from. "Where do we find the Redeemer?"

"The Voyeur knows." Death coughed and more blood spattered out of his mouth.

Arianne reached out to wipe the blood away, but a hand closed around her wrist. She looked up at Balthazar. His face up close looked even more handsome than from afar. He frowned down at her and shook his head.

"Learned the hard way not to touch him," he said in a dangerously quiet voice, like he mocked her, like she should have known better.

She bit down on her tongue. The pain broke the spell cast by staring at him. She yanked back, but she had a feeling he let her go because he wanted to. Her wrist still felt his fingers circling it. Not bruising, but strong enough that her puny yank wouldn't have dislodged the hold. His level stare said as much.

She turned on her heel and faced Tomas. "Are you sure I can do this?"

An expression really close to uncertainty crossed Tomas's face before he hid it beneath a blink. Then he nodded once. "You're the only one who can."

"Balthazar knows where to find the Voyeur," Death said from behind her, his breathing ragged like his lungs struggled to take in air. She had to force herself not to cover her ears.

"I don't remember saying yes to baby-sitting, D." Balthazar stepped back and crossed his arms. "Maybe I'll let you get sucked dry instead."

In a flash, Tomas had Balthazar by the scruff of his jacket and pinned against the wall. Arianne followed them with her gaze. She didn't actually see Tomas move from where he stood, just that he already had Balthazar pinned.

"Tomas," Death said. Although the warning sounded weak, it still brought goose bumps to Arianne's arms.

"I wouldn't do that if I were you, old man." Balthazar grinned down at Tomas. "I might just enjoy mopping the floor with you."

Arianne's gut told her Balthazar shouldn't be goading the Reaper of California. Tomas might have looked all refined, but something about the way he stood now, pinning someone as tall as Balthazar against the wall, said he could take care of business if he needed to.

Arianne understood then. In that room she might be the most insignificant. Yes, they needed her to find this Redeemer, but in terms of being able to protect herself, she played in the little leagues. Maybe even on the special team only.

As much as admitting she needed Balthazar's help seemed like the worst thing she could do, she forced herself to speak. "Tomas, please, we're wasting time. Tell me what I need to do and how I'm supposed to do it, and I'll go with Balthazar. The sooner I go, the sooner I can get Niko out of that coffin."

As if he had to force himself, Tomas let go of Balthazar and backed away slowly.

Balthazar adjusted his coat and pulled on his fingerless gloves. Then he grinned at her. "You don't know what you're saying, little girl."

Chapter 5

SOL

"I will help you," she said, sky-blue eyes shining with fear and determination, "but on two conditions." She didn't shrink away from D's deadly grin. Balthazar knew that grin well, having been on the pain-filled receiving end of it.

"I see you've learned something from our last encounter," D murmured. He grew weaker by the minute.

Like a shark, Balthazar scented blood in the water. Well, more like the life force he fed on. D's smelled oh so powerful. He suppressed his instinct to circle and hunt only because the conversation going on between a puny human and the Master of the Crossroads intrigued him. Shit. The girl had backbone.

He watched them both closely from his corner of D's office—soon to be his office. He flicked his gaze at Tomas. Damn the old codger for thinking he could threaten him. He'd get the Reaper of California for that when he took his rightful place as the new Death. Balthazar relished the thought for a second before he returned his attention to the dueling fools in front of him.

"Name your conditions," D said.

Arianne took a deep breath and squared her shoulders. She looked so tiny dressed in that ridiculous black robe. As a human in the Crossroads, she wore nothing underneath. Balthazar pushed the thoughts of her nakedness away with little interest. Teenage girls weren't his drink of choice. He'd scare her more than attract her, so why even try? But when she spoke, he listened.

"When I find this Redeemer and bring whoever it is here to pull that dagger out, I want you to give Niko his humanity without taking my eyesight or my memories. Our bargain before is erased."

Balthazar tightened his lips to suppress a grin. He liked her use of "when." She had guts, this one. Normally, humans hedged their bets by using the word "if." Less commitment that way. Arianne didn't know putting something into words gave it power. The fact that she said "when" pushed the Underverse to align everything needed for her to accomplish her goal. From experience though, just because the Underverse aligned didn't mean the job got any easier. In fact, because Arianne gave voice to the thought, things got more complicated for Balthazar. Now he had to say yes to D's request for help.

All amusement gone, a string of nasty, unvoiced curses spread through him like a rash. He should have stopped the girl from voicing her intentions. But, since everyone seemed to be committing acts of stupidity today, one more wouldn't matter much.

His ears burned at the mention of Niko's name. Could she mean that prick Nikolas? Only one Reaper went by the name Niko, so Balthazar's assumption couldn't be wrong. Arianne wanted his humanity. Would she still if she found out the truth about the Reaper of Georgia? Balthazar practically licked his chops. He'd have a field day with the little chit.

His day had just gotten more interesting. A plan swirled to life in his head. If he had to baby-sit the girl, he'd gain something out of it in the end. Nothing was free in the Underverse after all.

"For your help"—D's breath had an ugly rasp to it now, like he was preparing to hack up a lung—"I will negate our previous bargain and give you what you desire."

"Niko's humanity," she said. "Say it."

Balthazar's eyebrows went up. The chit had smarts. Somehow she knew she needed the word of Death for the deal to remain valid. In the Crossroads, D's word became law, which was one reason why Balthazar wanted the seat in the first place. After he had the minions clean away all the blood, of course.

"Once you return with the Redeemer and this dagger is pulled from my chest, I will give Nikolas his humanity and return you both to the human world unharmed. How is that?"

Arianne stayed silent for a long minute. On her face Balthazar read the way she digested the words. Maybe moving through the Underverse with her wouldn't be as difficult as he previously thought. At least she wouldn't be stupid and get them killed. Maybe. He still wouldn't bet on her. Being human had its disadvantages where they were going.

When she finally agreed to D's offer, the fear had disappeared and only determination remained.

"So," D addressed Balthazar, "will you escort her through the Underverse, using all the resources at your disposal to protect her, until she returns with the Redeemer?"

Balthazar grinned. "If she gets to make a bargain with you, so will I. My services aren't free, D, you know that."

For the first time, D's shoulders slumped. This little impromptu meeting was taking its toll on him, more than Balthazar first suspected. He'd make it quick. He may be a black-hearted jackass a majority of the time, but he did have a sense of mercy—a trait he'd gotten from his mother. The jury was still out on whether he thought it useful or not.

"For escorting the girl, I ask that, once you are back to your fighting weight and have put all your affairs in order, you will agree to my challenging you for your seat," Balthazar said formally. "And everything that results from the challenge. No counter offers, D. This is my price."

In the Underverse, they didn't need paper for a contract. So long as you knew how to word things properly, anything spoken became binding.

D nodded. "What about for protecting Arianne?"

"Ah, that…" Balthazar studied the girl. She didn't flinch under his scrutiny. Another point to her bravery. Foolish since she should be afraid of him. "For my protection and the use of all my resources in the search of the Redeemer, my bargain is with the girl."

"Arianne," she said. "My name's Arianne."

"All right." Balthazar raised an eyebrow at her. "My bargain is with you, Arianne, if you want my protection and help."

Arianne looked to D then to Tomas, who said, "He is the only one who can get through the lockdown, Ari. We're all tied here until we remove the dagger. I have to maintain order while the Master is incapacitated."

"No one else can come with me?"

Balthazar almost laughed at the hope in her voice. None of the Reapers would be powerful enough to face anything beyond the

Crossroads. In the Underverse only he had the kind of strength she'd need to stay alive. D knew this, as did Tomas, who shook his head at her.

Arianne grew quiet again. A knot formed on her brow. She seemed to be considering all her options. Balthazar was sure she was thinking about what she was getting herself into. She had just negated her bargain with D and now she was about to get into another one with someone she'd just met. The girl couldn't catch a break today. Balthazar thought of giving her some slack. Briefly. Damn his sense of mercy. He wouldn't budge for her knowing what lay ahead—facing the Voyeur would already be deadly enough, not to mention the journey to get to her domain.

Arianne swallowed and leveled an unyielding stare at him.

For a human, she had a pretty good stare.

"What do you want?" she said with only a slight quiver in her voice.

He reached out and took a lock of her hair between his fingers. She didn't flinch or pull away. Tomas growled, but Balthazar ignored the old Reaper. There was nothing he could do if he wanted his Master free of Brianne's Bitterness.

Balthazar twirled the red lock between his fingers and said, "For my protection and help, I ask for a year out of your life."

She gasped. Yes, she should be afraid now. He wouldn't have it any other way because he got a kick out of people being afraid of him. Plus, her fear would keep her safe from what they were to face out there. He waited.

"Balthazar, you ask a steep price," D said.

He looked at the being he once served without letting go of Arianne's hair and bared his teeth. "I only ask one year. She looks young and healthy. One year means nothing in the span of her human lifetime. Most take a year for granted. It's a good bargain for bringing her back alive."

"And in one piece?" she asked, bringing his attention back to her.

He shook his head. "That is all up to you, little girl. I can keep you safe, but I cannot account for acts of stupidity. If you don't listen to me, for instance."

"I'll listen."

"I admire your indignation, but you'll have to prove your word." He pulled on the lock of hair. "And, just so you know, I trust no one."

She didn't even yelp at the tug. He'd put enough force into it to let her know he was serious. She merely stared up at him with those blue eyes, the black dot at the center dilating slightly.

"Arianne," D said. She turned to him. "I wish I could tell you not to take Balthazar's bargain. I know I am asking much from you, but he is right. For his protection and resources, it is a bargain you must make. I cannot pay it for you."

She returned her intelligent eyes to Balthazar and held his gaze without blinking. She licked her lips then swallowed. Only a quick dart of the tip of her tongue wet her bottom lip, but Balthazar caught it without completely breaking eye contact. He knew her response even before she voiced it.

"A year of my life." She shrugged. "The price for keeping me safe and helping me find the Redeemer?"

Balthazar nodded once.

"All right."

"Say it," he said the same way she had with D.

Again her tongue darted across her lower lip. She swiped away the sweat dotting her upper lip before she said, "For your protection and help in finding the Redeemer, I give you a year of my life."

"Done!"

The word echoed around the room. A sense of finality settled on everyone's shoulders. Balthazar dropped his hold on Arianne's hair and shifted his gaze to Tomas.

"We should get going. I want to take advantage of the few hours in the day I have left to get as far away from here as possible."

Arianne looked at her robes. "Can I change my clothes first? I don't exactly want to run around bare-assed and with no shoes."

For the second time that day, Balthazar laughed. Tomas led her out of D's office without a word and he followed. But before he reached the double doors, he looked back.

"Are you sure about this?" he asked D.

D breathed in until his shoulders stopped drooping. He sat back as if he didn't have a dagger sticking out of his chest and said, "Is it the best situation? No. But it's all I've got to work with."

"Death painted into a corner."

"Protect that girl, Balthazar. She is an innocent in all of this."

"Why does she want Nikolas to gain his humanity?"

"She believes they are in love."

The absurdity of D's words hit Balthazar square in the gut. He would have doubled over if he didn't find the reason pathetic. Thankfully, he managed to keep the laughter in his head.

"Love? Nikolas?"

D nodded then turned thoughtful. "You know that he forced the Fade?"

Yet another ludicrous idea. "Nikolas? Reaper of Georgia allowing the Fade? I've been gone too long. I really should take your place, D. You're losing your edge. A thousand years ago you wouldn't have allowed such a thing."

"Maybe I am getting too old for this."

From the lack of wrinkles on D's face, Balthazar doubted that. But he did understand the impulse. Sometimes the job could wear on you. It was a testament to D's increasing weakness that he'd admit to Balthazar what sounded like a desire for replacement.

"You'll regret you said that to me, D," Balthazar said before he turned on his heel and followed after Tomas and Arianne. The double doors closed behind him and the darkness returned. The cloak would protect its master. But for how long?

Chapter 6

POV

In the room with no furniture other than the bed, mirror, and painting, Tomas snapped his fingers and several tables appeared. A table with clothes. A table with supplies. And a table with weapons.

Arianne moved toward the clothes first and picked out soft leather pants. Her dad told her once that leather didn't need washing as much as jeans did. Plus she'd always wanted to get a pair but they stayed out of the price range of her allowance. Now seemed like as good a time as any. Then the voice of her mother in her head said, *Light layers. You never know how cold or how hot it will be where you're going.* It was a memory from a vacation they took before her sister, Carrie, got really sick and had to stay at the hospital twenty-four seven. Arianne's heart twisted. How long had she been gone? It felt like weeks, and she missed her parents something fierce.

She picked out several tops and a badass looking jacket. "Aren't my parents going to start looking for—" She stopped herself. The word "us" almost came out. That word led to thoughts about Ben. When she could finally go back to her world, her best friend wouldn't be there with her. She pushed away the oncoming grief. She'd mourn him, she promised herself, but not now. "—me."

Arianne looked up at Tomas just in time to see him shake his head. "Time moves differently here. You don't have to worry about that."

"What about my body?"

"Niko's Caretaker will watch over it."

Arianne briefly imagined the crotchety ghost butler hovering over her still form. She liked Sickleton. When Niko had faded before her eyes, it was Sickleton who'd helped her bring him to the basement filled with souls. She shuddered at the memory of almost losing Niko. Arianne refocused half her attention back on Tomas. No point in dwelling on what had already come to pass.

From the set of his jaw and the tightness of the muscles in his neck, Arianne suspected Tomas was holding something back. Well, he'd either tell her or she'd have to live with not knowing. The one thing he got right? She had other things to worry about. She channeled her inner Girl Scout and stuffed a pair of jeans into a backpack along with several shirts and sweaters. A couple of pairs of underwear followed. She may not be in her actual body, but she wouldn't allow herself to travel feeling all icky. If she could—or if Balthazar would let her—she'd wash her underwear, if not her clothes.

"What can you tell me about the Redeemer?" she asked. "How will I know when I've found him or her?" She had a hard time thinking of the Redeemer as an it.

"How did you know how to bargain with the Master like that?" Tomas asked back.

Arianne paused before she reached for a pair of socks. She answered Tomas's question without looking back at him.

"There was a whole summer when Ben and I watched nothing but *Dealing with the Devil* reruns." Her chest ached at saying Ben's name. It still didn't feel like he was gone, like he was just wandering around somewhere doing something and she'd see him at the bus stop in the morning.

Tomas chuckled, relaxing a little for the first time since they entered the room. "I used to watch that show. They got so many things wrong, but the whole being specific part was right."

She shrugged. "I figured if I wanted something out of Death, I should be as specific as possible. Hell, if it weren't for being able to see the dead for years, I'd be freaking out right now. But after meeting Niko"—a twist of worry hit her chest this time instead of an ache—"there's nothing I wouldn't believe."

"Vampires, werewolves, fairies. Those aren't true."

"Aw man! I was hoping those were real too." She shook her head and smiled.

"Well…the romantic ones that sparkle in the sun aren't. But yes, there are what you might call vampires in the Underverse." Tomas smiled back briefly before his face turned serious. "You shouldn't have given Balthazar what he wanted."

Arianne zipped up the backpack and moved to the weapons table. She picked up a knife which was in a sheath with a strap. She couldn't be a hundred percent sure why she picked it out from the rest. The strap seemed too small for her waist. She glanced at her thigh. Ah. But did she really need a knife? The thought of what she'd given Balthazar for her protection made her knees go weak.

"Just what does giving him a year of my life mean?"

"With Balthazar, it can mean anything."

Arianne swallowed. "Can you give me an idea here?"

Tomas rolled his eyes to the ceiling and sighed. "Best case scenario, he'll take a year at the end of your life."

"Like if I'm supposed to die at eighty, he'll kill me at seventy-nine."

"Something like that."

"Doesn't seem so bad."

"But he can also keep you for a year, make you his slave."

Her heart jumped to her throat and beat there. "He can't really do that, can he?"

"Balthazar isn't exactly a humanitarian. Like the Master, he always does things for a reason. The reason why he's here is because he wants to challenge Death for his seat."

"He can do that?"

Tomas's frown spread all over his face. "The position of Death is a very powerful one. Imagine having power over all living things. It's an intoxicating position and many covet it. The Master has held the post longer than anyone else. And just as Lucifer challenged God for his seat in heaven, so did Balthazar challenge Death. The first time he did, he lost and was banished to the Nethers the way Lucifer was banished to Hell. But unlike Lucifer, who is content to rule over his kingdom of fire, Balthazar is single-minded. He wants Death's seat and he'll do anything to get it."

Now Arianne frowned. "Then why didn't he take it now? I mean, Death's all weak. Isn't it an easy win?"

"You should know this about Balthazar: he has a sense of honor and he knows mercy. He thinks of this as a flaw, but I think it's his redeeming quality. But don't let that fool you. He's the most dangerous thing you will face out there." Tomas tilted his chin toward an unseen distance. Arianne assumed he referred to whatever lay beyond the Crossroads.

"You know what they say, keep your enemies closer," she joked, but Tomas didn't laugh. His expression didn't even change.

"He's dangerous, Arianne."

"Okay, I get it."

"I don't think you do." Tomas pointed at the knife. "Take that with you. It's made of a special material that can kill Balthazar."

Arianne stared at the knife still in her hand.

"That knife chooses its owner. You may think you picked it out, but in reality—"

"It picked me," Arianne finished for him. And she felt it, too. Something about holding the knife told her it wouldn't leave her side, like it owned her as much as she owned it. Cool. "But I don't know how to use a knife against someone."

"The pointy end goes into the bad guy."

She tilted her head and pursed her lips. "I know that. But if Balthazar is as dangerous as you think, then he'll see me trying to stab him a mile away. I don't think I could do it."

Truth: she didn't know if she could bring herself to hurt someone else, no matter how bad they seemed. To her, Balthazar seemed more arrogant and annoying than dangerous. Sure, he'd scared her when he asked for a year of her life, but she figured he could have asked for something much worse. Losing all her memories of Niko, for example. And the whole losing her eyesight thing. A year didn't seem so bad in comparison.

"The knife is just for added protection." Tomas walked to her side and tapped the knife. "Ultimately, I believe Balthazar will uphold his bargain and keep you safe to the best of his abilities. He's dangerous, yes, but I think that works in your favor. He'll do anything to keep you safe." Then he looked Arianne in the eye. "But in case you need to protect yourself, the knife will just as easily kill other beings that stand in your way. There are few beings that it can't kill, and I don't think you will encounter those things on this journey."

"Why don't I find that comforting?"

Tomas put his hand on her shoulder and gave her a reassuring squeeze. "Arianne, you crossed into this world to save Niko. For *love*. Take strength in that. If it's for love, there's nothing much you can't do."

She remembered the time when Niko first became her Chemistry lab partner. Before that, he'd never even known she existed. She'd been equally nervous and excited, and had ended up dripping hydrochloric acid on her hand. What a total spaz she'd been, and in some ways, she still did spazzy things. But she couldn't deny what Tomas said. She'd walk through fire for Niko. They'd been through so much together already, and she wasn't about to throw all of that away just because she didn't know what would happen next.

And that scared her witless.

"I can do this," she said, more for herself than for Tomas's benefit.

He nodded then scanned the tables. "Is there anything else you might need that isn't here?"

"A picture of the Redeemer?"

"Alas, that I cannot give you. Redeemers are rare and difficult to find. But if there is someone who could find one it will be you."

"Because I'm human."

He followed the red thread coming from Arianne. "And because you're still tethered to the human world." He touched his fingertip to the center of her chest. "Trust in what your heart says. You'll know who the Redeemer is when the time comes."

Her gaze dropped until it landed on the red thread. "What about the thread? I feel like I need to protect it or something."

"Right now only someone from the Crossroads can see it, but that doesn't mean it isn't vulnerable. So, yes, you do need to be careful."

Then Arianne asked the question she'd been afraid to ask. "What happens when it breaks? Do I…" She couldn't finish the sentence. Ben had sacrificed himself so she could live. She didn't want his sacrifice to become useless by dying.

Tomas shook his head, suddenly even more serious than when they first returned to the room. "Worse."

"Define worse."

"Arianne, if the line is cut, you will eventually become a Wraith."

"Wraith?" The term made her skin cold all of a sudden.

"It's a creature who lives on the souls of others because it doesn't have one of its own anymore."

"So I die." She spat it out as fast as she could.

"Your body in the human world will slowly die, yes. But you will forever be trapped in the Nethers."

Another term she didn't know. "The Nethers."

"A place you don't ever want to go," Balthazar answered from the door. "What's taking so long? You don't need makeup where we're going."

Arianne took a deep breath. "I'll be right there. Just need to change."

Balthazar gave her one of those pointed looks she'd been getting since they met in Death's office. She started to think Balthazar looked at everyone like that.

He blinked. "Five minutes and then I'm leaving without you."

"You can't leave without me. What's the point?"

He seemed to think about it. "Then I'll come in here and drag you out with me in whatever state of dress you're in at that moment." Then he grinned before exiting the room.

Tomas twisted Arianne around so she looked up at him. "If your line is cut, even if you haven't found the Redeemer, you have to come back here as soon as you can," he said urgently. "We can fix it. Promise me."

"You can fix it?" Arianne repeated dumbly.

He shook her a little. "Promise me."

"Okay, all right. I promise."

That seemed to calm Tomas down a little. He let her go and proceeded to walk out of the room. "You better get changed," he said over his shoulder. "Balthazar was serious when he said he'd drag you out no matter what you have on. Or don't have on."

"How long do we have to find the Redeemer and get back?"

Tomas stopped at the door and bowed his head. "Balthazar will know. But hurry."

Chapter 7

STBY

Balthazar raked a discriminating gaze over the girl standing before him. Tight leather pants and a jacket over a sweater and a thin shirt replaced the shapeless robe. Who would have thought a girl as tiny as her—well, compared to his bulk and height—had curves that could tempt a man? He shook his head mentally and reminded himself she was human. A teenaged human at that. He'd gag, but he didn't want to waste precious minutes trying to explain why. The only thing in her whole get-up he approved of were the boots. At least the chit had sense enough to wear flats. Then his eyes landed on the knife strapped to her thigh. He crossed his arms and snorted.

"What are you?" he asked. "A Lara Croft wannabe?"

"Don't hate," she answered coolly then flicked her braided hair over her shoulder. "I'm surprised you know who that is. You seem like the shut-in type. You know…the Unabomber type."

"Just because I've spent the better part of a millennium in the Nethers doesn't mean I can't keep up with everything that happens outside the Underverse."

"Underverse?"

He spread his arms wide. "Everything and anything here. The Crossroads and everywhere else that isn't in the human world is part of the Underverse. I'd say you should know that, but you're human, so…"

"Don't look at me like I'm learning impaired, you jerk!"

"Ouch! That the best you can do?"

"No, but I don't want to hurt your feelings, pretty boy."

"I'm not gratifying that with a response, little girl." He leaned closer until his face stopped inches from hers. She still didn't flinch, so he grinned, making sure to bare his sharp canines. She stepped back then, but didn't gasp as he'd hoped. This girl had more backbone than he'd initially thought. "Good."

She tilted her head in question.

"For what we have to do, you need some backbone," he clarified. "But a knife? Do you even know how to use one?"

"Tomas told me it will know what to do when I need it."

Balthazar dropped his gaze to the knife again. When she opened her mouth again, he interrupted her with a word that would make the f-bomb blush. He reached for the knife, but Arianne danced away from him. She put both her hands on the knife's hilt as if it needed protection. To get at it, he'd have to get physical. He stepped back and exhaled long and slowly.

He raised his head toward the ceiling and said, "Damn you, old man! Where'd you find that knife?"

No response came, but Balthazar thought he heard a distinct chuckle from somewhere in the Crossroads. Needing release for his mounting anger, he growled at Arianne. She flinched and backed away shaking until a wall stopped her from moving any farther.

"If you so much as accidentally nick me with that thing, I don't care about our bargain, I will eat you alive. Do you understand me?"

She blinked at him several times. "I'm not gonna kill you, Baltha-zar, if that's what you're thinking."

"You say that now."

"I don't think I can hurt anyone with this thing."

"Again, you say that now." Balthazar shook his head for real this time then turned on his heel. "Come on. I want to reach the Sorrow Flats before nightfall." Then he walked away without looking back. A second passed before the patter of her footsteps caught up with him.

"Is that where the Redeemer is?"

"You have so much to learn."

"Then educate me," she said from his side.

He flicked a sideways glance at her before he took a left down a dark hallway. "No one just finds the Redeemer. You need to ask the

Voyeur for information." Even as he said it, Balthazar had to suppress a shudder. He'd rather carve out his own liver and feed it to crows than see the Voyeur again, but he had no other options. He could only hope she'd forgotten about the last time they'd seen each other. He still had the scars down his back to prove it.

"So the Voyeur is at the Sorrow Flats?" She grabbed his arm and pulled him to a stop. "Will you slow down?"

He glared at her hand until she yanked it back. "Don't do that," he said through his teeth.

She cradled her hand to her chest like he'd burned her. "Do what?"

"Touch me. Don't do it again."

"Well, if you slowed down a little, then I wouldn't have to take two steps for every one you make." Her tone was challenging, even if fear still showed in her eyes.

Balthazar breathed to calm his instinct to hit her. No one lived long after touching him without permission. Only his bargain with D prevented him from causing her any bodily harm. He had too much at stake to lose it now. It took him a full minute, but when his bloodlust went from a boil to a low simmer, he continued down the hall. He slowed his pace despite his purposeful stride. The girl had to learn to keep up or she wouldn't survive the journey. She already had so many things going against her, and being with him wouldn't help in the least. He'd increase his pace little by little until she could keep up with his regular stride. She may complain now, but when they had to run, her keeping up would help save their asses better than if he had to carry her.

"The Voyeur wouldn't be caught dead in the Sorrow Flats," he said in answer to her previous question. "We have to go see Granmare Baba."

"Okay, way too many names. Who's that?"

"Witch." Balthazar paused at the end of the entrance hallway of the main building. The number of wisps quivering and wailing seemed to have doubled since he'd last passed through here.

Arianne covered her ears. "Why are they all crying?" she asked above the panicky wailing.

Balthazar kept going. Whether whisps parted for them to pass or not, he had to get out of there before he snapped his fingers and regretted burning all of them. They were the souls of the unborn, for crying out loud. Harmless and fiercely devoted to D — or whoever currently held the title of Death. Killing them off wouldn't serve his purposes. But if he did step on one or two—which caused a sickening squelching beneath his boot—it wasn't the end of the world.

"Hey!" Arianne lifted her hands to push him, but she seemed to remember his threat and kept her hands to herself. "Don't crush them!"

"They're whisps, little girl. It doesn't hurt them."

"But they're so small. Don't hurt them."

"If this is how you're going to react the whole way, I might as well commit a murder-suicide here because we're not surviving this trip."

Arianne stopped at the entrance to the main building, her stance wide and her arms crossed. "You're such an arrogant ass."

"I don't apologize for anything that comes out of my mouth. Suck it up or I leave you here."

She glared fireballs at him, but he couldn't mistake the frightened quivers running through her rigid stance. "Then leave me, see if I care."

"I don't have time for this." He tossed Arianne over his shoulder in a fireman's carry and continued walking. She screamed and thrashed, which drew the attention of the shadow guards and minions. Balthazar ignored their stares and jeers. Let them find a distraction from the slow loss of control of their precious Master by watching him carry a thrashing teenager to the wall. He'd rule over them soon enough, and things would definitely change around here.

Arianne thumped her fists on his back, and he laughed.

"A little lower," Balthazar said. "I've had a knot down there for so long."

She froze and screeched. Then she became deadweight, her arms and legs going limp.

"Did you faint?"

"No," she mumbled.

"Good." He reached the wall. "Because you're about to."

Not giving her any warning, Balthazar jumped. Her answering scream followed closely by laughter baffled him when he cleared the wall and landed at the other side. He put her down, and she stumbled back, still laughing. He grimaced.

"Woohoo!" She jumped in place, clapping. "Can we do that again?"

Balthazar rolled his eyes to the pewter sky and walked past her. If he were a praying man, he'd have asked for strength, patience, and perseverance. But since he didn't pray, he contented himself with pumping his fists to release some of his murderous urges. What Nikolas saw in this girl baffled him.

She hopped to his side and adjusted the pack she'd brought with her. He didn't get why she needed supplies. She didn't have to eat or go to the bathroom. In fact, the pack would only slow them down.

Her slightly piercing voice broke the pleasant silence.

"Why do we have to see a witch?"

"Not a witch. *The* witch."

"I don't see the difference."

He heard the shrug in her voice. "Granmare Baba is the source. All the witches in your world draw their powers from her. Everyone has their own personal image of her. No one really knows what she actually looks like."

"Okay, I know I'm asking a lot of questions—"

"Could have fooled me."

It never occurred to Balthazar how much silence would mean to him until he'd begun this suicide mission with a human girl. He'd spent a good part of three centuries with no one to talk to in the Nethers, and it had almost driven him insane. Now D forced him to travel with someone who couldn't stop yap-yap-yapping. His luck must have run out somewhere along the way.

The bark in his words didn't stop her. "But why do we have to see Gran…what?"

He sighed. He wasn't the sighing type, but she brought it out in him. "Granmare Baba."

"Granmare Baba, right." She repeated the witch's name several more times as if committing it to memory. "Why do we have to see her?"

"There are many things out there—" he pointed at the vast land ahead of them "—that feed on residual energy." He imitated a snarling dog, bringing his teeth closer and closer to her just to see her flinch again. "You reek of residual energy. I need to do something about that before we go deeper into the Underverse. It would save me a lot of trouble."

Arianne smelled herself. "I don't know how long I've been here, but I don't think I need a shower yet."

"Little girl—"

"Arianne," she interrupted him.

Again he sighed. "Arianne, you're a soul. You don't need a shower. Nor will you need to go to the bathroom or eat. I would have thought Tomas would have briefed you about this."

"He did, but that doesn't mean I think it's all so cool."

"Sure, jail bait."

"I resent that."

"Honey, you're going to resent a lot of things before this trip is over."

"I hate you already."

Balthazar laughed. "Good."

When they reached the invisible barrier, his arm snapped to the side, stopping Arianne's progress abruptly. She bumped into his arm.

"What gives?" she complained. "You can touch me, but I can't touch you?"

"Will you keep your trap shut for one second?" He glared at her until she closed her mouth with a decisive snap of her teeth.

When she'd shut up long enough to satisfy him, he closed his fist and summoned his scythe. Her mouth opened. She stared at his scythe before looking up at him. A part of him wanted to gloat, but another part—the smarter part—kept quiet.

"You're a Reaper too?" she finally asked after the shock wore off.

He snorted. "Shit, no. I'd rather die than be part of the pansy squad."

Her face told him she took offense. "Niko's no pansy."

"He's the worst of them," Balthazar said. No mocking in his voice, only fact. She must have heard it because doubt rose in her blue eyes.

"You know him?" She seemed unsure of herself, like she wanted to ask him something else but didn't have the courage to. So unlike the girl who bravely made a deal with D and the devil himself.

Balthazar pushed away the emotion he had no name for which surfaced in his chest and used the blade of his scythe to rip open the barrier that protected the Crossroads from the rest of the Underverse. He motioned for her to step through. Arianne looked at her boots, then him, then her boots again, until he was ready to push her through himself. Oh he wanted to, but he kept his free hand to himself.

This is going to be a helluva trip.

Chapter 8

TMI

Lord help me, I wanna kill him.

They trudged along a barren landscape. Nothing but nothing stretched for miles around. There wasn't even the heat haze usually caused by rising temperatures. Arianne commended herself for her wardrobe choices. The jacket and leather pants protected her from much of the chill in the air, yet didn't restrict her movements. She scanned for a light source, but couldn't see the sun. The sky, gray as could be without clouds, stretched on and on.

She had no way of telling time, but it felt like they'd been walking for a while. She walked behind Balthazar, who seemed to know where they were going and was content not to clue her in. She didn't bother asking, not wanting to give him the satisfaction. He walked a couple of feet away, and her hand hovered inches from the knife at her thigh. It called to her, begging her to draw it and just stick it between his shoulder blades. No one had ever inspired murder in her the way Balthazar did. Not even years of bullying had driven her to the thoughts running around in her head right now. Maybe, deep down, she had violent tendencies.

Arianne stopped and breathed to calm down. No, she wasn't this person. She had to tell herself that at least three times before the killing urge went away. Balthazar had gotten under her skin, and they'd just begun their search for the Redeemer. She didn't understand half of what he'd said. All those names. Way too much information all at once. She blamed herself for not pacing the questions. Every time he answered one, even more popped up in her head. She stopped talking to him after he called Niko a pansy. So. Not. True.

Her heart ached when Balthazar summoned his scythe. The thing didn't look anything like Niko's, but it reminded her of the Reaper of Georgia anyway. There were seconds when she thought she'd gone absolutely crazy. Worrying about him sleeping in that crystal coffin wouldn't help her accomplish what she'd set out to do, but she worried anyway.

She must have been trapped in her thoughts for a long time because when she next looked up, the landscape had changed from barren to blinding white. Powdery hills randomly dotted the shining hexagonally cracked ground as far as the eye could see. The flats gave the illusion of a never-ending mirror, reflecting a sky with no sun. Arianne didn't know where to look. She shielded her eyes, wishing for sunglasses. The hills reminded her of salt, except finer and looser.

"The Sorrow Flats," Balthazar said, as if he'd anticipated her question.

"You're a mind reader now?" she asked, not taking her eyes away from the eerie and unreal sight. It was an odd name for a place filled with so much light.

"Just adapting."

"Okay, since you're adapting, what am I thinking now?"

He glanced at her from his shoulder and grinned, giving her a glimpse of fang. "For every innocent death, an angel weeps an ocean of tears." He gestured to the white hills of—not salt, technically. "Those tears collect here."

Arianne came to his side. "No dice, pretty boy. What I was actually thinking was what are we doing here?"

Pointing toward the distance, he said, "Beyond those hills is Granmare Baba's hut. She's the one who can help with your little human problem."

"I resent that."

"You'll have nothing to resent when you've been eaten." He snorted, which seemed to be his favorite thing to do because he'd been doing it a lot around her. That and sighing. "You don't have a body. What you're seeing right now is your soul, which is still tethered to your body. You're pure energy right now, and that's lunch for everyone and their uncle around here."

"Well, you've suddenly gotten chatty."

"You bring out the worst in me."

"Are you saying you want to eat me too?" Arianne dared to ask when the rest of what he'd said registered. The white hills were pretty distracting to look at.

"Hell no!" He stuck out his tongue and wiped his fingers over it. "I live on life force, the kind still inside whoever I'm eating. Residual energy has a bitter taste since it's no longer inside the being. Even if you're technically still alive, you're outside your body, so your energy is residual. Why the Reapers and a majority of creatures in the Underverse like it, I have no idea. No accounting for taste, I guess."

The way he said it—as if he didn't refer to what kept her alive—had Arianne backing away from him.

"Hey, where are you going?" Balthazar reached out for her, but she flinched back. Her hand went to the knife, and she pulled it out of the sheath. He grimaced. "I thought I made myself clear when I said no killing the protector?"

Hands shaking, breathing heavily, Arianne kept backing up. "You're gonna get me eaten. I think that earns me the right to protect myself."

Stopping his forward motion, Balthazar braced his hands on his hips and breathed through his nose, his nostrils flaring. "We've been walking for three hours and here you are still alive. Don't you think I would have allowed you to be eaten by now?"

"How would I know you're not just bringing me somewhere secluded?"

"Are you hearing yourself right now?"

Then Balthazar's eyes widened. He reached out for her without moving from where he stood. In a calmer voice, he said, "Arianne, stop."

"No." She kept backing away.

"Dammit, listen to me. You have to stop before you—"

She yelped when she backed right into one of the hills.

"Don't breathe in!"

But Balthazar's screamed warning came too late. Arianne coughed. The fine powder smelled like powdered sugar, coating her lungs with each inhalation. Her chest grew tight. The more she flailed against the hill in an attempt to get up the more the powder got into her nose, mouth, eyes, and everywhere else. Balthazar said something, but his voice sounded muffled. Arianne couldn't see him through the mist the powder created. Then the outline of a figure took shape in front of her.

"Balthazar, help!" She coughed then covered her mouth. A mistake since the stuff coated her palm. She coughed again then spat out as much as she could.

"Balthazar!" Her voice scratched against her throat. The powered seemed to cling to its walls. It got really hard to breathe.

"Ari," the figure coming closer said.

Arianne froze at the familiar voice. "Niko?"

The figure cleared the mist and stood a foot away from her now. She saw his boots first, then his jeans, then his T-shirt. When she reached his face, she gasped then coughed. He reached out and she took his hand. He pulled her up until she flew into his arms. She buried her face into his shoulder and called his name over and over, uncaring how much she coughed. His embrace tightened around her.

"Niko, how'd you get out of that coffin?" she asked into his neck. She felt his pulse on her cheek. He was alive and he held her close.

"Ari," he whispered her name again.

Her heart twisted. She didn't think she'd miss the way he said her name or the sound of his voice, but she did. They hadn't been apart for that long, but it felt like a lifetime. She missed him so much it hurt. He'd come for her. When she pulled back to get a good look at his face, the white mist disappeared. In the second that she'd crushed herself against Niko, he'd transported them into his Inbetween — a place in his mind he controlled. The scent of pine trees eased the ache caused by inhaling the powder. The breeze cooled her suddenly too hot skin. She looked up into his inky eyes and threaded her fingers through his equally black hair. She pulled him toward her, and he smiled, giving her what she wanted, what she craved.

Their lips only touched for a second when a voice she'd be happy never to hear again called her name. The voice was faint, but was definitely her name being called. Soon the voice got louder and louder. Arianne pulled away from the kiss reluctantly and looked behind her at the lake in the distance. The water rippled in time with the voice calling her name, increasing in volume now. Niko cupped her face with both his hands and turned her toward him again.

"Stay," he said.

She looked into the dark pools of his eyes, searching for the right answer. "Niko."

"Stay with me, Ari."

"Arianne! Dammit, answer me!" the voice said so loudly it drowned out Arianne's thoughts.

Arianne clung to Niko but suddenly he changed into something else. His handsome face melted away, revealing a grinning skull. She screamed and pushed away from him. The skeleton that replaced Niko wouldn't let her go.

"Stay with me, Ari," it said in Niko's voice.

She punched, kicked, and screamed but it was no use. Its bony fingers held her with bruising force. A siren blared, shocking Arianne into standing still. The skeleton let her go, searching for the source of the sound. Then Niko's Inbetween with its pine trees, placid lake, and charming dock melted like paint thinner had been splashed on a newly painted canvas. The colors bled into one another, threatening to take Arianne with the melting mess. She gave the skeleton one strong push. When it landed on its backside, Arianne bolted. But before she could get far, the same bony hand closed around her ankle, sending her face-planting onto sand that wasn't sand anymore. The white powder of the hill she fell into returned, choking her once again. The hand around her ankle yanked her back. She kicked and connected with something hard.

A grunt followed by a grumbled f-bomb resulted. Arianne stopped struggling when she recognized the voice. She rolled onto her back and came face to face with a red in the face Balthazar. He had a black bandana over his nose and mouth like a bandit from a typical cowboys and Indians movie. She would have laughed at how ridiculous he looked if the clouds of powder swirling around them didn't threaten to get into her lungs.

"Kick me again and I will cut off your leg," he threatened, his voice muffled by the bandana.

Arianne grinned. She couldn't help it. "You look stupid wearing that."

He reached down and pulled her to her feet. Then he did something she didn't expect. He dusted off her clothes. Shocked, she stood still. With every swipe of Balthazar's hand over her clothing the fine granules fell away and settled on the ground that reflected the sky. It didn't cling like she expected it to.

"You're such an idiot," Balthazar grumbled. "If you'd stopped when I told you to you wouldn't have fallen into the hill."

"If you hadn't scared me then I wouldn't have backed away."

"If you just listened to me then you'd know that I don't take residual energy from humans."

That stopped the next argument she prepared to toss his way. He looked into her eyes the way the fake-Niko did, and she dropped her gaze.

"What happened?" she asked, her voice still not quite working right from inhaling all that powder.

He finished dusting her off and stepped back. His gaze roamed her body, and for a second, Arianne squirmed. In the back of her mind she knew he was just checking her for any trace of powder left, but it still weirded her out having those black eyes with white centers staring at her. It was unnerving. Freaky, almost. Yet haunting.

When he completed his inspection, he handed her a wineskin.

"Drink."

One word, a command.

"I thought I didn't need food?"

He frowned. "Just take a damn sip, Arianne, before I make you."

She brought the skin to her lips and took a sip. A cold, sweet liquid splashed into her mouth. She wanted to drink more, but Balthazar snatched the skin away.

"I didn't say chug the whole thing down," he scolded.

She swiped her arm across her lips and swallowed the last of the liquid in her mouth. "What's in that thing?"

"Angel's blood."

Her eyes bulged. "Excuse me?"

His lips twitched, as if he held back a laugh. "Angel's blood is the best cure for inhaling Angel's tears. You learned the hard way that Angel's tears are highly hallucinogenic."

Arianne still couldn't believe she'd just swallowed the blood of a being which, until now, she'd thought only existed in stories. She would have gagged if the sweetness had let her. She hated to admit it, but if Angel's blood tasted like that, she'd drink it down like Iced tea.

"What were you hallucinating about anyway?" Balthazar's question pulled her away from thoughts of making a grab for the wineskin.

"You won't understand," she said.

"I'm pretty sure you tried to kiss me."

Chapter 9

BTW

Balthazar would have laughed if her reaction didn't insult him so much. Her face paled and her body shook like a leaf in the wind. A part of him wanted to admit that he'd been messing with her. That the entire time she'd been hallucinating, she'd thrashed a bit at the most, lost in the images brought on by the Angel's tears. But the worst part of himself held his tongue. Let her think she'd tried to kiss him. More suffering for her. He'd intended it from the beginning anyway.

Holding on to that thought, he removed the bandana and stuffed it into one of the many pockets inside his overcoat. Just because he'd helped her on this fool's errand D sent them on didn't mean he couldn't have a little fun.

"I almost…" Arianne's voice trailed away like she gagged.

"You were hallucinating. It's part of the territory. I'm here. You're here. Add a little Angel's tears and *poof.*"

"But I almost…"

Okay, that sounded like she'd vomited in her mouth a little. Balthazar reined in his fun before his ego took a major hit. If someone could tell him just how much time they've wasted, it would be Granmare Baba. They had to see her now.

"Pick up your knife and let's go." He pointed at the glinting blade. He would have made a grab for it, but the blade exposed like that could still harm him. It did have a life of its own. He'd bide his time and take the knife when it was sheathed, where it couldn't hurt anyone — especially him. He couldn't damn Tomas enough to the deepest pits of the Nethers for giving it to the chit. She'd poke an eye out with that thing.

Without breaking eye contact, Arianne bent down and felt for the knife. One of the more idiotic things Balthazar had seen. When would she learn that he would have hurt her already if he'd wanted to?

"Will you stop," Balthazar said, finally fed up. "I promise not to feed you to anyone. There, you happy?"

Only then did she drop her gaze and twist around. She reached for the knife, which lay a good six inches away from where she'd groped around for it, and returned it to her thigh. Balthazar breathed a sigh of relief. If she only knew the real damage that thing could do. He cursed his mother. Only the most powerful blacksmith in Heaven could conceive of the blade in Arianne's possession. His mother hadn't always been crazy. In fact, he remembered good times with her. But when his father left…Balthazar shook his head. Pretty soon after that, Brianne began to ramble on about how she needed to protect the world from him, how he was his father's son. She'd feared his powers so much — even as a boy — that she had forged the one thing that could easily kill him.

In a moment of clarity, Balthazar took back the curse. Maybe Brianne had been right. Maybe the world did need protecting from him. Everything he touched he destroyed. Who could say taking D's seat wouldn't be the same?

"I'm sorry," Arianne said when she stood up.

Lucky for Balthazar she turned around to pick up her pack at the same instant that his jaw dropped. He shut his mouth and convinced himself she hadn't just apologized to him. No one had ever uttered an "I'm sorry" to him before. To apologize meant weakness in his business. He never allowed himself to say the words, no matter how wrong he knew he'd been. When she turned back, he'd managed to put his mask of indifference back together.

"For annoying me with all your questions?" he asked nonchalantly.

Instead of the knotted brow and blazing eyes he'd come to associate with Arianne when he teased her, he got a frown. He couldn't be sure how he felt about that reaction. The insults just kept on coming. Who knew quiet expressions hid more hostility than actual words?

"You're going to make me say it," she said in a whisper. His ear told him she spoke through her teeth. She didn't meet his gaze. Such an emotional girl. If she only knew…

He laughed at her immaturity. "This whole Q and A has to stop. I don't know how many more questions I have left in me to answer. The solution's a mile away."

Her blue eyes lifted, but the frown on her face remained. He clearly disturbed her more than he gave himself credit for. Huh. Could he actually be better at his job than he thought? She tempted him to keep going, to open the wound a little more.

Maybe next time.

He wouldn't let his guard down just in case. He focused on what they had to do next instead. This detour into Granmare Baba's territory was unplanned. On good days Granmare Baba maintained a surly attitude. She became downright killer when annoyed. Walking in on her uninvited would raise her hackles, but if Arianne wanted to survive, she needed to get rid of her residual energy scent, and the only creature capable of masking energy like that was Granmare Baba. The last time he visited her, he managed to leave without much damage to his person. Then a thought hit him. Why did he never leave a place without pissing someone off?

He pushed away the question. "When we get to Granmare Baba's place there are a couple of rules you need to remember."

For the first time, Arianne waited for him to continue. This disconcerted Balthazar more than her reaction to their almost kiss that never happened. He pushed through the feeling and ticked off the rules by raising a finger for each one.

"Don't talk to her unless she first talks to you. Don't be rude."

She snorted—an almost perfect imitation of the one he did.

"What?"

Arianne rolled her eyes. "You expect me not to be rude when you're the one who insults people with every breath you take?"

"Of course I won't be rude to her. Much." The last part he added under his breath. "And last rule, don't—under any circumstances—leave anything. A lock of hair. A fingernail. Anything she can use to control you after you leave."

"Okay, so I won't remove my braid and cut my nails. Seems easy enough."

"This isn't a joke, Arianne."

"You actually used my name for once."

He sighed and rubbed his forehead. "Just do as I said and we'll leave there not dead."

"Why do I get the feeling dying isn't the worst thing she could do to us?"

"Because it's not. Trust me."

"Why should I when you don't trust me?"

Reaching his limit for this stretch of the conversation, Balthazar turned on his heel and marched away. He reminded himself to slow his pace—the last consideration he'd give her. He needed to feed soon. He felt the hunger, not in his gut, but in his chest, a pull that helped him locate the nearest source of life force. He hadn't been lying when he told Arianne he didn't consume residual energy. The time he'd spent in the Nethers had changed his appetites. Now he preferred something stronger. He hadn't planned on the need to feed, sure his energy supply would last him until they reached the Voyeur. Arianne's unscheduled romp among the Sorrow Flats had forced him to use his reserves to yank her out of a very powerful hallucination.

Angel's tears were the worst. Instantly addictive. No one trapped in their hold ever escaped until they wasted away. If he hadn't pulled her out and given her the Angel's blood, she'd have died within hours.

Walking by her side in silence, Balthazar glanced at the red thread trailing behind her. A part of it had frayed. The hallucination had done a number on her. The Angel's blood only cleansed someone; it didn't fully cure them. If he didn't get her to Granmare Baba soon, she would start jonesing for the tears again. Now he had to trade the witch three things instead of the two he'd initially planned. Being with Arianne was costing him more than a year of her life was worth. He should have asked for more.

"You said you have a solution for my questions," she said when they'd finally cleared most of the flats.

Balthazar gave her a sidelong glance. She seemed fine, but her twitching fingers told him otherwise. She didn't seem to notice that they moved involuntarily.

"Granmare Baba has the ability to upload some information into your head. Basically, we're asking her to help you understand a few things about the Underverse. You're handling things okay now, but I don't want you freaking out on me at the wrong moment."

"I'm sensing a bit of a control freak here."

"Let's see you not have the need to control the situation when you've faced down what I have through the years."

"And about me being human?"

"That's pretty easy. She's just going to give you something that convinces others that you're not what you appear to be."

"You sound like you've done this before."

"Hell no."

"Did I really try to kiss you?"

He almost missed a step at the sudden change of topic. "We're back to that?"

"I thought I was with Niko," she said.

"I take it the experience wasn't pleasant? Nikolas can do that to people."

"It sounds like you hate him for some reason. Why?"

If it weren't for the real curiosity in her eyes, Balthazar wouldn't have answered her question. "We do things we're not proud of. Nikolas more than most."

"You know him."

A statement with more truth in it than anything he could say. Everyone knew Nickolas. A little too well for more than most. There lay the problem. Arianne knew Nikolas as the teenage high school boy. Balthazar knew Nikolas as the take no prisoners Reaper who occasionally did D's dirty work. Nikolas could have easily been third in the rankings, maybe even D's right hand, but he maintained his Reaper of Georgia status to keep under the radar for the side missions he would be given. It baffled Balthazar that Arianne didn't seem to know this about Nikolas.

"You're in love with him," he responded.

"Since I started high school."

Nikolas? Entertaining love? From a human, no less. "And how's that going for you?"

She shrugged. "He finally noticed me when we became Chem partners."

Balthazar whistled. "That's rough." Yet completely understandable considering who they were discussing at the moment.

"It's not so bad. I mean, I was prepared to just like him from afar until we graduated. I guess the universe had other plans."

"It does that sometimes."

"It was all nice until he accidentally reaped Carrie's soul." She paused, a flash of sadness came and went on her face. "My sister."

"In case you forgot, the job of a Reaper is to reap souls, hence the unoriginal name."

"You don't have to be a jerk about it. If you knew Carrie the way I did, you wouldn't want her to die. She had this light in and around her. No matter how sick she got, she still managed to smile and make everyone around her feel safe. But being with Niko made me see there's a life beyond mourning Carrie's death."

Balthazar stopped when a hut made from the leather of demon's wings came into view. Smoke curled from the makeshift chimney at the top. Good, she was home. The sooner they saw her and he made the trade, the faster they could finish this godforsaken trip and Balthazar could move on with his life. If Arianne wanted to delude herself into thinking she loved trash like Nikolas, then that was her lunacy not his.

He faced Arianne. "Let's get one thing straight. We're in this together because of the bargain we've made. We are not BFFs or whatever you humans call it. We are not going to share sob stories. And we sure as hell are not going to treat this like some bonding road trip complete with soundtrack. Every step of this journey is dangerous. You almost died inhaling Angel's tears because you were stupid enough to put your fear of me above the fear you instead should have for everything around you. Remember this, little girl, everything about the Underverse is dangerous. I've lived more lifetimes than you can count and I still have to survive by the skin of my teeth here. You wouldn't make it a day without my help. So make this easier on the both of us by shutting up and following my lead."

Tears welled in her eyes, but she blinked them away. He wondered for a second how mean he'd have to be to get those tears to actually fall. Just when he thought he'd equated Arianne with the words "lost cause," she did something that completely surprised him.

"You done?" she grumbled.

"Not by half."

Chapter 10

CYA

Granmare Baba's house looked…weird. Some kind of black leather made up the walls, but it had red veins, which Arianne had never seen on cow leather before. The same boney material which made up the frame of the bed she'd woken up in stretched the leather. People around the Underverse sure liked their bones for furniture. Death's chair had been completely made of bone—definitely human judging by the skulls at the ends of the armrests. Something told Arianne they weren't a fashion statement either. Bleached bones—the next trend in home furnishing. She shook her head. Didn't have the right ring to it.

She opened and closed her hand. Her pinky wouldn't stop twitching. A slight tick had started in her right eye, and her lips felt really dry, like she'd become severely dehydrated. Tomas said she didn't need to eat or drink, so why did she crave water like the last thing she wanted before she died?

An itch sprang up on her elbow, which quickly spread to her upper arm by the time they reached the barbwire fence surrounding the little hut Granmare Baba called home. She scratched and scratched until her skin heated beneath her nails. She may be a soul, but she certainly felt like she had a body. Balthazar said something to her, but the itching had gotten so bad she couldn't focus on his words. What was going on with her?

Arianne's vision doubled for a second. She blinked it away.

She called Balthazar's name. To her ear it sounded more like a garbled mess.

"You're late," a crony, cackling voice bellowed from within the hunt. Certainly loud enough to pierce through the ringing in Arianne's left ear. Her tongue stuck to the roof of her mouth. Balthazar, who'd been facing the hut this whole time, finally turned and faced her. If she didn't know any better, she'd think he'd lost all the color in his already pale face. How weird was that? A pale guy getting paler. She would have laughed if her body hadn't begun to convulse.

"Quickly, bring her in," the voice said from somewhere.

Arianne's vision tunneled the second Balthazar swept her up in his arms. She would have resisted, but her limbs twitched too badly for her to control any of them. To be carried the way Balthazar carried her, like some Prince Charming, felt too intimate. Like she was betraying Niko somehow. Balthazar was only trying to help, the part of her brain that was still rational thought. But she wasn't exactly listening to that part anymore. She was too busy trying not to throw up.

Her legs went numb when Balthazar stepped into the gloom of the hut's interior. The place looked bigger on the inside. Despite her tunnel vision — the last step before passing out — she remained conscious. Oh she wanted to, no *needed* to pass out already. She begged for it. Maybe even heard herself beg aloud. She couldn't be too sure since the ringing now invaded her right ear too.

In a corner of the round hut, a hunched mound moved in a flurry. It murmured to itself about Angel's tears and careless Enforcers — whatever that meant. A kettle floated to a hook by the fire, and in seconds it whistled a shrill tune. A snap of fingers and the kettle unhooked itself and floated back to the mumbling mound that seemed to have a pile of scarves on its shoulders or back — they seemed like one thing.

All this time Balthazar still cradled her in his arms. He stood there, waiting. She wished he'd just let her go. Lying on the floor right now would be preferable to being this close to his broad shoulders and massive chest. She could feel him inhale and exhale, and if it wasn't for the ear-infection type of ringing, she'd hear his heartbeat too.

The mound pointed at a cot in another corner of the round hut. Arianne counted countless corners. So many of them. Balthazar inched his way to the cot, lifting her higher when she needed to avoid an assortment of pots, pants, and bottles with stuff in them. Was that a pig's head in one of the jars? She couldn't really focus anymore. Everything jumbled into one big mess, like the inside of the hut.

Balthazar finally settled her onto the cot and stepped away, but not before he brushed aside a lock of her hair that had fallen out of the braid and onto her forehead. Now, why would he do something like that? Did he actually look guilty? Impossible. She chalked it up to being delusional. Whatever caused her to twitch and itch uncontrollably also made her hallucinate.

Hallucinate.

The Angel's tears.

Did she inhale them again? No. They'd walked away from the powdery hills. And Balthazar had patted away the last of the powder on her clothing. It was not possible that she was hallucinating again, but it sure felt like it.

The mound, finished with whatever it mumbled about, moved closer until a face with a giant mole at the tip of its nose hovered above Arianne's. She turned away, but a callused hand forced her to face back. She closed her eyes. Too late. The image already burned itself behind her eyelids.

A strong arm cradled Arianne's shaking shoulders so she could sit up. She opened her eyes to blurry images. The tall, dark shadow near the cot must be Balthazar, while the smaller one beside her, helping her sit up, must be the mound. The rim of a wooden cup came to her lips. Someone said, "drink," and she did before coughing because of the bitter brew. It tasted of old tea and smelled like sweaty socks. She turned away again with a grimace. The same callused hand forced her head back so she could drink some more of the foul liquid.

"No more," Arianne whined, shaking her head.

"Just one last sip, dearie," the cackling voice said. Arianne forced one last sip before collapsing into the layers and layers of quilts on the cot. "That's a good girl."

"You should have brought her here sooner," the mound scolded in her cackley voice.

"She couldn't move fast enough," Balthazar answered. It was the politest he'd been since she'd met him in D's office.

"You should have carried her."

"I should have done many things."

The crone pointed a knobby finger at him. "Don't get smart with me, boy. I see the knife on this girl, and unlike her, I am not averse to using it."

Was that an actual flinch? Arianne's vision cleared enough to see Balthazar shrink away from the old woman—Granmare Baba, she assumed. The twitching stopped. So did the itching. Her lips no longer felt dry and parched. Whatever she drank had done its job. She tried to sit up, but the old woman held her down with strength surprising for someone her age. Balthazar said everyone had a different image of Granmare Baba. To Arianne, she seemed really old.

Granmare Baba laughed a cackling laugh. "Oh, my dear, you see what you want to see. What has the handsome Balthazar been filling your pretty little head with? Has he told you I am a witch?"

Arianne licked her lips before she said, "He said you were *the* witch. That I should not speak to you unless spoken to. That I shouldn't be rude. And most importantly, that I shouldn't leave anything you can control me with behind."

She laughed again. "Smart boy, isn't he? Always been too cautious for his own good."

Maybe some truth hid behind Balthazar's rules because, even if he looked like he wanted to say something, a muscle jumped on his cheek instead.

"How are you feeling?" Granmare Baba placed the wooden cup on a table that hadn't been there when Balthazar had put Arianne on the cot.

"Better." Arianne tried to sit up again. Her body still felt stiff, but she could move better than before.

"The Angel's tears shouldn't affect you anymore." To Balthazar, she said, "You did well."

"Thank you," Balthazar grumbled, apparently content to stare at the floor for some reason.

"I'm sure he's already given you my name," she said to Arianne. "But I would like to formally introduce myself. I am Granmare Baba. You can call me Baba for short."

Arianne caught Balthazar shaking his head at her. "I think I will stick to Granmare Baba if it's all the same to you."

The old woman's smile showed yellow, uneven teeth. "Good girl. You're very smart. I see what Nikolas sees in you. But for your sake, forget you even knew him." She stretched the hump she had for a back before returning to her hunched position. Arianne wanted desperately to ask her what she'd meant, but Granmare Baba was already continuing before she could form the proper question. "D is getting too soft in his old age. Being stabbed with Brianne's Bitterness isn't like him at all."

Arianne couldn't say anything anymore; neither did Balthazar since Granmare Baba didn't speak to either of them in particular. They looked at each other, and Balthazar gave her the subtlest of nods.

The crone went on. "Now he's sent you on a fool's mission to find the Redeemer. You should have known better than to accept, Balthazar."

"I get to challenge him for his seat when I return," he said.

"Ah —" she waved her finger in his face "— but you shouldn't let your greed cloud your judgment. There are other ways to gain what you desire."

"Not in the way I wish to achieve it, Granmare Baba."

"So you let him manipulate you into protecting this girl because she is the only one who can recognize the Redeemer. She's already proven to be a liability to you."

Arianne resented the insinuation. She hated that they talked about her like she wasn't there. Her gut told her the stupidest thing to do right now was interrupt. So, like Balthazar had done, she kept her mouth shut until Granmare Baba spoke to her again.

"The bargain has been struck," Balthazar answered her, all his rudeness replaced by a polite calm. "That's why I'm here now. I ask for your help in masking her scent so we may have safe passage to the Voyeur."

The crone huffed. "What do you want with that bitch?"

Balthazar dipped his chin once as if in agreement. "You know as well as I that she is the only one who can lead us to the Redeemer. She who knows all."

"A two bit gossip if you ask me."

"Your rivalries are legendary, but her beauty cannot match yours, Granmare Baba." Balthazar took her wrinkled hand and kissed it. What did he see that Arianne didn't? Could the old woman standing beside the cot really be as beautiful as Balthazar made her seem?

The old woman's gaze flicked to Arianne. "More beautiful than your limited imagination can ever conceive, my dear."

Arianne dropped her gaze and said, "I'm sorry, Granmare Baba. I didn't mean to be rude."

"You have a smart one here, Balthazar. I'm tempted to keep her for myself."

Arianne's heart kicked in her chest.

"As much as I want to leave her here with you to play with, Granmare Baba, I have use for her yet." Mischief sparked in Balthazar's eyes when he winked at Arianne. She wanted to roll her eyes but her fear of offending the witch stopped her. "I will trade the hoof of a Nightmare Steed for her residual energy scent to be masked from all who meet her."

Granmare Baba tapped her chin. The one long hair growing out at the tip of it quivered when she spoke. "A drop of your blood is my price for what you ask, nothing less."

"For a drop of my blood, you mask her scent and give her partial knowledge of the Underverse so she will stop asking me inane questions at every turn."

Arianne didn't like the direction this bargain took. Rule number three said she should leave nothing. What would it mean if he gave the witch a drop of his blood? Would she be able to control him? Arianne couldn't allow that, but an invisible force kept her mouth shut. She was unable to speak no matter how hard she tried. The haggling continued.

"For a drop of your blood and the Nightmare Steed's hoof, I will do both those things and even throw in a talisman that will tell you how long D has left." She waved her wrinkly hand. "I will not even charge you for the potion she drank because of her stupidity."

"Done!"

Arianne heard the exclamation mark in Balthazar's voice. Only then did the invisible force let her go. She tested her mouth, and it opened just fine. Now, as to who prevented her from speaking, she couldn't be sure.

"Go." Granmare pointed at the door. "Let me work in peace."

Balthazar didn't look back when he left.

"Now, my dear—" the witch turned to her "—let me give you what that foolish boy paid for."

"He's not foolish," Arianne said. For giving a drop of his blood, the least she could do was defend the annoying oaf. "He's going out of his way to help me, so if there's anyone foolish here it's me."

"My, my, my." Granmare Baba gasped, spreading her hand at the center of her chest. "You have a mouth on you. I will so enjoy watching what happens to you when the time comes."

A chill went down Arianne's back. She'd almost been afraid to ask, "What do you mean?"

Granmare Baba only smiled her yellow toothy smile before she went about putting things together in a large cauldron that seemed to have magically appeared in the center of the round room.

Chapter 11

RBTL

She'd defended him. To Granmare Baba no less.

Balthazar stood wide-eyed outside the hut listening to the witch and the girl. Either Arianne was a pure soul or was ignorantly assuming he held any good in him. And what did they say about people who assumed? It made an ass of everyone involved. He shook his head to clear it. He felt more comfortable thinking of her as an idiot who didn't know any better. She'd learn soon enough that he wasn't some project she could save. He'd been broken long ago. No fixing needed. He liked it that way, thank you very much. In fact, he'd spent years getting his abrasiveness just right—set to annoy even the saintliest of creatures.

He walked a few steps away from the hut the second he heard the clattering inside. Granmare Baba had something up her sleeve. When she didn't ask for a trade for the Angel's tears cure, it raised his guard. He'd barely kept his composure while they haggled. If his mask slipped, she'd figure out that he was onto her. But knowing Granmare Baba, whatever she planned didn't have immediate consequences. Balthazar prepared for every eventuality. Surviving meant being one step ahead of everyone else. That included the great Granmare Baba. Infinite possibilities presented themselves when it came to one of the witch's schemes. It meant having a plan for each letter of the alphabet.

Asking for a drop of his blood was standard. He'd expected it. A drop wasn't enough for her to control someone like him. He'd transcended petty tricks like that. Five drops maybe, but one wasn't enough for a decent spell. He didn't care what she did with his blood. As long as he got what he needed to make protecting Arianne a little easier, he'd consider the bargain fair. Nothing came free in the Underverse, and he'd willingly pay a high price for D's seat. His payment had begun with his banishment, but soon he would reap the benefits of his sacrifices. This trip with Arianne was a minor detour. He'd waited a millennium for his chance. A few more days didn't matter much.

Balthazar had no doubt Granmare Baba would be successful in masking Arianne's residual energy. The witch was good at her job. He itched at the thought of the first test. The Ghoul Woods. He had no choice. To get to the Voyeur's territory, they had to pass through the bleeding woods. Considering the time they had left—assuming his calculations were correct, and he prided himself on always being right—they didn't have any other options. The Ghoul Woods formed a straight shot to the Voyeur. Dangerous, but what wasn't here?

He squinted at the Sorrow Flats—probably the easiest part of their journey. Nothing called the flats home because of the hallucinogenic mounds of powder. Granmare Baba may be the second easiest—although they still stayed in the red. If you didn't play by the witch's rules, you might as well carve out your own heart. Arianne had enough smarts to understand, but how long would their luck last? Balthazar feared they'd maxed out already. His chest tightened from hunger. Damn. He couldn't hold out much longer. He'd have to hunt, and soon. He wouldn't walk into Voyeur territory with reserves running low.

After making up his mind to hunt once they'd set up camp for the night, Balthazar removed his overcoat and slung it over the barbwire fence. The spikes wouldn't scratch the material—things made of demon wing leather could take a nuclear explosion and all they'd need was a quick dusting off afterward. Things worse than nukes lived in the Underverse, and no amount of demon wing leather could stop them.

He checked the buckles all over his body, starting with his boots then moving up to his calves, thighs, hips, torso, chest, and each of his arms. He ended with the four around his neck. All strapped in nice and tight, he fished out an orange-sized crystal ball from one of the side pockets of his coat. He brought the ball to his lips and blew on it. A dark swirl formed at the center. It took a second for the smoke to solidify into a miniature version of D.

The Master of the Crossroads looked far worse than when they'd left him. The pool of blood around him had now become a lake. The lower half of his body was drenched. His breathing seemed shallower than before, and his skin looked more gray than white.

"Still stuck to the chair, huh?" Balthazar said.

"Still a grade-A a-hole, I see," D answered back without lifting his head.

Balthazar chuckled then winced when he heard Arianne yelp. Granmare Baba had begun. The girl would be pissed at him after. He actually looked forward to it. The fire in her eyes when she was angry warmed him. Grinning, he returned his attention to the crystal ball after giving the hut a quick glance over his shoulder.

"Still not telling me who stabbed you?" He shrugged. "I don't want any traitors when I start my rule of the Crossroads, D."

D finally lifted his head, his androgynous face in a grimace. A lock of his now-dull sunshine hair fell over a sweat-riddled forehead. The small image didn't give Balthazar a clear view of the emotion in D's light-fracturing eyes — never a single color at any given time. Not that he needed the facial cue to judge D's mood. Being stabbed brought out the worst in anyone.

"I trust you're on your way to the Voyeur and that Arianne is safe?"

Balthazar grinned. "Took a slight detour."

"What's going on in that devious head of yours, Balthazar?"

"I had to do something about her human scent. You know that. Something you neglected to tell her. The Underverse is a feeding ground and she's lunch. You like making my life just a little harder."

"I trusted you'd do something about it."

He growled. "You underestimate me, D. You know that's a mistake."

"Regardless of how you feel about me, Balthazar, I still believe there's good —"

Balthazar didn't let D finish the rest of his words. He chucked the crystal ball out into the flats until it landed quite a distance away in a broken heap. Shit. He shouldn't have done that. He'd have a hell of a time finding another communication crystal. Oh well. His lips twitched. It felt good throwing D away.

An explosion in Granmare Baba's hut whirled Balthazar around. A large plume of blue smoke rose from the chimney. He snatched his coat from the fence and shrugged it back on. Time to get going. He gave his communication crystal one last look before he returned to the hut.

"Get in here, boy!" Granmare Baba hollered.

Balthazar ducked into the hut and stopped at the door, letting his eyesight adjust to the gloom. His gaze skipped the tall, long-haired woman in leather pants and a corset standing by the smoking caldron and landed on the girl sitting on the cot. Arianne seemed in one piece. But with Granmare Baba, you could never be too sure. The only difference? A curling tattoo wrapping around Arianne's neck like a choker and a ring with a slowly pulsing black gem on her index finger.

"Admiring my handiwork?" Granmare Baba asked, her long fingers clutching her narrow hips. "It took a while for me to completely mask her scent."

"The tattoo," Balthazar said, never taking his eyes off Arianne. He let his other senses assure him Granmare Baba hadn't messed with the girl. No one else had that right.

"You were always a smart one." The witch gave him a flirtatious smile that he ignored. "A foolish boy, but a smart one." She reached for Arianne's neck. The girl had the sense to stay still. "The mark will deter anyone who thinks she is more than she is. They will see a slave, not a morsel from the human world."

Her hand shot out and wrapped around Balthazar's wrist. A burning sensation kept him from pulling away. The same blue smoke that curled out of the chimney escaped between his skin and Granmare Baba's hand. When the witch let go, she left behind the same tattoo design on his wrist.

"What did you do?" Balthazar growled. Screw the *don't speak until spoken to* rule.

She laughed—a scratchy throat sound that didn't match the sexpot standing in front of him. "I merely masked her scent with yours. For the duration of this journey, she is attached to you as your servant." She lifted her hand when Balthazar continued to growl at her. "You are facing the Voyeur. That jealous whore will not touch her if she thinks the girl is your slave."

Balthazar reined in the urge to ring the old hag's neck.

"Good boy," she said, treating Balthazar like a loyal hound. "You know I am right. I increased her chances of survival by tethering her to you."

"I would have protected her just fine." He was no longer growling, but Balthazar still bared his teeth at the witch and hissed. "You didn't have to bind us!"

She laughed again. "But it's more fun this way." Then she sobered. "Now, your payment, if you please."

"I shouldn't—"

A dark aura spiked out of Granmare Baba. Her hair danced like snakes around her head. Her eyes turned all white. "Don't even think of reneging on your payment, Balthazar."

Seeing no other way out, Balthazar took a needle from an inside pocket of his coat and pricked the tip of his finger. A ruby red drop gathered. The aura around Granmare Baba disappeared. She moved closer, groping for Balthazar's hand like a hungry street child. She took the tip of Balthazar's finger into her mouth and licked away the drop. Balthazar stood still, watching the witch closely. Before she could take more than his promised drop, he yanked his hand away and closed the wound. The witch licked her lips like a cat finished with a bowl of cream.

"I missed the taste of you, Balthazar. You have matured with age," she said between smacks of her black lips. "Your sweet, sweet blood has always been my favorite."

"The ring?" he asked.

"When the gem stops pulsing, you are too late," she purred.

"And the information?"

"She knows enough not to make mistakes."

Balthazar looked at Arianne, who nodded at him once. He hooked his finger at her, and she immediately stood up, slinging her pack over her shoulder. Granmare Baba closed her hand around Arianne's arm, stopping the girl from coming to him.

"Uh, uh, uh." She shook her head. "You must be forgetting something."

Reaching into another pocket, Balthazar tossed Granmare Baba the hoof of a Nightmare Steed. She caught it with her free hand. Then she sniffed Arianne from neck to temple. Arianne didn't flinch, but she visibly shook. With their new connection—annoying Balthazar already—he could feel the tight band of fear around her chest. He pushed away his predatory instincts to pounce and diluted her fear with his own calm until her breathing went from shallow to regular.

"See?" Granmare Baba said. "Isn't that much easier?" To Arianne she whispered loud enough for Balthazar to hear. "Fear is such a dangerous emotion to have in the presence of a predator."

Balthazar froze. His breath caught in his lungs. Damn the loose cannon old hag. He'd had to save Arianne from Angel's tears hallucinations because she got it into her head that he'd have her eaten. Having her actually think *he* might eat her despite his assurances… he couldn't fathom it. If Granmare Baba told her anything more, he didn't know how the girl would react. He didn't need a hysterical Arianne on his hands. She had handled things well so far, considering.

"Thank you for the advice, Granmare Baba," Arianne said, her gaze locked with Balthazar's. "I'll make sure to remember that."

Balthazar breathed easier again.

"Then go." Granmare Baba released Arianne. "Pleasure doing business with you, Balthazar. Don't let another millennium pass without coming to see me."

Lips a tight line, Balthazar nodded at the witch. When Arianne reached him, he ushered her out of the hut. He made sure to put the bulk of his body between the hut and the girl.

"Don't look back," he told her. He kept his hands on her shoulders to keep her from doing the exact opposite of what he'd said. "Keep moving."

"Consider what I told you about Nikolas, my dear," Granmare Baba called after them.

Arianne flinched at her words. The witch hadn't been off base in her warning. The sooner Arianne found out who Nikolas truly was, the sooner she'd realize he wasn't capable of love.

When they cleared the barbed wire fence, Arianne said, "For a really old witch, she seemed nice."

A thundering laugh came from behind them. Balthazar's lips twitched at the sarcasm in Arianne's tone. Oh, she was learning all right.

Chapter 12

SITD

New information swirled around in Arianne's head. She had to leave Balthazar alone—much to his relief, she could tell—just so she could sort through it all. She let him lead while she followed contently, watching the ground the whole time.

She had no idea what Granmare Baba had done to her back at the hut. The procedure involved drinking a couple more nasty potions—one smelling of armpits and the other tasting suspiciously like blood. Lots of chanting followed then just before the explosion, Granmare Baba touched her neck. Arianne lifted her hand to the tattoo. It still felt hot to the touch. She'd screamed when Granmare Baba branded her, but the explosion drowned out the sound.

The witch had connected her to Balthazar in a weird way. She could feel some of his thoughts. She wasn't sure how to describe it properly. She couldn't read his thoughts—nothing cool like that. And something told her she wouldn't want to know what really went on inside his coconut. Probably a lot of weird stuff a girl her age shouldn't know. More like she "felt" the moods connected to the thoughts, which gave her an idea of what he was thinking in connection to what they were doing. Like right now, Balthazar was zeroed in on something. Arianne assumed it had to do with where they were going. So, since he had reverted to his ignore-Arianne state, she focused on the information Granmare Baba "uploaded" into her brain.

If she imagined the universe like a coin, the human world would be heads to the Underverse's tails. The humans walked upright while the creatures in the Underverse walked upside down. That explained why the Underverse didn't have a sun. The sun belonged to the human world. The light in the Underverse came from a place called the Nethers. Arianne didn't know much about that place, maybe because it wasn't involved in their journey. She suspected Granmare Baba only gave her information connected to finding the Redeemer, who—she now knew—was a being created from the purest of souls. At any given time, there could only be one Redeemer in Haven—a place not quite Heaven. Beings called Heavenly Hosts stayed there when they needed to enter the human world, like the Crossroads for the Reapers.

Arianne felt badass knowing all these things. She didn't have to ask so many questions anymore. Only one other thing didn't make sense to her. Granmare Baba—while Arianne deliriously craved Angel's tears (an experience she'd never go through again if she could help it)—called Balthazar an Enforcer. Whatever that meant. Every time she groped for the information something blocked her, like with password protected files. Granmare Baba teased her with the information, but she had to unlock it herself like a character in a role playing game. Before she could level up, she needed to complete a few tasks first. Well, show her what to do and she'd get it done. Arianne didn't slack off. If she could accomplish something in a day, she'd have it done by lunch.

When she looked up, the scenery had changed again like when she and Balthazar moved from the Barren Lands—a stretch of nothing between the Crossroads and everything else in the Underverse—into the Sorrow Flats. She understood why now. Nothing stayed put in the Underverse. It didn't have a single location for a place. Things constantly shifted. If you didn't know what you were looking for you'd definitely get lost. And getting lost? Not good. She hated to admit it, but Balthazar was right. From what she knew, the Underverse made a Venus flytrap look tame.

"I'm always right," Balthazar said from over his shoulder.

"You can feel my thoughts, too," she said back matter-of-factly. Having Balthazar feel her too? Not as freaky as she thought. So long as he couldn't read the rest of her thoughts, she had no problems with him feeling what she was currently thinking.

Since it seemed he'd finished ignoring her, Arianne moved to a topic that had been bothering her after they left Granmare Baba's hut.

"What did she mean by forgetting about Niko?"

"I think she's right. You only know a part of who Nikolas is."

Arianne thought about it a second. How much could she really know about a single person? Reapers grew old and died then were reborn so they mingled with the next generation without causing suspicion. Niko had lived many lives before he met her. Whoever he was in his previous lives had nothing to do with the guy she loved now. No warning—from a witch or Balthazar—could change that.

"Just so we're clear, I'm not actually your slave."

Balthazar kept on walking. "Wasn't thinking of you that way. But I could easily change that if you piss me off."

"I can't promise that since you're so charming half the time."

He meowed. "Kitty has claws."

"And I have a knife with your name on it."

"Don't remind me."

The flats had turned into a mountain road. They trudged up the path for a while, the incline growing slightly steeper with every new turn. No plants or flowers. Just rocks and a whole lot of brown.

"We're making camp for the night."

Arianne considered Balthazar's words for a second. Convenient how he picked up on what she wanted to ask before she asked it, saving a lot of time and aggravation on her part. *Thank you, Granmare Baba.*

Balthazar snorted. "Don't let her catch you thanking her or she'll stew you for dinner. She's not big on gratitude, just payment. What did you see when you met her?"

"A hunched old woman with a lot of wrinkles and a big mole at the tip of her nose," Arianne said absentmindedly. She kept to the far side of the mountain road. They'd climbed high up already. One slip and she was a pancake.

"Typical human imagination." Balthazar's shoulders shook like he was suppressing a laugh. "I tell you witch and you go for the cliché image."

"Well, if you're so smart, what does she look like to you?"

"To me…" He became super silent.

"To you she's the slutty witch at Halloween, isn't she?"

Balthazar dropped the f-bomb. "This connection is getting on my last nerve."

"And here I was thinking it was pretty convenient. You answered most of my questions without me having to ask them." Arianne smiled. "I kinda dig it now."

"Keep your unicorn thoughts away from me."

Arianne looked up to see goose bumps at the back of Balthazar's neck. She unnerved him. She kinda dug that too.

"What's an Enforcer?" She threw it out there.

Balthazar turned around so fast, she almost tripped backward. He had her pinned against the mountainside a blink later. She gasped. Having his snarly face up close and personal shocked and awed her. Balthazar had one of those faces that looked better up close. Arianne had never had a vampire fetish, but that little hint of fang set off tiny tremors just below her navel. She focused on breathing instead of where the rest of her thoughts wanted to go.

"What do you know?" Balthazar said through his teeth. His breath tickled her cheeks, sending a cold shiver down her back. A low growl had begun in Balthazar's chest, vibrating into Arianne.

"Nothing."

He tightened his grip on her arms until she winced. "Liar."

"Feel my thoughts, Balthazar. I'm not lying."

He stared into her eyes, the white at the center unsettling her. When he spoke again, he sounded a tad calmer, but his grip didn't loosen. She felt herself bruising by the second. She may not have a body right now, but no one told her she'd still feel the damage.

"How do you know I'm the Enforcer?"

Arianne caught his use of "the," meaning he was the only one or the top dog if there were more like him. She had a sinking feeling the former was more true than the latter. She thought back to her delirium at the hut.

"I heard Granmare Baba call you that."

Balthazar let her go so quick, she had to grab on to the mountainside to keep her balance. He'd lifted her a couple inches off the ground when he held her, so when she dropped, she almost crumpled. Thank God for dodge ball giving her good reflexes.

"It's nothing," Balthazar grumbled. It sounded more like rocks rubbing against each other than actual words.

"She didn't give me the information, if that's what you're worried about." Arianne righted herself. "Although she did give me something."

When Balthazar eyed her like a hunk of beef he couldn't wait to sink his teeth into, she quickly added, "She protected the info. I can't get to it. And I don't know how, to answer your next question." She grinned when his eyebrows shot up. "See? Told you it's convenient."

For the millionth time that day, Balthazar sighed. This time he coupled it with running his fingers through his silver streaked hair. All the black he wore really made the strands stand out. The fingerless gloves weren't working for her, though.

"Live with it," he said in response to her thought.

"If you haven't heard, the eighties died a long time ago," she snarked back.

Balthazar pointed at his glove-covered palm. "This isn't a fashion statement, little girl."

"Tell me about it." She rolled her eyes. "Where are you taking me this time?"

"We'll make camp at the top of this mountain. We'll be safe there for the night."

Balthazar led the way again, but this time Arianne positioned herself by his side. He put her close to the mountainside and himself near the outer edge of the mountain's road. She got an inkling he protected her even now. Determining whether it was conscious on his part or not was beyond the scope of the connection she shared with him. She couldn't tell unless he actually thought about it.

"I don't want to walk into the Ghoul Woods at night," he continued.

Arianne swallowed when the information about the Ghoul Woods filled her head. "Are you sure it's the only way?"

"I just enjoy putting my life in more danger than it is now."

"Really?"

"Of course not." He huffed. "It's the shortest way to the Voyeur."

"Don't be mean. I wasn't gonna ask about it."

Weird trees filled the Ghoul Woods. Usually trees resembled umbrellas, which was why forests were called canopies. The Ghoul Woods' canopy looked like bowls with braided stems for trunks. They didn't provide the kind of shade normal trees did because of their bowl shape. The sap in the trees was the freakiest part. Cut the trunk and it looked like the tree was bleeding. Arianne shivered, rubbing away her own set of goose bumps.

The trees alone wouldn't make the Ghoul Woods so bad. They had to be careful of what lived in the woods.

Balthazar spat out more than the f-bomb this time.

Arianne agreed with him. Carelessness in the Ghoul Woods equaled royally screwed. She for one didn't want to be roasted on a spit and made the main course. But, then again, it was nothing new in the Underverse. If something didn't want to eat her, it wanted to kill her. Insert the incident with Angel's tears here. She hated that it used the likeness of Niko to try to do the killing. Had she said yes to staying with him, Balthazar wouldn't have been able to do anything to get her out of the hallucination.

At the top of the mountain a stand of pines swung in an imaginary wind. Arianne stopped and stared. She had a feeling she'd be doing a lot of stopping and staring during this trip. Like the Sorrow Flats, the Dancing Pines were something to look at.

"They can't kill me, can they?" she asked Balthazar, who stopped at her side, looking up at the pines like she did. According to what she felt of his thoughts, he didn't look at them because he admired them. He was making sure nothing stayed with them up there.

"Just don't piss them off and you should be fine," he finally said.

Arianne followed him into the outcropping until they reached a cleared-out center. Balthazar quickly fashioned a makeshift shelter for them out of fallen branches. Then he dug out a fire pit and surrounded it with rocks. He dumped the rest of the branches into the pit and took out a Zippo. He flicked the lighter open, and the branches in the pit burst into flames.

"Cool trick," Arianne said. "You're such a Boy Scout."

His brow furrowed. "Don't mock me. Remember our bargain? I have to use all the resources available to me to help you. That includes making sure you're comfortable. You don't look like the roughing it type to me."

"I've been camping before."

"And how'd that work out for you?"

"I didn't know it was poison ivy, okay!"

Balthazar threw back his head and laughed. Arianne crossed her arms and stewed. She'd gone to the bathroom and accidentally sat on poison ivy. Ben had laughed at her the whole time too. If it hadn't been so embarrassing, she'd be laughing too. Then the thought of Ben hit her fully. She rubbed her chest, and Balthazar sobered.

"Don't you dare cry on me," he warned in response to what he felt from her.

Arianne looked away. "I'm not." She swiped at the tears and reminded herself she'd mourn after they found the Redeemer. When her eyes were finally dry, she returned her gaze to Balthazar. "What now?"

"Gather as much wood as you can, but don't leave the protection of the pines."

"Why do I get a feeling you're going somewhere."

He grinned enough to show his fangs. "I'm going hunting."

Chapter 13

NIMBY

Not pissed off at all. Not an ounce. And Balthazar had no idea why. He'd been prepared for Arianne to chew him a new one after what Granmare Baba did. Hell, he wanted to chew someone a new one, too. He'd been ready for any barbs Arianne would throw his way, ready to annihilate her. Connecting them like that was underhanded. He still wasn't clear on what Granmare Baba had planned, but the tattoos were a part of it. Now Arianne invaded his head as he invaded hers…and he hated every second of it. Arianne called it convenient; he called it annoying. No one had any right to his thoughts but himself. Sure, she didn't have to ask him questions anymore. He spoke the answers before she could breathe, but he felt whipped doing it, like she had all the control.

He left her open-mouthed at the top of Mount Deus. She'd be safe there so long as she didn't leave the Dancing Pines. He needed to hunt and maybe even burn off some of the frustration the old hag had caused him.

Bringing Arianne to Mount Deus wasn't about protecting her, or having a safe place to camp for the night. Only the hunt mattered. What he needed called the other side of the mountain home. He'd felt his prey even before they started the climb to the top. It took all his concentration not to leave Arianne then and there to satisfy his increasingly painful hunger. His chest crumbled into itself. If he let it go on any longer, he'd lose all control, and there was no upside to that for anyone within a hundred mile radius.

Light steps stopped the buckles from jingling. Not that he needed to be completely silent. Ogres were big, with brains the size of peas. Two or three would be more than enough to sustain him until he got to the Voyeur. She had prime hunting land. Balthazar could get anything he wanted there. He hoped he could persuade the Voyeur to let him poach on her land — or maybe she'd be so busy that she wouldn't miss a demon or two. Right now, Ogres were on the menu. Saliva gathered in Balthazar's mouth. His fangs lengthened as he swallowed.

He reached the bottom of the mountain in record time. The loud grunting masked any remaining noise he might have made. But he couldn't be too careful. A branch snapping at the wrong moment would be most inconvenient. He hated playing with his food.

If his ears were correct, a nest of them lived in a cave at the bottom of Mount Deus. A softer grunt indicated a young one, no more than a few hundred years old. He swallowed again. The wet garbage smell that wafted at him like a hot wall of smoke confirmed what his ears heard. Balthazar breathed through his mouth. Just because he liked a little Ogre once in a while didn't mean he appreciated their ripe aroma.

His scythe manifested without him having to call it. His anticipation and the urge to kill was more than enough. Balthazar gripped its staff in one hand and kept running.

About a hundred feet away Balthazar spotted a bald, knobby head. Ogres came in different shapes and sizes. This one had the snout of a pig and wicked elephant tusks. A hairy chest, beefy hands, and stubby legs completed the picture. It must have been twice as tall as Balthazar and three times as wide. Just the way he liked it. The Ogre grunted, chewing on something. Balthazar had no interest in finding out what it was. A second Ogre — this one with a full head of hair and a mouth filled with sharp teeth roughly the size of his forearm — hobbled toward the first. It handed over a leg of something big. Saber mammoth maybe. The behemoths didn't come from the human world as the humans suspected. They were accidentally brought there when a demon thought he could play warlock. Caused a big snafu in the Nethers. Totally hilarious. Balthazar thanked his lucky stars he'd been present for that fiasco.

Balthazar counted, pretty sure there had to be another Ogre hanging about — the young one. He made a mental note to find it the second he finished with Dumb and Dumber. He licked his lips and raised his scythe. He jumped off the ground to strike at baldy when a whip wrapped around his neck and snapped him back. He slammed onto his backside, robbing his lungs of air. The crash alerted the Ogres. They turned to him and charged. Ogres killed first and didn't ask questions later. To them he was food as much as they were to him. Balthazar struggled against the whip, but it wouldn't budge. He used the blade of his scythe against the whip. The contact caused a grinding sound. Balthazar froze. Dammit. Why couldn't it be an ordinary whip?

The ground shook from the charging Ogres. They were on him in seconds. He swung his scythe around and the blade connected with the arm of Baldy, lopping it off. Baldy screamed and green blood spurted out of the stump where his forearm used to be. The long-haired Ogre growled at its companion before returning its attention to Balthazar. Before it could move, he swept his scythe across its legs. The second Ogre fell to the ground, wailing in agony. The first Ogre finally came to its senses, now twice as pissed. It uprooted a pine and swatted Balthazar with it. An ugly snap filled the air as Balthazar's body flew one way while his head remained where the whip kept it.

The whip finally let up, followed by a whistle. Balthazar dragged himself off the ground. It would take more than a broken neck to kill him. But that didn't mean it didn't hurt like a mother f—

On his feet, he took his head with both hands and snapped his neck back into place. He groaned, disoriented by the pain for a second. He grabbed on to a tree trunk to stay upright. Whoever had whipped him better be ready to become the dessert to his Ogre dinner. When his vision cleared, he saw the creature with the whip finish off Baldy by snapping its neck. The huge body fell to the ground with a loud rumble. Balthazar glanced at the second Ogre who'd lost consciousness some time ago.

"Before I kill you, mind telling me why you interrupted my dinner?" Balthazar said to the lady demon with the nasty whip. The breasts tipped him off. But, then again, many things in the Underverse had breasts and weren't necessarily of the female persuasion.

She—for the lack of a better word—coiled her whip and hung it on a belt around her hips. She flicked her leathery wings twice before folding them tightly behind her back. Then she focused yellow eyes on him.

"My mistress forbids hunting on her land," she said in an echoing voice, like she spoke with more than one.

Balthazar quickly picked up on what the demon meant. "When did Mount Deus become Voyeur territory?"

"Since she killed the king of the Ghouls."

That put a kink in Balthazar's plans of passing through the Ghoul Woods. "And why would she do that?"

The demon picked dirt out from under her long fingernails. "She takes the prince for her lover."

Another kink in the plan. Oh this was just peachy. The Voyeur collected lovers like jewelry. What she saw in the Prince of the Ghouls he had no idea. But before he could start figuring things out, first things first. He flipped two fingers up and the whip on the demon's belt uncoiled and wrapped around its master. The demon fell to her side.

"I wouldn't struggle if I were you," Balthazar said, grinning.

She hissed at him, forked tongue flicking in and out of her mouth.

Balthazar closed his fist, and the whip coiled tighter, choking the demon into silence. "There, that's better." He raised his index finger at her. "One, I didn't know this was Voyeur territory now. Two, I don't give a damn. And three, you're next."

The demon's yellow eyes widened. She shook now. Balthazar inhaled a lung full of her fear. If she hadn't snapped his neck, he would have let her go. No, scratch that. He'd still eat her. The mercy was that he would save her for last. She could watch.

He walked toward Baldy and kicked the carcass until it lay on its back. Dead. The bitterness of the residual energy in the air stuck his tongue to the roof of his mouth. Grunting, he moved to the one bleeding out. He knelt down and sank his fangs into its neck—not for blood. Balthazar didn't drink blood. He used his fangs to suck out the Ogre's remaining life force. He called it recharging, and it felt damn good. He would have preferred the Ogre still fully alive, but beggars couldn't be choosers, especially really hungry ones.

After draining the Ogre, he wiped his hand across his lips to clear the blood that came with the kill and spat out any that spilled into his mouth. Balthazar relished the heat of its life force. He felt so much better already. The hunger he'd been battling all day receded.

Done with the Ogre, he turned around and faced the demon. She trembled openly now, finally realizing what he was. She might not have recognized him, but his reputation did precede him.

Balthazar knelt beside her and sat her up. She snapped her teeth at him. Her struggle to live only whetted his appetite.

"Shhh. Don't be afraid." He smiled. "I can make this pleasurable for you if you like."

She spat at him.

"I like them feisty," Balthazar said in a deadly whisper. "Tastes better." He sank his fangs into the demon's neck without bothering to wipe the spittle sliding down his face. She jerked and screamed. She opted for the painful way, so Balthazar gave it to her. He wasn't such a monster that he couldn't make the experience the best of her life, but she spat at him. He didn't tolerate insolence from his food.

As her life ebbed, Balthazar eased up a little. He'd been pretty much full about halfway through. But he wouldn't waste the life force she provided, so he didn't stop. He took his time. He loosened the whip the second he felt her go limp. At the last second of her life, he injected pleasure into the demon. She raised her hand and touched his cheek. Her heartbeat sputtered twice before it stopped completely. Balthazar unhooked his fangs from her neck and stared at her smiling face. She stared blankly at the dark gray sky. He swept his hand over her eyes, closing them.

He'd gotten his wish, a demon. The energy she'd given him would definitely help. If what he suspected about the Ghoul Woods was correct, he'd need every ounce. The tricky passage just got trickier. He'd been right—like always. He and Arianne had run out of luck.

Balthazar laid the dead demon back down gently. He got to his feet and took out his trusty Zippo. One lift of the lid and all three bodies burst into flames. He murmured the death rites as they burned. They'd given him sustenance. The least he could do was provide them with a decent burial. He wasn't a complete barbarian.

Chapter 14

BRB

Typical. Arianne huffed. Balthazar had left without further explanation. He'd said he was going hunting. For what? She didn't need food. In fact, she hadn't been hungry this whole time. She didn't even need to go to the bathroom when normally a pee break would have happened by now. If she didn't need food, then what was Balthazar hunting for?

Hands on her hips, Arianne surveyed their "camp." How she wished for a tent right about now. The night was tolerably cold rather than freezing, so the fire didn't make any sense other than to provide light. She looked up at the darkening sky and missed sunsets. Basically, in the Underverse, the sky went from light gray to dark gray. Just gray, gray, and an even more gray. No wonder the creatures she'd met so far had attitudes. If she didn't see the sun at least once a day, she'd be all depressed and surly too.

Balthazar was the worst of them. He didn't just have an attitude. He had the attitude problem of all attitude problems. His sarcasm and up to the minute annoyance of her went beyond being a simple defense mechanism. It seemed the guy liked to be in a constant state of grumpy sourpussness. If he didn't shout at her or say mean things, he grumbled curses under his breath like she couldn't hear him. Most of his favorite curse words she hadn't even heard until now. The only reason she knew he cursed was because of the venom the words dripped with. If someone needed a big hug, the prize went to Balthazar.

"No point obsessing," Arianne said to herself. She sighed. Let Balthazar be all mean and nasty. As long as he kept her safe and helped her find the Redeemer, she didn't have a problem with him. Well, maybe she wasn't entirely problem free, but she'd tolerate him. A little.

The wood feeding the fire popped, bringing her attention back to the camp. She glanced around. Balthazar said she'd be safe within the outcropping of pines. Might as well make herself useful and pick up more firewood.

In the human world, fire kept predators away. Maybe the same could be said in the Underverse. None of the information Granmare Baba gave her confirmed the thought, so she assumed. If fire was a bad thing, then why would Balthazar leave her with it?

With a mission, Arianne searched for fallen branches. She started in a circle around the clearing. Once her hands were full, she dumped her load by the fire and started all over again. She went into wider and wider circles until she decided she had enough wood to keep the fire going for the rest of the night.

Having time on her hands, and not sure when Balthazar would return, Arianne stacked the branches she'd gathered the way they did at the back of their house at winter time. An unexpected pang of loneliness hit her. Tomas said time flowed differently in the Underverse, so what could be hours here could be seconds in the human world. When Niko brought her to his Inbetween for the first time, they'd spent a whole afternoon there though when they returned to school, they'd only been gone a few seconds. But just because time flowed differently didn't mean she didn't miss her parents.

The last time she'd left her house on one of her midnight walks after Carrie's death, her mom had been swallowing pills like candy and her dad had barely been keeping it together. Their whole family had become a mess. Arianne had been so out of it that she didn't even see the car barreling toward her when she'd stepped out in front of it. If it weren't for Niko's stalking tendencies, she'd be roadkill by now. It hadn't helped that Darla had been the one driving the car.

Arianne pushed away thoughts of her high school bully and focused on finishing her wood pyramid. She'd gone on this mission because of Niko. She couldn't care less what happened to Death, but if she didn't help him then he couldn't bring Niko out of his sleep in that crystal coffin. Her gaze landed on the ring. The pulse seemed weaker than before, even if it still blinked constantly. Granmare Baba said if the ring stopped pulsing they were too late.

She got the feeling Balthazar would have charged through the Ghoul Woods that night if it weren't for her. Ghouls littered the place—hence the name. They ate anything and everything with a pulse. Their appetite made them dangerous. Once caught, you might as well say your prayers. Arianne rubbed away the goose bumps on her arms. She hadn't come this far just to be eaten by ghouls. The picture of them in her head wasn't very clear, so she couldn't tell what they really looked like. Maybe something went wrong with the information upload. Or could it be another blocked piece of info Granmare Baba wanted her to unlock.

Arianne hated the old witch.

With that thought, she fed the fire then dusted her hands. She stretched to her full height and stared at the lean-to Balthazar had created for her. If she didn't know better, she'd think he was being sweet. But Balthazar didn't have a sweet bone in his body. His bargain with Death forced him to build the shelter. Basically, he protected her from the elements too. Arianne shrugged. No matter how much he denied it—and he definitely would if she asked him—the lean-to was still a nice gesture.

She had just decided to clear the space of pebbles when the pines rustled behind her. She froze. Something grunted. To Arianne's knowledge, Balthazar didn't grunt. Plus, this sounded more guttural than his smoother, deeper voice. A soft gravelly mewling followed the grunt. Arianne closed her eyes and thought really hard for Balthazar to get back. If he could feel her thoughts then she didn't need to scream. Who knew what a scream would attract around here? So Arianne bit the inside of her cheek and slowly turned around. She forced herself not to close her eyes. If she needed to run, she needed her eyes to see.

Whatever grunted when it arrived sneezed now. Arianne flinched. What did her dad tell her about dealing with predators? No sudden movements? Play dead?

Let's see what you're dealing with first, Ari, she scolded herself.

Once she completed her one-eighty, Arianne's eyes popped. The information in her head dinged almost immediately. Ogre. And it hunched at the other side of the camp. Eight feet tall—maybe a bit bigger—it had a bald head except for a tuft of hair at the very top. Big hands, big feet, but what scared Arianne the most were the teeth. Two boar-like tusks the size and length of her forearm jutted out of the Ogre's lower lip. She shook now; she couldn't help it. The Ogre's beady black eyes watched her every move. It grunted again, bringing its beefy hands to its chest.

Arianne reached for the knife on her thigh and pulled it out. She held the hilt with both hands and pointed the blade at the Ogre about to eat her. Okay, it actually just stood there staring at her, but she didn't doubt that it would eat her.

"Don't come near me," she said, but at some point her voice broke, so she cleared her throat and tried again. "I'll cut you. If you come near me, I swear I will."

Threatening it didn't seem like a good idea, but she had to show it who was boss. Her hands shook so the blade shook too. The wood in the fire popped, startling the both of them. The Ogre reached out, and Arianne stumbled back. When she landed on her backside, she screamed. The Ogre screamed too. Then it curled into the biggest trembling ball she'd ever seen. Arianne's jaw dropped. It covered its face with its massive hands and wept. It sounded like rocks tumbling down the mountainside, but Arianne recognized sobbing.

Hand still shaking, she returned the knife to the belt on her thigh and stood up slowly. "It's okay," she crooned. She reached out trembling hands. "It's okay. See, the knife is gone. If you're not going to hurt me, I won't stick the pointy end into you. Okay?"

Arianne knew how ridiculous she sounded comforting an Ogre twice as big as she was. But something about the trembling ball tugged at her heart. She took a step forward and—she didn't know how it happened—the Ogre managed to create a smaller ball of itself. Its wet garbage smell made Arianne hesitate getting any closer, but the poor thing sniffled and whimpered. So she slowed her pace instead, taking one agonizing step at a time. It occurred to her that the Ogre could be faking and at any second could leap up and swallow her whole. But the poor thing was crying. She cursed herself for being a sucker. She supposed her need to comfort anyone in distress came from all those hours with Carrie at the hospital. Sometimes the sunshine in her sister's smile didn't shine quite as bright.

When the Ogre came within touching distance, Arianne reached out until her hand patted its semi-bald head. The tuft of hair felt softer than she expected against her palm. The Ogre froze mid-sniffle. Arianne snatched her hand back, but when she saw one teary, beady eye staring up at her with a loss she recognized, her hand went back to its head.

"It's okay," she whispered. "Don't cry."

"Parents," she thought it said. The words were garbled by the tears.

"Your parents?"

The Ogre nodded. At least she thought it nodded.

"Are you lost?" Arianne asked.

It shook its head. Her hand seemed so small compared to it. The Ogre seemed to understand her, so she might as well continue the questioning.

"Why are you crying?"

"Dead," it grunted.

Arianne's heart twisted. She'd been right. What she'd seen in the Ogre's eyes looked like the kind of loss she'd seen when she stared into a mirror after Carrie's death. She forced herself to keep speaking.

"How did they die?"

The Ogre looked up at her then. Arianne forced a smile on her face, but her lips wobbled. It didn't seem like the Ogre would eat her any time soon, but fear still tied her stomach in knots.

The Ogre swiped its massive hand across its face, whipping away tears and snot. "Man come. Eat them."

Arianne understood him better now since he wasn't crying as hard. "What man?"

"Arianne!" Balthazar barked from the other side of camp. "Step away from the Ogre."

Chapter 15

DILLIGAS

The Ogre pushed Arianne behind its massive body as if to protect her and bellowed. The Ogre's cry shook the ground and rattled the trees. Every dangerous thing for miles around heard that sound. If Balthazar didn't dispatch the Ogre soon and leave the mountaintop, predators of the night would come after them, and then they'd truly and royally be screwed. At least Arianne was still alive. Balthazar took the consolation prize. But he couldn't be sure how long that status would remain unchanged.

"Balthazar," Arianne said, pulling his attention to her.

"Arianne, I need you to shut up right now."

The Ogre bared its large teeth and growled. Balthazar raised his scythe and pushed off from where he stood. The Ogre was young—not more than a toddler. It would be easy to dispose of. Balthazar didn't need its life force since the demon he'd drained filled him to bursting. He raised his scythe, the blade ready to chop off the Ogre's head when Arianne suddenly appeared in front of the massive creature, her arms spread out like a fence.

"Balthazar, no!"

Unable to stop his forward momentum, Balthazar used his feet to kick off the Ogre's chest high above Arianne's head and back flip. He landed a few yards away. The Ogre raised its fists at him and grumbled, not happy about being used as a springboard.

"What the hell's gotten into you?" Balthazar barked at Arianne, which made the Ogre growl at him.

Arianne turned around and patted the Ogre's stomach—the only place she could reach. She raised her head and made calming noises until the Ogre dipped its head to look at her.

"That's it," she said to the Ogre. "He's not going to hurt you."

"Who's not going to hurt him?"

"I'm going to need you to shut up now, Balthazar," Arianne said over her shoulder. She accompanied the words with a pointed look.

Balthazar planted his scythe on the ground, giving him easy access to it once whatever stupidity Arianne had gotten herself into played out. Didn't she know never to trust an Ogre? They were brutes who lived for nothing but violence. A group of Ogres in any army made the best infantry. They were strong and easy to command. The best for ramming into an opposing military.

"See?" Arianne said to the Ogre. "He's not going to hurt you. You just surprised him, that's all."

"Surprised my ass," Balthazar grumbled under his breath. He crossed his arms and waited for the inevitable carnage.

Shockingly—causing Balthazar to raise both his eyebrows—the Ogre grunted and sat on its haunches.

Are those tears in its eyes? Balthazar snorted in disgust. Babies. Aside from being icky and sticky, the waterworks they produced totally annoyed him. He scratched his head. Only Arianne could make an Ogre heel like a puppy. A humongous puppy with huge teeth that could tear her apart.

Arianne dried its tears, her fingers really close to the giant tusks that could easily impale her. Despite his calm appearance, Balthazar couldn't deny holding his breath the entire time. If he didn't have his arms crossed he wouldn't be able to suppress the urge to snatch her away. At the back of his mind he still formulated a plan to actually do that. If she wasn't standing so close to the Ogre, he could take her into his arms and run as fast as he could in the opposite direction. He didn't have to kill the Ogre. Arianne didn't seem to want that, so as a favor to her, he wouldn't, but he had to get her out of there. The hair at the back of his neck stood up. He felt the ghouls coming for them. They were still a few miles off, but they had heard the Ogre. Alone he could deal with the ghouls, but he had Arianne to think of now.

"Arianne, we have to go," he said calmly. He made sure to leave out his annoyance. If he pissed her off she might get stubborn on him and refuse to budge. By the wrinkle on her forehead when she faced him, she came close.

"But we just set up camp."

"Your little theatrics woke up the ghouls." He hiked a thumb over his shoulder. "They're on their way here now. We need to find a new place to camp."

She frowned at him then turned to the Ogre and asked it, "What's your name?"

If Balthazar was prone to dropping his jaw, he would have then. What could the crazy girl be thinking? Ogre's didn't have names.

"Uluru," the thing said in garbled speech.

Or they apparently did. Balthazar tilted his head. Sometimes he couldn't tell the sex of an Ogre, but if he wasn't mistaken, the two he'd hunted must have been the parents of the toddler Arianne now treated like a puppy.

"Okay, Uluru," Arianne said in a friendly tone. "You heard Balthazar. The ghouls are coming."

Uluru bared his teeth and huffed, ruffling Arianne's hair. She raised her hands and shook her head.

"No, we can't fight them. They're too dangerous."

"Uluru eat ghoul before. Good eats."

Huh. An Ogre with an appetite for ghoul. That could come in handy. Balthazar pushed the thought away. What was he thinking? They weren't using the Ogre to fight the ghouls. In fact, the less bloodshed the better. Balthazar didn't want to fight unless he absolutely had to.

"We have to go, Arianne," he repeated.

She ignored him and kept her attention on the Ogre. "We have to go, Uluru. Come with us."

"Hold on a f—" Balthazar caught himself and decided on a different word. "Freakin' minute!" He stepped forward and pointed. "That thing's not coming with us."

The Ogre growled at him.

"Yeah, that's right," Balthazar challenged. "Growl at me again and your head will roll before you even feel me cutting it off."

"Balthazar!" Arianne gasped. Anger quickly replaced her surprise. Worse, he saw the determination in her eyes. "Uluru just lost his parents. He's an orphan."

"And that matters to me because?"

Arianne looked at Uluru with sadness in her eyes Balthazar couldn't understand. "He has nowhere else to go." She brushed her hand over the Ogre's head. When she looked back at Balthazar, it was clear that she'd made up her mind. "He's coming with us or I'm staying here. And since you already left me once, you owe me to stay and protect us."

For a second time that night, Balthazar stood shocked. When did he suddenly become the protector of all? Coming up against Arianne, a.k.a the roadblock, and having no more time to argue, Balthazar snuffed out the flames and pulled his scythe off the ground.

To the Ogre he said, "You better keep up. If they catch you, I am not coming back for you." To Arianne he added, "Am I making myself clear?" When he saw them nod, he pointed at the Ogre. "Can you carry her?"

Without another word, Uluru picked up Arianne and placed her on its shoulder. "Hold on," it grumbled at her.

Arianne hugged its neck tight. Satisfied she wouldn't fall off, Balthazar bolted in the opposite direction of the coming group of ghouls. Heavy stomping steps followed. A pine or two toppled. He would have liked a less noisy getaway, but when an Ogre was involved, nothing muffled its movement.

Getting them out of there as fast as he could became Balthazar's priority.

They hadn't been running long when the ghouls' laughter—a series of *yip, yip, yips*—surrounded them. Balthazar skidded to a stop at the foot of the mountain when a group of five ghouls blocked his way. He turned around but another group blocked the way they came. Their green eyes glowed in the dark like two pinpoints. The Ogre growled, baring its teeth. But the ghouls—with their sharp claws, numerous teeth, and crumpled faces—weren't intimidated in the least. They only laughed all the more, their tattered clothing hanging on rail thin bodies. The weird thing about ghouls was that no matter how much they ate, they never gained an ounce. That made them doubly eager to keep eating. They were like the hyenas of the Underverse. Vicious. They didn't stop until they captured their prey.

Balthazar didn't wait for the ghouls to make the first move. He struck out with his scythe, cutting down three of the five in front of him. The other two dodged his attack and hissed. Quick as bullets, the ghouls shot out of the night and came at them in all directions. Balthazar prepared to attack and create a hole for them to get through when Arianne was suddenly thrust into his arms.

"Go!" the Ogre bellowed.

"No!" Arianne reached for him.

But Balthazar didn't wait. He jumped as high as he could to clear the closing in ghouls, leaving the Ogre to fend for itself.

"Balthazar! No!" Arianne screamed in his ear. "We have to go back. We have to help Uluru. They're going to kill him."

And as if to prove her point, the Ogre let out a gurgled cry. But Ogres were resilient creatures. No matter how young, the Ogre would last against the ghouls for quite a while.

Balthazar jumped from one pine to the next. "My bargain is with you," he said. "To protect you. I'm doing that right now."

"Forget the bargain," Arianne begged, tears clearly in her voice. "We need to help him. We need to go back! We can't just leave him!"

With each sentence, Arianne grew more and more hysterical. Balthazar ignored her and kept going. He knew of a cave they could hide in for the rest of the night. It would keep them safe until morning. An Ogre would provide the ghouls with enough distraction. Ghouls didn't have very long memories. In minutes, all their attention would be on the Ogre and they'd forget about the other two running away from them.

When the Ogre's growls and grunts seemed farther away, Balthazar said to a now limp Arianne, "You can't let his sacrifice be in vain, Arianne."

In the saddest voice he'd ever heard, Arianne said, "I hate you."

Chapter 16

IMHO

In a cave, miles away from where they'd left Uluru, Arianne cried. It started as sobs, then after what seemed like hours, settled into hics and huffs. She lay on Balthazar's coat with her back to him while he stood watch at the cave's entrance. She didn't know why she cried. She'd only met Uluru tonight, but something about the Ogre had touched her. Now seemed like as good a time as any to mourn everyone she'd lost. She had nothing better to do until morning when she and Balthazar continued their journey. Right now, she cried. For Carrie. For Ben. For Uluru, who must be dead too.

In the morning — or at least she thought it must be morning when Balthazar woke her — Arianne asked him for water so she could wash out her sore eyes. He nodded and left. Minutes later he came back with a clear plastic bag filled halfway. Balthazar pinched a corner until the water trickled out. Arianne cupped her hands over the stream and splashed her face with what she collected. The coolness felt good on her hot eyes.

Balthazar didn't meet her gaze when she looked at him. Was that guilt on his face? She couldn't be sure because he kept his expression pretty blank.

Arianne breathed in deep and let the cool air in the cave wake her up. She still had a long way to go mourning her best friend and sister, but after last night, she could make it through the rest of the trip. She could always fall apart again when she returned to her body. By then she'd have Niko back.

"What next?" she asked as Balthazar dumped the rest of the water outside the cave.

He snorted. "You talking to me again?"

"Don't be such a baby." Arianne stood up from where she spent the night and rolled out the cricks in her neck and back. "I'm pissed that you left—"

"In case you're forgetting, you're the one I'm supposed to protect."

She ignored his interruption. "You left Uluru to die. I'm still pissed at you for doing that. You could have taken all those ghouls."

"How can you be so sure?" he challenged.

"You want to be the next Death. Isn't that why you're helping out? If you weren't strong enough to take on the current Death then you'd be stupid to challenge him. But something tells me you're not stupid. So, yeah, forgive me for thinking you are strong enough to wipe the forest floor with those ghouls."

The guilt left his eyes, replaced by his usual seriousness. "You done whimpering?"

"Is there a way we could—"

"No." Balthazar knew she wanted to search for Uluru. Their connection and all that.

"Come on!"

"Don't make me command you to come with me." He pointed at the tattoo on his wrist.

Arianne's eyes widened. "You wouldn't."

"Granmare Baba said so long as I have this that you're my slave." He grinned. "Slaves do what their masters tell them to."

"I'll see you try. Slaves revolt."

"This isn't a negotiation, Arianne. We don't have time to run around the Underverse in search of an Ogre." He tilted his head toward the ring on her finger.

Arianne watched the pulse. Definitely weaker now. She closed her hand into a fist. "Then I want to make a grave for him."

"You've got to be kidding me."

Done arguing, Arianne stomped out of the cave and gathered as many rocks as she could. When her arms were full, she dumped her load at one side of the cave entrance. Balthazar, his coat back on, joined her. He stood at the other side of the entrance and crossed his arms.

"You might as well make yourself useful and grab more rocks," she said over her shoulder.

Rocks floated to join the ones she arranged into a small mound. She glanced over her shoulder at a bored looking Balthazar. He had his eyes on the sky, seeming not to pay attention to her at all.

"Neat trick."

He grimaced. "Just hurry it up. I want to get to the Voyeur before nightfall."

Arianne continued her rock arrangement. "Something tells me you're not as bad as you make yourself out to be."

Another one of those nasally snorts. "You on the Angel's tears again?"

"I'm serious." Arianne grabbed the rocks that floated toward her and added them to the mound. "If you're Mr. Bad Guy, why are you helping me with Uluru's grave?"

"You said you wanted me to be useful," Balthazar said. "So I'll be useful if it's going to speed things up."

Arianne used a small smile to banish the coming sadness again and focused on her work. Then something Uluru said to her made sense. "Were you the one who killed Uluru's parents?"

The long pause confirmed her suspicions.

"It's eat or be eaten here," he grumbled.

"That's not an answer to my question." Arianne wanted to hear Balthazar say it.

"I needed the life force. I wasn't going to see the Voyeur at less than full strength."

"Still not an answer."

"All right!" Balthazar snapped. "I killed the Ogre's—"

"Uluru."

He sighed. "I killed Uluru's parents for their life force. There, you happy?"

"No." Arianne stood up when she finished putting the mound together. Her heart felt heavy. What did she think? That Balthazar could be more than who she thought he was? A sinking feeling told her it might be foolish to hope he had some real kindness in him.

Just when the last of her hope drained away, a bright pink flower floated her way. Arianne stared at Balthazar a long time. He still had his eyes on the sky. She moved her gaze from him to the flower then back again. Forget where he found the pretty thing, the fact that it floated to her gave her hope some life.

"What's wrong?" Balthazar looked at her then, no emotion on his face or eyes, but Arianne knew better. She felt the embarrassment in his thoughts. "Don't they put flowers on graves where you come from? Stupid practice if you ask me. They just die anyway."

Letting the last of what he said go, Arianne plucked the flower out of the air and placed it on top of the mound she'd made for Uluru. She said a silent prayer not only for the Ogre but also for everyone she'd lost. For Carrie, that she might be happy wherever she found herself. For Ben, that he would find his way back to Carrie, knowing how much he loved her sister. And lastly, she thanked Uluru for sacrificing himself without really knowing the big picture. Balthazar was right. She shouldn't let the Ogre's sacrifice be in vain.

She wiped away the last of her tears and faced Balthazar. He stood a few feet from her. He had the same serious look in his eyes.

"What's the plan?" she asked.

He blinked. "I got some information last night that leads me to believe the Ghoul Woods are chaotic right now. If we're careful, I think we might make it through without any problems."

Arianne raised an eyebrow at him. "And where did you get this information from exactly?"

Balthazar grinned, showing her some fang. "Let's just say I ran into more than just the Ogres."

She frowned.

"Too soon?"

She waited until Balthazar continued.

"Look, it seems the Ghoul Woods have become Voyeur territory. She killed the king and took the prince for her lover."

"Ghouls aren't very organized. Even with the monarchy." Arianne dug through the information in her head. Ghouls had kings and queens only because they needed someone to lead them. The process of choosing who led them was a brutal and bloody one—often the winners ate the losers. May the strongest ghoul win, basically. She swallowed.

"With their prince shacking up with the Voyeur, it means they're more disorganized than usual. We might just have a chance."

Arianne shivered. "After seeing them last night, why would anyone...*you know.*"

A corner of Balthazar's lips twitched. "You'd be surprised. The ghouls you saw last night were the bottom feeders. Not all of them look like they stepped out of a *Walking Dead* set."

"You know that show?"

"Arianne—" he grinned fully now "—there's so much about me you don't know."

"That's what I'm afraid of."

Balthazar turned away from her and walked to the edge of the entrance of the cave. She was so preoccupied with her grief and the need to honor Uluru's sacrifice that she hadn't noticed that the cave opened out to a cliff face high above the ground. In the distance spread the tall top-heavy trees of the Ghoul Woods. The shiver that rattled down her back didn't come from the prospect of walking into the place the ghouls called home but what Balthazar said next.

"You should be afraid, little girl."

Chapter 17

SH

Confusion plagued Balthazar. For every tear Arianne shed last night, he felt a knife go through his chest. Very irritating, if you asked him. With each hour she sobbed, he wanted to run away. To find a place where he couldn't hear her hiccups and hitches. But he stayed at the mouth of the cave all night, keeping guard. He endured her pain. He'd caused it. He should have been happy about it, but he wasn't. Still disturbed that he wasn't, actually.

He shouldn't be feeling all torn up over some tears and puffy eyes. But he couldn't help himself. Had he gone soft? He shuddered. *Oh hell no!*

At the entrance to the Ghoul Woods, Balthazar stopped.

"What is it?" was the first thing Arianne had asked him all day. He had to admit—only to himself—that having her quiet unnerved him more than when she yammered. A quiet chick was a chick stewing. In his experience, nothing good came from a stewing chick.

The silence within the woods raised Balthazar's guard. Normally, smaller creatures, mostly wood nymphs and several species of birds, created enough background noise. Today, the woods were dead still.

"I don't like it," Balthazar finally said, his eyes flicking from shadow to shadow within the wood. "No matter how many ghouls are in these woods, it's never this quiet."

"Maybe they're not in there?"

Balthazar raised an obnoxious eyebrow at Arianne. She shrugged it off. He approached the nearest Blood Tree and pointed at the braided trunk.

"Make a cut here."

Arianne approached to stand beside him. "Why?"

"Just make the cut, Arianne."

She pulled the blasted knife that seemed to tease him every time he stared at the blade out of its sheath and made the cut he'd asked for. Sap the rich red of blood oozed out. The tree shuddered as if in pain. Balthazar cupped his hands over the wound and collected as much sap as he could. Then he rubbed it on Arianne.

"Hey!" She danced away from him, wiping at the sap on her jacket.

"Shhh!" Balthazar froze and listened. Then in an angry whisper he said, "Keep it down. We can't risk the ghouls hearing us."

Arianne frowned, pulling her hand — now sticky with sap — away from her jacket. "Then what's this for?"

Balthazar cupped more of the sap and began rubbing it all over himself. "This will mask our scent from the ghouls. If they can't smell us the chances of them finding us decreases."

"Eeww!" Arianne grimaced.

Typical girl. Balthazar snorted. He prepared for another argument, but she proved him wrong once again by making another cut on the tree and rubbing the sap all over her body. Balthazar hated being wrong, and this little girl proved him wrong more and more often the longer they stayed together. He had to finish this mission before he lost his mind completely, or bruised his ego enough that he'd lose his will to challenge D for his seat.

They rubbed sap all over their bodies in silence, until Balthazar said, "Make sure to get it on your face too." He demonstrated by rubbing some on his cheeks.

She grimaced, but didn't complain. "Hair too?"

He grinned. "You're learning."

"It smells like pee."

"Better pee than something else."

"Oh don't even go there. I'm pretending this is a mud mask. A really stinky mud mask."

"Whatever gets you through the day, little girl."

Arianne rubbed some into her hair and whimpered. "This is so disgusting. Please promise me there's a bath at the end of this neck of the trip. I may not be in my body right now, but I still feel the need to stay clean."

Balthazar barked a laugh. "When we get into Voyeur territory, the mansion will have amenities for a shower, or a bath if you prefer."

"I know I've lasted this long without needing a shower." Her nose crinkled. "But now I really, really need one."

"Stop being such a girl."

"Well, sor—ry!" She huffed. "For a pretty boy you're so annoying."

"Better annoying than whiny."

Arianne opened her mouth to say something else, but a thought crossed her mind and she shut her mouth instead. Balthazar felt the curiosity in that thought. Damn the connection for not being any clearer.

Finished covering himself with sap, Balthazar checked Arianne. He twisted her right, then left, running his eyes over every part of her exposed to him.

Once satisfied their scent—which they shared now because of Granmare Baba—had been masked, he said, "Watch your step and try not to make a sound. Stay behind me at all times. Keep your eyes on my back the whole time. Ignore anything you hear and see. Move with me. Am I making myself clear?"

The determination on her face answered his question way before she said yes. Finally, maybe they were on the same page about this trip. He nodded at her once before he turned around and began their trek through the Ghoul Woods.

He was banking on the fact that Arianne knew enough about the woods that she'd listen to him. Ghouls weren't the only residents of the Ghoul Woods. They were the most dangerous, but that didn't make the rest of the inhabitants less deadly. He didn't quite manifest his scythe, but he kept it close—a shadow by his side. He just had to wrap his hand around the staff and it would fully materialize.

Soon the gloom of the top-heavy trees surrounded them. Not a sound. Not even a bird chirped. It had been a while since Balthazar had been to the Ghoul Woods. It couldn't have changed so much that the birds disappeared. He suspected the Voyeur had a hand in the silence. Expanding her territory didn't mean anything good for the Underverse. Greed never did. She grabbed power. He couldn't keep up with all the jostling for power in the Underverse from the Nethers. Granted, he'd had other things to worry about at the time. Now the bigger picture became clearer. Things shifted, changed. If he didn't make his play for D's seat soon, someone else would. He could feel it in his bones. Balthazar was D's best bet for a successor to the Crossroads. Others would just take advantage of all that residual energy. He snorted. Well, he couldn't promise there wouldn't be any advantage-taking on his part, but he certainly had more self-control than the Voyeur — if he made comparisons.

About halfway through the woods the silence reached an unnerving peak. Balthazar almost exhaled in relief when he spotted the first ghoul patrol. He grabbed Arianne and pushed her into a hollow made by two entwining trees. She opened her mouth. He felt the question coming on, so he shoved his hand over her lips. Their softness shocked through him for a second. Her eyes grew wide then narrowed. He grinned. Anger sparked those blue eyes to life. And damn if he didn't like it.

Pulling himself away from the useless — and potentially dangerous — thoughts, Balthazar raised his free forefinger to his lips in the universal sign for shut up. Only when Arianne's breathing calmed and she nodded once did he drop his hand from her lips. He pointed at the nearing group of ghouls. She flicked her gaze at them and trembled. Balthazar screamed at her using his eyes, his lips in a tight line. If she so much as squeaked, not even their bargain would keep her safe from him.

Balthazar didn't give thanks much, but when Arianne managed to keep her mouth shut despite her trembling as the ghouls passed them, he breathed a quiet thanks. He inched his way out of the tree and completely manifested his scythe. He swung it once and beheaded all five ghouls in one go. Their bodies slumped to the ground in soft thumps. He gestured for Arianne to leave the protection of the tree.

"That's harsh," she whispered when she reached his side.

"There's more where that came from. Think of it as payback for the Ogre."

"Thank you."

Even through the blood red sap, the smile on her face charmed him unlike anything he'd seen — and he'd seen many things in his life, most of them despicable. He snorted and turned on his heel, resuming their journey.

To distract himself from Arianne's smile, he considered the patrol they encountered. The first one this deep into the woods? He'd expected them half a mile in. Something had changed in the Ghoul Woods beyond his comprehension. He pushed down his curiosity. Now wasn't the time to play detective. He had no power over what happened in these woods. He stuck to his goal. Get Arianne to the Voyeur. They still had half the woods to traverse to get there. He didn't return his scythe to its shadow form, taking strength from its solid presence in his hand.

He was so caught up in his thoughts, Balthazar almost missed the yips coming from their left. Shit. Relying on instincts honed by countless battles, Balthazar repositioned himself into a defensive stance. He pushed Arianne directly behind him and raised his scythe just in time to block the first slash of claws. He pushed against the ghoul and slashed it in half before it could regain its footing. Three more jumped at him. A second patrol so close to the first? It baffled Balthazar enough that he almost didn't block the combined attack. He forced himself to focus. He whipped his scythe in a wide arch and knocked the three advancing ghouls over like bowling pins. He made mincemeat out of them fast enough. He could manage them in groups of five. Piece of cake.

"One's getting away." Arianne pointed at the retreating ghoul.

Shit. He'd celebrated too soon. He took a step forward to pursue it then stopped. Too late. Ghouls moved fast. The thing likely ran to invite his buddies to the party. Instead of leaving Arianne, he whirled around to face her.

"How fast can you run?" he asked.

"Fast enough," she said.

He doubted the truth in her statement. "We're going to need to run. That guy's spreading the word. You need to keep up. I can't carry you because I have to cover our asses, do you get me?"

"Point in the direction we need to go."

Balthazar tilted his head in confusion.

"Just do it," Arianne commanded in a powerful voice he'd never thought her capable of.

He did as she'd asked. Arianne took off in that direction. He grinned and licked his lips. The girl continued to surprise him. He gave chase, making sure to keep her in the lead.

Chapter 18

LMAO

Running through the Ghoul Woods, and trying her best not to trip, Arianne thought she'd been doing well at following Balthazar's instructions. She'd let him take the lead when they entered the woods. Stayed directly behind him. She kept her eyes on the ground most of the time so she didn't accidentally step on a branch. She even ignored how distracted he'd been. Balthazar completely missing the second ghoul patrol seemed like something that shouldn't have happened. Now they were running for their lives—again. Arianne had a feeling this happened a lot in the Underverse.

She'd been doing well until she spotted the Nixies—fluffy pink, round creatures that lived in wooded areas all over the Underverse. No one knew much about them except that they barely showed themselves. Some help Granmare Baba's information was. Couldn't she have given Arianne the comprehensive version? She muttered her hate for the witch again. The Nixies laughed—their voices the tiniest things.

Arianne ignored them until they started calling her name.

"Ari, Ari, Ari."

Shut up, shut up, shut up, she thought and kept running. Somewhere in the distance the distinct yipping of the ghouls reached her ears. She couldn't be sure which direction they came from because sound traveled weirdly in the woods. Her lungs burned, but she kept running. Balthazar hadn't said anything since she'd sprinted in the direction he pointed to, but she felt him close behind her. Once in a while he pushed her forward. She knew he could go faster and that she slowed him down. She tried to pick up her pace. The blood in her thighs magically transformed to acid. She may not need food or drink in the Underverse, but she sure as hell still got tired. She'd never really been a fan of gym in school. Now she cursed that fact, hearing her gym teacher lecturing her about the importance of exercise.

"Ari, Ari, Ari," the Nixies called.

Arianne glanced at a group of them floating to her right.

"Keep going," Balthazar growled behind her.

She grunted. Her braid bounced painfully against her back — a *thump, thump, thump* that almost matched her heartbeat. The yips sounded closer now too.

The Nixies started again. *"Ari, Ari, Ari, we can help. We can help."*

"What?" Arianne said around the burning that moved from her lungs to her throat now. She couldn't keep running any longer.

"We can help you."

"Arianne, don't listen to them," Balthazar said.

"You can hear them too?"

"Over here. Over here."

The group Arianne saw gestured for them to come nearer. It seemed like no matter how far Arianne ran the Nixies managed to follow. When she took her eyes off where she was going to look at them, she spotted the first group of ghouls too. An army of claws and teeth. Balthazar wouldn't have a hope of holding them off and keeping Arianne safe at the same time. She had her knife, but against a battalion of ghouls, it might as well be a toothpick.

"I'm making an executive decision," she said to Balthazar over her shoulder.

"Arianne, don't!"

But she didn't listen to him. She veered toward the Nixies. They beckoned her with their tiny hands. When she reached them, a hole opened up and some of them jumped in. Arianne skidded to a stop. Balthazar slammed into her. He grabbed her arms for support and by some miracle kept them both from falling into the hole.

"Inside, inside. Quick!" the remaining Nixies said at the same time.

"No!" Balthazar said.

Arianne turned her head so she could see around Balthazar. A wave of ghouls crashed their way. She could make out the drool streaming out from between their lips. Without thinking, she turned in Balthazar's arms. She grabbed his jacket and kicked off the ground until they both fell back into the black void. The remaining Nixies leapt after them. Arianne saw the light from where they'd jumped from snap shut. A ghoul stuck its arm in at the wrong time, and the closing hole cut it off. Arianne closed her eyes and pulled Balthazar closer. She felt his arms wrap around her as they plummeted toward whatever.

Balthazar twisted, and Arianne felt them switch positions. She suddenly lay on top of him as they fell.

"Don't argue with me," he said so calmly that she almost didn't believe he spoke.

"But we don't know what we're landing on," Arianne whispered. She didn't know why she needed to be quiet, but the blackness around them closed in so tightly she didn't want to disturb it.

"Should have thought of that before you jumped in."

Arianne shook her head. "Better than being ghoul food. You should be thanking me."

Balthazar grinned, his white hair whipping around his face. "Jury's still out on that one. We might not survive the fall."

The bubble of worry in her gut transformed into boiling panic. Suddenly, she couldn't breathe. Her fingers went numb from clinging tightly to Balthazar's coat. They'd been falling for a long time now. A plunge this long never had good consequences. *Pancakes,* she thought, her heart in her throat.

"No worries. No worries." The Nixies fell with them. Or around them, Arianne corrected herself. Their fluffy, puffy fur ruffled with the wind from their fall. They looked so much like those fuzzy balls on some key chains. She would have thought of them as cute if they weren't all skydiving to their deaths.

Blinding light closed Arianne's eyes for her. She screamed while a chorus of *wheeee* surrounded them. Arianne rested her head against Balthazar's chest and focused on his heartbeat. Hers must be beating a mile a second, but his kept a perfectly calm rhythm. She drew unexpected comfort from the strength of his heartbeat. If Balthazar wasn't worried, then why should she be? He promised he'd protect her and she believed him.

A loud splash cut off Arianne's scream. Something cold and wet enveloped them. Arianne opened her eyes a second after cannonballing into the water. She pushed against Balthazar to swim to the surface. She swam a couple of feet up when she noticed Balthazar didn't follow her. Arianne looked around and spotted him plunging deeper. He had his eyes closed. The impact must have knocked him out.

Arianne switched her course and swam toward Balthazar. She reached for his coat and pulled him up, but his weight kept dragging them down. Panicked, Arianne kept pulling, struggling to get them to the surface. She used one of her arms to paddle upward. No use. They still kept sinking. If she thought her lungs hurt when she ran for her life, they turned into a furnace now that she couldn't breathe. But she wouldn't let him go. She'd only made it this far because of him. Screw the consequences, she wouldn't leave him.

Arianne just about lost the last of her breath when the Nixies crowded around her and Balthazar. They each grabbed a part of his coat and pulled. Arianne nodded at all of them in thanks, and they all heaved and heaved until Arianne's head broke the water's surface. She gulped in as much air as her lungs could accommodate. Balthazar broke the surface too, but remained unconscious. Arianne's summer as a life guard kicked in. She hooked her arm over Balthazar's shoulders and doggy paddled to shore. The Nixies helped tug him the whole way. They must not have needed to breathe because Arianne suspected the only reason Balthazar floated had to do with the furry little things supporting his weight under the water.

Reaching shore, Arianne stumbled forward, her clothes waterlogged. She balanced her footing and pulled Balthazar the rest of the way until only his feet were in the water. Working fast, she put her ear on his chest. He still had a heartbeat, but it seemed weaker than before. She moved her ear to his nose and couldn't feel him breathe. She tilted his head back and opened his mouth. Pinching his nose, she breathed into his mouth. Then she began chest compressions. After a count of five, she repeated breathing into his mouth.

"Come on," she said between her teeth as she pumped Balthazar's chest. She breathed into his mouth again. "Wake up you, jerk!"

Water gushed out of Balthazar's mouth, and while he coughed like his life depended on it, Arianne rolled him onto his side so he wouldn't choke the water back down. Every time Balthazar spit water out an ugly curse followed. To Arianne they sounded like the best words anyone could ever listen to.

"Shit," Balthazar said. He coughed some more. "Damn…" *Cough.* "It…" *Cough, heave.* "All…" *Cough.* "To…" *Inhale.* "Hell," he spat out.

Arianne sat back on her haunches and pushed back strands of her hair that had escaped from her braid. She needed to retie the thing once her hair dried. Relieved laugher bubbled out of her chest.

"So damn not funny." Balthazar groaned before he sat up slowly. "Felt like I slammed into a brick wall." He shook his head like a dog would after a bath. Arianne squealed when the cold drops hit her face. She raised her hands to block the rest.

The Nixies squealed with her. The little things had crowded around them while she'd been busy saving Balthazar's life.

She smiled at them. "Thank you."

They jumped up and down and cheered like an army of Lilliputians, except round, pink, and fuzzy — even the water-logged ones.

"*Yay, yay, yay!*" they cheered, their tiny hands in the air.

Arianne laughed. They were too cute! Then she caught Balthazar staring at her from the corner of her eye. He sat very still, just staring. She locked gazes with him and tilted her head to the side.

"What?" she asked.

The Nixies quieted down, like they knew something was about to happen.

"You saved my life," Balthazar said.

Did she hear awe in his voice? Arianne couldn't believe it. Maybe she'd heard his tone wrong. He just came back to life, after all.

"I think you're in shock." She came closer and checked his white pupils to see if they were dilated.

Balthazar leaned away from her. "I'm the one who's supposed to be saving you," he grumbled, dropping his gaze.

Arianne reached out and paused, remembering how Balthazar didn't like to be touched. She dropped her hand to her lap. "You did save me. You took most of the impact of that fall. I wouldn't have survived if you hadn't."

He touched his lips, and at first she didn't know why, but she blushed, realizing what she'd had to do to save him. This was becoming super awkward, so she scrambled to explain.

"I was a lifeguard one summer," she babbled. "I went into lifesaving mode the second I felt you weren't breathing. You would have done the same thing."

She gasped from the way Balthazar looked at her. His expression could only be called confused, like he stared at something he couldn't understand. The words sprang out of Arianne's lips before she could censor them.

"Don't make a big deal out of it." She focused her gaze on the Nixies. "I still need you to find the Redeemer. I have a feeling this trip is far from over. Let's call it even."

At the corner of her eye, she saw Balthazar's face turn blank. But before he could stand up, the Nixies jumped all over him. He struggled, but so many of them swarmed him that they soon covered him from head to toe. The all-black Balthazar covered all over by pink Nixies. Arianne couldn't help herself. She laughed and laughed.

"Not funny!" Balthazar barked.

"It's a little funny," Arianne said. She covered her open mouth, but the laughs kept coming.

The Nixies laughed too and began jumping up and down on Balthazar.

"Get them off me!"

Chapter 19

FWIW

Balthazar lay there stewing, ignoring the jumping Nixies on top of him while Arianne laughed. She'd saved him. Damn it! He should have been the one doing the saving. Now he owed her, and he didn't know how to feel about it. The thought of her lips on his as she breathed life back into him disturbed him as well.

Plunging into the water had knocked him out cold. He'd seen nothing, felt nothing. If it weren't for Arianne's quick thinking, it might have taken him longer to recuperate, and time wasn't a commodity they had a lot of these days. D had been worse when they'd spoken last. That had been more than a day ago. When he'd gotten a glimpse of the ring on Arianne's finger as they ran away from the marauding ghouls, the pulsing seemed distinctly weaker. They needed to keep going.

He rolled onto his side, sending the Nixies flying in a chorus of *yahoo, yippee,* and *wahoo.* He grunted, but tried not to crush any of the too-pink creatures. Arianne had reacted horribly when he'd crushed the whisps, and he wanted to avoid the meltdown squashing the Nixies would bring. She apparently thought they were cute. At least the feeling from her thoughts told him so. If he was the type of creature that puked, he'd lose his gourd right about now. He pushed to his feet and shook off the dizziness that came with being knocked unconscious.

Arianne's laugher redoubled, almost knocking her over. She hugged herself, her cheeks pink from something hilarious that Balthazar couldn't understand. He narrowed his eyes at her.

"What?" he asked with an almost wicked trepidation. Did he really want to know?

She pointed up at him, still laughing. Her legs flailed about.

He raised an eyebrow, waiting for actual words to come out of the girl.

Arianne gulped in a lungful of air and forced herself to speak around the giggles. "Your face." Another round of giggles.

Balthazar refused to touch his face. "What about it?"

"It's full of kiss marks."

His eyes widened before he ran for the water's edge — they'd fallen into a massive lake, now that he got a good look at it — and stared at his reflection. The damned Nixies had left their mark on every available surface of exposed skin he had, even on the tips of his fingers where they weren't covered by the fingerless gloves. He saw red then. He didn't care how cute Arianne thought the puffy pink creatures were. He manifested his scythe and growled at them. The pink balls scattered amidst tiny, squeaky screams.

"Oh, you better run!" He continued growling like a rabid dog.

Arianne pushed off the grassy embankment they'd been on this whole time and raised her hands, no hint of concern on her face at all, just a playful smile across her lips.

"Come on, Balthazar," she said, stepping a little closer. "They were just having some fun."

Balthazar's nostrils flared. "You call this a bit of fun?" He pointed at his face filled with countless red spots. "My head looks like a giant pimple."

Arianne made it worse by giggling some more. Balthazar dropped his head and returned his scythe to its inert state. What had happened to his carefully built bad guy reputation? The Nixies were right to run. Arianne, on the other hand, represented a whole different bowl of beans. The crazy kind. She'd gotten too used to him. She no longer saw him as something to be afraid of. He had to remedy that, and quickly.

"Don't think for a second that just because you saved my life we're in any way even, little girl," he said, adding bite to his words.

Her brow furrowed when she said, "Don't bark at me. The Nixies saved us from the ghouls. If I hadn't listened to them we wouldn't be here."

"Here" was a small island surrounded by the lake Balthazar had used as a mirror earlier. At the middle of the island grew a stand of trees with orange leaves. The grass looked green, at least, and the water clear. A massive cavern enclosed the rest of the space. They seemed to be in an underground cave of some sort. Balthazar knew of these places, but had never been in one. The Underverse had many facets that lay undiscovered. The home of the Nixies seemed to be one of them.

"You were wrong," Arianne said, distracting him from his thoughts.

He looked down his nose at her. "Wrong about what?"

She pointed at the cowering Nixies. Grouped together, they resembled a giant, trembling pink clump.

"Not everything in the Underverse is dangerous."

Balthazar snorted. "Just because they haven't attacked you yet doesn't make them any less dangerous."

"Don't snort at me." Arianne frowned. "Just because you're wrong doesn't mean you have to get snippy. The Nixies helped us. They could have just as easily ignored what was going on, but they brought us here instead."

"Don't be naïve, Arianne." Balthazar indicated the "here" she mentioned. "If you haven't noticed, we're in a place that doesn't look like it has any exits. How are you supposing we're getting out of here? In case you're forgetting, we have a date with the Voyeur."

Before Arianne could respond, a brave Nixie separated from the group and said, "*We can take you to the Voyeur.*"

"See?" Arianne said to Balthazar like they had nothing else to argue about then smiled at the still shaking thing. "You'll help us?"

Nixies nodded using their whole body since they didn't have a distinct head. Of course, Arianne found it adorable. Balthazar, on the other hand, found it gag-worthy. He hated having his initial impression of the Underverse as a killer world shattered. He didn't trust the Nixies, no matter how small, cute, and pink Arianne thought they were. He shuddered at his use of the word *cute*. Never in his considerably long life had he used that word to describe anything.

"*We can take you through the Ghoul Woods without the ghouls finding out.*"

"And why would you do that?"

"Balthazar!"

He pretended he didn't hear the admonishment in Arianne's tone. "You don't need to help us, yet you do. Explain yourself, Nixie."

The pink fluff pointed at Arianne. "*She is a pure one.*"

"That doesn't explain anything." Balthazar glanced at Arianne and his gaze landed on the red thread no one else but those from the Crossroads could see. The fray he'd spotted before looked worse now. The blood drained from his face. She didn't survive the fall as unscathed as he had originally thought. Tomas had warned her about what would happen if she was separated from the thread. She'd turn into a Wraith, a being so consumed by hate that it lived on the souls of others. Balthazar wouldn't hesitate ending her if that happened. He made a mental note to keep a close eye on the fraying section of her thread. Arianne didn't seem to notice, and that could be bad, maybe even add to her carelessness.

"*Believe what you want, Enforcer,*" said the Nixie, no longer trembling.

The mention of his identity drew Arianne's attention again. In Balthazar's periphery he saw her go very still. She stared at the Nixie intently. Balthazar had to tread carefully now.

"If you know what I am, then you know what I can do if you betray us," he said softly.

"*We know many things, Enforcer.*" The Nixie turned from him to Arianne and back. "*We know when we will die, and this is not that day.*"

"Why did you help us?" Arianne asked.

The Nixie faced her, joined by several of its companions. "*We pledged to aid the purest of souls.*"

"I'm not pure."

Balthazar would have laughed if the situation wasn't so serious. Arianne knew so little about what she was. Her purity was one of the reasons why he'd risked bringing her to Granmare Baba in the first place. Now she lived on the witch's radar. Pure souls were hard to find and held so much power in them, they could feed the Crossroads for a long time. Arianne walking into Death's den, even without knowing that, was a ballsy thing.

"*Be careful of this one.*" The Nixie pointed at Balthazar. "*He means you great harm.*"

Arianne looked at him, but not with fear.

He shrugged. "I've never lied about what I am."

She returned her gaze to the Nixie. "Can you give us a moment before we go?"

The Nixies nodded in that full-bodied way they did and moved away from where Balthazar and Arianne stood.

"I'll just change my clothes and then we'll go," she said when the Nixies went out of earshot.

"I don't trust them." Balthazar knelt by the water and washed the Nixie kiss marks from his face and hands.

"You don't trust anyone."

He looked over his shoulder at Arianne and looked away quickly when he saw she'd removed her jacket. "It's what's kept me alive this long."

"I have a feeling you're not the fast-dying type."

"Yet you saved me anyway." How did he get back to that topic? Balthazar splashed more cold water on his face to relieve some of the heat residing there. He heard Arianne move toward the stand of trees. She wanted privacy while she changed. Not that he found anything she had to offer body-wise appealing, but he gave her what she asked for by keeping his gaze on the placid underground lake.

"I did what I had to." Arianne grunted, sounding like she struggled against her clothes. The Blood Tree sap was pretty sticky. "You'd do the same for me."

"You sound so confident about that."

"Let's hope I don't have to put it to the test. You can be so unreliable sometimes."

Balthazar stifled a laugh by coughing. Arianne was starting to get him. It didn't sit comfortably with him. Someone who knew too much knew your weaknesses. And Balthazar would rather die than expose himself that way to a girl who wasn't even old enough to understand what he'd gone through in his life.

"Okay, all set," Arianne said.

She'd re-braided her hair when Balthazar turned around to face her. His plunge had washed away most of the sap from his clothes, so he didn't feel the need to change like Arianne did. She still wore the leather pants he wished didn't hug her curves the way they did, but she'd changed into a new shirt and sweater before shrugging on the jacket she'd discarded previously.

"I still don't feel like we should let the Nixies help us," he said, eyeing the pink balls coming near them again.

Arianne pursed her lips at him. "You said it yourself. The pulse on the ring is getting weaker. We don't have much time. I for one don't want to fight my way through the ghouls, do you?"

She had a point. Balthazar hated it. Of course, he could just order her not to let the Nixies help them, but he'd be a hundred kinds of stupid to do that. As much as he hated admitting that they needed help since he didn't know where they were, he let Arianne do all the talking with the Nixies.

"We're ready," she said, giving him one last glance that said she could handle it from here. He raised an eyebrow at her but didn't say anything more.

Chapter 20

OIC

The Nixies opened another portal for Arianne and Balthazar to walk through, this one bigger than the one they'd fallen into to get to Nixie Island. The Nixies hopped in first. Arianne inched toward the portal and stuck her head in. She didn't want a repeat of the endless fall. She breathed a sigh of relief. The portal opened to a long tunnel lit by spherical orbs floating along one wall. The tunnel seemed like it had been cut from what she assumed was the inside of a mountain or somewhere deep underground.

Not trusting the solid ground ahead even if the Nixies had already gone ahead of her, Arianne took a tentative step, keeping one foot outside the portal just in case.

"Oh for suck's sake," Balthazar said. He grabbed Arianne by the waist and lifted her into the other side of the portal before joining her. She yelped a little too late. She'd already been set on her feet when the pathetic sound escaped her lips.

"You keep forgetting we don't have time," Balthazar added, the snort in his voice.

"Suck's?" Arianne raised an eyebrow at him. "Don't get all gentlemanly on me now."

Balthazar dropped a nasty case of the f-bomb. "Better?"

"Much."

He gestured for her to lead the way. Arianne didn't argue. Considering how little Balthazar trusted the Nixies and vice versa, having her in between both parties seemed like the better option. The Nixies seemed content to move ahead of them, not bothering to look back to see if Balthazar and Arianne followed. They hopped and skipped, bumping into each other and giggling tiny giggles. Arianne envied what seemed like such an uncomplicated life. They lived on their little island, once in a while saving someone like her from killer ghouls. What did they call her? Pure?

She shook her head. After everything she'd been through, pure wasn't the word she'd use. Exhausted. Drained. Running on fumes. Okay, the last bit was three words, but she didn't care. She held on to her motivation—saving Niko—so she could keep going.

"You really are pure," Balthazar whispered from behind her.

Without looking back, Arianne said, "What do you know about that?"

"It's not about knowing." She heard the shrug in his voice. "I've been alive long enough to know how to spot a pure soul, and yours is as pure as it comes. Even Redeemer quality."

Arianne laughed at that. "Me? A Redeemer?" She shook her head. "I don't consider myself that bad of a person, but I've had my share of mean girl moments."

"I doubt that."

"I once *outed* this girl in front of the cheerleading squad."

"And why did you do that?"

She recalled the memory like it happened only yesterday. Darla had bullied Arianne for years because she got it into her head that she was in love with her. Arianne admitted to being partially at fault for leading Darla on. She became friends with Darla at the time Carrie had just been diagnosed with kidney disease and needed a transplant. It had been a pretty rough year for everyone, and Darla welcomed her with open arms. When Arianne refused Darla's advances, the bullying started. Darla lost everything the day she threatened to hurt Niko. Not that she could because of Niko's Reaper status, but Arianne "outed" her anyway in order to keep Niko's secret. Arianne guessed that was why Darla wanted to run her over. Niko saved her, which caused Darla to swerve into a pole. Darla had been unconscious and bleeding when the ambulance drove away that night. Since Arianne had been in the Crossroads and now the Underverse shortly after that, she didn't know if Darla had survived the crash.

In some ways, it did feel like only yesterday that she had jumped in front of Niko to save him from the wrath of Darla. "She threatened to break Niko's kneecaps. I guess I just had enough of her constant bullying."

"Amateur."

"I almost didn't give my sister the kidney transplant she desperately needed." Arianne didn't know why that slipped out. Call it a desperate move to prove Balthazar and the Nixies lied about her being pure.

"The way I'd do it? Just to be un-pure? I'd drug someone, cut out their kidney, and leave them in a tub of ice. Now that's as far from pure as you can get."

"You just have an answer for everything don't you?" She turned around and walked backward, glaring at Balthazar with each step she took.

He stared back, unfazed. "Our actions don't dictate the purity of our souls. Sure, they taint our souls, but you would have to do something truly heinous to really do some damage to your soul. I'd say you're just looking for excuses to deny what's clearly the truth. Why don't you just accept it and save us the aggravation? The Nixies wouldn't have helped you if you weren't a pure soul."

Arianne turned back around and considered Balthazar's words. Just because he spoke of the truth didn't mean she had to agree. "If there was someone with a really pure soul, it would be Carrie. She was the nicest person I know…" She paused, swallowed around the lump in her throat, and corrected herself. "Knew. When Niko reaped her, she had the brightest soul I'd ever seen."

"You can see the souls of the dead?"

Did she just hear awe in Balthazar's voice? Arianne shook her head. The acoustics in the tunnel must be messing with her hearing. She shrugged, never liking to make a big deal about seeing the dead. "Happened after the transplant. I died for a second on the operating table. When I came back, I started seeing souls. I wish I hadn't. No one told me they were naked."

Balthazar chuckled. "Clothes don't follow into the afterlife, Arianne. As you well know."

"Hollywood always gets it wrong, huh?"

"You don't know the half of it."

Arianne grew quiet for a second, thinking back to what the Nixies said about Balthazar. They told her he would hurt her. A part of her believed them, but like he'd said, if he'd wanted to hurt her then he would have already. She refused to give up on him. Balthazar had redeemable qualities. Sure he'd left Uluru to die amongst the ghouls, but he did give her a flower to leave on the memorial she'd put together for him. Then the first part of the Nixies' conversation with Balthazar surfaced.

"What does being an Enforcer mean?" she asked, keeping her gaze on the Nixies yards away from them cheerily chatting with each other.

"I told you, we're not here to share sob stories," he grumbled, but she heard him giving in. His tone didn't sound as stringent as the last time he'd barked at her.

"We're not sharing sob stories." Arianne thought fast. "I'm just trying to understand. Granmare Baba didn't unlock that piece of information, but she clearly put it in my head. Why would she do that if it wasn't important?"

"That old hag can be malicious sometimes. Who knows why she put that shit in your head in the first place? For all I know she did it to torture me."

"I get the feeling you really hate everyone."

"Not much to like in the Underverse."

Arianne veered away from the topic of why Balthazar seemed to hate all things and returned to her original line of questioning. "So being an Enforcer?"

She waited with baited breath. They'd been traveling together for some time now. She believed she deserved a little information about him.

"It's what I used to be," he finally said. "A long time ago."

"You don't seem happy about it."

"Because I'm not!"

"You don't have to yell."

Balthazar cleared his throat. "There's really no point in rehashing the past, little girl. We're here to find the Redeemer, that's all. The sooner we do that the sooner I get to challenge D for his seat and you get your precious Niko back."

She didn't miss the venomous hate Balthazar sprinkled around Niko's name when he'd said it. "What is it about Niko that gets you all riled up? What did he do to you?"

"I'm pretty sure you don't know anything about him," Balthazar challenged.

Arianne shifted through what she did know and said, "He's the Reaper of Georgia. He owns a Mustang. He likes cooking." Arianne realized she didn't really know much about the guy she loved. Sure, she'd been observing him over the years. He drank soda at lunch every day, but hardly ate anything. He'd been hanging out with Darla's crew since he transferred to Blackwood High from Atlanta. What else?

Nothing.

She wracked her brain for more. And nothing.

Little by little doubt spread in Arianne's chest. All the information in her head seemed superficial at best. Kids' stuff. Suddenly the ground didn't feel as solid underneath her feet. Granmare Baba's warning of forgetting about him added to her mounting confusion. What were they keeping from her?

Balthazar made things worse. "And you say you love him? How do you know it's really love when you hardly know anything about the guy's past?"

"I just do."

She swallowed. Her words sounded hollow to her ears. For the first time Arianne questioned her feelings for Niko. Her heart ached. Then she stopped herself. She did love him. She couldn't be wrong about her feelings. With everything that had happened, they'd hardly had any time to get to know each other. After she found the Redeemer, she'd have all the time in the world with him.

"Have you ever been in love?" she forced out calmly.

"No." He said it so quietly that Arianne wouldn't have heard it if solid rock didn't surround them on all sides.

"Then you shouldn't accuse me of not knowing if I'm in love with Niko or not."

"Ari, Ari, Ari." The Nixies called excitedly.

They'd reached the end of the tunnel during her argument with Balthazar. Well, it wasn't exactly an argument when only one person raised her voice. It surprised her that Balthazar managed to keep his cool most of the time. Weird, since he'd done nothing but snap at her before. They should have been tearing each other's heads off by now.

Arianne wanted to point out that they were all standing in front of a dead end when the Nixies opened another portal. Nifty trick. A sprawling garden with a massive X-rated fountain and lewd sculpted bushes appeared at the other end. She averted her eyes. Sure she'd seen lots of naked souls, but having the naked bodies displayed in various sexual positions was a whole different peanut. Once Ben had dared her to watch Japanese Anime porn. It involved a lot of tentacles and women in positions that shouldn't be possible. She'd barely kept her eyes open while watching. From her short glimpse, she recognized a couple of tentacles on some of the shrub sculptures.

"Where are we?" she asked the ground, the only safe place to look.

"The Voyeur's mansion," Balthazar answered, disgusted. "Her gardeners are getting really creative with the shrubbery." He whistled. "I haven't seen that one before. Or that one. Oh, and that looks uncomfortable."

Arianne had a feeling Balthazar was trying to get her to look up. She shook her head, letting what he said enter one ear and exit the other. Was this even legal? She was way too young to be exposed to a freaky garden. No amount of therapy would erase some of the things she now wished she could un-see. She had a bad feeling about this.

One of the Nixies walked up to Arianne until it stood directly below where she glued her eyes to the ground. Oh she wasn't looking up. So not looking up.

This is as far as we will take you, the Nixie said.

"Are you sure this is where we can find the Voyeur?" she asked, her voice shaky.

"Just think of them as nude art."

"Not helping," she said to Balthazar, who'd pushed past her. He stepped out of the tunnel into the garden of ill repute—she'd heard the term from her mother once when they'd watched the news about some strip club burning down. Her mother had said other things, but Arianne didn't want to repeat them.

"Be careful, Ari." The Nixie's words returned Arianne to what she had to face. *"You must not let go of yourself. Remember why you are here."*

Arianne thought about what the Nixie said. Sure she wanted to save Niko, but that didn't seem enough anymore. Balthazar—as much as she hated him—had planted a seed in her she wished he hadn't.

She set aside her growing confusion for another time. Doubting someone who didn't have a chance to defend himself seemed unfair. If she asked Niko about himself, he'd answer. Right? She shook her head. Not now. She had to focus.

Arianne bent down until she rested her hands on her knees. "Thank you so much for helping us."

"Remember what we said."

Even if only one Nixie spoke, the fact that they all gathered around Arianne told her it spoke for all of them.

She nodded. "I'll remember."

The Nixies jumped around and cheered. She missed them already.

"You comin'?" Balthazar called from the other side of the portal. "We don't have all day."

Arianne waved goodbye to the Nixies and breathed in the cloying scent in the air. She'd hate to find out what perverted things the gardeners did to the flowers the fragrance came from. She steeled herself, looking straight ahead, not focusing on any particular thing in the garden when she stepped out of the portal. The second her feet hit the grass, the portal closed. She glanced over her shoulder. For the first time since she and Balthazar had started their search for the Redeemer, Arianne wished she were home asleep under the covers of her bed.

Chapter 21

WEG

The Voyeur's mansion — a massive white three-story building with columns and wraparound porches — loomed over Balthazar and Arianne against the gray sky. Contrasting with the greenery, it stuck out — not really like a sore thumb, but it did make a statement. Lesser demons — ones without wings and with less power — dressed in various kinky maids' uniforms, ran around carrying sheets, buckets, and various other things. One even carried a whole host of whips and a variety of handcuffs. Balthazar raised an eyebrow. Someone had a fetish. He shrugged. You only came to the Voyeur if you had something that needed satisfying.

"Maybe you should stay out here," he said without looking at her. "I'll go in, get the information we need, and meet you back here in an hour."

"Oh no you don't," Arianne said. He winced at the determination in her voice. When she got this way, no argument would convince her otherwise. This was why he hated chicks. "You're not leaving me in this porn garden."

"What you're seeing out here is tame compared to what's in there."

"I already know this is a whorehouse, Balthazar. I pretty much get what happens in there. I know about the birds and the bees."

"If you have to call it the birds and the bees then you don't know anything." He faced her, blocking her view of the mansion with his body. He stared into her clear blue eyes. "This is the Underverse, Arianne. I don't know what's in that human head of yours but I guarantee it doesn't measure up to the depravity in there." He hiked a thumb at the mansion. "Trust me, it's better that you stay here."

Arianne stared daggers back at him, her brow crumpling.

"I don't like that look." Balthazar shook his head.

"Better get used to it, buddy, because I'm coming with you."

"If that's really what you want." He pulled a leash out from inside his coat and somehow attached one end to the tattoo on her neck. Arianne jerked back, but he tugged on the leash until she returned to her original spot. She grabbed the leash with both hands and glared at him, fireworks in her eyes.

Balthazar scratched his eyebrow. "That pissed off look doesn't work on me, little girl."

"I'm not a dog, Balthazar." She hissed like the leash hurt.

"If you want to survive untouched in there, you better start acting like my slave." He tugged on the leash again, yanking Arianne forward. He held her chin so she couldn't look away from him. "This is one of the reasons why Granmare Baba attached us together. Whatever you do, keep your eyes on the floor. Act as meek as you possibly can. And no matter what you hear in there, don't react."

"Gosh, so many rules," she spat back.

"You can be a bitch about it, but the 'tude doesn't change what goes on in there." He let go of her chin and sighed. "I told you to stay here, you said you wanted to go in with me. Now that I'm giving you a chance at safe passage, you're fighting me on it. What do you want, Arianne?"

She dropped her gaze as if his words defeated her, but Balthazar knew better. He'd been with Arianne long enough to know she considered everything he said and was searching for a middle ground she could live with. It didn't take more than a minute. She looked up at him again, the same hard determination in her eyes.

"Fine," she said. "But this has nothing to do with being a slave." She pointed at him. "You're not gonna make me do slavish things. Are we clear?"

He grinned. "You're lucky I didn't cuff your wrists together."

Her jaw dropped for a second, a hot blush burning across her cheeks. Balthazar inhaled sharply. He liked her when she was feisty, but this blushing thing had its charm too. For a second he imagined licking her plump bottom lip. He shook his head to clear it. Wrong time to indulge childish fantasies. They had work to do.

"Are you clear on what you have to do?" he asked.

"Promise that you won't make me do anything slavish."

He stared into her eyes, searching for a chink in her armor. Finding none, he broke eye contact and said, "I promise. But if I ask you to do something to prove you are my slave in public, you don't question me or I will punish you. We clear?" He looked back at her and saw in her eyes the argument she wanted to push against him, but like any good slave, she held her tongue. "Good girl."

Balthazar turned around and headed for the back entrance of the mansion. He tugged on the leash when Arianne didn't move fast enough to keep up with the slack. A good slave walked a step behind her master. Balthazar didn't tell Arianne that anymore. Schooling her in the art of submission would take more time than they both had. And something told him she wouldn't appreciate the lesson as much as he would.

He skirted the great fountain called Desire.

It was aptly named since it depicted nymphs being chased around by satyrs and doing all manner of naughty things to each other. Basically, take every position in the Kama Sutra, use mythical creatures instead of humans to act them out, and you got an orgy of a fountain. The splatter of water only enhanced the sculpture. Balthazar had admired this fountain once. Now it only looked cheap. But what could he say? He and Arianne were entering the biggest, baddest brothel in town. If creatures in the Underverse had an itch that needed scratching, they had the Voyeur's merchandise scratch it for them. He hid a laugh into his free fist when he heard Arianne gasp.

"What happened to not looking up?" he asked over his shoulder.

"That fountain is just gross!" she said indignantly.

"You sound like a virgin. I thought you said you know a thing or two?"

A quick pause followed. He imagined a blush accompanying it. Then Arianne said grudgingly, "What's wrong with waiting for the right time with the right person?"

Balthazar laughed then, but he checked his volume, not wanting to attract the wrong kind of attention. In any case, when in Voyeur territory, any kind of attention was the wrong kind.

"Not funny," Arianne grumbled, which fueled Balthazar's chuckles even more.

When he could finally speak again, right around the time they climbed the veranda steps, he said, "No offense, but I don't believe there's ever a right time."

"You would say that."

"Okay, we're going in. Shut up."

Balthazar stood before the double glass doors of the back entrance with Arianne right behind him. An Oni—a species of Ogre who made Japan their home when a portal into the human world opened by accident—guarded the back entrance. Oni—like many Ogres—came in different shapes and sizes. This one sported green skin and white hair and was the size of a minivan. It grunted at Balthazar.

Balthazar had to think for a second where he'd hidden his token. Not just anyone could partake in the pleasures the Voyeur's establishment offered. You had to be invited. It had been a while since Balthazar made a visit—being in the Nethers had deprived him of many things. He raised a finger at the waiting Oni then patted his coat, sure he had the token somewhere. He hoped he hadn't thrown it out in a fit of rage. He'd done that on occasion. The communication crystal, anyone?

"Balthazar," Arianne murmured behind him.

"Shut up," he whispered back.

"That thing's eying us for dinner, in case you haven't noticed."

"Shut up, shut up." He smiled at the Oni. "I have the token. Just a sec."

The double doors flew wide open. Balthazar looked up just as a woman—at least he'd like to think she belonged to the female sex—in a floor-length velvet gown of deep purple that overflowed with her curves glided forward. The color of her long nails, which currently grasped her thin hips, and the color of her pillowy lips both matched her dress. She'd gathered her mass of black hair with purple streaks to one side of her head so it would fall over her slender shoulder. Balthazar had thought her beautiful once. In a predatory-flower sort of way.

"He doesn't need a token," she said in her smoky voice. Her purple eyes filled with mischief. "Balthazar is always welcome here."

The Oni bowed its massive head before resuming its stoic stance by one side of the doors.

"I wish I could say it's good to see you, Solara," Balthazar said.

Solara tilted her head back and laughed, giving him an unobstructed view of the curve of her neck and décolletage in the deep V of her dress. The sugary scent of hers burned up his nose. "You always say that. But when you get a taste of me, you don't seem to complain. How long has it been since you came to me?"

Balthazar barely kept his hate for the Voyeur in check. He wanted so badly to bare fang and growl. But if he wanted information about the Redeemer, he had to play nice. Arianne inhaled sharply behind him, and he tugged on the leash, hoping she wouldn't say anything.

"Who have you brought with you, dearest Balthazar?" Solara looked around him. He had to force himself to stay still when everything inside him begged to cover Arianne from the view of one of the vilest creatures in the Underverse. "Is she an offering for tonight's auction?"

Nausea hit Balthazar hard. They couldn't have come at a worse yet more opportune moment. The Voyeur hosted the Underball every half century, where all the patrons of the mansion gathered to purchase whatever exotic flesh Solara had collected for them at an auction. Balthazar once bought a night with a mermaid. He gave the creature points for most creative lay. He stifled a grin at the memory. Seriously, he had to concentrate.

"No," he said.

Solara's purple eyes returned to him with curiosity. One perfectly shaped eyebrow coming up. "No?"

"She's my slave."

Solara placed one of her hands over her chest. "Oh my," she said in a breathy, almost turned on voice. "The great Balthazar finally has a slave. I find that quite…amusing." When she smiled, she exposed blindingly white teeth. "I assume you'd like your usual room?" She raked hungry eyes over Arianne again.

Balthazar bristled. "We won't stay long. I'm here to ask you about the Redeemer."

"My, my." She pursed her lips and tsked at him. "This keeps getting more interesting by the second. Balthazar asking about the Redeemer. Your angelic blood finally calling for something more heavenly?"

Balthazar held his tongue. The Voyeur knew all. He wouldn't be surprised if Solara had already heard about what had happened to D and why they needed the Redeemer. But he had to play her games if he wanted them to leave the mansion alive.

Solara confirmed his suspicions when she said, "It's too bad what happened to D. He must be hurting so much by now."

"Then you understand why we must find the Redeemer," he said between his teeth. The muscles on his neck bunched with tension.

"Well—" she gestured into the mansion "—you need not look far. But you? Helping D? It's priceless."

Balthazar's heart stopped for a second. "Cut the crap, Solara."

Solara snapped, and a lesser demon appeared by her side in a puff of smoke. "Take them to suite five."

"I just said we can't stay."

"Oh, but you must." Something cruel entered the Voyeur's eyes, changing them from deep purple to gold. "I insist."

Trapped, Balthazar nodded. He went through a string of curses in his head.

Solara clapped. "Very good. Make yourself presentable for tonight. I promise the auction will not disappoint you." She turned around and moved deeper into the mansion, exaggerating the sway of her hips, no doubt for Balthazar's appreciation.

Balthazar rolled his eyes instead then grunted at the lesser demon. It jumped, all nervous energy, and led the way to the room he used whenever he visited. If he had ever considered praying, now seemed like a good time to start.

Chapter 22

TTYL

The Voyeur's mansion — whorehouse to the stars. Well, at least the VIP of the Underverse. *Girl's gotta make a living.* Arianne understood as much. She didn't care what the Voyeur, Solara, did with her time or how she made a living. She did care about the auction as she walked behind Balthazar on the stupid leash while they followed a lesser demon (according to Granmare Baba's info) in a freaky maid uniform. The information got fuzzy here. At this point, what exactly qualified as help from the old witch confused Arianne. From what she understood, useless info or not, the auction was the main event of the Underball. Basically the party of the century where all the very important creatures of the Underverse, the most depraved of them anyway, gathered.

Balthazar got really quiet again, the way he always did when keeping something from her. Solara had let it slip — or did she really slip? Arianne couldn't tell since she didn't directly look at the woman — that Balthazar had angelic blood in him. Nothing about Balthazar screamed angel. In fact, if Arianne was totally honest, Balthazar leaned more toward the bad side.

"Angels can be bad too," he said over his shoulder.

"Reading my mind right now isn't good for you," she said in a low hiss.

They'd been climbing a countless number of steps since entering the mansion. Hadn't the Voyeur heard of elevators?

Like the garden, the mansion's furniture carried the same sexed-up theme. Arianne happily pasted her gaze to the marble. Seemed like a good idea until she started making out weird shapes in the veins of the slabs. Worse than a Rorschach Test. If she closed her eyes, she'd surely stumble and break her neck. Keeping her eyes open, on the other hand, felt like she was intentionally corrupting herself.

"What can you expect from the premier bordello in the Underverse?" Balthazar said when she gasped at the marble and saw male body parts she shouldn't be seeing.

"But the marble too?" she whispered in utter shock.

Arianne only breathed a sigh of relief when they reached the stairs. At least plain carpet covered the wood. No chance of seeing anything porny there. The PG went to R-rated quickly after they passed by the closed doors lining the hallways to the next flight of stairs. First, the rhythmic thumping. Then the moaning. And then the slapping and giggling.

"What's that thumping?" she dared to ask when the curiosity got the better of her.

Balthazar looked over his shoulder at her, mischief glinting in his eye. "A headboard hitting the wall."

"Ugh! I wish I could un-hear all this," Arianne said, wincing when she heard what sounded like a whip crack. "I'm so gonna need therapy after this."

"Suck it up," Balthazar mumbled.

His pointed stare when Arianne flicked her eyes up for a second kept her quiet until they reached Balthazar's private suite. Oh, she didn't hear Solara wrong. Balthazar had a room in this place. No surprise there.

When the Voyeur said Balthazar didn't need a token to enter, Arianne's ears had burned. According to Granmare Baba's spotty info, special tokens the size of silver dollars were given to a select few. Apparently, Solara ran a classy joint. Arianne snorted to herself at that. If Balthazar didn't need a token, what did that make him? Balthazar had never struck her as the man-whore type.

"More important than the VIPs?" he volunteered.

"I thought you wanted me to shut up," she grumbled. "And this leash chafes." She tugged on the leather strap and Balthazar tugged back.

The lesser demon led Arianne and Balthazar to the end of the hall of the third floor and took out a key card.

"Don't look up," Balthazar warned.

"Wasn't planning to."

She didn't want to, but telling her not to do something made her doubly curious about doing it. She flicked her gaze up once. The image of Balthazar naked in the arms of an equally naked Solara was branded into her mind forever. Based on their position, they weren't playing tickle.

"Eww!" Arianne covered her eyes. "Ah, that's going to scar me for life. I feel like I need to wash out my brain."

"Excuse me?"

Balthazar's insult curled in Arianne's mind. She didn't care. She was too busy cursing her natural curiosity. "A little warning would have been nice."

"What part of 'don't look up' didn't serve as a warning?"

"I need soap."

"What for?"

"To scrub the grossness out of my eyeballs. So much eww!"

Balthazar snorted his classic snort. "Pretty tame if you ask me. You've seen the fountain."

"Yeah, but that wasn't depicting someone I know." Arianne scrubbed her eyes. "Now I know way too much about you. Way to make a statement that the room is yours. A nameplate would have worked just fine."

There was the click and squeak of doors opening then Balthazar demanded, "Open your damn eyes before you break something." Then to someone—the lesser demon maybe—he said, "Leave us."

Only when the doors closed did Arianne drop her hands. She carefully opened her eyes one at a time then scanned the room.

"Huh," she said.

Balthazar removed the leash and coiled it before hiding it within the endless number of pockets Arianne suspected he had in his coat.

"Too normal?" he asked back.

Normal wasn't the right word. Considering they were in a whorehouse, Balthazar's room passed for tame. The silk sheets on the large bed in the next room did scream one night stand, but everything else seemed pretty okay. No lewd paintings. No weird furniture. Only the balcony that opened to the porn garden said freaky. Arianne guessed they had to compromise there.

"I'm surprised it's not like the rest of the mansion," she said after she finished taking in the room. "It actually comes pretty close to what a presidential suite might look like."

"Solara thinks it's funny that this room is so much like something that could be found in the human world." Balthazar removed his coat and slung it over the large couch dominating the living area.

"Those doors aren't funny." Arianne scrunched up her nose, remembering Balthazar's bare chest.

"It's not anatomically correct." Balthazar's million buckles jingled when he fell back into the couch.

"Eww!" Arianne said again when his words made sense. "Will you stop?"

"What?" He shrugged before tucking his hands behind his head. "It's true."

Arianne stuck her tongue out at Balthazar then continued her exploration of the room. Sometimes she'd prowl the Internet for pictures of hotel suites. Not in any weird way. She just liked seeing how the hotels decorated the rooms. She always had this fantasy of having a room like it for herself one day. It seemed like a silly memory now after what she'd been through.

She plucked out a white rose from the centerpiece by the icky double doors and thought back to what Solara said about Balthazar not needing a token. "I'm guessing you're a regular here."

Balthazar had his eyes closed when he answered, "Back in the day. All work and no play and all that. Solara's not so bad, if you take away her tendency to eat her lovers."

Arianne dropped the rose and blinked. Then she shrugged. "Can't say I didn't see that one coming. But you survived."

"Only because I wasn't stupid enough to stay the night. Niko, on the other hand…" Balthazar stopped suddenly, like he'd caught himself about to say something.

"Niko what?" Arianne's voice grew very soft. Her chest deflated. When Balthazar didn't say anything, she rephrased her question. "What about Niko?"

Balthazar opened one eye to look at her before he grimaced. "Slip of the tongue. Forget about it."

Arianne rushed the couch and thumped Balthazar's chest, completely forgetting he didn't like to be touched.

"Don't growl at me," she said, but took a step back just in case. Those fangs did look like they could cause some serious hurt if they sank into her. "Just finish what you already started and I'll shut up about it."

Balthazar tsked before he closed his eyes again and settled back into the couch like he hadn't been ready to pounce a second ago. He breathed in deeply then exhaled slowly. Arianne waited, twisting her fingers together.

"There are some things you're better off not knowing, little girl," he finally said.

"I'm not a little girl anymore, Balthazar. If it's about Niko then I have the right to know."

He opened his eyes and locked gazes with her. "No, actually you don't."

"I *need* to know."

A shiver ran down Arianne's back by the way he stared at her, like he was measuring her worth. She steeled herself. Whatever he had to say about Niko she would accept without judging. She promised herself that.

Balthazar moved his gaze from her to the ceiling before he closed his eyes again. "Niko frequented this place as much as I did. In fact, we even came together once in a while."

Arianne's heart fell into a heap in her stomach. Then she picked the poor thing up and put it back into her chest. She couldn't judge. Niko was a guy. A Reaper who'd lived countless lifetimes. If he came here to…Arianne couldn't let herself think about it.

"Don't obsess, Arianne," Balthazar said in a grumbly voice, like he forced himself to speak. "Niko's done far worse things than be at a whorehouse…"

"What do you mean 'worse things'?"

His lower lip jutted out. "I'd rather not say. If you think he's a good guy, then maybe he is now. I haven't seen him since I got banished to the Nethers. Maybe he's changed."

"Are you actually trying to comfort me, Balthazar?" Arianne put together her best "aww" face.

"Don't get all mushy on me," he barked, but his words didn't have the same bite. "I'm more the bang 'em then leave 'em type."

Gross, but Arianne smiled anyway. Balthazar did have some good guy in him. He could deny it all he wanted, but she believed. He coughed out the f-bomb, apparently in reaction to her thoughts, but said nothing to contradict her. "So," she began, taking a seat on a chair opposite the couch. She'd chew on the latest piece of information Balthazar had given her another time. "What happens next?"

"We wait."

"The Underball."

"Yeah." Balthazar's brow crinkled, but he didn't open his eyes. "What are the chances you'd stay here while that's going on?"

"Slim to none."

"You're such a stubborn bitch."

The doors opened. Arianne and Balthazar both looked to see who'd come in. The Voyeur, still dressed in her Elvira-inspired gown, stood by the doorway flanked by two lesser demons in equally revealing maids' uniforms. So little cloth covered them that their clothes couldn't be considered decent, not even by hooker standards.

Balthazar flicked his wrist and Arianne found herself kneeing on the floor, her eyes glued to the carpet as if commanded by an unseen force. She bit her tongue to keep from reacting. The impact hurt her knees, but she'd complain to Balthazar later. Right now she had to play the role of obedient slave. She placed her hands flat on her knees and waited. She figured Balthazar had sat up based on the feet he planted firmly in front of Arianne's line of sight.

"Twice in less than thirty minutes," he said. "I can't say I like it."

Arianne got the feeling Balthazar hated the Voyeur more than most. He coated his words with honey every time he spoke to her. Like he forced himself to be extra nice, but in a sarcastic way.

"You've always been my favorite, Balthazar," Solara said in a voice that reminded Arianne of smoke and secrets.

"I'm the only one who's still alive. Eaten the Prince of the Ghouls yet?"

"I brought my two most prized demons to help with your slave," the Voyeur said, her tone clipped.

Arianne froze at the mention of slave and demons. What the hell was happening? Why would the Voyeur bring two demons to help her? She instantly didn't like where this was going and hoped Balthazar had the sense to refuse.

"I'm saying no to whatever you're offering."

Arianne had almost sighed in relief when the Voyeur said, "Oh, but I insist. She's not dressed properly for a slave belonging to someone like you."

"Solara."

She didn't think it possible, but Balthazar managed to growl out the Voyeur's name in a respectful manner. Arianne had really hoped he'd win this one. Unfortunately for her, it didn't look like she could escape whatever the Voyeur had planned. If they wanted information on the Redeemer, they had to play nice.

"Whatever it is I'll do it." The words shot out of her mouth without her thinking twice. If she kept thinking, she'd chicken out. Just to relieve some of the tension she felt coming from Balthazar and Solara like lightning bolts, she'd agreed. She immediately regretted it.

Chapter 23

RTFM

Arianne would be the death of him. Balthazar's heart stopped when the stupid girl agreed to be dressed by Solara's demons. She didn't know what she'd gotten herself into, yet she boldly — foolishly — agreed. He wanted to smack the girl so hard her fraying thread would snap. He'd come close to helping her get out of all this. A quick stare down with Solara would have worked. Or maybe not.

What the hell had possessed her to suddenly say she'd do it?

The satisfaction on Solara's face bruised his ego the most. Arianne agreeing made him look weak, like he didn't control her like a master should a slave. Oh, he'd remedy that as soon as she finished playing dress up.

Liking the idea more and more every second he thought about it, Balthazar licked his lips and grinned. With Arianne's eyes firmly on the carpet, she couldn't see the thoughts surfacing in his expression, but she could feel them. The shiver racking her body — the ones she tried really hard to hide — were too obvious to his hunter's eyes. He looked to Solara and wiped the grin off his face. He didn't want to give the Voyeur the wrong idea.

"She changes in this room, nowhere else," he said.

Solara nodded her head once. "But you must come with me."

"And miss all the fun here?"

The Voyeur gave him a pointed glare. "We have much to discuss, Balthazar. Come with me."

He felt the push in her words. Part of the Voyeur's charm was her ability to make creatures of the male persuasion obey her by adding a mental push into her voice—almost like a combination of subliminal persuasion and hypnotism. Balthazar blocked it but nodded anyway. The way she looked at him said more was going on here that he hadn't picked up on.

He pointed at Arianne and said to Solara, "She does not leave this room." He added his own push. Solara wasn't the only one who knew this little parlor trick.

"You heard him." She tilted her head at her demons. Both bowed deeply before they entered the room and flanked Arianne. They took one arm each and eased Arianne from her kneeling position.

Balthazar ignored the apology in Arianne's eyes. He pushed off the couch and shrugged on his coat. Only then did he saunter toward Solara. The Voyeur moved out of the way, giving him just enough room to exit the suite. Once he had his back to the doors, they closed with a soft click. Oh, he'd be back, he promised himself. And Arianne would learn what it meant to have him as a master. He gestured to Solara, and she swayed her hips down the hall.

"Your seduction won't work this time, Solara," Balthazar said when he took his place at her side.

She snaked her long arms around his. He allowed the contact, knowing a dead Voyeur would be no use to him. She seemed to believe the time they'd spent together bought her some leniency from him. He continued to give her that impression by bending the arm she hugged so she wouldn't have a hard time holding on to him. Then he patted her hand.

"Am I not beautiful anymore?" she asked in a whisper that had her lips touching his ear.

Only a fool would deny the beauty of the Voyeur. He'd been telling Arianne the truth when he said Solara had the tendency to eat her lovers like a praying mantis. Balthazar plastered a grin on his lips.

"You're as beautiful as the day I first met you."

His words garnered him the desired effect, an almost girlish giggle. No matter how powerful, the Voyeur was vain. Stroke her ego a little by telling her how pretty she looked and she'd give up most things.

Of course, Balthazar reminded himself, he entered a tricky trail now. Say the wrong thing and his head would roll. Literally.

Solara led him down the flight of steps to the second floor. The sounds of creatures getting it on rang out. Balthazar remembered Arianne's reaction. He knew just by feeling her thoughts how much she blushed. The girl truly was a virgin if she turned red at the sounds of sex. To him, it sounded no different from watching two women play tennis. Close your eyes and it sounded the same. Dirty. Noisy. And full of sweat.

"Business is doing well," Balthazar said.

Judging from Solara's silent agreement, the creatures of the Underverse still patronized her establishment.

"The auction this year is more popular than ever," she commented.

"I'm not here for that."

"Oh, I know." She gave Balthazar a sidelong glance. "But you're already here. Might as well."

A couple of maids carrying various whipping canes scurried past them. Balthazar raised his eyebrow at the pair. Solara waved her hand in dismissal.

"You know we live to serve."

"Oh, how well I know." Balthazar guided her down the last flight of steps to the first floor. He'd guessed they were heading for her office. He didn't have to ask. If Solara wanted to speak to him, her office gave them the most privacy.

"I trust you know the way," she said, her purple lips pulling up into a seductive smile.

He steered them to the back of the mansion past the grand ballroom. Several lesser demons scurried about, preparing the massive room that housed three large chandeliers for the night's festivities. Several male demons — at least Balthazar thought they were male, hard to tell sometimes — built a platform at one end of the floor space. It would serve to showcase the different auction items for the evening.

Solara must have noticed him staring at the platform a little too long because she said, "Are you sure you don't want to participate in the auction? We have another mermaid up for bidding tonight. And this one is triple jointed."

Balthazar's mouth watered, but he quickly swallowed. *Focus*, he barked at himself. It may have been more than a thousand years since he'd tasted the pleasures a mermaid could offer, but he wasn't here for that. After he'd completed his task, he could always return and ask Solara for the mermaid. She'd oblige one of her oldest and most prominent clients. He'd slit her throat if she didn't. She knew that.

They crossed the ballroom into a secret hallway hidden by a column. Mirrors for walls gave the long passage the illusion of continuing forever. Walking through it could confuse the uninitiated. Solara did it on purpose when she built this particular part of the mansion.

If you didn't know about Solara's office, you'd miss the entrance to it. Only a handful knew. Mostly her past lovers. Solara didn't trust anyone any more than Balthazar did. She hardly invited anyone to her inner sanctum. Balthazar had been in her office twice before, and both times not really for business purposes.

"Not tonight." Balthazar pushed against the mirror at the end of the hallway. It slid to the side, revealing Solara's office. Several lamps gave the room its soft lighting. Solara never cared for bright lights when alone. The softer the better. On one wall hung a tapestry of naked women dancing around a fire. Statues of naked men flanked the fireplace. Solara liked the human form. Throughout the mansion she chose more mythical themes for her erotic sculptures, but for her office, sculptures of humans dominated all the art, some by the great Michelangelo himself.

Solara let Balthazar go and arranged herself on a daybed by the crackling fire. The light from the flames danced over every curve and hollow she possessed, every move a show for his benefit. Balthazar watched her intently. He couldn't blame her for trying to seduce him. The Voyeur hadn't gotten her name for being meek. He moved to the reading chair opposite Solara's daybed and took a seat, stretching his legs out toward her.

"Unfortunate what happened to D," she said when she'd positioned her body to her satisfaction. "Brianne's Bitterness isn't a joke."

Balthazar shook his head. "Straight to business."

She stabbed him with a glare. "You made it perfectly clear that you weren't here for anything other than business. Has your mind changed?"

Again he shook his head, meeting her purple eyes. She shivered.

"Those eyes of yours." She ran the tip of her finger over her lower lip. "They scare me and turn me on at the same time."

"The Prince of Ghouls. Is he still alive?"

She huffed, leaning her elbow against the curled lip of the daybed, her body lying sideways now. "He's such a bore."

"He's still alive."

"The Ghoul Woods is all I'm after. Eating him would throw the place into more chaos."

Balthazar tapped his fingers on the chair's armrest. "The Ghoul Woods have never interested you before."

A perfect eyebrow quirked up. "It's the easiest way to get into my territory. The woods serve my purpose of protecting what's mine."

"It's none of my business."

"Not yet." Her lips smiled but her eyes didn't.

"Ah." Balthazar leaned back further into his seat. "You know I'm challenging D for control of the Crossroads."

"I've known since you left the Nethers."

"Keeping tabs on me. I'm touched."

She waved her slender hand. "Don't feel special. I keep tabs on everyone."

"That you do," Balthazar agreed. "Tell me what you know about the Redeemer."

"Only one knows the location of what you seek."

"Don't play cryptic with me, Solara. I don't have time for games."

"I'm not playing games. Even I don't have that far a reach into Haven."

Balthazar frowned. Haven, the sanctuary of Heavenly Hosts when they traveled between worlds. Many mistook Haven for Heaven. Only the Heavenly Hosts had seen the real Heaven. Heck, he'd grown up in Haven, and he still had no idea what Heaven looked like. Balthazar pushed away disturbing images of his childhood and returned to his conversation with the Voyeur.

"The Redeemer's in Haven?" A useless question to ask because Haven stretched as vast as the Underverse. No map. He barely remembered the ins and outs of the place. Without a guide it would be useless.

Solara nodded. "Zakariel is attending the auction tonight."

Balthazar sat up and leaned forward. "What's that bastard doing here?"

Not like Heavenly Hosts didn't seek alternative companionship from time to time, but as a rule, they avoided the delights of the Voyeur's mansion like the plague. They said being within its walls tainted their wings. Heavenly Hosts were particular to the point of being OCD about keeping their wings a pristine white. His mother had slapped him once for accidentally rubbing his grubby hands — her words — on the tips of her wings. Brianne hadn't always been cruel. In fact, he had some happy memories. Until everything changed when his father betrayed her. Solara's nonchalant response pulled him away from the painful memories.

"I believe he would like to purchase one of my auction offerings."

Balthazar thought about the Voyeur's words. Zakariel being at the auction made his life a little easier. He'd know the location of the Redeemer, being a high level Host. But he hadn't seen Zakariel since he was a child. Sure, Balthazar's reputation preceded him, and in this case that might not be a good thing.

"He controls Haven now, did you know?"

Balthazar's jaw would have dropped if he didn't clamp down on it so hard. "When did this happen?"

Of all the shitty things, this had to be the worst.

Solara stretched like a cat in the sun. One side of her mouth pulled up. "You've been in the Nethers a very long time not to know Zakariel had ascended. I'm not so sure he'll be inclined to help you, considering who your mother is."

Fuck.

Chapter 24

TYVM

The second the lesser demons left the suite, Arianne regretted having said yes to "changing" for the Underball. Changing had been the Voyeur's word. Apparently, she wasn't dressed appropriately for the event. The lesser demons, not breathing a word, had moved quickly. Regardless of how much Arianne struggled, they removed all her clothes, leaving her covering all her girly bits while they prepared a bath. This must have been what Balthazar had meant about not worrying about bathing until they reached the Voyeur's mansion. The plunge into Nixie Island's lake washed off most of the sticky stuff from the Blood Tree, but parts of her still felt glued together.

Once steam curled from the bath, Arianne gladly sank into the large tub of rose-scented water. She'd leaned in to relax when the terrible scrubbing began. Like Liza Doolittle in *My Fair Lady*—a movie her mother watched almost every weekend—she kicked and screamed while the demons washed every nook and cranny they could reach with their brushes. Arianne felt like the underside of a pot being scoured. When they finished, her skin glowed pink.

For a soul outside its body, Arianne had never felt cleaner. Who knew souls could be washed?

They pulled her out of the tub with a no nonsense attitude, like she wasn't the first "slave" girl they had cleaned. Arianne only had time to take a deep breath before they smothered her in bath sheets.

This time she felt like a car passing through the last part of the wash. She coughed out towel fluff afterward.

The dressing quickly followed. The demons re-braided her hair into the most intricate French braid she'd ever seen. Her red locks fell over one shoulder and looked shinier than they'd ever been. They painted her lips a pale pink and blushed her cheeks, not talking—even to each other—the entire time. Arianne had wanted to chat, find out a little more about the Underball and the auction. Disdainful looks met each of her questions until they showed her the depths of their mouths. No tongues. A pang of hurt twisted her stomach.

That's one way to ensure silence, she thought to herself while staring into the mirror.

Arianne had never really liked wearing makeup. A bit of lip gloss here. Some concealer there. She didn't even use mascara. Now that the lesser demons used her face as their personal canvas, she barely recognized herself. They used too much eyeliner, but the black kohl brought out the blue of her eyes. She had never thought her lips had a bow shape until one of the lesser demons painstakingly applied the lipstick like she was painting the ceiling of the Sistine Chapel.

Once they'd overhauled her head, they stood her in the middle of the room. The robe came off. Arianne attempted to cover her girly bits again, but the demons wouldn't let her. One even raised an eyebrow at her. She got the point. So, with much embarrassment turning her pink from head to toe, she stood still while they applied glittery lotion all over her body. Like literally *all over* her body.

Arianne didn't think she could have been any more mortified until they dressed her. Well, dressed seemed like a relative term at this point. She was more a one-piece kind of girl at the pool. Her outfit now showed way too much of *everything*.

Okay. Maybe she exaggerated in her head. The bikini she wore covered all her PG-13 bits. Considering her reflection, twisting left then right, she reminded herself to be mindful of her movement. Less moving around meant a lower potential for a wardrobe malfunction.

She didn't think her situation could get any worse until the lesser demons manacled her wrists together. Arianne's protest stuck to her throat when she remembered she played the role of slave in this Comic-Con horror story. The tattoo around her neck said so. She cursed Granmare Baba for not thinking of a better way to hide her humanity. She paced the living area of the suite in the gladiator sandals they'd put her in, trying to think of a way out of walking around the Underball attached to Balthazar by a leash while in tiny pieces of cloth masquerading as appropriate clothing for a slave.

She took consolation in the fact that Granmare Baba had done such a good job of hiding her. The information she'd been given about the Voyeur indicated Solara liked humans — like…for dinner. She craved them like expensive chocolate. The fact that Solara hadn't sniffed her out as one during the entire time she'd been in the Voyeur's mansion was a miracle in itself. Solara made the witch in the story of Hansel and Gretel seem tame by comparison.

Arianne had worn a path in the carpet when the door to the suite opened. Balthazar had his eyes firmly on the ground until he saw her. He stopped by the door, as still as any statue. Arianne stopped pacing too, frozen in place by Balthazar's blatant gawking.

They stood absolutely still for the longest minute of Arianne's life. She barely breathed while Balthazar's eyes roamed her body. She swallowed, feeling each part of her where his gaze landed turn pink, like he was actually touching her. How was that even possible? When Arianne thought she could breathe a sigh of relief because his eyes locked with hers again, the most devilish grin she'd ever seen formed on Balthazar's lips. She inhaled sharply. When had his grin become less arrogant and more…sexy?

Arianne realized the mistake of her thought the second Balthazar's grin turned into a full-on smile complete with a show of fang. Now she cursed herself. She'd completely forgotten about their connection. Balthazar felt her thoughts the second they materialized in her brain.

Oh Lord, give me strength.

Her lungs hurt until she realized she'd been holding her breath.

Balthazar entered the room and closed the door behind him. Arianne jumped at the click of the lock.

"Why'd you lock the door?" she blurted, eyes wide.

"I can't say I'm not liking this transformation," Balthazar said, stalking toward her.

Arianne swallowed again, trembling slightly now. She raised her hand to keep him from coming any closer only to realize she'd also forgotten the lesser demons had bound her wrists together. *Ah, crap!*

"That's right." Balthazar continued to smile. "I bet you're completely regretting saying yes to this now."

She shook her head. "I shouldn't have."

"Yes, you shouldn't have." She'd backed herself into a wall and Balthazar reached her in two steps. She flinched when Balthazar spread one hand on the wall beside her head. He shifted his weight there as he leaned over her and whispered, "You smell like roses."

"I-I-It's the bath water. They used rose oil," she stammered. Having Balthazar so close frazzled her brain. He seemed bigger somehow. Like he'd grown ten feet since she'd last seen him. And so broad too. When did his shoulders and chest get so broad?

Balthazar touched the tip of his nose to the base of her neck and traced a line up to her jaw, inhaling as he went. The move sent Arianne slumping against the wall for support, her knees threatening to give way beneath her. She raised her shackled hands until they spread over the center of his chest. She clutched at the buckles there, the cool metal digging into her palms. Balthazar tsked after he'd pulled away far enough to stare into her eyes — eyes now lined with kohl. She found herself shaking her head along with him.

"You shouldn't have spoken over me the way you did," he said with the softest threat. The kind that sent tingles down her spine.

"I didn't." At least she didn't stammer anymore. Instead, her voice sounded breathy, which seemed so much worse.

He touched her lips with the tip of his finger. "Oh, but you did. I'd pretty much convinced Solara that you didn't need to change for the Underball, but you had to go and ruin it by agreeing without my consent. Not that I'm complaining." He raked his gaze over her body again. Like a bomb exploding, Arianne felt all her blood rise to the surface. "But something has to be done about this master/slave relationship we have here."

"W-W-What do you mean?" Great, the stammering returned. The muscles in her abdomen quivered in the most delicious way. Arianne tried to ignore it and focus, but her body betrayed her more and more the longer Balthazar stood this close to her. She only noticed now, so close to him, that he smelled like sandalwood. The spicy earth scent brought her back to the time her mother burned incense around the house. She went through a whole New Age-y phase before Carrie got sick. Standing a nose away from Balthazar sent a sense of comfort surging through her body with a hint of something more. A feeling Arianne didn't care to acknowledge. Hot. Drugging. Dangerous. She knew if she let herself cross the line she wouldn't find her way back.

Balthazar moved his hand from the wall to her cheek. Arianne fought against leaning in to the touch. Even with the fingerless gloves, she could feel the warmth of his hand. The calluses on his exposed skin didn't feel rough on her face at all.

"You put us both in danger if you don't act like an obedient slave, Ari." He whispered her name like the sweetest candy on the tongue. A part of her wished he'd say it again. The other part of her struggled to continue the conversation.

"I won't disobey you. I promise." And she meant it too.

"Remember when I said you shouldn't force me into teaching you a lesson about what it means to have a master?"

She nodded. They'd had that conversation right before they entered the Voyeur mansion. Balthazar had warned her, yet she'd forgotten all about it the second Solara came into the room with her demons. Arianne thought she'd done something good by agreeing. Unfortunately, her good deed backfired in the most frightening yet insanely delicious way.

She hardly recognized the guy standing before her. The sarcasm and gruff nature had disappeared, leaving behind someone who oozed sex appeal like some cologne he'd sprayed on. Heat pooled inside her stomach, causing every muscle below it to clench. If Balthazar didn't step away now, she'd find herself flat on the floor.

"You know what happens now, don't you?" His eyes locked with hers again. His voice grew even softer.

She shook her head into his touch.

"I punish you."

The way he said punish blew the last of her knees' power to support her body weight. The second she began to slide down the wall, Balthazar's other arm snaked around her waist and pulled her forward until her body fused against his. Every buckle that touched her skin made her shiver.

She looked up and Balthazar's lips descended.

Arianne stood there in shock before her brain caught up with what her body was doing. Somehow, even without prompting from her, her lips danced with Balthazar's. He easily slipped his tongue between her lips and took control. Arianne's tongue quickly joined the game. When she grazed the tip of his fang, she just about self-combusted. The sharp sensation of his fang against her tongue might be the sexiest thing she'd ever experienced. She understood the appeal of vampire novels now. She only had two options at this point: either pull away or pass out. But she didn't want to do either. She wanted to live within his kiss, to stop time so they wouldn't have to part.

Why she waited so long escaped her until Niko's face flashed in her head. Arianne gasped and, with strength she didn't know she possessed, pushed Balthazar away. He stumbled back but regained his balance just before he hit the low glass coffee table. He blinked at her, dazed.

Arianne covered her wet, still warm lips with the back of her hand. She slumped against the wall and breathed. She whimpered when she still felt Balthazar's lips on hers. How good they felt.

"What the hell?" Balthazar asked when his shock wore off.

"You can't kiss me," Arianne stammered out, on the verge of tears.

Balthazar grinned. "I thought that was what we were doing. You seemed to be enjoying yourself. My ears don't lie."

Had she been moaning? Her eyes welled up. Balthazar's grin disappeared. He returned to her in two steps, slamming his hands against the wall on either side of her head. She flinched, still covering her mouth. His breathing was hard and deep.

"We didn't do anything wrong," he growled.

The tears flowed then. They *had* done something wrong. At least she had.

"You can't kiss me again," she said through her hand. Tears streamed down her face. "Promise me."

"I won't."

She couldn't understand why Balthazar decided to be stubborn.

"Promise me," she insisted, more force in her words. Her breathing turned into hics and sniffs.

Balthazar breathed in deeply and closed his eyes. On the exhale, he opened his eyes. When he moved his hand to dry her tears, Arianne flinched away. Thankfully, he returned his hand to the wall beside her head. If this was his punishment for disobedience, she'd follow orders from now on.

Balthazar sighed. "I promise not to kiss you again…"

Relief flooded Arianne. She breathed easier. She'd deal with her overwhelming guilt later. For now, she had work to do. She'd have nothing to feel guilty about if she didn't save Niko. She wiped away her tears.

"Good," she said.

The grin on Balthazar's face should have been a red flag. His next words definitely were.

"…unless you ask me to."

Chapter 25

SWAK

Three chandeliers hung from the ceiling, along with pixies dancing like floating ballerinas from some freak version of Cirque de Soleil. It all seemed a bit excessive. But the Voyeur wouldn't have anything less. Solara lived in excess. She ate, breathed, slept in it. Her guests, in their finest, drank from diamond champagne glasses. Not diamond encrusted. Actual glasses made from polished and cut diamonds. Platinum platters, not silver. Hors d'oeuvres and an assortment of finger foods decorated the platters, some of them actual fingers for the more carnivorous types. For the blood drinkers—vampires weren't the only creatures in the Underverse that enjoyed drinking from the vein—various females from different species were tied along the walls. Some already had blood dripping from various cut points on their bodies. The life force and residual energy drinkers were offered the same refreshments at the other side of the room. Balthazar spotted a unicorn and made a mental note to drink from it before they left.

The Underball packed the ballroom of the Voyeur's mansion with the Underverse's elite. Heavenly Hosts, Demon Kings, Warlocks, Fairy Queens. Even Granmare Baba made an appearance. The witch gave him a wink as she mingled with an assortment of the worst the Underverse had to offer. Balthazar swallowed the sudden flood of saliva in his mouth when a Demon King—the biggest, baddest of demon kind with their large leathery wings—ambled by. He hadn't had a Demon King since the Nethers. Their life force tasted the best, the most potent. It could keep him full for a month without depleting his reserves no matter how much power he used. Maybe a Demon King would be better than a unicorn?

Balthazar shook his head and forced himself to focus. The only beings missing from the gathering were Reapers. Nikolas had accompanied him to an auction once. He'd purchased a siren while Balthazar went to bed that night with conjoined twins. He rolled his eyes to the ceiling. The wild days.

Because of the lockdown, none of the Reapers could make an appearance, not even those in the human world. They needed the Crossroads to get into the Underverse, like the Heavenly Hosts needed Haven to enter the Underverse or the human world. Of the many entry points into the Underverse, specific creatures had specific places they used—a safety mechanism in place since before Balthazar became a thought in his mother's head. He didn't question it, and neither did anyone who made the Underverse their home. But, of course, like with the Oni, accidents happened.

Just as well.

Balthazar had other things to worry about than Reapers not being in attendance at the auction. Mostly, that he'd kissed the girl. Totally not the plan. Damn if he didn't enjoy himself. Called her by the name the Nixies used too. Ari. Rolled off the tongue like a bell note. Ari. And the taste of her almost brought him to his knees. If he'd known humans tasted so good, he would have kissed one a long time ago. Yet, in the back of his mind, he knew not just any human would do.

Ari.

He tugged at the leash, causing her to stumble forward, pushing up against his back. She grunted but didn't complain. He grinned. Since they'd left the suite, she'd been playing the silent slave girl. He'd like to think he had a hand in her obedience instead of the promise he'd made her. He intended to keep it too. Oh, how this game had progressed. What better way to ruin Nikolas? If the Reaper of Georgia truly had feelings for the girl who tried to save him at the expense of her own life, then taking her away from him would be the best kind of torture.

Arianne had become an unexpected prize. Those curves he cared nothing about before suddenly took on a new light. Maybe under the light of the damn chandeliers everything changed. That sinful bikini didn't do him any favors either. He noticed a few pointed stares at his slave from several attendees. Some leers more than stares—hungry. Balthazar scowled back at them. The creatures knew better than to mess with him. The stares he could forgive, but if someone so much as drooled in the presence of Arianne, he'd have them for dinner.

The change in his mindset toward the girl disturbed him profoundly.

When he'd walked into the suite, he'd been ready to hand out her punishment. Teach her a lesson. Instead, he ended up making out with the chit. How was that possible? He blamed the damnable slave's uniform Solara's lesser demons had put her in. A little slip of a thing. It barely covered the important bits. Balthazar didn't know if he wanted to curse the Voyeur into the nine circles of hell or kiss her on each cheek for handing him a tasty morsel she'd wrapped nicely.

Or should he say, barely wrapped?

"They're staring at me," Arianne mumbled.

"Took you long enough to notice," he said, not looking back at her. He gave a passing Fairy Queen a smile. The creature's glamour couldn't fool him. What might look like a wondrously beautiful woman to others hid a tentacled creature with a taste for young demon boys. Balthazar barely suppressed a shudder. He considered himself depraved, but he had some standards and quite a few limits. Some of the creatures walking around in the Underball looking all tame and urbane made a mockery of the civility in the ballroom with the things they liked to do behind closed doors. Sometimes blood-curdling screams filled the mansion when they stayed under its roof.

"I hate Solara for putting me in this…I don't even know what to call it," Arianne complained.

"You're a slave."

A long pause. Balthazar grinned when he felt her thoughts. She imagined their little interlude in the suite. Likely she blushed. Oh how he wanted to face her and see. But he couldn't draw attention to them. His presence in the Underball already created ripples. If he acted like he cared too much for his slave, he'd be putting Arianne in needless danger. He didn't want to get bloody tonight if he didn't have to. Tempting on any other day, but the ever weakening pulse on Arianne's ring didn't afford him the luxury of a massacre.

Once she'd convinced herself the kiss wouldn't happen again—not if Balthazar could help it—Arianne spoke again. "I'm just not used to being looked at like an object."

"Honey, right now, you are." Balthazar sobered. "Solara's heading this way. Suck it up and shut up." He gave the leash one more tug before he plastered a smile on his face. "You've out done yourself, Solara."

The Voyeur had exchanged her velvet dress for a revealing sequined gown that left little to the imagination. She smiled back at him before she leaned in and kissed him on both cheeks. Balthazar endured the touch, although he couldn't stop his shoulders from tensing. He forced himself to relax by grabbing two diamond glasses filled with Nectar, an elixir that gave a better buzz than any alcoholic beverage, and handed one to Solara. Blacking out on Nectar meant worse things than waking up with an ugly tattoo.

"You don't think the pixies are a little too much?"

Balthazar looked up. "So long as they don't rain pixie dust on everyone, I think you'll be fine."

Pixie dust was the strongest aphrodisiac known to exist. If they started raining dust, the party would quickly turn into one big love fest. And considering the perverse proclivities of many of the creatures at the ball, an orgy would be the worst outcome.

"Oh, I had them drained of dust. In fact, that's one of the auction items." She wiggled her eyebrows at him. "I trust your slave is satisfactorily dressed?"

Balthazar cleared his throat to hide Arianne's whimper. "She's adequate."

Delight sparkled in Solara's radiant face. "She's already been getting lots of attention. Are you sure you don't want to put her up for auction, even just for tonight? She does seem so exotic."

The way Solara said exotic coupled with the intense interest in her eyes worried Balthazar. The Voyeur might know the secret he shared with Arianne. But with several humans used as entrées tonight, he doubted the Voyeur's attention focused enough on a slave that smelled more like him.

"She's mine, Solara." Balthazar bared his fangs.

The always smart, sometimes opportunistic, Voyeur tilted her head and pursed her lips. "If you ever reconsider, you know where to find me." She finished her glass of Nectar. "Zakariel has arrived."

Balthazar tensed. A Heavenly Host as powerful as Zakariel shouldn't have gotten past him without detection. He'd been so preoccupied with his slave girl that he'd totally dropped the ball on noticing Zakariel. He cursed his distraction.

He took a moment to focus and quickly found the Heavenly Host surrounded by a contingent of lesser angels. Why someone like Zakariel attended an auction as sleazy as Solara's escaped Balthazar's understanding.

"I need five minutes with him," he told Solara.

Her eyes narrowed. "What will you give me for it?"

Sometimes Balthazar cursed the barter system of the Underverse. "Three drops of my blood to auction off tonight."

Solara's eyes changed from purple to gold. "That would be fantastic. The price of the blood from someone like you…oh!" She shivered in delight.

Balthazar removed a small vial from one of the pockets in his coat and a needle from another. He pricked his finger, squeezed out three drops into the vial and sealed it. Then he dangled the blood in front of Solara.

"Do we have a deal?" he asked.

Solara nodded, never taking her golden gaze away from the vial. "I'll set the meet."

"You do that." He tossed her the vial.

The Voyeur caught it in mid-air and hugged it close to her chest. "You don't know what you've done."

"I'm pretty sure I do."

"Very well." She licked her lower lip. "The auction's about to start." She turned and walked away.

"What is it about your blood?" Arianne whispered from behind him.

Balthazar frowned. "Let's just say it's a very rare commodity around here."

"Granmare Baba seemed like she would lose her mind after tasting it. What the hell's that about?"

He barked a laugh. "Hell? Really, Arianne?"

"You're not the only one who can curse around here, you know."

"Saying hell isn't cursing."

"Well, from where I'm from it is."

Balthazar had a ready answer when he noticed the auctioneer, a giant lizard that walked upright in a tuxedo, moved to the podium positioned to one side of the platform. Red curtains covered the rest of the stage, presumably to give the assistants time to move the items in and out without the bidders seeing.

The Voyeur kept the list of items confidential until the auction, but sometimes information about certain items were leaked. Balthazar considered this in relation to Zakariel's presence. But what would he buy in an auction geared toward the carnal arts? Last time he'd checked the Heavenly Host wasn't really into sex toys. So why? It couldn't be chance that D had sent him and Arianne to the Voyeur only to meet with the one creature who could give them information about the Redeemer. It seemed way too easy.

The lizard banged a gavel three times on the podium, capturing the attention of everyone in the ballroom. A hush fell. Only the servers moved among the guests, keeping them fed and happy while the main event proceeded.

Like anything in the Underverse, the auction used the barter system as payment. Anyone who bid the highest exchange possible for the item up for auction won said item. Cash meant nothing in the Underverse, although gold and jewels did have some value. It depended on the kinds of jewels and the number of chests of gold. The best currency in the Underverse? Power.

Balthazar swallowed. Suddenly he had a very bad feeling about this scenario. Everything up until their arrival at the Voyeur's mansion had been a walk in the park, like an invisible hand led him and Arianne to where they needed to be. Like they were part of some big plan. Balthazar hated being manipulated. He couldn't get a handle on the grand plan…yet. But when he found out, heads would roll. Someone clearly pulled the strings.

He squared his shoulders and kept his eyes on the platform then said to Arianne, "Whatever you see during the next few minutes, don't react. Do you understand me? You scream, we die."

Chapter 26

IRL

Balthazar's warning tickled down Arianne's spine, but not in a good way. Suddenly, the large ballroom got so very quiet. It didn't even seem like anyone breathed. A crackling tension filled the air.

For the first time since she joined the party with Balthazar, she didn't feel like eyes were on her. Wearing tiny pieces of cloth did that, brought attention. But in the back of her mind, Arianne would rather be in public dressed in a bikini than fully-clothed in private with Balthazar. Her lips still remembered his kiss too well. The little nips he'd treated her bottom lip to had sent unwanted warmth below her navel.

Every time she flushed, she hoped Balthazar wouldn't feel her. She couldn't be sure since he had his back to her the whole time. Part of being the master, he'd said before they entered the ballroom. She had to walk behind him the whole time and not bring attention to herself. Fat chance in the itsy bitsy slave bikini.

Everything that went bump in the night and then some seemed to have gathered in the Voyeur's mansion. A strangely beautiful vampire sucked on the neck of an innocent girl who seemed to be enjoying it a little too much. It figured that Hollywood got vampires right. The pixies bobbing up and down on what seemed like a bungee cord executing acrobatic stunts looked sad, like someone was forcing them to entertain the gathering. No one really looked up at them. Arianne only got a peek at them when she entered the ballroom. Most of the time she kept her eyes on the polished floor.

But she had to admit to being a bad slave. She kept glancing up, catching glimpses of the party.

A ghoul—one that looked more like a human than the scary ones she and Balthazar encountered in the woods—snacked on steak so rare it still oozed blood. At least, Arianne thought it was steak. The trippy fairies were the prettiest things in the party in their flowing dresses and long, braided hair. She suspected a creature that pretty—with its graceful movements—had to be twice as dangerous.

Mental note: stay away from the fairies. And Tomas, that big liar.

She couldn't forget the huge Demon Kings, wearing nothing but what looked like black Speedos. Bigger than any linebacker. She felt Balthazar's hunger when one passed him by. It still unnerved her to know that, unlike the Reapers, who took energy from the souls they reaped, he drained energy from creatures in the Underverse. And based on Balthazar's intense reaction to the leathery-winged beast here, Demon Kings were his favorite.

Arianne shivered.

Each new thing she learned about Balthazar weirded her out more. At least with Niko, she could pretend he was human. They had gone to school together, attended classes, eaten at the cafeteria. She had a hard time imagining Balthazar in the same situation. Balthazar in high school...*that* would go over well. He'd never pass as human.

And yet a part of her had enjoyed his kiss, even participated in it. Despite her initial shock at the sudden contact, he'd drawn her in quickly. She'd parted her lips when his tongue asked for entrance. In their dance, he led and she willingly followed. Balthazar's kiss filled Arianne's head with thoughts she shouldn't be having when she was on a mission to save the boy she loved. Even when guilt wracked her, she couldn't help but squeeze her thighs together from the discomfort brought on by the mere memory of Balthazar's lips on hers.

"Do you understand me, Arianne?" Balthazar asked again, bringing her back to the Underball.

"Why?" She didn't think she had the nerve to question him, considering the seriousness of his words, but the question still came out.

He snorted. "Can't you just obey me without asking questions for once?"

Her yes stopped short when what the Voyeur said earlier—the information Balthazar sold his blood for—sparked her curiosity. "Who's Zakariel?"

"Not now." Two words he said through his teeth.

"Fine." She knew it seemed like she gave up easily, but really she didn't. Arianne knew how to bide her time. Balthazar couldn't hide things from her for long. She'd find out about Zakariel even if she had to follow him to that meeting Solara would set up.

Balthazar relaxed his shoulders a little.

"How's the masking of your scent working for you?"

Arianne jumped at the sound of Granmare Baba's voice. The witch stood beside her all hunched over. The mole on her nose twitched when she smiled.

"What are you doing here?" Arianne whispered harshly.

"Granmare Baba has something she wants," Balthazar answered without looking back at them. Did that count as speaking to the witch when she clearly didn't speak to him? Arianne stared at the center of his broad back. He seemed determined to keep his eyes on the platform. The lizard in a tux cleared its throat, ready to announce the first item up for auction. Shuffling came from behind the curtain.

"He's right about that," Granmare Baba said. She cackled softly. "How are you doing?"

The nudge the witch gave Arianne clued her in that she spoke to her. The first question she assumed Granmare Baba gave as a freebee. Arianne had no idea what such an old woman needed in a whorehouse. She forced herself to focus.

"The information you gave me isn't complete."

Granmare Baba clucked her tongue. "Not satisfied with the product, eh?"

The glint in the old woman's eyes scared Arianne into shaking her head. "No, it's not that. It's just there are some things that are blocked. I can't *access* them."

"Some things you will know in time."

The second time Granmare Baba smiled it seemed so sweet that she could pass for any old lady, except Arianne knew better. She swallowed and stood straighter. She wasn't about to let the witch intimidate her. Arianne knew she was playing way out of her league. She'd known this from the beginning. She put on a brave face about it, but most of the time she wanted to run home and forget about all the scary things she'd found out during this Redeemer search with Balthazar. She figured she wasn't dead yet, so she must be doing something right.

"Like the information about Balthazar." Arianne saw his shoulders tense again after she spoke. Making him uncomfortable satisfied her…a lot. She remembered how he'd tortured her before the kiss. *Payback's a bitch.*

"Ah!" Granmare Baba cracked her gnarly knuckles. "I thought you meant the information about the Redeemer and a certain item up for auction."

Balthazar whirled around then, his eyes wild. "What the hell's going on here?"

Arianne's brow furrowed. Maybe all rules didn't count outside of Granmare Baba's territory because the old witch didn't react to being spoken to without her speaking first.

"The Voyeur's mansion is neutral territory," Balthazar said as an aside in answer to her question without really looking at her. He currently glared down at the witch.

Granmare Baba's wrinkled lips stretched into a grin. "I heard the Redeemer sent Zakariel here on a hunch."

"Don't play games with me, old hag."

Did Balthazar just threaten Granmare Baba? Arianne stood in open-mouthed amazement. Some of the creatures nearest them glanced their way, but most of the time they had their heads turned toward the stage. Arianne barely heard the first auction item—a night with a succubus—sold for the head of Rubin—whoever that was. She flicked her gaze to the platform just as the red curtains closed around the barely clothed woman with small leathery wings and a tail. By the frown on its face, the succubus wasn't happy about being an auction item. Arianne returned her attention to Balthazar and Granmare Baba.

"Better not be threatening me," the witch responded.

"What are you getting at?" Balthazar asked, seeming to ignore the dangerous narrowing of the witch's eyes.

Arianne opened her mouth to speak up, but Granmare Baba beat her to it. "Just know that this auction is important to the Redeemer." She looked over Balthazar's shoulder and said almost distractedly, "I believe the item I want is up. If you will excuse me."

Arianne watched the witch waddle away before she looked up at Balthazar who stared death daggers at the witch's back. "What's she mean about this auction being important to the Redeemer?"

Balthazar didn't look at her. He faced the stage again. They both watched as Granmare Baba battled it out with a Fairy Queen for the jar of pixie dust. The Fairy Queen Arianne got, but what would Granmare Baba want with an aphrodisiac?

She shuddered at the possible answer.

Just when she thought Balthazar wouldn't answer her question, he said, "Zakariel is the Heavenly Host currently in control of Haven. He's the one who knows where the Redeemer is. And it looks like he'll bid on something in this auction."

Whoa! The information flooding Arianne's brain almost overwhelmed her. Every time Balthazar said something new, Arianne instantly understood a part of what he'd meant. Like Granmare Baba said. The information unlocked when the right time came. Haven was like the Crossroads. Heavenly Hosts, basically Archangels, and the lesser angels used it as a halfway point between the human world and Heaven. And the most important information of all? The Redeemer lived in Haven and the Heavenly Host called Zakariel knew where. Arianne's stomach tumbled. They were so close. Her gaze fell to the ring. The pulses were spaced farther apart now, so weak that it frightened her.

She sent a silent prayer to whoever might be listening for Death to be able to hold on a little longer. They'd almost found the Redeemer. Just a little bit longer.

The second Arianne finished her prayer, her eyes landed on the platform. The curtains opened. First she saw the cage then her blood ran cold. The cage enclosed someone she thought she'd never see again.

"Ben," she said, barely heard even to her own ears. Balthazar glanced at her from over his shoulder.

"Ben?" he asked.

Arianne felt like a fist closed around her heart. She never took her eyes off the pale slumped figure inside the cage. He still wore the robe Tomas had given him when they'd first left their bodies to save Niko from Death. He didn't wear the smile she was so used to seeing on his face. He seemed thinner than before. It took everything she had not to run to the platform and rattle his cage until he looked up at her. Right now, even from afar, Arianne could see that his eyes were glazed, like he'd lost all hope.

"Ben's my best friend." Tears welled up in her eyes. She blinked them away and forced herself to continue. "I had a Death Certificate out on me. Ben put himself in my place so I could live. Why's he here?"

The lizard spoke over the greedy whispers Arianne only noticed now. Everyone in the room seemed to want Ben, ready to bid for him. The lizard described Ben as a human soul still fresh from a reaping, unprocessed — whatever the hell that meant.

Without thinking about the consequences, Arianne grabbed Balthazar's arm. "We have to save him," she begged.

He looked down at her then at Ben in the cage. "We're not here for him."

Arianne squeezed his arm harder. "I don't care." Her voice shook along with the rest of her. "We have to save him. God knows what they'll do to him."

"I can just imagine."

"This isn't a joke!" she said through her teeth. "We *have* to help him. Please."

A movement caught Balthazar's eye and he looked away from Arianne. She followed his gaze to a tall man with long blonde hair in white linen pants and nothing else. But what got Arianne really staring were his pristine white wings. Each feather glimmered under the chandelier light. Beside and behind him gathered a group of four lesser angels, Arianne knew from their not-as-white wings. The creatures around them took a step back — whether unconscious or because they really tried to avoid the heavenly crew, Arianne couldn't be sure.

"It looks like we finally know what Zakariel is after," Balthazar said.

Arianne looked from the Heavenly Host to the sad face of her best friend. "Ben."

Chapter 27

BFF

Seeing the Heavenly Host in all his glory momentarily stunned Balthazar. The last time he'd been in the same room with Zakariel, Balthazar still had baby teeth. His mother had been walking with him toward the park in Haven where newborn angels played. He'd been bullied the day before for being "different" and had been hugging his mother's skirt ever since. This was before his mother went crazy. He had taken comfort in hiding within the shelter of her magnificent wings.

If anyone thought Zakariel's wings were beautiful, they paled in comparison to his mother's. She'd been prized for the purity of her wings, so white they looked almost translucent. Rainbows formed when light reflected on the feathers. Staring at Zakariel now brought back all the painful memories that came with remembering his mother.

Balthazar bit his tongue until he tasted his own blood to clear his head of the ghosts that accompanied an encounter with Zakariel.

Granmare Baba said the auction was important to the Redeemer. He suspected the boy in the cage — the one Arianne called Ben — had something to do with Zakariel visiting the Voyeur's mansion. The Heavenly Host wouldn't be caught dead in such a place if it weren't a matter of absolute importance. He was too honorable to find pleasure in what Solara had to offer within her walls. Balthazar dropped his gaze to the tips of Zakariel's wings. One side of his lips twitched up.

The controller of Haven didn't even let the tips touch the wooden floor. It took great muscle strength to keep wingtips aloft like that. Zakariel's angel posse couldn't even manage it for long, which was why they didn't have the whitest of wings. Even dirt tainted angel feathers.

Zakariel had all his attention on the cage. A plan quickly formed in Balthazar's head. The Heavenly Host must not have known he'd attend the Underball too. Again the feeling of being manipulated by some unknown force irked Balthazar. Oh, he'd get to the bottom of all this shit after he'd delivered the Redeemer. D looked less and less innocent in all this than he did when Balthazar first found him with Brianne's Bitterness sticking out of his chest.

"You have to save him," Arianne begged from his side.

He'd forgotten all about her for a second. He glanced down at her then flicked his gaze to her hands gripping the sleeve of his coat. She didn't let go immediately. When he didn't move, just kept looking at the contact between them, she uncurled her fingers one at a time. Once she let go of him, he returned his gaze to her face. He didn't see the defeat he'd expected. The girl had backbone. She stared on with all the courage and determination she possessed. Balthazar had a feeling that if he didn't do something to save the boy, she'd go rogue and save him herself. That would ruin everything.

He closed his eyes and sighed. When he opened them again, he said, "Are you willing to do whatever it takes to save your friend?"

She worried her lower lip before she nodded.

"You have to be a hundred percent committed," he insisted. "No backing out."

She nodded again.

"Say it."

"I'm sure."

He nodded at her once then returned his attention to the stage, giving Zakariel one last glance. The Heavenly Host hadn't shifted his stance, waiting along with the rest of everyone in the room for the bidding to start.

The lizard banged his gavel three times.

Zakariel said in a deep, rumbling voice, "One of my feathers."

Whispers rippled all over the room. The feather of a Heavenly Host, especially one from someone like Zakariel, held powers untold. It could be used in many different ways. Balthazar raised his eyebrows.

The bidding got stiff pretty fast. What value did the boy possess? Last he'd checked human souls didn't fetch the prize of a Heavenly Host's feather. Balthazar ran through the inventory of items he had with him. He'd have to pull out all the stops.

The lizard acknowledged the bid and scanned the crowed.

"The trident of Poseidon," a Demon King from one corner of the room said.

The whispers grew louder now. Balthazar thought the trident of Poseidon had been lost when the god perished in one of the wars. He couldn't remember which. The Greek gods always fought about something. Not many of them were left now.

As expected, the bidders upped the ante. He wiped the grin off his face, not wanting to look too eager.

"The Book of Arcana," he said.

A collective gasp came from the crowd. Every head, including Zakariel's, turned toward Balthazar. He inched Arianne behind him so no one saw her. The Heavenly Host's silver eyes widened before they narrowed. Balthazar tipped his head at Zakariel in greeting, adding a lopsided smirk for good measure.

Zakariel faced the lizard. "The Sword of Michael."

Balthazar almost dropped his jaw. Created by his mother, the Sword of Michael was one of the most powerful artifacts in Heaven's arsenal. It had enough power to level worlds if wielded properly.

The lizard looked at the Demon King for a counter bid. The Demon King fluttered his wings, giving the cage one greedy look before shaking its head. The lizard turned his gaze to Balthazar. In his periphery, he saw Solara eyeing him closely. He ignored the question in the Voyeur's gaze.

He showed fang when he said, "The Sword of Lucifer."

The crowd went from whispers to all out talking now. Zakariel's eyes widened in complete and utter shock. Balthazar stood in self-satisfied silence. If they talked about swords, Lucie's trumped Mike's any day. The sword of Heaven's greatest betrayer? Hell yeah! Being God's favorite Heavenly Host once had its perks—the reason why after the Great Heavenly War, God refused to have a favorite ever again.

"You don't have Lucifer's sword," Zakariel accused when he finally recovered from his shock.

Balthazar raised a finger before reaching into the depths of his coat. He pulled out a mighty sword in a weathered scabbard. The shining gem at the pommel shone brighter than the light of three chandeliers. Many of the creatures in the room hissed and cowered away. For the third time that night, Zakariel stood in stunned silence. Balthazar returned the sword into his coat before its power killed some of the lesser attendees of the Underball. Such was Lucifer's Sword — merely showing it was enough to do great damage. A part of him understood where his mother's insanity came from. If she was powerful enough to forge Lucifer's sword, there had to have been darkness already in her before she even met his father.

Once the heavenly light of the sword disappeared, Zakariel blinked several times and returned his gaze to the platform. He said to the lizard, "One night with Jezebel."

Wow! Balthazar's eyes practically popped out of their sockets. Jezebel — the renowned prostitute turned Heavenly Host. At one time, she'd held the distinction of being Lucifer's consort. One night with her changed your life forever. Or so they said. That definitely trumped swords, especially in the Voyeur's mansion. Zakariel played dirty. Unfortunately for him, Balthazar invented playing dirty.

Balthazar stepped aside to reveal Arianne to the rest of the room. She had her head bowed and her bound wrists lowered. And in that skimpy bikini? She made the pretty little picture.

"One night with my human slave, Arianne. She is still attached."

The crowd roared.

Arianne's head snapped up. She glared at him with the purest hate he'd ever seen. The boy in the cage whipped his head toward them. Recognition sparked in his eyes. He pushed off the cage's floor and slammed against the bars, rattling them.

"Arianne!" he screamed. "What are you doing here? What does he mean *slave?*"

Before Arianne could respond, Balthazar blocked the boy's view of her with his body. A corner of his lips quirked up when he moved his gaze from the fire in Arianne's eyes to the defeat in Zakariel's. He'd won. A night with an attached human soul equaled the ultimate prize. Granmare Baba's meddling when she'd connected them finally made sense. An attached human soul carried some weight, but one kept as a slave tasted even better, bringing with it certain expectations in the bedroom.

Zakariel bowed his head at Balthazar then at the lizard, conceding. The lizard—after shaking its head to clear the shock from its face—banged his gavel three times and declared Balthazar the winner. The red curtains closed. The lizard announced that Balthazar's item would be kept for him until the time he wished to claim it.

Solara appeared beside Balthazar in a heartbeat. She bent down and sniffed Arianne from the base of her neck to the top of her head. Arianne tried to flinch away, but Balthazar pulled on the leash, keeping her in place against her will. For some reason, the betrayal in her eyes punched him in the gut. He ignored the discomfort and focused on the Voyeur. They were still in grave danger for what he'd done.

"You dare hide an attached human soul from me?" she said then hissed. "How is this possible?"

"You should ask Granmare Baba."

Her glare turned venomous, eyes of hot gold. "That bitch!"

"I think you mean witch." Granmare Baba sauntered toward them, her lush curves encased in the tightest leather. She stopped right in front of Balthazar and pointed at him. "I didn't think you had the stones to bid her."

Balthazar laughed. "Why does everyone continue to underestimate me?" He saw Arianne about to say something. He touched his thumb to his middle finger and her jaw shut. Her eyes bulged. He felt her panic through her thoughts.

The Voyeur turned her poisonous glare from Balthazar to Granmare Baba. "How dare you meddle?"

Granmare Baba covered her laugh with delicate fingers. "I do always love ruining your day, dear sister."

"Don't call me that!"

"Ladies." Balthazar raised both his hands, ready to separate them if needed. "Please. Although a catfight between the two of you would be so entertaining, let's not make a scene. There's still more than half the auction to get through." He looked at Granmare Baba. "Be sure I will not forget what you have done for me."

Granmare Baba tilted her head toward him in silent acceptance.

Then to Solara, he said, "I'll take those five minutes with Zakariel now. We have much to discuss, the Heavenly Host and I. It's been a while since we've spoken."

Solara pieced together her composure and flicked her gaze at Arianne. "My lesser demons will take her to your suite and prepare her for service tonight."

Balthazar froze for a millisecond. Not long enough for both women to notice. Yes, he'd bargained Arianne away. She did say she'd do anything to save her friend. Now she had to pay up.

"Very well," Balthazar said.

Two demons approached them and Balthazar handed the leash to one. Balthazar did not meet Arianne's gaze when they led her away. He'd had enough of her drama for one night. He had other things to focus on if they wanted to make it to the Redeemer in time. The boy's soul gave him leverage against Zakariel. If the Heavenly Host bargained away Michael's Sword and a night with Jezebel, then the boy's soul played an important role in all this.

"I think I will claim my price and take my leave," Granmare Baba said. She turned on her stilettos and left.

"I'm not done with you, hag," Solara called to her.

Granmare Baba gave her the finger without looking back.

Balthazar shook his head. The sisters always had to one up each other. Granmare Baba won this round. Solara—competitive to the bone—wouldn't take that lying down. She'd get her sister back, and Balthazar didn't want to be in the room when that happened. Someone usually died when the sisters clashed.

"So, those five minutes?" Balthazar said to get Solara's attention back.

She waved a finger in his face. "Don't think I'll forget your deception, Enforcer."

He winced. She knew how much he hated that particular moniker. "Like I haven't done worse."

"That remains to be seen." She let out a deep breath before turning her back to him. "Come with me, please."

Balthazar looked toward where Zakariel once stood. He wasn't surprised that the Heavenly Host had left. He likely waited for him in Solara's office, ready to bargain for the boy's soul. Balthazar licked his lips. Oh, he was ready. He was born ready.

Chapter 28

DBEYR

Arianne walked behind the two lesser demons in a daze. They were the same ones who'd dressed her. No point in asking them for help. Something told her the two were loyal to the Voyeur. And where would she escape to even if she managed to convince them to let her go? She didn't know where to find the Nixies short of returning to the Ghoul Woods. Plus, she still had to find the Redeemer. Balthazar said that angel with the really white wings would know.

The thought of Balthazar twisted Arianne's insides. One second they were making out, the next he used her to bid for Ben in the Underball auction. She felt all kinds of betrayed. Seeing the way Ben reacted made everything worse. He'd screamed her name over and over. Even through the uproar of the crowd in the ballroom, she'd heard him. She shook her head at him and mouthed an apology, then refused to look his way again. Thankfully the red curtains closed, blocking his reaction.

For one night with Arianne, Balthazar had saved Ben. It shouldn't feel as scary as it did. Cold sweat dotted her brow. Her palms were slick. She tangled her fingers together to keep them from shaking too badly. The air in the mansion nipped at her exposed skin now when before she'd hardly felt the cold.

What did one night with her mean? Just what exactly did Balthazar sell her for?

With every step she climbed to the third floor, Arianne's hope for Balthazar fell away. She'd agreed to do whatever it took to save Ben, but she never expected to be sold like some object. She bit the inside of her cheek until she tasted blood. She had to coat the bitterness of betrayal on her tongue somehow. She should have known when Balthazar said the word "anything" he really did mean anything. He had no morals. No matter what they'd been through, or whatever they'd shared during this insane quest for the Redeemer, he still didn't think twice about bartering her away.

For the hundredth time, she cursed Granmare Baba. If the witch hadn't connected her to Balthazar to mask her human scent, he wouldn't have had the power to use her in his scheme. Did Balthazar call selling her using everything at his disposal to help her? Did he consider whoring her out protecting her?

Arianne's skin crawled the second the thought entered her head. Oh god, what did one night with her mean? Would they force her to…

Arianne doubled over and puked. She didn't have anything in her stomach to hurl out, so she dry heaved instead, which hurt ten times worse. Her stomach squeezed then tumbled inside her like it wasn't attached to her body. To her ear, she sounded both horrible and pathetic.

Again and again the same thought repeated in her head.

She'd been sold to save Ben.

The lesser demons gathered around her. One rubbed her back while the other held her shoulders. When the dry heaving stopped, Arianne wiped the back of her hand over her wet lips. Just because she didn't have anything in her stomach didn't mean she didn't have spit. She swallowed, then took a deep breath before straightening. One of the lesser demons gave her a sympathetic smile.

Arianne tried to smile back but her lips wouldn't stop trembling. She took a couple more deep breaths and reminded herself what she did all of this for. Her knees shook when Niko's face came to mind. Would he still want her after tonight?

Arianne shook her head.

She'd saved Ben. That had to count for something. Ben had given his life for hers without thinking twice. Surely she could survive a night. Just one night.

Arianne took one last deep breath and nodded at the demon still smiling at her. She gestured for them to lead on. They climbed one more flight of stairs until they reached the hall that led to Balthazar's private suite. Arianne closed her eyes. She didn't want the image of him naked in her head.

She opened her eyes when she heard the doors open. The lesser demon to her left ushered her in before closing the doors behind her. Arianne turned around and stared blankly at the doors. Then she turned in a tight circle inside the empty room.

"What now?" she asked the still air.

Arianne's eyes landed on her folded clothes on the couch. On top lay the knife Tomas had given her. She ran for it and clutched it to her chest. Considering her slave outfit, she had no way to hide the thing on her body. Shaking, she moved away from the couch toward the bedroom.

Thinking fast, Arianne stuffed the knife under one of the pillows. No one said she couldn't defend herself against whoever was spending the night with her. When the doors opened again, she froze. She stared at the entrance to the bedroom.

A large Demon King filled her line of sight. The thing must have been over seven feet tall and all muscle. She recognized him as the one who'd bid for Ben before the angel and Balthazar had outbid him. He looked bigger up close with skin blacker than the darkest night. His eyes burned a fiery red, watching her carefully. His massive wings spanned the entire height of him. The tips curled toward each other to keep from touching the floor. He had hooves for feet and long claws at the end of his fingers. He kept his lips firmly closed, but Arianne suspected he had a wicked set of teeth under there. Her fingers itched to inch back and grab the knife beneath the pillow. If it could kill Balthazar, then surely it could kill a Demon King.

"You look lovely," he said in a gravelly voice, like he had a sore throat. He inhaled. "You smell lovely too."

"It's the rose oil," Arianne said, surprised she managed to speak without trembling. The muscles in her stomach quivered. She leaned against the side of the bed's headboard.

The Demon King licked his black lips with an impossibly red tongue. "I've never been with an attached slave soul before. I will relish spending the night with you."

Arianne thought fast. If she could make a deal with Death himself, surely she could do the same with a Demon King. "Are you the one who will spend the night with me?"

The Demon King hesitated before he nodded. Arianne wondered what that second's hesitation was about, but she pushed forward with what she had in mind. If she could get the Demon King to somewhere public, maybe she could still escape, or at least buy some more time until she could find someone willing to help her.

"You must be very powerful for a Demon King," she said. Rule number one in getting any guy to do what you want: stroke his ego. She'd learned this from Carrie. Hopefully it would work.

His chest puffed up like a silverback gorilla. "The most powerful."

Arianne batted her eyelashes through her fear. Predators smelled fear. She'd learned this from her father. "I thought so." She adjusted her stance so she looked curvier. This she'd learned from her mother. She never thought it would come in handy, but the bikini helped, too. Little did her family know when they were teaching her all these tricks that their lessons would be used to get what she wanted from a Demon King.

"Then you can take me to where the auction items are being kept."

The Demon King snorted. "Of course I can. But why would I?"

"Because…" Arianne paused, thinking about what to say next. Then something Ben told her long ago about bad boys came to mind. "Wouldn't it be cool to get a look at what else they have down there? Maybe there's something we could use."

Bad boys equally liked bad girls, according to Ben. Arianne couldn't remember why they'd had that conversation, but judging from the smile on the Demon King's face, it worked. She never in a million years thought it would.

She raised her chin to seem haughty, staring at him through her eyelashes. She'd seen an actress do it in one of these teen dramas she'd watched over the summer. The episode was about seducing the lead male away from the lead female. Arianne thought it might help now.

"Show me the way?" she said.

Instead of leaving the room, the Demon King hauled Arianne over his shoulder. She struggled against him, but she might as well be pounding on a brick wall. The Demon King laughed.

"Do you honestly think I will fall for your attempts at distracting me?" he said.

Arianne stopped struggling immediately. She should have known her little seduction wouldn't work. The Demon King had agreed way too easily to what she wanted. She cursed Balthazar one more time for putting her in this position. She wasn't about to become demon bait. Not if she could help it.

"I'm new at this," she said softly, like someone helpless.

The Demon King grunted. "I find that hard to believe."

"And why's that?"

"Any slave of Balthazar's should be of the highest quality. Why do you think bidding you managed to win him the soul of that boy against a night with Jezebel?"

Arianne didn't know who this Jezebel person was. Her name didn't ring a bell, so it meant Granmare Baba didn't include that piece of info. But she did give Arianne ways to kill a Demon King. Arianne steeled herself. If she wanted to survive the night, then she had to work around her aversion to hurting another living thing. She quickly realized the only person who could help her out of the situation was herself. Balthazar had been right all along. Everything in the Underverse was dangerous. If she didn't man up now then she didn't deserve to survive.

She swallowed and forced herself to say, "If we're going to do anything, I'd rather do it on the bed, if you don't mind."

The Demon King slapped her backside and tipped his head back, laughing loud enough that the walls vibrated from the inhuman sound. Arianne raised her hands to cover her ears then realized her wrists were still shackled together. The Demon King—still laughing—flipped her onto the bed. Arianne yelped, her breath catching in her lungs. She struggled to inhale. Before the Demon King could position himself above her, Arianne raised her wrists.

"Can you undo these?" she asked in the sweet voice she used when she wanted something from someone—specifically a male someone.

The Demon King blinked at her, confusion clear on his face.

"I can hold you better if my wrists aren't tied," she added, ignoring the twist in her stomach at having to say those words.

Finally getting what she meant, the Demon King used one of his claws to cut off the shackles holding her wrists together. Arianne sighed as if she hated being tied up and rubbed the aching skin on her wrists. Then she did something she didn't think she could do under these circumstances: smiled like she meant it.

"Go on," she said. "Take your…" She meant to say clothes but the Demon King only had that tight Speedo looking thing on.

She didn't have to say much more because the Demon King backed away then turned around, presumably to do what she'd asked. Arianne averted her eyes and reached for the knife beneath the pillow. She pushed it out of its sheath, leaving the leather where it was. She clutched the hilt and hid it behind her back.

The Demon King turned back around then leaped on top of her. Arianne saw nothing but blackness. At first she thought she'd blacked out. But when the Demon King shifted above her, she got a glimpse of the ceiling. Her heart hammered a million beats a minute, sending roaring blood to her ears. The Demon King smelled rancid, like rotting road kill. He dipped his head and licked her neck from base to chin. Forcing herself not to squirm from the gross touch, Arianne steeled herself for what she had to do. If she didn't move now it would be too late.

Just as the Demon King grabbed her breast, she pulled the knife out and screamed.

Chapter 29

ISO

Solara left her own party without a second thought. She didn't even leave instructions. Like D, the Voyeur liked order in her entire operation. She didn't need to micromanage anything. The party would go on flawlessly even without its mistress keeping a close watch. The guests were already thoroughly entertained, judging from the cheers and jeers. Which was no surprise given the amount of Nectar circulating. Most of the creatures in the ballroom were already hammered.

Balthazar trailed the Voyeur as she weaved through the increasingly boisterous crowd. The auction resumed around them as if tonight's excitement had never happened. Balthazar should have known better than to expect that his antics with the honorable-to-a-fault Heavenly Host would leave a lasting impact. Call it ego. Call it whatever you wanted. Balthazar had at least wanted to make an impression. Sadly, he played for a jaded crowd. They'd quickly moved on.

He sighed under his breath. Might be better this way. The more waves he and Arianne created tonight, the harder their escape would be. Solara wouldn't take their deception lying down. The thought of Arianne led to other unexpected things. Or should he say emotions. Chief among them: guilt, something Balthazar never had any use for until now. It ate at him like a parasite. The look on Arianne's face bothered him every time he blinked. The betrayal in her eyes haunted him. When had his chest grown so tight?

Balthazar forced himself to ignore the irritating guilt picking at him. Instead, he concentrated on following Solara. They ducked into the concealed entrance without anyone else being the wiser. Balthazar hadn't seen Zakariel among the crowd, so the Heavenly Host must already be waiting for him inside Solara's office.

Not once did Solara look back at him. Balthazar expected it. He'd managed to outwit her and he used her sister to do it. The Voyeur's relationship with Granmare Baba had always been a tumultuous one. Over the centuries they'd made a game of one upping each other. Anyone who got in between the battling bitches usually lost their heads.

Balthazar rolled his head from side to side, popping the vertebrae in his neck, the muscles there tense. He had to find a safe way out of the mansion with Arianne.

None of his plans would work if he didn't play it right with Zakariel. The Heavenly Host held the key to the Redeemer. Balthazar reminded himself to take things a step at a time. He was so close, so very close to his goal. The thing now would be not to trip and unravel everything he'd worked so hard for.

At the mirrored hallway, Balthazar caught a glimpse of Solara's face. Her lips had disappeared into a white line and her brow crumpled. He grinned, unable to help himself.

"Stress causes wrinkles," he said.

Solara stopped abruptly and faced one of the mirrors. She raised her hands to her face and leaned closer, checking for the wrinkles Balthazar had mentioned. When she found none, she straightened and faced him.

"What are you playing at here, Enforcer?" She raised an eyebrow at him, her gaze damning.

He used every ounce of will power he had not to react to her use of his dead title. He hadn't been the Enforcer for the longest time. Nothing made him happier. Unfortunately, the memories of the creatures in the Underverse lasted millennia. When someone like Solara held a grudge, a thousand years in hiding wouldn't be enough. Balthazar had to keep things simple.

"Last I checked, you're not my mother. And even then I wouldn't feel like explaining myself to you."

Solara crossed her elegant arms and waited.

Balthazar narrowed his gaze for a moment. "I made a bargain to protect her."

"You're saying you did the honorable thing by taking her to that bitch?"

"You keep confusing witch for bitch."

"With my sister? Same difference."

"I wouldn't call going to her honorable. I have a reputation to maintain."

"What reputation?" She sneered at him. A very unladylike move for someone so powerful. "You've been stuck in the Nethers too long, Balthazar. Things are changing in the Underverse, and they're going to keep changing with or without you."

"Your expansion into the Ghoul Woods—"

"Is just me protecting my assets."

"Bullshit."

She whirled around in a blur of shinny fabric. "You want your five minutes with the Heavenly Host or not?"

Balthazar didn't say another word. He followed Solara the rest of the way. She pushed open the door and gestured for him to enter. He looked into her now-golden eyes as she stared into his. He couldn't find a chink in her armor, or even a clue to how she really felt about Arianne being in her mansion. For now maybe they were safe, but what she'd said about everything changing concerned him. Maybe things weren't as they used to be. If he didn't evolve and get with the program fast, he might not survive. Adapt or die.

"You have five minutes," she said evenly.

He nodded once then entered the office. Solara shut the door behind him. Zakariel stood by the fire place, a deep frown already on his magnificent face. Balthazar had to remind himself he no longer admired the Heavenly Host. He and Zakariel stood on an even playing field now. He had nothing to be intimidated about. Then the voice of his mother reminding him to respect his elders whispered in his head. He pushed the thought away and told himself to get down to business. He had to get back to Arianne before Solara thought to do anything stupid. He wouldn't put it past the Voyeur.

"Solara has always had a perverse fascination with the human form," Zakariel said in greeting.

"Of course you'd say that." Balthazar stepped closer until he reached one side of Solara's gold leaf desk. Its carvings were just as suggestive as everything else in the mansion. His suite really was the only PG part of the place. If Solara took the time to preserve his suite, maybe she didn't despise him as much as he initially thought. He and Arianne stood a chance of getting out of here intact.

The Heavenly Host turned away from the fireplace to face him then. "What gives you that impression?"

"You're a Heavenly Host." Balthazar tilted his head. "You're snobby."

"On the contrary." Zakariel ran his gaze over one of the naked statues. "You should know better than most that angels have always envied humans. God may not say it, but he does favor them above all others."

He snorted. "Free will is a bitch. They're an experiment gone wrong. God just won't admit it."

"And yet you escort one of those so called failed experiments around the Underverse. Your mother, for all her faults, always believed in the good in you."

"You still have a hard-on for her? Is that what this is, Zakariel? That ship sailed. And sadly, you weren't on it."

The Heavenly Host charged Balthazar and pinned him against the opposite wall, a hand around his neck. Balthazar grinned.

"Your mother may have chosen demon scum over me, but I don't think any less of her because of it. She was beautiful and well-respected within Heaven, Haven, and the Underverse. It would do you good to show some of that respect."

During one of her trips within the Underverse to collect an assortment of special alloys for weapons, Brianne had encountered Balthazar's father. Some in Heaven said she'd been seduced by him. To Balthazar, that was just a PR stunt the higher ups spread to keep the reputation of Heaven clean. Anyway, Brianne had started seeing him on the sly. She told Balthazar once that she really loved his father. He believed her because his father's betrayal drove her crazy, tainting her once pristine wings until they slowly turned black and the feathers fell away, barring her permanently from Heaven. Worse than Lucifer's Fall, some whispered. She took out all her rage on the closest thing to his father — Balthazar.

The day she died couldn't come fast enough for him.

Zakariel gave Balthazar's neck one more squeeze before releasing him, letting him fall to the ground. Balthazar rearranged his coat and cleared his throat. Zakariel could have broken his neck. The bastard didn't have the balls though.

"What do you need with the boy that you would sacrifice the tethered soul of a girl for it?" Zakariel asked after his breathing calmed. He moved back to the other side of the room.

"Leverage." The word came out scratchy. Balthazar cleared his throat again. Zakariel damaged his vocal chords. The asshole. He'd pay the Heavenly Host back with interest later.

Zakariel stared. His silver gaze narrowed.

"I need to see the Redeemer," Balthazar clarified.

"And what makes you think I'll grant the audience?"

"You just bid Mike's sword and a night with Jezebel for the boy. I figure he's important to you."

"Not to me," Zakariel grumbled. He leaned both his hands on the mantel. "The Redeemer heard the unprocessed soul of a boy would be auctioned off. I was sent here to save him."

That Balthazar didn't quite get. "Why would a Redeemer care about the soul of one boy?"

Zakariel barked a sad laugh. "I asked myself that over and over on the way here. But my will is to serve. I was given the task of bringing the boy back and I lost him to a half-breed like you."

"How racist."

The Heavenly Host whirled around again, but instead of charging he just growled. "You're always pushing buttons. One day you'll push the wrong one and it will kill you."

Balthazar showed fang in an arrogant smile. "Looking forward to it."

Deflating, Zakariel relaxed his stance. "There's no winning with you."

"You're just learning that now?"

"So, the boy."

"All you have to do is bring us to the Redeemer and he's all yours."

Doubt entered Zakariel's silver eyes. He crossed his arms, his wings twitching as if he ached to take flight. "I don't believe it's that easy."

"You're questioning an easy bargain. Suspicious much? The boy for an audience with the Redeemer. That's all."

"It's never that easy with you, Balthazar. I'm not that stupid." Before Balthazar could comment, he added, "No matter what you think."

"A selfish angel?" Balthazar rubbed his nose. "Isn't that against your rules?"

Zakariel's eyes widened. "Don't turn my status against me. I may have my doubts, but that doesn't mean I will not help."

"Good." Another shocker for Balthazar. "I thought I was gonna have to play dirty."

"I would have let you, but as you might have noticed, the boy doesn't have much time."

The room grew very quiet. Balthazar had thought he imagined things when he got a look at Ben. He'd been too pale, even for a soul. Since he was unprocessed, and who knew how long it had been since he'd been separated from his body, it meant only one thing.

"Let me get Arianne and the boy. We'll leave for Haven immediately."

"You collect Arianne and I'll collect the boy."

"Uh, uh, uh," Balthazar said. "The boy stays with me until we see the Redeemer."

"Don't you trust me?"

"Don't think you're special. I don't trust anyone."

Right before Balthazar turned to leave, the door to Solara's office opened. The Voyeur poked her head in and smiled.

"Time's up, fellas," she said in a too cheerful tone.

Balthazar faced her. "I'm buying Arianne from you for the night."

Solara pursed her lips and tilted her head. "Too late."

"What?" Balthazar stood frozen. *Shit.* He felt all his blood drain from his face. "What did you do?"

The Voyeur's smile that followed chilled Balthazar to the bone. "I thought you would think this appropriate. I sold her to that Demon King who bet against the two of you."

Like a whip crack, Balthazar ran out of the office. He made sure to use excessive force when he shoved Solara aside. She slammed against one of the mirrors, breaking it into a thousand jagged pieces. To a lesser being, the impact would have hurt. Solara just laughed hysterically.

The sound of her laughter followed Balthazar through the ballroom and up the three flights of stairs. No matter how fast he moved,
it felt like he wasn't getting to the suite fast enough. For the first time
in his miserable existence, his heart hammered in his chest until it
bruised. Somewhere along the way, he'd forgotten how to breathe.
His lungs burned.

At the door to the suite, he heard Arianne scream. The sound—so
full of fear—rooted him on the spot for a second. A new wave of
guilt slammed into him. When he remembered how to move again,
he didn't bother opening the double doors.

Chapter 30

RT

The knife jumped out of Arianne's hand. At least it felt that way to her. She barely managed to hold on to it when, as if by magic, it sank into the stomach of the Demon King. Arianne's heart beat in her throat, choking the second scream she wanted to let out.

The Demon King grunted.

Arianne's mind raced. She had a freakin' huge naked demon over her. Didn't he feel the knife go in?

The knife's handle suddenly felt hot and slick. Arianne struggled to pull it out and try for another stab. She hitched up her knee in an attempt to kick the Demon King off her. He must not have really felt the knife go in because despite the bleeding all over her midsection, the creature still managed to lick her with his forked tongue from chin to temple. She whimpered, turning her head away. The move only gave the Demon King access to her ear. He hummed as if he liked the way she tasted. She shook so badly, the bed beneath her creaked. She had to do something before her situation got worse.

Taking a better grip on the knife, she willed it out of its hold on the Demon King's belly. They were harder to kill than she initially thought. Just as she braced herself for a second stab, an explosion caused the Demon King to hiss at the entrance to the bedroom. Arianne turned her head just in time to see wood splinter everywhere into the living room.

Everything happened so fast after that.

A black blur rushed into the room and pulled the Demon King from on top of her. The air around her whooshed. She blinked and immediately recognized Balthazar. The feral look on his face scared her more than what almost happened with the Demon King.

Staring at her the whole time, Balthazar restrained the Demon King with one arm around his bleeding waist. He used his other hand to tilt his head to the side and sank his fangs into the Demon King's neck.

The creature howled and twitched, but couldn't do anything against Balthazar's hold. Blood—blacker than the Demon King's skin—oozed out of where Balthazar's lips met jugular. Not once did Balthazar take his eyes off of Arianne, and Arianne couldn't convince herself to look away either. She stared back, still shaking. A new kind of fear came over her as she watched Balthazar take his fill. Her grip on the knife, the only thing that seemed real, tightened.

Several panicked breaths later, the Demon King hung limp in Balthazar's arms. Its red eyes were glazed over, unseeing. With a swift twist of his hand, Balthazar broke the creature's neck before letting him go. He fell to the floor with a loud thump. Balthazar blinked then, breaking the spell his stare had on Arianne. She pushed away from him and the now dead Demon King until she reached the opposite side of the bed. Her teeth chattered and she kept the knife pointed at Balthazar. He spit out the blood in his mouth and wiped his lips with the back of his hand. He wobbled back as if drunk, using his other hand for support against the wall.

"Ari," he said into the back of his other hand. A trail of blood still remained on the corner of his lips down his chin.

"Stay away from me!" Arianne said, voice shaking the whole time. The knife shook too, but she continued to hold it up, pointed toward Balthazar.

Without taking her eyes off him, she sat up then climbed out of the bed one leg at a time. Her lower half trembled as badly as her hands and voice. Unable to support her own weight, she stumbled back into the wall behind her.

She leaned hard against it, letting the wall take most of her weight.

Balthazar moved toward her in drunken steps. "Ari, you okay?"

"Shut up," she spat. "Don't come near me." The last part came out as a sob. Tears welled up in her eyes then.

"Ari." He paused, a few steps away from her.

"You sold me," she bit out, tears spilling from her eyes. "You sold me to *that*." She pointed her knife at the dead Demon King then back at Balthazar. "I thought you were good. That some part of you was good."

In a blink of an eye, Balthazar stood right in front of her. Arianne yelped. He took her wrist and brought the tip of the knife to the center of his chest. With his other hand, he tilted her chin up so she could look into the white center of his black irises. His silver hair rained over his forehead, covering the crease that marred its usual smoothness.

"You think I'm the good guy?" he whispered. She continued trembling, worse now. He leaned down until his lips touched her ear. "I'm not."

Every breath she took smelled of the Demon King. She whimpered at the memory of the gross thing lying on top of her. Her skin crawled.

"That should scare you."

She swallowed, but maintained eye contact. When he looked at her the way he did now, like he carried all the pain in the universe on his shoulders, she couldn't turn away.

"Why?" she managed to say.

He leaned forward until his forehead touched the wall she leaned on. Arianne felt the knife slice through the buckle into the leather of his shirt. She inhaled sharply. She tried to pull back, but his grip tightened, keeping her in place.

"Because I have nothing to lose," he said softly, dangerously.

Arianne's trembling turned into shudders. Like before, the knife wanted to jump out of her grasp. Arianne tightened her grip on it. She felt it beg her to let go so it could bury itself into Balthazar's chest. She considered it. But now, while his blood dripped down her hands, she couldn't seem to go through with killing him anymore. He might be a killer, but not Arianne. Balthazar had been right. She wasn't as bad as she thought she was—no matter what she'd done in her life. No longer looking into Balthazar's intense gaze, she closed her eyes. She had to think, and think fast.

"Do it." His voice trembled too now. "Just do it and save us both the trouble."

She licked her bottom lip and forced the fear caused by her encounter with the Demon King out of her mind. *Nothing happened,* she told herself repeatedly. Balthazar got there just in time. He saved her. If he'd really wanted to sell her to the highest bidder for the night, he wouldn't have pulled the Demon King away. Right?

He'd killed for her.

He'd saved her.

She repeated the words until she believed them.

Still with her eyes closed, she said his name.

"What are you waiting for?" His grip tightened on her wrist, forcing the blade further.

Opening her eyes wide, Arianne said, "No!"

That one word sounded like a bullet out of a gun.

Balthazar stilled, his hard breathing the only movement he made above her. The way the blood trickled from the wound the knife had created in his chest, his heart slammed as hard as hers. Quickly, Arianne realized she had to make this right. If she really wanted to find the Redeemer, she had to be the bigger person — like Carrie had taught her.

Gritting her teeth, she forced herself to breathe. When her heart didn't feel so much like a fist inside her chest, she uncurled one of her hands off the knife's handle. Slick with Balthazar's blood, she curled her fingers around the back of his neck. When she squeezed at the tension there, she felt Balthazar take a shuddering breath. His grip loosened against her wrist, and he dropped his hand to his side. Arianne quickly lowered the blade and used her free hand to staunch the bleeding on Balthazar's chest. In her palm, she felt his powerful heart beating.

Staring up at the ceiling, she channeled Carrie and leaned against Balthazar until their cheeks touched. Into his ear she whispered, "I forgive you."

For the third time that night, Balthazar stilled like a statue.

Like Carrie had always told her, forgiveness wasn't for the benefit of the person being forgiven. It set the person doing the forgiving free. Arianne let go of what Balthazar did tonight. He'd asked her how far she would go to save Ben. Because she agreed, he took it to the extremes. She should have known better. Now she did.

"You got here in time," she repeated.

Balthazar pulled away from her. "Don't pity me."

His words shocked her. "Pity you?"

He pinned her with an unforgiving glare. "You forgive me? *You* forgive *me?*" He punched a hole into the wall too close to her head.

Arianne flinched, but didn't move away. Plaster tumbled down her shoulder when Balthazar pulled his fist out of the hole he'd made.

"Don't make me want to kill you again," she said, eyes wide, unable to believe the turn of events. Did she really think someone like Balthazar would take her act of kindness graciously?

He tilted his head back and laughed.

Balthazar had gone from homicidal to suicidal and now to hysterical. She stared, unbelieving. He'd saved her, and when she'd forgiven him for being a complete jerk, he laughed in her face. Nothing seemed to be going right in this scenario. In her head, she'd imagined this going another way, a much more sane way.

It took Balthazar a minute to compose himself. He wiped a tear of laughter from the corner of his eye, then shook his head. He chuckled a couple more times before he resettled his gaze on Arianne.

He took a couple of deep breaths. "Get dressed. We're out of here."

"Huh?"

Arianne now had the strength to push away from the wall. She trembled more from anger than fear. One day, what happened with the Demon King would haunt her. For now, adrenaline and a prayer were the only things keeping her together. She could fall apart later… when all this was over. Why process what Balthazar had saved her from and give herself additional worries? Instead, just to get moving, she pushed against his chest. He didn't bleed anymore.

"That's all you're gonna say?"

Balthazar stepped back as if she'd pushed him hard enough to actually unbalance him. She knew it wasn't the case because he was built as solid as a brick house. Nothing could move him if he didn't want it to.

"Zakariel's waiting for us downstairs. We still have to pick up your friend from his holding cell."

Hearing about Ben got Arianne thinking straight again. "We're taking him with us?"

Balthazar nodded. "The Redeemer really wants him. So I made a deal with Zakariel. We get to see the Redeemer in exchange for Ben."

"You're not really thinking of giving him to the Redeemer, are you?" Arianne frowned. She picked up the knife, silently thanking it for helping her out too. It warmed in her hand, as if saying "you're welcome." She smiled. At least it knew how to accept gratitude. Unlike some people.

"Not your choice."

"And why's that?"

He sighed, looking away from her. "Ben's slowly turning into a Wraith."

Arianne's stomach twisted. "You're lying."

"Not about this."

Ben? A Wraith? A creature so filled with hate it fed on the souls of others. If Ben turned into a Wraith, he'd be cursed forever. Arianne couldn't let that happen.

"What's the Redeemer going to do with him?" she asked.

Balthazar shrugged. "Like I'd know. But like the name means, the job of a Redeemer is to redeem."

"And if we don't get to Haven in time?"

"I kill him."

Chapter 31

NP

*L*ike a girl possessed, Arianne moved quickly. She sprinted out of the bedroom, presumably to change back into her regular clothes. It couldn't happen fast enough for Balthazar. He preferred seeing her in her leather pants and layers of shirts and sweaters than the slave uniform Solara deemed appropriate. The less skin she showed him the better. His blood still ran a little too hot for his taste when it concerned Arianne.

She'd taken the knife that almost ended everything for him with her. So much for swiping, and possibly getting rid of it. The crazy part? He'd been ready to give her his life. He'd made it easy for her by making the first stab. All she had to do was shove the blade the rest of the way. His heart would have exploded, the special blade preventing it from regenerating. The end of Balthazar. He wouldn't have been missed.

He felt her consider it for a second, too. Then in a sick twist, she'd forgiven him.

Balthazar's gut crumpled.

No one had ever forgiven him for anything. His mother never had to. Thankfully, she didn't live long enough to see what had become of him—to see that she'd been right to create the knife. And now this girl, tethered to her human body by a single flimsy thread, had taken it upon herself to forgive him.

He moved his gaze from the bedroom entryway to the Demon King's limp body. When he'd burst into the room, he'd seen its massive body on the bed, and just underneath it a squirming Arianne. His gaze tunneled, seeing nothing but red. He blacked out after that.

The next thing he remembered, he'd let go of the dead Demon King. From the marks on the demon's neck, he'd drained him. Fresh life force filled his body to bursting. If he could puke out the excess energy, he would have. But why did he have to break the creature's neck? That seemed a little excessive even for his standards. He usually left his dinner alone after he'd finished with it. Balthazar's gaze shifted to the stab wound in the Demon King's belly.

Come to think of it, Arianne had been holding on to the knife when he'd regained consciousness.

So, the little girl got a stab in, did she?

Balthazar rubbed his chin, a grin playing on his lips. He knew she had fire in her, but to actually defend herself against a Demon King? The creature might not have even felt the stab. His mother's blades could kill, but the victim wouldn't feel the blow. His mother, insane yet humane until the bitter end.

Arms crossed, Balthazar wondered what to do with the body.

No use hiding it.

Burning it might set the room on fire too.

After the Underball, the rooms would be cleaned and the guests accounted for. If the Demon King didn't make an appearance, Solara would be pissed. Bad for business to have customers croaking.

In the end, Balthazar decided to leave the body alone. Located at the end of the hall on the top floor, his suite would be the last to be cleaned. Except…that meant they had to leave. Like, *yesterday*.

Turning on his heel, he reentered the living room, catching Arianne strapping the knife to her thigh. His finally cooler blood boiled to raging again. Unthinking, Balthazar grabbed her by the waist and pushed her up against the wall. She looked up at him like she always did when he leaned over her this way. He liked this position. Perhaps his favorite so far. He searched her face and found a question mark there.

"I thought we're in a hurry?" she asked, confirming the thoughts he felt in her head.

"Ask me to kiss you," he said impulsively. He couldn't take it back now. His eyes dropped to her lips. He had to taste her again.

Like a flower retreating into itself, Arianne's lips disappeared into her mouth. A pained groan escaped him. He couldn't help himself. He'd asked for his current humiliation, so he had to man up and take it. Arianne met his gaze and shook her head.

Unable to get what he wanted most, Balthazar thumped his forehead on the wall three times before he pushed away from her rose-scented body. He noticed that she'd washed off as much of the Demon King's stench from her skin as she could without having to bathe. Just thinking of the scum pinning her down made him see red again. His fangs ached to sink themselves into the demon's neck and tear it open.

As he backed away, Balthazar took solace in the fact that Solara would definitely be pissed when she found the body. He took a deep breath, keeping his gaze anywhere but on Arianne.

She pushed away from the wall and gathered her things, shrugging on her jacket and slinging the pack over her shoulder.

"Did you really have to turn the door into toothpicks?" she asked, dodging the splinters while making her way to the gaping entrance to the suite.

Balthazar strode out and said when he passed her, "Never liked that door anyway."

"If I didn't know any better, I'd think you actually cared."

"Don't push it."

He felt her smile in his head instead of actually seeing it. He kept his eyes straight ahead because if he stared at her too long he'd end up pinning her against another wall. One humiliation for the night was enough.

Maybe he was coming down with something?

He must have contracted something before he'd left the Nethers. Something nasty. He'd never been this way with anyone. Sure, he'd had lovers out of physical necessity. None of those encounters resembled relationships in any way.

Relationship.

Balthazar shuddered at the word. What did they say about relationships? It wasn't one unless someone was in pain?

The thorn in his side reminded him she existed by asking, "What about the Demon King?"

He grunted, feeling the proverbial pain. "What about it?"

"Oh, I don't know. Maybe a couple people won't like the fact that he's dead?"

He liked it a little too much when she turned sarcastic on him. Balthazar pushed away the useless emotion when they reached the first flight of steps. "Zakariel is waiting for us outside the mansion. We'll grab Ben and leave."

Arianne did her best to catch up with him. She moved faster already. His plan of having her match his pace by slowly increasing it had worked.

"How does that answer my question about the Demon King?" She lowered her voice when they passed a lesser demon at the second floor.

"The sooner we leave the better our chances of making it out of here alive. Solara won't check on the guests until after the party." Balthazar made a sharp left when they reached the ground floor. They skirted the ballroom to get to the holding area at the back. "Nobody will know about the Demon King until morning. So, if I were you, more hurrying and less talking."

"Well, gee, there's the Balthazar I know and love."

The word "love" made Balthazar sick to his stomach. Hearing it come out of her lips made the experience even worse. They had to finish this mission soon so he could once and for all rid himself of this strange affliction of wanting to kiss the girl running by his side. Emphasis on the word *girl*.

At the end of a long hallway that ran parallel to the ballroom, another set of red curtains hung from the ceiling down to the floor. Balthazar pulled the tacky fabric aside and let Arianne through.

Behind the curtains, a makeshift area housed the auction items. Arianne squeaked when she spotted the centaur. From the way she shielded her eyes, he could hazard a guess as to why. Centaurs weren't called studs in the Underverse for nothing. From the tag on its cage, a Fairy Queen had won him for the night.

Balthazar looked away from the centaur in time to see Arianne running for the boy's cage. He grimaced. The boy looked unwell—definitely worse than he'd been at the auction. They had very little time left.

Running out of time seemed like the recurring theme in this journey of theirs. Couldn't things just slow down? Give him a second to think and to piece things together?

Arianne was speaking frantically with her friend when Balthazar noticed the fraying on her thread. The phrase "hanging on by a thread" came to mind. The damage looked so much worse. Anything could detach Arianne from her body. Dammit. He had to keep an extra eye on her.

"I don't know what happened," the boy said, bringing Balthazar back to the conversation. "After I agreed to take your place, I disappeared into this dark place. I stayed there for a long time, but I never got hungry or had to use the bathroom."

Arianne held the boy's hands through the bars. A low rumble started in Balthazar's chest. He forced himself to stay calm by focusing on Arianne's voice.

"When you're a soul you don't need food anymore, much less go to the bathroom."

Tears were clear in her voice even if none were in her eyes. She was attempting to keep it together for her friend. Balthazar breathed a silent thanks for that, because he couldn't take another bout of the waterworks.

"I hate to interrupt this little reunion you're having here," Balthazar said, "but we have to go. We have an angel to catch." He touched the lock on the cage and it snapped in two.

Arianne pulled the door open and yanked Ben into a fierce hug.

"What part of 'we have to go' don't you understand?" Balthazar scowled. His hands tingled to yank them apart.

"We'll talk some more later," Arianne said to Ben. She let him go, but she kept hold of his hand. Balthazar grunted.

"What's going on here?" one of the lesser demons sent to guard the items asked, accusation on its face.

Balthazar appeared beside it in a flash and snapped its neck. He didn't have time to explain why they had to make a hasty exit. It would only rouse Solara's suspicions.

"Run for the back door," he said to Arianne. She nodded and towed Ben out of the room. Balthazar turned to follow when a voice he'd hoped he didn't have to hear for the rest of the night called his name. He whipped around to face the Voyeur.

"Solara!" He plastered a smile on his face. "What are you doing here?"

She eyed him. "Your blood's up next and I thought to fetch it myself."

"Why would you do that when you have lesser demons to do that for you?" Balthazar put a hand behind his back and summoned the vial of his blood to him. It floated to his hand, and he closed his fingers around it.

"Do you really have to kill my lesser demons?" Her glaze flicked to the dead demon at their feet.

"I thought I'd have a snack." Before she could speak her displeasure at the killing, Balthazar dangled the vial in her face. "Here you go. You don't want to keep the crowd waiting." He grabbed her hand and placed the vial in it, closing her manicured fingers around the glass container. Then he turned her around and practically shoved her out of the room.

"I think you're trying to get rid of me," she said over her shoulder.

"Not exactly." Lying came easily for Balthazar. He thanked his centuries of practice. "I just hate for the masses to wait long for my blood, that's all."

"Well, when you're done, we need to talk about you pushing me into that mirror."

"I'll pay for it," he gritted out. In his head he cursed her to the Nethers multiple times and in several colorful languages.

"You better."

With one last push, he nudged the Voyeur through the curtains before she could ask him about Arianne and the Demon King. The crowd cheered at her appearance. Probably she'd told them about the vial of his blood before she came in to get it. Balthazar didn't wait to see what his blood fetched — no matter how much he wanted to. He turned on his heel and followed after Arianne.

Chapter 32

OT

From the auction storage room, Arianne beelined it to the back door of the mansion that led to the veranda and ultimately the porn garden. She prepared herself for the mental image of those explicit bushes and Kama Sutra fountain. No amount of therapy would ever erase the images of this place from her brain. She'd be scarred for life. She silently cursed Balthazar for ever bringing her here.

Okay, not really his fault.

They *had* to come to the mansion to meet the Voyeur, but he could have at least warned her about it first. Arianne rolled her eyes and immediately regretted it. Of course the ceiling looked even worse than the marble. If the roof of the Sistine Chapel had an x-rated version, you'd find it in the Voyeur's mansion.

"Did you see that centaur?" Ben's voice pulled her attention away from the ceiling.

She squeezed his clammy hand. "Don't even go there."

"The equipment on that guy—"

"Ben!" She rolled her eyes again despite the ceiling. She had to because she really missed her best friend. It was either roll her eyes or start crying. She'd maxed out her cry card for the duration of this trip.

He laughed. God, she'd missed the sound of that laugh more than the sound of his voice. Actually—she corrected herself—both ran neck and neck for the number one spot. Having Ben back, even if in the back of her mind she was fully aware it could never be a permanent thing, still warmed her heart. When he'd sacrificed himself, it had happened so quickly that she didn't have time to say her goodbyes. Maybe this time…she stopped herself.

For now, they had to get out of the mansion. No more detours.

She glanced down at the ring as she moved toward the glass double doors. Its pulse was much weaker now. A pulse for every five seconds instead of the one second pulse from before. Death got worse and worse by the hour now, and Arianne had no idea how long she and Balthazar had been gone. It seemed like two days, but it could be more than that since time wasn't as linear in the Underverse as it was in the human world.

Arianne pushed away the pang of homesickness that blossomed in her chest. She wanted to click her ruby slippers three times and wish herself home. And not just any home. She wanted to be back to a time when Ben was alive and Carrie wasn't sick. Good times. But wishes like that weren't really possible. The sooner she accepted that fact, the faster she could accept that Ben and Carrie weren't in her life anymore after this mission.

She sniffed.

"Getting a cold?"

She smiled over her shoulder at Ben. Despite his sickly gray coloring, unlike any soul she'd seen before, he managed a warm smile. The kind of smile she'd been used to. Maybe she still had some credits left on her cry card after all. She faced forward again and wiped them away.

"I just missed you, you dork," she said.

"Missed you too, Ari," he said back.

Heart lighter, Arianne pushed open one of the glass doors and walked out into the veranda. Crystal tiki torches lit the garden, casting the porno bushes in a weird light. Almost romanticizing them. Ick!

What now?

"Wait, isn't there supposed to be an Oni guarding this door?" Arianne looked around for said ogre.

"Oni, as in Japanese ogre?" Ben asked. He stood beside her now, but he didn't let go of her hand. Arianne took comfort in that.

"I took care of it."

Arianne jumped when Zakariel landed in front of her and Ben. She all-out stared at his uber white wings—she'd never seen anything prettier.

"You're an angel." Ben took the words right out of her mouth. Because of Granmare Baba's magic info, she knew what Zakariel was, but having Ben say it aloud made Zakariel sound more real.

Zakariel nodded once. "Heavenly Host."

"What's the difference?"

"They're higher in rank. Their wings are much whiter than those of regular angels." Arianne finally found her voice. She concentrated on Zakariel's face. Zakariel had long hair, and she suspected his blond to be the natural kind based on the smattering of hair on his bare chest. Add to that the broad shoulders and the ab-tastic situation he had going on and he was ready for a cover shoot.

"And how do you know that?" Ben looked from Zakariel to her.

She tapped her temple. "Let's just say a witch gave me an info boost."

His brow wrinkled, but he shrugged. Arianne's heart flipped. She'd missed that shrug too. It always meant Ben trusted her enough not to question how she knew things. He'd done the same thing the first time she'd told him about seeing dead people. Ben was awesomely accepting that way, and she loved him for it.

"It's good to meet you, Benjamin," Zakariel said, forcing Arianne and Ben to return their attention to him.

"How'd you know my name?"

The Heavenly Host gave him a small smile, his silver eyes flashing. "I'm here to retrieve you."

"The Redeemer sent you," Arianne said.

He nodded once. "I came to save you, and would have if it weren't for Balthazar."

Arianne heard the bitterness in his voice. She smiled a secret smile for Balthazar. She'd be annoyed too if someone took away what she was sent to save. But because of what Balthazar did, they had a chance to see the Redeemer. It all made sense now. Arianne shivered. The last thing she needed was rehash the Demon King episode.

"Cold?" Balthazar asked when he finally joined them.

"Just remembering something," she answered back, giving him a quick glance.

"You took care of the Oni," Balthazar said to Zakariel.

The Heavenly Host tilted his head in a slight nod.

Arianne guessed that was as close to a "thank you" Balthazar would ever give and the little nod was Zakariel's way of acknowledging it. She huffed.

Zakariel broke the second of silence by saying, "My retinue has already flown back to Haven. We can all fly there together. I can take the boy and you can take the girl."

Arianne's eyes bugged out when she looked up at Balthazar who frowned like he tasted something nasty.

"You can fly?"

He aimed a poisonous glare at Zakariel, not meeting her gaze and totally blowing off her question. "Let me stop you there. The boy's not going anywhere with you."

"You need to stop this utter mistrust you have for everything, Balthazar. I, of all people, will not renege on our bargain. You will get to see the Redeemer. That is my vow."

Balthazar snorted his signature snort. "Excuse me for being me. We'll meet you at Haven's gates." He gestured at him in a shooing motion. "Go fly away and make your preparations. I want this meeting with the Redeemer to be a quick one."

Zakariel's thick blond brows came together. "Enough of your stubbornness, Balthazar. You know flying will save time."

"We are *not* flying there," Balthazar said through his teeth, flashing fang.

The memory of running her tongue over that fang chose that moment to make an inappropriate appearance. Arianne dropped her gaze and willed herself not to blush. When she felt Balthazar tense beside her she could have died of embarrassment then and there. He'd felt her thoughts. Fan-freakin'-tastic.

In a calmer voice, Balthazar said, "We'll use Charlie."

Zakariel sucked in a breath. "You're going through the Strait of Gwen?"

"Got a problem with that?"

"No." Zakariel cleared his throat. "I just thought that with two souls in tow, you wouldn't risk using the strait."

"It's still the shortest path to Haven, right?"

"That is if Charlion will allow you passage."

That half grin Arianne now found super sexy on Balthazar revealed itself again. "The big guy owes me one. We'll get through."

Zakariel gave Balthazar a pointed look Arianne couldn't understand. When the Heavenly Host mentioned the Strait of Gwen, a stretch of ocean came to Arianne's mind.

"What's the Strait of Gwen?" Ben whispered to her.

"Remember the River Styx in Lit class?" she whispered back while Balthazar and Zakariel continued to converse with each other.

Ben shuddered. "Don't remind me."

"The Strait of Gwen is something like that. Only red." The next thing Zakariel said caught Arianne's attention.

"You've got to get over this insecurity of yours, Balthazar."

What did the Heavenly Host mean by that? Balthazar…insecure? No way. But from Balthazar's glare, Arianne knew he used everything he had not to throw a punch. She certainly felt the intention in his thoughts—among other less savory things he wanted to do to the angel.

Before an actual brawl broke out, she said, "Aren't we supposed to be escaping here?"

As if snapped out of his anger, Balthazar said to Zakariel, "Just meet us at the damn gates. I'll handle getting us there."

Despite looking like he wanted to argue a bit more, the Heavenly Host zipped his lips and spread his wings. In a single wing beat, he executed a perfect vertical takeoff.

"Color me impressed," Ben said, tilting his head back and watching Zakariel—like Arianne did—until the Heavenly Host looked like a dot in the dark gray sky.

"Let's go," Balthazar barked at the both of them and ran for the garden.

Arianne took off after him, pulling Ben in her wake.

"Can you keep up?" she asked him over his shoulder. Recently, she realized she'd been moving faster. When she and Balthazar first started out, she could barely keep up with him. Was she actually getting stronger? Growing quicker? She liked that thought very much.

"You're worried about me?" Ben jogged up beside her when they reached the fountain. "How you can move so fast? I'm pretty sure you skipped gym class almost every chance you got in Blackwood."

Balthazar ran just a few steps ahead of them. He still had to slow his pace down, but not by much anymore. Could he have planned this all along? Balthazar seemed to have picked up on her thought because the answering feeling she got felt a little too smug.

Jerk.

He did plan it all along. She didn't know how to feel about that. Did she actually want to thank him for "training" her, for lack of a better word.

"Let's just say I've learned a lot since coming here," she said in answer to Ben's comment.

They ran through the garden, trailing Balthazar wherever he would lead them. He may not trust others, but Arianne trusted him. How could she not? She stared at the center of his back. Sure, he had his moments where she wanted to cut him, but he more than made up for those by saving her more times than she could count. But then he had said something about not being the good guy and that she should be afraid because he had nothing to lose. She doubted he had nothing to lose because he wouldn't be helping her if that were true.

Balthazar snorted. "Keep going. I have a feeling we're about to have a pissed off Voyeur on our hands."

As if in response to Balthazar's words, a terrible shriek came from the direction behind them. When they reached the edge of the property, Arianne stopped for a second. For the first time that night, she let go of Ben's hand so she could stare back at the mansion, far away now.

The first jagged lightning strike came down then, pretty close to where she stood. It exploded with flashing light and left behind a distinct ozone smell. Balthazar appeared at her side and yanked her away in time to avoid the second strike. It landed where she once stood.

"Move!" he yelled over the booming, blinding light.

Chapter 33

ADIH

Lightning rained down on them in crackling, sizzling, potentially lethal bolts. Everywhere. It made the edge of the Ghoul Woods a war zone. Debris flew in every direction. As they said, hell hath no fury and all that shit.

Balthazar wanted to run at full speed, but leaving Arianne and her almost-a-Wraith best friend behind wouldn't go over well with Zakariel. So now, instead of clearing Solara's attack and hopping a raft to Haven, he had to play "dodge the lightning strike" and pray the next one didn't hit where he landed.

A zigzag pattern worked best.

The ground around them exploded as if cannonballs were falling from the sky. Dirt bounced off every part of Balthazar. He raised his hands to block the stones kicked up by the lightning. The sour ozone in the air wreaked havoc on his sense of smell. He'd be breathing through his mouth for a week if this kept up. Damn the Voyeur for being a vindictive bitch.

"I think she's not happy with what we did," Arianne said through the cacophony. She jumped away from another strike.

"You think?" Ben added.

"No shit. Burned that bridge," Balthazar shouted over the noise.

"More like threw a nuclear bomb on it."

"Don't be overdramatic, Arianne."

As soon as Balthazar used a Blood Tree for cover, a lightning bolt burned it down.

They had to skirt the Ghoul Woods to get to the Strait of Gwen. At least they didn't have to deal with the ghouls, but every time a strike hit too close to home, Balthazar wondered if the ghouls wouldn't be easier. At least the boy could keep up with them. He had to admire that. Arianne chose her friends well, based on the agility Ben showed.

Right, 'cause agility was part of the friendship criteria. Balthazar rolled his eyes at his own logic.

"I don't think I'll ever be invited back," he added. "Now, shut the hell up and keep going. At some point the lightning will stop."

"I don't see why you'd want to go back there anyway." Arianne ducked behind a boulder. It disintegrated in seconds. She ran forward full tilt, rocks and dirt pelting her as badly as they did him and Ben.

Balthazar's heart stopped for a second. He wanted to throw her over his shoulder and make a run for it. But her weight combined with Ben's would hinder more than help. Plus, they would only make a bigger target for Solara to aim for, so he threw the idea away.

"You don't know me well enough if you think that," he replied, shoving her behind a Blood Tree a second too slowly. The lightning grazed his sleeve, lighting it on fire. He patted at the flames and glared at the sky. "Is that the best you got, whore of Satan?"

"Taunt her some more because that's all we need." Ben joined Arianne and glared at him. Arianne, being a fast thinker, grabbed Ben's arm and dragged him to the next tree just as a bolt split the one they'd hidden behind in two.

"How far?" Arianne shouted.

About to reply, Balthazar opened his mouth only for it to be filled with dirt from another explosion. He coughed and spat.

Busy hacking up a lung, he stayed in one place too long. The bolt shot through him in less than a second, throwing him aside like a rag doll. He collided with a Blood Tree. The force of the impact sliced the braided trunk, toppling the tree over in a crash just as loud as the explosions. Somewhere in his dizzy spell, Balthazar heard Arianne scream his name. He landed on his backside and skidded until a large root from another Blood Tree got in the way. Balthazar shook his head, the smell of something burning choking his nose. He rolled to his side and coughed, clutching his ribs. This time, instead of dirt, he spat out blood.

Arianne called to him again when she reached his side, Ben directly behind her. Then they began shoving dirt at him. He covered his face and cussed.

"What the hell are you doing?" he barked, blood streaming down one side of his mouth. He coughed again, his lungs burning.

"Putting out the fire, you ninny," Arianne said as she shoveled more dirt all over him.

Balthazar picked up the panic in her voice. He blinked to clear his vision and saw two of Arianne and Ben. He focused on his hand. His fingerless glove was gone. Then his gaze went up his arm. Instead of black leather, red skin with bits of black fused together. Once his vision cleared fully, he saw the extent of the damage. The strike might not have hit him head on, but it had burned one side of his body. His heart twisted when he realized what that meant. Blocking out as much of the chaos around him as he could, Balthazar patted at the buckles holding him together. Arianne and Ben looked on in bewilderment, but he didn't care, and he didn't explain himself. He only let himself breathe in relief when all but ten of the restraints held. He pushed himself off the ground and toppled over when his burnt leg couldn't support his weight. Ben rushed to his side and helped him up. The urge to push him away almost overwhelmed Balthazar. A soul helping him. He'd sunk to a new low for letting it happen, but if they all wanted to live, he'd allow the lesser evil.

"I don't think you should stand." The worry in Arianne's blue eyes touched a part of Balthazar that scared him to explore. Suddenly, it didn't matter that deadly lightning exploded around them. Suddenly, all he wanted was to take the worry away. It took all his will not to reach out and touch her cheek. Instead, he made a fist and gritted his teeth against the pain. He had to heal himself, and fast.

"Reach into my jacket pocket," he said, breathing hard.

Arianne searched his singed jacket. Her hands shook like she was afraid to touch him. "Which pocket?"

As soon as she asked the question, another strike hit to their left. Arianne covered her ears from the deafening boom. Balthazar forced himself to concentrate by staring at her face. The real fear there — not for herself — pushed him.

"Arianne," he urged. "I need you to concentrate." He leaned heavier on Ben. The boy adjusted his stance to accommodate the extra weight. Arianne's eyes returned to his. Only when he saw the determination peek through did he speak again. "Left inside pocket. There's a vial there."

Arianne reached into his coat tentatively. Balthazar had to force himself not to scream at her to hurry. Her hand shook too much for comfort as it was. If he screamed, she might drop the vial and he'd have to content himself with healing naturally, which, considering the ugliness Solara had caused him, would take longer than they had time for. He had to speed things up, and the vial Arianne fished out of his coat was their only hope.

When she had the vial with clear liquid and a pearl floating inside in her hand, he said, "Okay, remove the cork. Be careful!" He had to scream that one. Arianne froze with her fingers around the cork. If she pulled the wrong way…Balthazar shook his head mentally and took a calming breath. As calming as the situation they were in could provide. The strikes got closer and closer, but not directly hitting them. *Vengeful who*—Balthazar stopped the rest of the thought, no matter how satisfying it would be to finish it. He returned his full attention to Arianne, who still stood frozen in front of him.

"Pull the damn cork out slowly. That's it." The cork popped open, the liquid inside sloshing slightly. A spasm of pain rolled through Balthazar before he continued, "Shit. Okay." He breathed. "Bring the vial to my lips then tilt it until everything is inside my mouth. Can you do that without spilling anything?"

She glared at him like she knew he treated her like someone learning impaired. He'd shrug if his shoulder hadn't collapsed. Arianne's gaze dropped to her hand holding the vial. Her eyebrows shot up as she finally noticed the dangerous shaking of her fingers. She returned her gaze to Balthazar and nodded.

Just in case, she wrapped her free hand around her wrist to minimize the shaking. Balthazar opened his mouth and tilted his head back as far as the burnt skin on his neck permitted. The pain almost killed him. His eyes actually rolled back into his skull. He fought hard against the impending fainting spell and swallowed down the bitter liquid Arianne poured down his gullet. When he felt the ball tumble into his mouth, he rolled it to his back molar and bit down, crushing it immediately. He chewed around the rotten egg taste. Once the ball was a fine paste, he forced himself to swallow the foul concoction. His stomach rebelled. He let go of Ben to cover his mouth. The powder had to stay down for it to work.

Solara picked that time to end her little game. The next strike landed on Arianne. Balthazar watched everything happen in slow motion. He couldn't do anything to stop it.

The bolt shot down from the gray sky in its jagged pattern of light. The spear tip landed square on Arianne's head and went straight down. For the longest second of Balthazar's life, blinding hot light engulfed Arianne. Ben screamed her name.

Just as he felt the healing take effect, repairing his broken bones and burned skin, the light blinked out and Arianne's burning soul lifted off the ground as if pulled by an invisible fisherman who'd caught her in his hook. Before she could land, Balthazar pushed away from the ground in a burst of speed his still healing body wasn't prepared for. He caught her in his arms—her clothes on fire. He crouched down and folded his body over hers. The speed of his movement snuffed out the flames.

Not thinking twice about what he had to do Balthazar pinched her chin and opened her mouth. He stuck his tongue in and rubbed the last of the powder he hadn't swallowed onto hers. She wouldn't be happy when she found out, but it wasn't technically a kiss when he did it to save her life. Done transferring the last bit of the powder, Balthazar closed her mouth and massaged her throat so she swallowed. When he felt her do so, he gathered her closer to his still-mending chest and stood up. His legs bore her weight and his.

"Is she…"

Balthazar had forgotten about Ben until the boy couldn't finish his sentence.

"No," he said, more to comfort himself than Ben. The relief in the boy's face was enough for him to keep going. He looked down at Arianne. The lightning had damaged her soul, making it appear like her skin was peeling off. He returned his gaze to Ben and said, "You better keep up."

Ben nodded once, the same determination Arianne would get showing in his eyes. Balthazar had to grudgingly admit he liked the kid. Before he could grin, another bolt reminded him why they had to get away. Arianne wouldn't survive another hit. She was barely surviving already.

Balthazar turned on his heel and ran in the opposite direction of where the lightning bolts were coming from. He didn't bother checking if Ben managed to keep up. He weaved in and out of the forest perimeter, using the Blood Trees for cover. If the tightening in his chest meant he'd started having a heart attack the second the lightning bolt struck Arianne, then it was another first Balthazar couldn't believe he'd had.

Sucking it up against his own painful healing, Balthazar gave Arianne one quick glance and winced. She looked pretty bad — red skin alternated with black, her hair singed, and angry, smoking wounds littered every exposed part of her. Then his gaze landed on the red thread — the tether to her body in the human world. His eyes widened. Again his chest tightened.

Chapter 34

TLC

Eyes closed. Body warm but heavy. The acrid smell of burnt flesh faded. The explosions receded, replaced by voices. A couple of them, speaking in hushed tones. Both familiar, both voices Arianne thought she'd never hear again. She shifted her body as her consciousness surfaced from the darkness she'd plunged into the second everything around her exploded. The last image she had was of Balthazar on his hands and knees after he'd swallowed the pearl thing he'd asked her to help him drink. From the way his face looked, the pearl in that vial couldn't have tasted good. But the instant it went down his throat, he seemed much better, so maybe the vial's contents helped heal him.

As she lay on her side, whatever they'd put her on felt springy against her weight. Also, something cocooned her in awesome warmness. She never wanted to open her eyes.

One side dipped. The distinct sound of bedsprings woke her further. A soft hand, unlike the roughness of Balthazar's, touched her forehead. In surprise, Arianne's eyes shot open. Similar blue eyes, the same flaming red hair, and the heart-shaped face of her mother stared back, a small smile on her coral lipstick lips.

"Mom?" Arianne said in a scratchy voice. She moved her gaze from the face to the white power suit. Must be a weekday if her mother was dressed for work.

"Good," she answered in her soft but authoritative tone. "I thought I'd have to drive you to the hospital if your fever didn't break."

"Fever?" Arianne heard her mother's words but they didn't register properly in her head. What fever?

"Figures you'd get sick on the first day of school," the second voice chimed in.

Arianne's heart sputtered. "Carrie?" She tried sitting up. Her mother's hand pushed her back gently into bed.

"You don't want your fever to come back, do you?" She stared pointedly at Arianne—a look that dared her to disobey under pain of death.

Her body felt like lead anyway, so she sank back into her bed, sheets pulled up to her chin. She angled her head so she could see around her mother's body. Her chest ached at the sight of Carrie all ready for school in a summer dress and espadrilles, leaning against the door, her pink backpack at her feet.

"Carrie?" she called her sister's name again. She had to. Carrie standing there all pink-cheeked and shiny hair seemed so unreal.

"I think she's delirious, Mom," Carrie said.

"But the fever's gone." Her mother checked again by touching Arianne's forehead then cheeks. She frowned. "Maybe I should bring you to the hospital just in case."

Arianne didn't know what to say. One second she was skirting the Ghoul Woods to get to the Strait of Gwen—dodging nasty lightning bolts—and the next she was opening her eyes to find herself home in bed with her mom checking if she still had a fever and her sister—who her family had just buried—was standing by her door. Weird, freaky—*The Twilight Zone* couldn't come close to describing the scene playing out in front of her. Maybe if she pinched herself she'd wake up and she'd find herself back with Balthazar and Ben.

About to close her eyes to test her dream theory, Arianne caught the look that passed between her mother and Carrie. She shared that look with her mother right before they took Carrie to the hospital. If they brought her to the emergency room now, she wouldn't be able to figure out anything.

Thinking fast, she said, "I'm fine, Mom."

Her mom's frown shifted to a straight line. "You sure?"

Arianne clutched the sheets to her chin and settled deeper into her bed. "Yeah. I think I'll just sleep the rest of the day."

The look on her mother's face said she wasn't buying what Arianne was selling. So Arianne looked to Carrie for some help. Carrie rolled her eyes before her lips pulled into a wicked grin.

"I'm gonna be late, Mom," she said in that patented whiney voice that never failed to get their parents to comply with whatever she wanted.

Their mother glanced back at Carrie then sighed. She turned back to Arianne just as she inhaled to heave a sigh of relief. Arianne held her breath, blinking up at her naturally suspicious mother.

"Make sure you call me if you feel like the fever's coming back," she instructed.

Arianne nodded, afraid if she said anything more her mother would change her mind.

"There's chicken soup in the fridge—"

"Heat it up in the microwave, blah, blah, blah," Carrie interrupted. "She's a big girl, Mom. Ari can take care of herself."

With an exasperated frown, Arianne's mother planted a kiss on her forehead then rubbed away the lipstick mark she'd left behind with her thumb. It freaked Arianne out how normal everyone was acting.

Seriously, all this had to be a dream.

No matter how fantastical being in the Underverse seemed right now, being there was Arianne's reality, not Carrie being alive and her mother worrying over her being sick. She couldn't let herself hope for it or she'd fall apart. Sure, at some point, Arianne wished to go home, wished everything that had happened so far never had, but for that wish to actually come true shouldn't be possible. It couldn't be. Her chest ached thinking about it.

"Anything you want for dinner?"

Her mother's question brought Arianne back to the strange present she currently found herself in. She forced herself to focus. Not particularly hungry for anything, she said the first thing that popped into her head.

"Pizza."

"Extra cheese," Carrie piped in. She slung her backpack over her shoulder. "Come on, Mom. Don't wanna be late."

Her mother gave Arianne one last assessing glance before she pushed off the bed and flattened out the unwrinkled front of her pants. Her mother never wrinkled—at least the dream got that right.

Yup, totally a dream.

Arianne decided that unless she had more proof which told her otherwise she'd keep thinking of it as a dream.

"Leave the door open," she said when her mother's hand closed around the knob. Her mother complied then left.

Carrie waited a beat then mouthed, "You owe me."

Arianne mouthed a "thank you" back then stuck her tongue out at her sister. She missed Carrie so much it hurt.

Seeing her healthy hurt even worse because she couldn't remember the last time she'd seen Carrie that way. Her last memory of her sister involved a hospital room and a dialysis machine. Arianne took a deep breath to dissipate some of the pain lodged at the center of her chest.

Carrie stuck her tongue out too before she sprinted after their mother. Arianne waited. The front door opened then shut. The deadbolt slid into place. Then car doors opened then closed. An engine started. Arianne counted to twenty after she heard her mother's car pull away. She waited an extra ten seconds. No other sound followed. Her father must have left for work before everyone else.

Arianne finally breathed the sigh of relief she'd been holding in. She didn't know how she could deal with seeing her dad. When her mother spent most nights with Carrie at the hospital, she and her dad had become a team, battening down the hatches while they weathered the storm. If she saw her dad now, she might not want to leave.

Once enough time without anyone else making a peep inside the house passed, Arianne sat up and pushed aside her comforter and blanket. She swung her legs over the side of the bed and got up.

On her feet, she wobbled. The blood rush to her head doubled her vision. She padded her way to the bathroom then to the sink. After splashing water on her face, which didn't help end the dream — because pinching was just crazy — Arianne grabbed a towel and dried off.

Leaving the towel by the sink, Arianne stared at herself in the mirror. Her hair was still a mess, and she had dark circles under her eyes. Saying she looked like crap would be a lie because she looked worse than crap right now. She gathered her hair into a ponytail then left the bathroom to change.

After leaving her pajamas on the floor and slipping into jeans and a T-shirt, Arianne stepped out of her room. She considered making her bed but didn't see the point. Although, for a dream, everything sure seemed way too realistic. She rushed down the stairs and padded to the kitchen. Maybe the chicken soup her mother promised would help.

"Hey, you."

Arianne whirled around to come face to face with Niko. The grin on his handsome face sent a familiar shiver down her spine. Her belly quivered like jelly. Without thinking twice about it, she ran into his arms and held on. She inhaled his fresh minty scent, burying her fingers into his black as midnight hair. Then—just as he gathered her closer—a thought made her pull back. She stared into his eyes—a rainy night couldn't compare to their darkness.

"You're not some Angel's tear hallucination, are you?" she blurted out.

Niko tilted his head to the side and stared back at her for a second before he said, "How'd you know about Angel's tears?"

"So you're still the Reaper of Georgia?"

"Last time I checked." His hands on her hips tightened. "Ari, what's the matter? You're acting weird."

Blinking several times, Arianne had to remind herself about the dream. This couldn't be real. Yeah, a dream. A really awesome one, but a dream nonetheless. She forced herself to step away from Niko's arms and dropped her gaze.

"You're not real," she said, more for herself than to hurt him in any way.

"Ari, what are you saying?" Niko reached for her.

Arianne moved away from his touch even if she wanted to drown in it. "The last time I saw you, you were in a crystal coffin surrounded by milky water."

"Can you hear yourself right now?"

"Yeah." She backed up until her lower back hit the kitchen table. "All this isn't real. Carrie's dead. My mom's a mess. My dad's barely holding it together. Ben's dead too. And I have to find the Redeemer before it's too late." She glanced at her finger. The ring wasn't there. Why would it be in a dream?

"I skipped morning assembly to check on you." Niko stopped his advance, a confused frown on his sexy lips. A lock of his hair fell over his wrinkled forehead. "Should you be out of bed?"

"I'm fine." Arianne voice shook. She didn't feel fine. What was she saying? Maybe this — being in the kitchen with Niko — was reality and the rest of it was the dream. Arianne's heart twisted. She rubbed her forehead when a dizzy spell sent her leaning against the kitchen table until she practically sat on top of it.

"Ari."

"No!" She held up her hand. "I have to figure this out. All of this isn't making any sense right now. I should be with Balthazar and Ben."

"Ben's in school."

Her head whipped up. She narrowed her gaze at Niko, who'd since stuffed his hands inside the pockets of his jeans. "What? What do you mean Ben's in school?"

He shrugged. "Coach called him in for morning practice."

"Ben hates morning practice." Arianne pushed away from the table, able to think straight again. The dizzy spell still made her feel off balance, but she managed to stay on both feet.

"Tell me about it. But he's a pretty good basketball player."

Arianne's heartbeat kicked up. "Baseball."

"What?"

She stepped closer, staring into Niko's face, searching for the truth. "Ben plays baseball, not basketball."

"Arianne!"

Arianne whipped around, searching for the source of the voice. This time she couldn't mistake Balthazar calling for her. She returned her gaze to Niko. His expression went from calm to worried.

"Stay here, Ari," he pleaded.

"Arianne, open your eyes!"

Balthazar's voice grew insistent. The dizzy spell got worse.

"What do I really know about you, Niko?" she asked around the need to puke. The room felt like it spun around even if she was standing still.

"I love you."

Those three words pulled her to him. She loved him…so much. She loved the way he smiled at her. She loved the way he'd hold her hand while he drove. She even loved the way he teased her. The only reason she agreed to help Death was so she could get Niko back.

Her Niko. Not this pretend guy standing in front of her.

"Arianne!"

She looked away from him. "I have to go."

When she moved past him, Niko grabbed her arms and pulled her to his chest.

"I won't let you leave. I can't."

Arianne's heart jumped into her throat. She spoke around it. "If I want to save you, I have to go."

"No!" Niko's grip tightened around her arms.

Arianne winced. "You're hurting me."

Even after she said it, Niko wouldn't let up. In fact, his grip bruised.

"You can't leave. Stay here. Stay with me."

"Arianne, open your eyes!"

Chapter 35

AFDN

On the white sands of the Strait of Gwen, fresh out of options for how to revive Arianne — because calling her name obviously worked like a charm — Balthazar shook her. She'd healed enough the second he and Ben made it out of Solara's lightning strike range. She likely wasn't in any pain anymore. The powder had done its job, as it had done on him. Her skin stopped looking like burnt meat — replaced by flaking, new pink skin. Other than having to cut her hair, her face remained relatively untouched. He focused on her closed eyelids instead of her tattered clothing. He'd have to replace what she wore. She'd dropped her pack when they made a run for it. Ben had been busy stomping out the flames at the end of Balthazar's coat when Balthazar laid Arianne on the sand.

Now Ben stood by his shoulder, looking down at Arianne. They couldn't board Charlie's raft to Haven if she didn't regain consciousness. Charlie wouldn't allow her passage if she didn't pay the fee herself. To do that, she had to wake up.

He shook her again, harder this time. If she didn't open her eyes soon, he'd resort to head-butting her.

In the distance, lightning bolts continued to explode. Even out of her reach, Solara still attempted to kill Balthazar and crew. He looked back over his shoulder at the Ghoul Woods. A plume of smoke rose up from the burning Blood Trees. The air reeked of ammonia from the boiling sap. Solara wreaked havoc on her new territory—all because Balthazar and Arianne escaped her clutches.

"Come on," he said, returning his gaze to the still unconscious Arianne. "Open your goddamn eyes!"

"How're you sure she's in there?" Ben asked.

"Oh, she's in there." Balthazar tapped her cheeks. "See how her eyes are rolling around?" He pointed at her fluttering eyelids. "Her dream doesn't want to let her go."

"How is that a bad thing?"

Balthazar held the profanity inside. He'd had just about enough of the boy. He bargained with Granmare Baba for the sake of avoiding having to answer these inane questions.

"If she stays inside the dream then we might as well give up. She won't ever wake up." What Balthazar left out was if she didn't wake up, she would return to her body and she'd be in a coma for life. If she was no longer attached to her body, her soul would fade into nothingness.

He stared at the cut red thread. Eventually, it would erode, and when it completely disappeared without Arianne's soul processed, she'd turn into a Wraith. Balthazar had searched for Ben's life string when he'd freed him from the cage. He had about an inch left then. Now less than that remained.

The disasters kept on coming.

Why he ever agreed to all this escaped him. Was D's seat worth all this aggravation? To date, he'd almost died more than three times already. Sure, being in the Nethers was far worse, but he should be sitting as the new controller of the Crossroads instead of helping a silly girl save her equally silly Reaper boyfriend. Well, technically, his task was to help D remove Brianne's Bitterness from his chest so he could challenge him for the seat, but who could keep track at this point?

Frustration bubbling over, Balthazar lifted Arianne up and brought his forehead down against hers. She yelped, blinking her eyes rapidly. Then she groaned, reaching up and massaging the redness Balthazar's forehead had left behind. With no regrets, he eased her back onto the sand.

"About goddamn time you opened your eyes," he grumbled, sitting back then stretching his legs on either side of her.

Arianne kept rubbing her forehead. "Why do I feel like I hit a brick wall?"

"Maybe because Balthazar head-butted you," Ben said, a silly grin on his goofy face.

Balthazar snorted, casting his gaze over to the red water. It lapped at the white sands, turning the shoreline pink. The sea breeze wafted at them the water's coppery, tangy scent. A blessed reprieve from the burning sap. Along the coast, hexagonal stones were stacked like a toddler haphazardly left his blocks on the floor.

"Thanks."

Arianne's voice drew him back to her. He stared into her ever blue eyes, clear as the human sky. What could he say? The customary "you're welcome" stuck to the walls of his throat. Like he'd ever acknowledge her gratitude. Ben saved him from having to.

"What's with the largest *Q*bert* set?" Ben hiked his thumb at the ballast columns.

Arianne followed his gaze and said, "They were formed by Gwen. Nobody knows what she really was. Some say she was a god, others say she was more powerful than that."

Balthazar almost breathed a sigh of relief at not having to explain to the boy what the almost forty-foot high columns were. He'd never met Gwen, but from what he'd heard, she'd gone crazy. The varying sizes of the columns indicated her lack of control except for what they called the Giant's Organ. Sixty ballasts more than thirty feet high with three shorter tiers created the whole thing. It gave the effect of an elaborate pipe organ.

"They say she fell in love with a Heavenly Host who betrayed her. That's why the water is red. She cut off the Host's wings and let them bleed over the ocean. And those columns are the Host's bones," Arianne continued. Her voice took on a lonely turn that called for Balthazar to soothe her.

His hand reached for her when Ben said, "It's freaky how you know all this stuff."

She rolled her eyes toward the gray sky. "You don't even know the half of it." Then she turned those eyes on Balthazar. He immediately dropped his hand. "Do I even want to know how you saved me this time?"

Her question brought out his more normal side, the one not hanging on her every word and thought her hair looked pretty. "You're not gonna like it."

Ben's face crumpled. "He had his tongue down your throat."

Arianne blushed immediately before she slapped him in the chest. "You kissed me!"

He grinned, showing fang. He couldn't help himself. The fear he'd felt when she'd died on him almost broke his sanity. She walked in his realm now, no longer tethered to the human world. He felt partially responsible. Whether to tell her or keep it to himself until he returned her to the Crossroads presented another question he'd deal with later. For now, they had a boat to catch.

"It was either kiss you or let you die." He stood up and dusted white sand off his backside. "Easy choice to make."

"Don't ever do it again."

Despite the admonishment in her tone, she reached up. He wrapped his hand around hers and gave her a tug until her body stood close enough to his.

"By that blush on your cheeks, I'd say you enjoyed yourself." Balthazar knew he fanned the flames in the worst possible way, but he couldn't help himself, not when he stood this close to Arianne, her lips inches from his.

"Are you two actually flirting?" Ben didn't hide his disgust. Balthazar had the urge to slap the boy upside the head. The urge became actuality when his hand did what his brain wanted. Ben's head snapped to the side. "Ow!"

"Balthazar!" Arianne said indignantly. She pushed away from him and stepped closer to Ben. She examined the place where Balthazar's hand had connected with Ben's head. Balthazar had to stop himself from pulling her away from the almost-Wraith. Technically, Ben didn't represent any danger yet. But Balthazar still had to keep an eye on him.

When had he become a baby-sitter?

Instead, Balthazar concentrated on stomping down the ugly jealousy rising up from the darkness within him. To be jealous of a twerp like Ben when he could have anyone he chose meant Balthazar really had come down with something. Arianne infuriated him half the time. The other half, on the other hand…

Not going there.

If Arianne wanted to mother-hen her best friend, then let her. It didn't mean he had to watch, so he scanned the shoreline.

Not all the ballasts littering the coast were large. Some of them were short enough to walk on. The shortest of the columns formed a makeshift dock, and at the end of the line bobbed a raft made from Blood Tree wood. On the raft stood the ferryman, Charlion, in his hooded white robe. Like D, Charlion preferred to hide his true face beneath the cowl of his robe. No one knew why. The sleeves of his robes were so voluminous that they covered his hands clutching the oar he used to steer the raft.

Balthazar turned his back on Charlion so the ferryman wouldn't see him fish out two coins from his coat and hold one in each hand. On one side of the coins was the morning star, the symbol of Lucifer back when he was still God's favorite. You met him at the Heavenly Gates, not Peter. Before he fell from grace, of course. Someone else had the job now—a new morning star. The other side of the coin remained smooth, symbolizing the Nethers. A cold shudder went through Balthazar at the memory of spending more than a thousand years in that godforsaken hellhole.

"You two done fawning over each other?" he grumbled.

Arianne stepped away from Ben to frown at him. "What's the matter with you?"

"You keep forgetting why we're here," Balthazar barked back.

"Sometimes I think you like being mean and pushy."

He laughed. "I am mean. Now, shut up and listen."

"Don't talk to her like that." Ben took a step toward him, his chest all puffed up. Thank God Arianne had the sense to stop him by placing a hand at the center of his chest.

"What? You think you can take me? I'll *eat* you." Balthazar showed fang. "I'm running out of patience for your kind of bullshit. Just shut your trap and obey."

For the second time that day the thought of baby-sitting twisted Balthazar's insides. When had he sunk so low? *Oh, that's right, when I agreed to help.* Even his thoughts sounded bitter.

"Open your mouths," he said through his annoyance.

"I thought you just said to close them?" Arianne asked. She was being sarcastic for the sake of it. He knew she knew through his thoughts why he asked them to open their mouths.

"Do it or I shove this in your mouth."

Arianne complied, sticking out her tongue and eyeing him like the worst creature in the world. Some days Balthazar felt that way. Her reminding him stung for some reason.

Not letting her get to him any more than she already did, he placed the coin on her tongue, the morning star symbol up.

"Hold the coin in your mouth," he said. "Don't swallow it." He raised the other coin to Ben's lips. The boy jerked back.

"I'm not putting that thing in my mouth."

"It's not dirty," Arianne said around the coin. From the sound of her voice, she struggled not to swallow it and drool at the same time.

"It's payment for a ride on Charlie's raft," Balthazar said through gritted teeth. Forget Arianne getting on his last nerve. He had the urge to chuck the boy into the Strait of Gwen and let the waters feast on his pathetic soul. Unfortunately, if he wanted an audience with the Redeemer he couldn't act on the impulse. He pointed toward the raft, and Ben wisely looked in that direction. He continued. "You need to place the coin on your tongue. As soon as you get onto the raft, the coin will disappear."

Ben looked back at Balthazar. Despite the skepticism in his eyes, he accepted the coin and placed it in his mouth. He winced, probably from the metallic taste. Balthazar took great pleasure in knowing those coins had stayed in his coat for a long time. Who knew what stuck to them. Not that they'd get sick from germs. Souls didn't get sick—not in the human sense.

"What about you?" Arianne asked, pushing the coin around in her mouth so she could speak clearly.

Balthazar shrugged. "Don't need one."

Chapter 36

AOAS

The eerie red water rocked the raft gently. Charlion didn't say a word when Balthazar brought Arianne and Ben onboard. He'd been right, the coin disappeared the second Arianne stepped onto the rickety raft. She sent a silent prayer to whoever was listening that the sodden ropes would hold the thing together until they reached Haven's Doorstep on the opposite shore.

Balthazar had been standing with the ferryman he kept calling Charlie at the rear of the raft ever since they cast off. Charlion didn't seem to mind the nickname…at least he didn't say anything about it. According to what Arianne knew, the ferryman didn't speak at all.

Arianne gave the pair—one in black, the other in white—another quick glance over her shoulder from her spot at the front of the raft. She hugged her folded legs to her chest and rested her chin on her knees. A chill she'd begun to feel since she opened her eyes at the beach wrapped around her tighter now. No matter how small a ball she made of her body, she couldn't seem to shake the cold. She turned her head until her cheek replaced her chin on her knees and watched the ring pulse. After the light went out, she counted.

Ten seconds.

It took ten scary seconds for the light to come back on. They were cutting it close. Death must be so weak by now, and maybe in so much pain. The knife on her thigh warmed as if in response to the cold she felt. Weird that she took comfort from a piece of metal used to kill things. She shrugged, returning her chin back to her knees.

"Cold?" Ben settled beside her and imitated her pose, pulling his knees to his chest. "I'd give you a jacket if I had one. Balthazar should lend you his."

Arianne reached out and squeezed Ben's arm. "He's not the lend-a-girl-a-jacket type."

"Yeah, he seems to keep everything in there. Did you see him pull out that sword? Where the hell did that thing come from?"

At the mention of the auction, Arianne shivered again. Ben misunderstood her reaction and slung his arm over her shoulders. Sadly, her best friend felt even colder, but she didn't have the heart to tell him. She prayed they'd make it to Haven before he became a Wraith. Balthazar had warned her against staying too close to Ben when they walked from the beach to the raft. He'd pulled her aside, letting Ben walk ahead of them, and quickly whispered the words into her ear. Forget the hot blush his breath tickling her earlobe caused, she didn't believe Balthazar. Ben wouldn't hurt her, Wraith or not. Even now, she felt Balthazar's eyes boring a hole at the center of her back. Something in his mind went beyond normal protective instincts. Arianne wanted to dissect Balthazar's thoughts more, but Ben didn't give her enough time.

"You gave me a heart attack back there."

She gave him a sidelong glance. The icky blood-smelling breeze ruffled his sandy hair, paler now in his spirit form. She reached up to her own hair. Because of the burn caused by the lightning bolt, Balthazar had needed to cut off her braid. Now chin-length, her hair stuck out in wild wisps. Balthazar assured her it would grow back after the rest of her body finished healing.

She itched in weird places because of the healing he'd told her about. The skin on her hands didn't look so bad anymore. As for her clothes, Balthazar's magic coat provided the shirt, jeans, and jacket she now wore. Since she'd worn less during her stint as Balthazar's slave at the mansion, she didn't freak out when she realized most of her clothing burned away. He'd let her change before they boarded Charlion's raft. The leather pants, shirts, and cool jacket Tomas had provided, including her pack, were all gone.

"Was it that bad?" she asked after she finished mourning the loss of the jacket. Maybe she'd find one when she got back to her body. She made a mental note of it.

"Seeing you almost die again?" Ben shook his head. Then he puffed out a breath. "Not cool, Ari. When that lightning bolt came down and hit your head, I thought my heart stopped. Well, technically I don't have a heart to beat anymore."

She nudged him with her shoulder. "Not funny."

"Yeah? Try watching your best friend be swallowed by burning white light. See if that's funny."

"I promise not to stand under any lightning bolts ever again." She crossed her heart. "I don't even remember it happening. Everything went black as soon as I felt the bolt hit. It was like I blew a fuse or something."

"And then when Balthazar stuck his tongue down your throat..." Ben continued as if he wasn't listening to her. He exaggerated a shudder.

Arianne hid her blush by tucking her face between her knees. God, it sucked that she blushed every time Balthazar kissing her came up. At the mansion, he'd begged her to ask him to kiss her again. She hated that the rumble in his voice alone tempted her to say the words. She'd thought she had herself under control when she managed to deny him. And now she'd woken up from a dream of her perfect life to find out Balthazar had kissed her to save her. How was she supposed to feel about that? Niko had begged her to stay. A part of her had wanted to. If she'd stayed, she'd be living the perfect life right now. Her sister would be healthy. Her family would be whole. She'd have the best boyfriend in the world. And her best friend would play basketball.

"What's with the smile?"

Ben's voice brought her back to the gently rocking raft. Blush finally subsiding, Arianne returned to her original position — chin on knees.

She sighed and said, "You know when I was — "

"Unconscious," Ben finished for her.

"I had this dream where you played basketball instead of baseball."

"Basketball?" Ben scrunched up his face like he'd sucked on a particularly sour lemon.

Arianne laughed. "Yeah. That's how I knew I was really dreaming."

Ben sobered. "Balthazar said you wouldn't wake up if you decided to stay in the dream."

"I wanted to. It was the perfect dream."

"How can you say that when I'm playing basketball in it?"

Her heart twisted at the memory. "Carrie was healthy. Like really healthy. Pink cheeks and shiny hair healthy."

Ben whistled then paused a second before he said, "You're right. That is the perfect dream."

Arianne smiled a tight smile. She remembered catching Ben with Carrie. They'd kept their relationship under wraps for a whole year. They didn't even tell Arianne about it until she'd caught them kissing in Carrie's hospital room. She'd been so pissed at them for not telling her. But Arianne couldn't stay mad at Carrie. Deep down she understood why her sister wanted to keep her relationship with Ben a secret. She'd wanted something for herself since everyone else saw the rest of her. Being sick did that.

The look of longing on Ben's face as he stared out at the seemingly endless stretch of red water hurt Arianne's heart. She reached out and took his cold hand in hers. She inched closer until she sat shoulder to shoulder with him.

"I miss her too," she whispered, staring at the sea with him.

Ben nodded before he buried his face in his knees.

"I miss you too," Arianne added. She squeezed his hand harder.

Balthazar had told them they couldn't touch the water or it would suck their souls dry. Despite sitting close to the edge, Arianne's and Ben's spot was still safely out of the water's reach. She sighed and steeled herself. Never really a good time to talk about what she wanted to talk about. Since they had no escape from the raft, might as well.

Seeing no better way, Arianne just went with her gut. "Why did you volunteer when Death asked for a soul to replace mine?"

Without facing her, his voice muffled by his legs and chest, Ben said, "I had nothing else to live for. You still did."

Somehow she had known this would be the answer, but it didn't mean she was any more prepared for it than if she hadn't known. Her stomach fell at Ben's confession. She willed herself not to breakdown. Tears wouldn't help. They might even cause Ben to feel guilty. So — like Balthazar kept telling her — she sucked it up and stared quietly out into the open waters instead.

Ben broke the silence that followed. "What happened with that anyway?"

Arianne thought back to the room Tomas had led her and Ben to. Niko had been tied to a board by his wrists and ankles. If she didn't know any better, she'd think Death had tortured him. Arianne pushed away her rising anger and reminded herself why she had agreed to helping Death in the first place.

"After Death took you…" She paused, swallowing the hard lump in her throat. She had to make it through without crying. She had to. "I made a bargain with him to give Niko his humanity. He wanted my memories of Niko and my eyesight."

"Oh, Ari."

She pretended not to hear the disappointment in her best friend's voice. "Before you judge me, let me remind you of the sacrifice you made for me."

"Mine was different."

"Why don't you look me in the eye and say that?"

Ben shook his head, still hiding his face from her. His grip on her hand slackened. The sea breeze picked up, forcing Arianne to turn her head away from the sudden gust. When Ben completely let go of Arianne's hand, she twisted around to ask why. Her heart fell. Ben's skin had turned completely gray in a matter of seconds. His breathing was ragged, like he fought for every breath.

"Ben?" Arianne whispered his name. She got on her knees and inched closer to him. He groaned like a hurt animal—a keening painful to the ears. "Ben, can you hear me?" Despite her gut telling her to run, she reached out and placed her hand on his hunched back. Ben trembled badly. She moved her hand from his back to his nape and flinched away at the freezing feel of his skin. The groans grew gravelly.

Ben grabbed at her with a bony hand, his fingers more like claws. She pushed back before he caught her, but she had nowhere else to go. She'd reached the edge of the raft, only inches away from plunging into the water. She breathed as hard as Ben now.

Before Ben could lift his head, Balthazar was suddenly behind him. He lifted his fist and hit Ben at the back of the head, knocking him to his side. Arianne yelped then covered her mouth to keep herself from all-out screaming. She curled into the smallest ball she could become without falling into the water. Her eyes widened when she got a look at Ben's face. Not a face she knew anymore. Sunken eye sockets, gaunt cheeks, black lips, and serrated teeth.

Balthazar didn't look at her. She shook badly. Ben had turned into a Wraith. They were too late.

"No," Balthazar said, still not looking at her. "He's close, but no dice. If he'd taken your soul then the transformation would have been complete."

"How could he take my soul if I'm still attached to my body?" she asked through her shaking hands. Wraiths couldn't consume attached souls.

"Charlie, we need to hurry," Balthazar said over his shoulder before he finally looked at her. The blankness of his expression scared Arianne more than if he'd had emotion there.

"Balthazar?" She swallowed, never dropping her hands from her lips. "Ben can't eat my soul."

He shook his head. "The lightning strike."

Arianne's brain suddenly refused to work. "I don't understand?"

"You're not attached to your body anymore."

Chapter 37

LABATYD

The damn dam broke.

Big, fat tears leaked out of Arianne's eyes. Snot everywhere. Balthazar cursed the vilest curse he could think of under his breath. Arianne sitting there bawling was the most unflattering look a girl could have, and yet like a hundred times before, her crying brought out a primal need in him to comfort her. He hated chicks so much—working with them especially. The waterworks. He vowed never to partner with a female again.

Balthazar ran his fingers through his hair in self-disgust. Even if he wanted to comfort her—a totally big *if*—he couldn't move from where he stood over Ben's body. His transition into becoming a Wraith made him doubly dangerous around Arianne. As much as possible—and Balthazar had no idea where this irrational urge came from—he didn't want to cause her extra pain by having to kill her best friend.

Wraith-to-be or not, Ben still mattered. At the back of his mind he did all this for more selfish reasons beyond taking the Crossroads throne—maybe something connected to Arianne, helping her. But he chose to think Ben mattered because he was their ticket to see the Redeemer. Yeah, thinking that way made him more comfortable. The blubbering girl had nothing to do with anything. Just a means to an end.

He glanced down at Ben. The boy breathed evenly, still out cold. How long that would last, Balthazar had no idea. They had to get him to Haven and to the Redeemer before he followed through on

Arianne as a snack option. Then he stared straight ahead. The red water remained placid. Barring a storm, which never happened when Charlion had passengers on his raft, they'd get there soon.

"Put your back into it, Charlie," Balthazar said over his shoulder. He dropped his gaze to Ben again. The urge to kick the bastard off the edge almost overwhelmed him. "We've got a Wraith in the making and a soul ready for the eating."

The raft jerked forward like a motor had been switched on. Balthazar suppressed a grin. Charlie liked a leisurely ride to Haven, so it must be killing him to have to row faster. Charlie was made of residual energy, which meant having a Wraith on his raft pissed him off. Balthazar refused to glance back at Arianne. She continued to whimper on her side. So long as she stayed clear of the edge he wouldn't have to move away from Ben. And right now—weird as it sounded—he felt safer with the Wraith-to-be than the sobbing girl.

In a quivering voice, Arianne said, "I'm dead?"

Balthazar swallowed. Ah, she sounded so pathetic, and yet his arms ached to pull her to him. He made tight fists instead and nodded without glancing her way. He kept his gaze on the water. If he looked ahead long enough, he wouldn't have to watch her suffer the shock of realizing what being dead meant.

To humans the experience was far worse than for anyone else. They tended to be attached to things and to people. By now Arianne must be thinking of her family, friends, her cell phone. Whatever teenage girls like her thought about. He made it a point to stay away from inside her head. The chaos outside only reflected the turmoil inside. He'd rather choke than get a front row seat to the Arianne's dead freak show playing in there.

The raft rocked, forcing him to glance at Arianne. She'd gotten up without care that she stood perilously close to the edge. Still sniffling, she turned in a circle like a dog chasing its tail. She searched for her thread. The length of it reached her knees, but he doubted she saw it through the flood of tears.

"Arianne, stop," he said, exasperated. "You'll be fine."

She did stop. Her head whipped up, a champion glare on her puffy face. "I'll be fine?" she asked dangerously. "I'll be fine! What the hell's that supposed to mean?"

Balthazar opened his mouth to speak when Arianne launched herself at him. He leaned back and caught her. Her fists pounded against his chest. He barely felt the blows, but if her being angry stopped all the crying, then he'd rather have her hit him as many times as she wanted.

"I'm dead! I'm dead!" she repeated over and over again. "Why didn't you tell me sooner?"

"I just told you."

Wrong answer because Arianne went from enraged to manic. Her eyes widened the second the thought hit her.

"Tomas said he could fix it." She stepped away from Balthazar's arms and stared at her hands. "He said if my thread broke, I had to get back to the Crossroads. He'd fix it. He told me before we left." She lifted her crazy gaze at Balthazar. "You have to take me back."

He knew he'd be digging his grave deeper, but he had to say it. "I can't."

"What do you mean you can't?" Balthazar didn't think Arianne's eyes could get any wider than they did that second. Her chin quivered, and he cursed.

Instead of tears, Arianne growled. She launched herself at Balthazar again, kicking and screaming. He barely managed to keep his balance on the rocking raft. Red water sloshed dangerously around them.

"Take me back!" she shouted at the top of her lungs. "You have to take me back. Tomas has to fix this."

"I can't!" he screamed, matching her volume with his own. "We have to get Ben to Haven." He shook her, and Arianne stopped struggling. She glared up at him. "Ben's turning into a Wraith. If we don't get him to the Redeemer, he'll spend the rest of his existence consuming souls. Is that what you want?"

"I'll turn into a Wraith too if you don't bring me back," she answered with so much venom.

"Really? That's what you're going with?" Balthazar hated taking the high road, but if it meant ending this madness then he sucked up his pride. "Your best friend is turning into one of the most dangerous creatures in the Underverse. Are you really willing to leave him behind?"

Arianne's pupils practically consumed all of the blue in her eyes. She'd gone over the edge.

"Take me back to the Crossroads," she said slowly. "I'm not turning into a Wraith, Balthazar."

He moved one of his hands to her wrist and lifted her hand up so she could stare into the weakly pulsing ring. "You see this?" He shook her again. "Look at it," he threatened.

Arianne stared at the gem on the ring.

"If I bring you back, the knife will suck out the last of Death's powers and all this would be for nothing." He growled until she returned her gaze at him. "So you don't care about your best friend. I'm fine with that. I have a bigger stake in all this than you do. I'm taking the Redeemer back to the Crossroads. Whether you're coming with me or not is entirely up to you." Balthazar dropped her wrist and returned his hand to her arm like the other one that continued to hold her in place. If she stumbled and fell into the water now, they'd be in bigger shit.

"You selfish jackass!" She kicked out, nailing him on the thigh. Balthazar swiveled so her next kick wouldn't hit more precious body parts.

"I *am* selfish!" he said through the pain climbing up his thigh, "Bad guy here, remember? D's challenge is all that matters to me. So excuse me if I don't feel like taking you back to the Crossroads when I'm so close to getting the Redeemer." And just because, he added, "What happened to I'm doing this for love? Huh?"

"I hate you!" she screamed. "I hate you so much!"

"You can say it all you want. Doesn't change anything."

"Take me back! Take me back! Take me back!"

It became a mantra followed by punches and kicks, with some clawing too. Balthazar widened his stance to accommodate her thrashing body better. In his periphery he could make out the shore, and beyond, the mighty rock columns of Haven. The greenery growing on the columns stood out vividly even at a distance. White-winged angels and Heavenly Hosts flew from peak to peak. Almost there. Zakariel would meet them at the shoreline and take them directly to the Redeemer. Balthazar licked his bottom lip. So close.

Arianne's crazy-fueled struggling pushed Balthazar to the limits of his patience. He raised his hand and slapped her across the face, sending her stumbling until she fell flat on the raft's floor. She rolled onto her side, clutching her already reddening cheek. Balthazar bit the inside of his own cheek, thankful he hadn't hit her hard enough to draw blood. She had to shut up, and hitting her was the only way he could think of that didn't involve kissing her into silence. Anyway, the insanity had stopped. Now she just glared up at him, her crystal blue eyes filled with hate.

"Yeah," he spat out. "I'm not afraid of hitting a girl to get her to shut up."

"Asshole."

It was the first real curse word he'd ever heard come from Arianne's lips, and somehow Balthazar didn't like the sound of it. He pushed aside his growing scruples and sneered at her.

"Been called worse. Hate me. You do that. Life's a bitch and then you die." He grinned. "The sooner you get that, little girl, the easier it will be for all of us."

Arianne dropped her gaze and curled her body into the smallest ball she could manage. Balthazar's heart spasmed. What he didn't add? He'd rather she hated him than she hate herself when she realized she would leave her best friend to become a Wraith just so she could save herself. In all that crazy, Arianne was still Arianne. Balthazar knew that. He'd been a bad guy most of his life. But Arianne? In the time they'd spent together, he knew she didn't have a mean bone in her body. In her right mind, she wouldn't freak out about dying. The torn thread could be fixed if they made it back to the Crossroads. In fact, she had little to worry about. But she was only human.

Balthazar snorted. The girl who had the stones to bargain with Death still lived in her. Right now, she was locked up because of all the pain from realizing she'd died. Only Arianne could get herself out of the mire she'd found herself in. Keep Ben away from her. That was what he had to do. Comforting her wasn't part of the job description.

After he was sure Ben stayed unconscious and Arianne moved from crying to staring out into space in an almost catatonic state, Balthazar took his watchful gaze away from them. The shoreline grew bigger and bigger the closer they got. Balthazar calculated what he had to do to get the Redeemer out of Haven. The Heavenly Host now landing at the shoreline wouldn't make it easy. Zakariel was sworn to protect Haven, and the Redeemer by extension.

Chapter 38

HAR

In the days after Carrie's burial, Arianne had lived in a constant daze. She breathed in and out, yes, but smelled nothing. She opened and closed her eyes, but really saw nothing. She chewed her food, but didn't taste a single bite. It was a feeling of loss so deep, she couldn't feel anything at all. That same numbness enveloped her now as she lay curled up on the damp raft floor. The tears had stopped. Thank God. Tears did nothing for her. The gentle rocking of the raft didn't comfort her like it had done before everything exploded in her face.

Speaking of face…she inched her hand up and touched the place Balthazar had slapped. Her skin still remembered the feel of his rough hand, leaving heat and sting behind. The throbbing had subsided some, but not before it had done its job of bringing Arianne back from the pit of insanity she'd fallen into the second Balthazar told her the thread connecting her to her body had been cut.

Arianne Wilson was dead.

Well, technically her body had died. Tomas said he could fix it. But it didn't change anything. She'd still died.

She sniffed the last of the snot left over from her latest crying jag. It got embarrassing. How many times had Balthazar witnessed her break down? She'd lost count. It didn't matter anymore. Even hope left her cold now. She'd taken too many emotional hits. Each blow left her exhausted. Her battleship had been sunk.

Normally, she didn't advocate men hitting women. She should have condemned Balthazar for laying a hand on her. But she couldn't deny that what he did gave her clarity. Head clear of all the crazy, guilt ate at her. She'd been willing to sacrifice Ben to save herself. She'd cry again if she had any tears left.

All this time she had convinced herself she needed to find the Redeemer so she could help Niko, but in truth she went on this trip so she wouldn't lose him. She'd accused Balthazar of being selfish when at the end of the day she'd been the most selfish one of all. Balthazar said she didn't know Niko well enough to truly love him.

Maybe he'd been right all along.

Maybe she did this not because of love. Maybe she did this because she wanted the boy who she thought she loved back so she wouldn't be alone anymore. She'd lost so many people in her life already. She wasn't willing to lose Niko on top of everything else.

But what if she did lose him?

Would it be that bad?

The question scared Arianne. To even consider losing Niko sent a nasty shiver down her back. Had she been doing all of this for the right reasons? She twisted so her forehead touched the wood of the raft. Then she thumped her head several times, causing a dull ache to form at the center of her forehead. It chased away some of the numbness, clearing her mind even more.

Then something else Tomas had said pushed away the rest of Arianne's self-imposed pity party. Her eyes widened, and she sat up slowly. The shore of Haven inched closer and closer with each rowing motion of the ferryman. On the crystalline sand stood Zakariel. He'd be escorting them to the Redeemer.

Balthazar stood by Ben's body the whole time. He'd been keeping her safe all along. Hate him or not, Balthazar had always done right by her — no matter how twisted some of his methods might have been. He had to know what she'd just realized. He had to know they wouldn't be able to bring the Redeemer with them back to the Crossroads.

Because she'd been careless.

Arianne's heart lodged itself in her throat. She fisted her hands until her knuckles lost all the blood circulating in them. She forced herself to speak around the beating of her heart. Nothing came out at first.

She cleared her dry throat and tried again.

"Balthazar." His name came out as a whisper.

"What?" He said it like a curse. She winced. After the insanity she'd showed him, she deserved his attitude. If he was pissed now, she could just imagine how he'd feel after she told him what she had to say.

No way around it but forward, so Arianne said, "Tomas said I'll be able to recognize the Redeemer because I'm still attached to my body."

There, she'd said it. She'd put the truth out there.

Balthazar remained quiet. Quiet enough for Arianne to look up at him. Instead of the rage she expected, his expression stayed blank. Arianne bowed her head, hopelessness coating the numbness that enveloped her. She'd failed Balthazar. She'd failed herself. She'd failed them all. The one thing they counted on her to do and she couldn't anymore because of a freakin' piece of string.

Just as she felt sick to her stomach, Balthazar said, "I know."

"What?" She sucked in a breath of coppery air. The red water's smell made her nauseous. "What do you mean you know?"

He snorted. "I was there when Tomas said you'd be the one to recognize the Redeemer. I'd been keeping an eye on your thread this whole time, not only because I hate Wraiths."

"Then what are we gonna do?"

Balthazar glanced down his nose at her. "I have a plan. Just play along. Zakariel will be too busy with Ben. Since you're still bound to me, he may not notice. If you follow my lead we might make it through this."

Arianne's molars squeaked against each other when she gnashed her teeth together. "How's that supposed to work?"

"Shut up and follow my lead. How hard can that be?"

The raft glided into shore. It came to a stop on the sand, jerking forward. The motion cut off the rest of Arianne's argument.

Zakariel came forward, his brow wrinkled. "The boy?"

Balthazar picked up Ben and handed him over to the Heavenly Host. "We had a situation. He's not fully a Wraith yet since he doesn't have access to an unattached human soul."

Arianne gulped. *Act natural. Act freakin' natural.*

The Heavenly Host looked Ben over when he balanced him in his arms. "The Redeemer can still save him."

A sigh of relief exploded from Arianne's lungs. Balthazar stood over her before Zakariel could notice anything off. He reached down and picked her up off the raft floor like a doll. Then he stood her up and patted her body down like he was dusting her off. Too woozy with relief, Arianne didn't argue. She stood in stunned silence and let Balthazar do what he wanted.

He kneeled before her and tied a shoelace that had come lose. She didn't quite understand why. The boots she'd worn had burned away, so he'd given her sneakers instead. Now he tied her shoelace for her. Was he deliberately being sweet?

He looked up at her and grinned the second the question entered her head. Arianne tsked. The link between them. When would it disappear?

"Soon," Balthazar whispered. He pointed at his wrist. The tattoo looked faded.

Arianne didn't know if she should be relieved or disappointed.

Her conflicting feelings continued as Balthazar held her by the waist and lifted her off the raft onto the beach. Arianne stared at the sand that sparkled like little diamonds while Balthazar thanked Charlion for getting them safely to Haven. She looked over her shoulder just as the ferryman pushed off the beach. Creepy how she saw nothing of him, just that cowl casting a shadow where his face should be. By the time a shiver had gone through her body, Charlion had become a speck in the vast horizon. She briefly wondered what favor he'd owed Balthazar, and whether it was settled by bringing them to Haven.

"Quit standing there," Balthazar called.

Arianne whipped around to see him and Zakariel already several yards away. She waved because she didn't know what else to do. Idiot. The nerves tied her muscles in knots. When she could move from the spot Balthazar had left her in, she jogged toward them.

Once she'd caught up, Balthazar eased her behind him while he walked side by side with Zakariel.

After they cleared the beach the sand bled into a dirt floor, Arianne forgot her worries for a second. Information flooded her brain about Haven. Her connection with Balthazar may be fading, but the info download still worked. Arianne tuned out Balthazar and Zakariel's conversation to take in her amazing surroundings.

Towering limestone pillars made up most of Haven. More than thirty thousand of them. No one really kept count of the exact numbers. The columns rose up several stories — some as high as forty feet into the air. A light fog covered the tops, obscuring the actual height of some of the higher pillars. Leafy trees peppered the columns. The nests were the most amazing part. Arianne had to crane her neck while she walked just to catch a glimpse of them. Angels who stayed in Haven before they made their way to the human world or Heaven lived in nests. Mothers took care of their young in nests too.

The air in Arianne's lungs whooshed out when a group of angelings — baby angels — ran around her. They turned her in a circle because of their game of tag. Zakariel barked something at them and they ran away, giggling the entire time. Arianne glanced up at the Heavenly Host and caught a small grin and a twinkle in his eye.

"The little ones are always a menace," he said with great humor. "Do you remember when you used to run around like that, Balthazar?"

Arianne's jaw dropped at the new piece of information about her traveling companion and bodyguard. "You used to live here?"

Balthazar snorted in response to her question.

The Heavenly Host was more than happy to fill her in. "Balthazar was born here."

It was like Zakariel had dropped a bomb. Balthazar? Born in Haven? Shut the front door!

"My mother was a Heavenly Host," he grumbled.

Arianne staggered. Too much shocking information all at once. Her brain couldn't take it. Balthazar's mother was like Zakariel?

Shocked, she asked, "Where are your wings?"

Balthazar's shoulders stiffened. "I think you should know, Ben's going to be fine."

A distraction. Really? And dang if it didn't work.

"Is it true?" she asked Zakariel.

The Heavenly Host nodded once without looking back at her. "You got him here just in time. He'll be processed and sent on his way."

Touching her chest, both happiness and sadness swirled inside at the news. Happy because Ben wouldn't be condemned to a life of consuming souls. Sad because this might be the last time she'd see him. Her eyes went to his unconscious body in Zakariel's arms.

"Will I get to say goodbye to him?"

Zakariel smiled at her then. "I'm sure that could be arranged."

The relief flooding Arianne's insides didn't last long when Zakariel added, "That is, after you pick out the Redeemer."

She stumbled on an invisible rock. "How does that work exactly?"

Patiently, Zakariel answered her question. "It's very simple really. We will present you with several candidates and you will pick out the Redeemer. If you succeed, you get your audience."

Yeah, simple.

Arianne swallowed. Her hands began to shake. She stuffed them into the pockets of her jeans. Balthazar stared at her for a second over his shoulder. Zakariel led them into an amphitheater at a clearing. He handed Ben off to another Heavenly Host and continued forward. He descended the steps toward the sunken center of the amphitheater.

Just as Arianne stepped forward to follow, Balthazar whirled around and caught her shoulders in his hands, stopping her momentum. He looked into her eyes and said, "You can do this."

Arianne had lost count of the shockers today. "Are you actually giving me a pep talk?"

"Just make your choice and I'll take care of the rest."

"I don't like the sound of that."

Balthazar didn't answer the hidden question in her statement. Instead, he turned around and made his way to where Zakariel stood at the center of the amphitheater. Arianne followed solemnly. How hard could it be to pick out the purest soul of them all?

At the bottom of the steps, Arianne stopped. Zakariel nodded at her then waved his hand at the angel standing off to one side. Arianne looked from Zakariel to Balthazar. Her heart did mini somersaults. Her palms inside her pockets began to sweat. When she looked back at Zakariel, a line of women stood behind him. The candidates he'd mentioned.

Zakariel stepped aside and gestured for Arianne to choose. She looked at each face of the candidates then her heart stopped. Arianne forgot everything she had to do and ran for the line of could-be Redeemers.

Chapter 39

GMAB

For the first time in his life, Balthazar stood slack-jawed. Arianne didn't take a second to think about her choice. Before he could stop her, she bolted toward the line of seven Redeemer decoys. What the hell? Pins and needles ran up and down his left arm. His chest tightened. If a heart attack felt like this, he'd drop dead in seconds.

Did she stop and think? No! What Niko saw in this impulsive chick escaped him. Balthazar snapped his mouth shut. He saw their deaths. Plain as day this would be the last they'd exist together. He'd slap her again. If they made it out of this alive, he'd slap her silly. His hand itched for it. His only consolation? Watching Zakariel look as dumb as he did. Two powerful creatures in the Underverse bested by a human girl. Balthazar shook his head. He had to admit it was funny. Downright hilarious. Maybe he'd taken a hit of the Angel's tears after all, and this entire thing was just a stupid hallucination. But in what hallucination would he get to see the Heavenly Host's eyes bug out of their sockets?

Zakariel's wings twitched in a way that told Balthazar he was too surprised to control the muscles holding them still. His great dignity was shattered. Balthazar forgave Arianne her impulsive nature. She had managed to shock the unshockable Zakariel. There was hope for her yet.

Arianne ran for the second to the last girl farthest from where Zakariel stood. The Redeemer decoy Arianne zeroed in on had long brown hair with hints of red mixed into the strands. In the right light, she'd have flames for highlights. Her heart-shaped face turned from calm to surprised. The white Grecian gown she wore enhanced her curves instead of drowning them in fabric. Balthazar would have thought of her as beautiful if his eyes weren't riveted to the flame-haired girl risking her life on a hunch. Well—Balthazar corrected himself—she didn't have a life to risk. Her soul. Yes, she risked her very soul. He had to admire her for that. He couldn't be too sure if she really did go on a hunch because their connection was fading by the second. He guessed they didn't need it anymore. Granmare Baba's magic always had an expiration date, and he couldn't tell if he liked that their connection faded or was disappointed.

Then the unexpected happened. The girl Arianne ran to opened her arms and Arianne flew into them. Balthazar cocked his head to the side. Both girls jumped into each other's arms before the one in the gown pulled back and cupped Arianne's face in both her hands, tears glistening in her eyes, a wide smile on her Cupid's bow lips.

Balthazar's brows rose a fraction. Now that both girls stood together, he made out the similarities in the slant of their eyes, the shape of their cheekbones, the curve of their lower lips. What were the chances?

"This can't be," Zakariel sputtered. "How?"

Arianne and the girl turned toward the still-in-shock Heavenly Host, question marks on both their pretty faces. They looked so much alike Balthazar wanted to kick himself for not noticing it sooner.

"What's the matter, Zakariel?" Balthazar grinned because his job just got easier. Sort of.

Zakariel pointed a trembling finger at Arianne and continued to sputter. "She couldn't have been able to pick out the Redeemer."

The surprise on Arianne's face and the calm smile on the girl—who Balthazar suspected to be Arianne's younger sister—confirmed it all. He could have laughed then if he wasn't too busy searching for the whistle he kept in one of the pockets of his singed coat. He may have to replace it after all this craziness was over.

"Are you saying you stacked the deck against us, Zakariel?" Balthazar clucked, shaking his head. "That isn't very sporting for a Heavenly Host."

"Oh shut up." Zakariel's face crumpled. "You know as well as I she's no longer attached to her body. Did you really think you could hide it from me?"

The girl who held Arianne frowned. "Is that true, Ari?"

Balthazar's heart cracked at the question.

Arianne bowed her head and nodded. "I didn't think I'd ever see you again, Carrie. I should have known you'd be the Redeemer. When Niko reaped you, your soul was different from the others."

"What?"

"I'll tell you all about it later."

Carrie stepped away from Arianne and spread her arms at an angle. Golden light engulfed her. Arianne shielded her eyes as did Zakariel. Balthazar stood far away enough that he didn't have to shield his own. In the distraction the Redeemer created for him, he finally found what he was feeling for.

He fished out what resembled a dog whistle and blew on it. Only one creature in the Underverse would hear the subsonic call. Balthazar could only hope it came in time as he returned the whistle into his coat.

The golden light receded and concentrated behind Carrie. Electrical sparks outlined her transparent wings. As the Redeemer, she had a set of four — two on each side. They stretched out and dispersed the excess energy manifesting them caused. The air in the amphitheater crackled. The six other decoys backed away from Carrie and returned to wherever Zakariel had summoned them from. Balthazar didn't need to know the whats and whys of it. Arianne — by sheer luck — had picked the right one. She didn't need to be attached to her body. This new information niggled at Balthazar. Could it be that D and Tomas had known all along? Had he worried about Arianne's thread for nothing? His molars rubbed against each other hard, the tip of one of his fangs piercing his lower lip. Oh, they were going to pay.

While Balthazar mulled over the various tortures he'd inflict on D and his liar for a right hand man when he got back to the Crossroads, Arianne stood dumbstruck, her mouth open. She stared at her sister like she didn't recognize the other girl. She blinked several times before closing her mouth again.

"That's better," Carrie said as a sigh. She folded her transparent wings behind her in a flutter of golden sparks. "I hate having to hide my wings. It always feels like stuffing tissue in a bra." She giggled, the girliest sound Balthazar wished he'd never ever heard. "When Zakariel told me we'd have visitors, I never in a gazillion years thought it would be you, Ari."

Swiping away yet another flood of tears that twisted Balthazar's insides, Arianne laughed. "Cool wings, sis."

Carrie twirled around. "Aren't they just awesome? They came when I got here."

"So, Ben?"

"Yeah." Carrie pursed her lips. "The second I heard the rumor, I sent Zakariel to the auction." Her eyes widened. "Don't tell me you were there."

Balthazar frowned when Arianne averted her gaze in an effort to hide her blush. Did she feel ashamed of being at the mansion? He'd warned her against it, but she insisted on going in with him. She shouldn't feel guilty about her decision.

Balthazar rolled his eyes. Why did he worry about that when they had other things they needed to do? *Focus,* he thought.

"Way too many reunions. We've got to jet, Arianne." He pointed at the ring on her finger.

"What does he mean?" Carrie asked Arianne.

Arianne raised the hand with the ring, the pulse dangerously weak now. "You have to come with us, Carrie."

"And why do I have to do that?"

"Because you need to pull out a knife from Death's chest." Arianne looked into her sister's eyes. "I promised I'd help him in return for Niko's life. If you don't do this, Death will lose his powers and that's going to cause a butt load of problems in the Crossroads and our world."

Carrie's face softened. "I'd love to help, I really would—"

"She can't leave Haven," Zakariel interrupted, finally getting his wits back, much to Balthazar's irritation. Was it too much to ask for that they leave without incident?

"Bullshit," Balthazar said in response to Zakariel. In the distance, he heard the distinctive neighing of their ride.

Zakariel leveled a pointed glare at him. "That was your plan all along, wasn't it? To take the Redeemer away from here. I will not stand for it."

"Not like you can do anything." Balthazar shrugged. "I'm borrowing her for a bit. Once she's done pulling my mother's blade out of Death's chest you can have her back."

"Brianne's Bitterness is your mom's knife?" Arianne's question held as much shock as her face showed.

"Who do you think Brianne is?" Balthazar spat back, never taking his eyes off Zakariel. He slowly manifested his scythe, keeping it invisible for as long as possible.

"Well, sorry for not putting that together fast enough for you."

Balthazar loved it when Arianne got sarcastic on him. It brought out the fire in her blue eyes. Again with the not focusing. He cursed himself for easily being distracted by Arianne. He had stayed with her far too long already. She was beginning to rub off on him.

"Who's he, Ari?" Carrie touched Arianne arm.

"Balthazar," Arianne said. "He helped me get here." She turned and faced her sister head on. "Carrie, you have to come with us. Please. You're the only one who can pull the knife out."

"No!" Zakariel answered when Carrie opened her mouth to respond.

The Heavenly Host moved toward the Redeemer when the Nightmare Steed arrived. One side of Balthazar's lips quirked up. Just in time. Zakariel froze, watching the giant blue-black stallion with black flames for hooves, mane, and tail land on the center of the amphitheater. The magical animal pawed at the ground, bobbing its head up and down. Black flames flared out of its nostrils.

Before Zakariel could recover, Balthazar fully manifested his scythe and cut across his palm. He pushed off from where he stood, letting the blood pool in his cupped palm. Reaching the Nightmare Steed, he placed his hand under its mouth. The steed sucked up his blood and neighed. Once it accepted the bargain of transport back to the Crossroads, Balthazar sprinted toward Zakariel. The shocked Heavenly Host didn't have time to react. Balthazar sliced up with his scythe, taking one of Zakariel's wings with it. Then he de-manifested his scythe so he had his hands free.

As the severed wing landed with a thud on the ground and Zakariel fell to his knees, clutching at the wound, Balthazar grabbed a screaming Carrie and hauled her over the back of the steed. He climbed up after her then reached out for Arianne.

"Let's go," he commanded the wide-eyed girl.

Arianne looked from the bleeding Zakariel up to him. "You cut off his wing."

"It'll grow back."

Carrie twisted and slapped him across the face. Balthazar's head didn't even twitch to the side despite the force of the blow. She wasn't strong enough. The Redeemer saved, not hurt. The guilt in her eyes for slapping him showed her nature loud and clear. He glared at Carrie just to show her who was boss before he returned his gaze at Arianne.

"What the hell are you waiting for?" he shouted.

A fleet of angels gathered above them. If they didn't leave now, they wouldn't make it out of Haven. But Arianne stood frozen. He'd given her another reason to believe he played the bad guy in this scenario. If it wasn't for his bargain to protect her, he'd leave her where she stood like an idiot staring up at him.

At the end of his patience, Balthazar leaned down and grabbed Arianne by the arm. With one heave, he pulled her behind him onto the steed. Then he grabbed the steed's black fire mane and pulled, kicking it at its sides. He felt Arianne's arms snake around his waist just as the Nightmare Steed took off.

With a maniacal grin on his face, Balthazar called for his scythe once again. *Time to make some room.* As the Nightmare Steed flew into the gray sky, angels and their not-so-white wings fell.

Chapter 40

DEGT

Icy air whipped Arianne's short hair all over her face. She tightened her grip around Balthazar's waist. Not that she'd die if she fell; at least, she thought she wouldn't die, but she sure as hell didn't want to test the theory. She could barely keep her eyes open from their speed. She peeked down and regretted it. The landscape of the Underverse zipped by at a dizzying pace.

"Why couldn't we use the Nightmare Steed all this time?" Arianne asked through the whipping wind. She wasn't sure if Balthazar heard her, so it surprised Arianne when he replied. The guy had good ears. She'd give him that.

"Nightmare Steeds can only be used once. I figured now is that time."

"You didn't have to cut off his wing, you know," she heard Carrie say, the wind carrying her words to her ears before completely taking them away.

"Bought us time." Balthazar snorted. "I don't even know why I'm defending myself. I cut off his wing because it was fun to see him suffer. There."

"You're lying, I can tell."

"And how do you know that?"

Arianne had to crane her neck so she could catch their argument, clenching her teeth against the cold that had been steadily creeping into her body since her thread had been cut. Did death—the real kind—feel like this? Cold and lonely? Arianne clawed at the buckles on Balthazar, drawing comfort from their metallic hardness. Carrie's next words distracted her from thoughts of eventually turning into a Wraith and what Balthazar would do if that happened.

"I'm the Redeemer. You can't lie when you're this close to me."

Balthazar snorted again. She couldn't connect with his thoughts anymore so she couldn't be a hundred percent sure what he was thinking, though. Her heart ached at their connection being completely gone. A part of her missed it already.

"It'll grow back," Balthazar grumbled. "I'm pretty sure he's already on his way here."

"Kidnapping the Redeemer. You have balls. A guy with your name should have a set."

Arianne almost laughed. Carrie always had a way of telling the truth and making it sound so funny.

"Where'd you find this guy, Ari?" Carrie twisted so she could look at Arianne around Balthazar's bulk.

Arianne smiled at her sister, still not used to seeing her so healthy. "He got roped into helping Death pull out the dagger in his chest."

"Mr. Charming Personality got conned into helping out?"

"It's like you already know him." Arianne wiggled her eyebrows and Carrie wiggled hers back. Carrie always had the knack of reading people even before actually interacting with them. She got Balthazar spot on. Well, maybe not the bad guy aspect of his personality, but Arianne decided to give her a couple more minutes.

"I should just chuck the two of you overboard," Balthazar said through his teeth.

"You do that and you lose what little chance you've got at ruling the Crossroads," Arianne bit back.

"You want Death's job?" Carrie asked Balthazar.

"Chicks suck," came his venomous reply.

Something about the way Carrie looked up at Balthazar disturbed Arianne. She understood why Carrie had to sit in front with Balthazar's arms around her. He didn't want Carrie to fall or escape. She got that loud and clear, but it didn't mean she had to like it. Arianne shut her eyes and pushed away all thoughts of jealousy. Why would she be jealous of something as little as who got to sit in Balthazar's arms? She loved Niko. She'd done all this for him. How could she be jealous? No matter how strong the urge to kick Carrie overboard was, Arianne had to remind herself that she loved Carrie and Carrie loved Ben. Heck, she sent Zakariel to bid for Ben at that auction. Arianne's eyes opened then.

"How'd you know Ben was dead?" Guilt replaced Arianne's irrational jealousy after she asked the question.

Carrie twisted around again. "I was only going on a rumor. When Zakariel came back, he confirmed it was Ben." Her eyes watered. "How'd he…" She swallowed.

"Please not you too with the waterworks."

"Shut up, Balthazar." Arianne slapped him on the shoulder and he grunted.

In the silence that followed, Arianne put the right words together while Carrie waited—her expression openly expectant, which made things much harder for Arianne. She couldn't bear to break her sister's heart—Redeemer or not.

Finding no other way to soften the blow of the truth, Arianne dropped her gaze. "After you died—" she swallowed around the prickly lump in her throat "—Ben sacrificed himself so I could live."

The confusion in Carrie's face forced Arianne to summarize everything that had happened between her and Niko. She hadn't spoken so fast in her life, spilling out as much detail as she could. When she'd finished, she could hardly breathe no matter how much air sped past them.

"Niko's a Reaper," were the first words out of Carrie's lips, her eyes wide.

"Of Georgia," Arianne added.

"A total asshole if you ask me."

"No one's asking you, Balthazar!" Arianne slapped him on the shoulder again.

"Keep slapping me and I'll forget that I have to protect you." He glared at her over his shoulder. Arianne didn't cower at his murderous glare. He could bark all he wanted—and he really did have a bite worse than his bark—but right now, the only thing that mattered was her conversation with Carrie.

Arianne debated whether to tell Carrie what Ben had said on the raft.

"Tell me," she said as if reading Arianne's mind. Carrie read expressions as well as people. She didn't need mind reading powers.

"Ben said after you died he had nothing else to live for."

"Ben didn't want to live without me?" Carrie's heart showed on her face. Half hurt, half clearly touched, which equaled to a whole lot of love.

Arianne couldn't be sure of the tone of Carrie's question. "What happens now that he's at Haven?"

Carrie blinked away her tears and pulled a smile on. "He'll be safe."

A measure of relief blunted the guilt in Arianne's chest. Ben's rightful place was with Carrie. Even when they were alive, seeing them together, how he hovered over her, always told Arianne what she should have known from the beginning. She'd just been too blind, or her attention had been somewhere else the whole time.

Niko.

Did she really love him? Did she do all this for the right reasons? Being with Balthazar added a grain of confusion. She shouldn't be doubting her feelings. So what if she didn't know enough about Niko?

"So."

One word and Arianne's attention returned to Carrie. Her sister's expression changed. She became more formal, her face looking older and far wiser than her sixteen years. Arianne waited for Carrie to continue.

"You need me to pull out Brianne's Bitterness from Death's chest to get Niko back."

"I crossed the Underverse to find you."

"That's not what I want to hear, Ari."

Dropping her gaze, Arianne nodded. "Yes. I need your help pulling out the dagger in Death's chest."

Carrie rolled her eyes. "You should have said so."

Arianne's jaw dropped. "I thought that's what I just said?"

"Ari, if you asked me to help you I would have."

"What?"

"Redeemers are sworn to help when asked," Balthazar grumbled like the information annoyed him. "But Zakariel wouldn't have let you go."

"I could have convinced him to let me go." Carrie fearlessly thumped Balthazar's chest. "I can be very persuasive. Now you have half of Haven after you."

At the same time, all three of them looked over their shoulders. In the distance, a cloud of white neared.

"I didn't think the Underverse had white clouds," Arianne said.

"It doesn't." Balthazar's lips disappeared into a thin line. He faced forward again. "Hold on."

Arianne's reply died when her stomach jumped into her throat. They plummeted at breakneck speed. Going up she didn't mind. Going down from this height, on the other hand, she hated like broccoli. In true Carrie fashion, her sister raised both her arms and screamed in delight, like they were riding a roller coaster.

The Nightmare Steed landed in a swirl of dirt and dust. Balthazar reached behind him and grabbed a fistful of Arianne's shirt from behind. In a swift tug, he lifted Arianne off the horse and plopped her on her feet. Balthazar quickly followed. Carrie reached out to him and he pulled her off the horse too. Arianne gritted her teeth at Balthazar's gentleness toward her sister. Why couldn't he treat her more like that?

Balthazar manifested his scythe and twirled it like a baton before he ripped an opening through the Crossroads barrier. Without speaking, he grabbed Arianne again and manhandled her into the hole he'd made. Carrie followed without having to be pushed in.

"Hey!" Arianne lost it. "Quit the physical abuse."

"I'll hold them off," Balthazar said to someone behind Arianne. "Get them to D's office. Then bring the Redeemer back here."

As soon as Arianne whirled around to see who Balthazar was barking at, Tomas touched her shoulder and the scenery changed. Her vision tripled when they arrived at Death's office. She didn't have time to worry about Balthazar facing down an army of angels and one pissed off Heavenly Host.

Her shoes stuck to the ground when she tried to move. She looked down and made out something dark. Her gaze followed the spot and quickly realized she stood in the pool of blood coming from Death. She gasped. If she thought Death couldn't look any worse than he did before they'd left, she'd been so wrong.

The once androgynous being who had oozed power had been reduced to skin and bone. His golden hair hung limp and white, clinging to his sunken cheeks and sweaty forehead. His skin rivaled the gray of the Underverse sky. His once alive robe only twitched on the floor around him, soaking in his blood. The room had a sickly sweet smell. It choked Arianne every time she breathed in.

"What…" he rasped out.

"Don't speak, Master," Tomas said—the weight of worry on every word. "Arianne has returned with the Redeemer."

Like staring at a wreck, Arianne couldn't take her eyes away from Death. Carrie moved forward, uncaring if her white gown soaked up the blood on the floor. She wrapped her hand around the hilt of the dagger. With one quick tug and a sickening squelch, the blade slid out of Death's chest.

Death inhaled as if for the first time. His frail shoulders rose in relief before a blinding light engulfed him as if he were on fire. Tomas grabbed Arianne's arm and pulled her and Carrie out of the office. The double doors shut after them with a loud bang.

"Is he gonna be all right?" Arianne asked, never taking her eyes off the doors. In her head she could still see Death at the brink of death—or something really close to it since Death couldn't really die. Not in the human sense.

"He'll be fine now." Tomas sounded as relieved as Death's gasp had sounded.

Carrie called her name, and Arianne turned to face her sister. The blade she held in her hand glowed red. She let it go, and it hovered in the air in front of her. Before Arianne could ask about the blade, Tomas touched her shoulder again and she found herself back in the room she'd woken up in the first time, Carrie right by her side.

"You really have to warn me before you do that teleporting thing, Tomas." Arianne clutched at her stomach, ready to puke.

"Your thread has been cut," Tomas said in response.

Arianne's already queasy stomach flipped like a pancake. "You said you could fix it."

"Not me." The worry in Tomas's wise old eyes worried Arianne tenfold.

"Death," Carrie said.

Unable to speak, Arianne faced her sister. She'd begun to tremble, and breathing got really hard all of a sudden.

"Only Death can fix this," Carrie finished for the benefit of Arianne's speechless state.

Again Arianne found herself painted into a corner. She could see it now. If Death really was the only one who could reattach her thread to her body—or whatever he had to do—another bargain would have to be struck. Ben had sacrificed his life to save hers. She'd sacrificed her life to save Niko's. What more could she give? Had Death played her this whole time? Could he have known Carrie was the Redeemer? Arianne fell to her knees when the realization struck her like a physical blow. A chill ran down her spine.

She hugged herself. "In the Underverse, nothing is free."

Chapter 41

BIO

Outside the Crossroads, just beyond the barrier, ten angels surrounded Balthazar in a loose circle. He flicked his gaze at each one of the faces he could see and used his sixth sense to keep tabs on the ones he couldn't see behind him. He'd sent away the Nightmare Steed so it wouldn't get in the way of his scythe. He'd hate to accidentally kill another one.

No one moved except for Balthazar who was spinning his scythe. The air the rotation kicked up ruffled the feathers of the angels nearest the scythe. Zakariel stood at a distance, his arms folded. More angels gathered behind him. The wing Balthazar had lopped off had healed like he'd told the sisters. He grinned at the twitching wing. The new feathers growing in must itch, and Zakariel—with his pride as Heavenly Host—refused to scratch.

"Itchy?" Balthazar asked. He'd dug his grave already. A few more feet wouldn't matter much. "Bitch to be you right now."

"You cut off my wing," Zakariel said, enunciating each word like they tasted bad in his mouth. "I should have let your mother kill you when she had a chance."

"Wow, that's the best you can do?" Balthazar's smile reached his eyes. He'd laugh if it wouldn't distract him from the horde of angels waiting for their leader's attack signal. He couldn't let his guard down, not until Tomas returned with Carrie in tow. "I get it, my mother hated me. At least she had the decency not to sleep with a prick like you."

Zakariel's nostrils flared. "If it wasn't an insult to your mother, I'd call you a son of a bitch."

"Ah, but you just did."

A pinch of pride at chopping off Zakariel's wing made getting beaten to a pulp by a bunch of winged pansies worth the bruises. He'd always wanted to catch the Heavenly Host by surprise, and now that he had, he didn't care what they did to him. The angels couldn't kill him. They could try, and it would hurt when they did, but the only one who stood a real chance at ending him itched like a madman a few yards away. Maybe a laugh wouldn't be so bad after all.

"Come on, Zakariel. I was just doing what I had to. A bargain is a bargain." Balthazar planted his scythe on the ground by his side and shrugged dramatically, adding a head tilt too. "I needed the Redeemer. You wouldn't have let her leave Haven, so I took matters into my own hands. Basically, nothing you wouldn't do."

"I wouldn't hurt someone to get what I want."

"That's the difference between you and me." He folded his arms, puffing out his chest. "Bad guy, remember?"

"You cannot just take the Redeemer from Haven, Balthazar. There are consequences."

"From the looks of your goon squad, I see that. But if you wait a little longer, I'm pretty sure she's done pulling my mother's blade from D's chest. Then we can move on and no one has to die." He eyed the closest angel and showed fang. The angel stood firm, but Balthazar couldn't mistake the slight wing tremble.

Zakariel dropped his arms. "Brianne's Bitterness?"

Not the reaction Balthazar expected. He hid his own surprise with a smirk. His mother, still a monumental headache from beyond the grave. What had she done now to deserve utter shock from Zakariel?

"The one and only. My mother—" Balthazar shook his head "—always made the most annoying things. She even made a blade that could kill me. Can you imagine that?"

The Heavenly Host pointed at him. "Don't speak of her that way."

Oh, Balthazar was scared now. He rolled his eyes. The big bad angel threated him by pointing. "Come on, Zakariel. This doesn't have to get bloody. Tomas will return Carrie soon. If you just wait—"

"You forget what pulling out Brianne's Bitterness means for the one who does the act, you bastard. You just condemned the Redeemer."

This caught Balthazar off guard. He never knew of any consequences involved in the removal of the blade. Yes, only the Redeemer could handle the blade. He assumed this because his mother was a Heavenly Host and had a penchant for all things heavenly—well, except for his father. Balthazar almost spat at the thought, but he swallowed his ire and continued his conversation with Zakariel. The more time he bought, the less likely it was he'd have to fight off the angels. He had to conserve his energy for his showdown with D. The Crossroads would be his soon. Just a little more patience.

"Then tell me what I'm missing," Balthazar said nonchalantly.

A self-satisfied smile spread across Zakariel's face. "Finally, something I know about your mother that you don't."

"What are you? The encyclopedia of all things involving my mother? You need a hobby." Balthazar bit the inside of his lip. "Spit it out, you dick."

The sobering of the Heavenly Host bothered Balthazar more than it should have. The gray clouds above them grew darker. In the distance lightning still reverberated from Solara's anger. Balthazar had a lot of thinking to do when it came to pissing off powerful chicks. But in seconds, what he thought didn't matter. Zakariel might as well have stabbed him with his next words.

"The one who removes the blade stands as replacement."

"Replacement?" Balthazar asked, the word not making sense in his head right away.

Zakariel cocked his head along with an eyebrow as if accusing Balthazar of being slow. He spread his wings then folded them back in place. "Oh, I think you know what I mean."

"Son of a bitch!" Balthazar didn't know if he should be pissed or delighted. He went for pissed instead. It seemed like the right emotion to have. "You mean to tell me the Redeemer is the new Death?"

"Until you find the original Death, the Redeemer stands as the replacement."

"I call your bluff."

The Heavenly Host merely shrugged at him. "Why don't you go see for yourself? We'll wait out here."

Balthazar had heard enough. He picked up his scythe and slashed at the angels. Most of them managed to avoid the blow except for the last one who didn't quite time his jump right. The black blade sliced cleanly through the angel's legs from the knees. The screaming distracted the rest enough for Balthazar to run up to the barrier, cut his way in, and sprint toward the Crossroads. Dust swirled in his wake.

Carrie the new Death? It's not fucking possible.

As soon as the thought entered Balthazar's mind, he knew the "not possible" part was a lie. His stomach dropped. No wonder Zakariel hadn't attacked him himself. The bastard of a Heavenly Host had been waiting for the inevitable. Balthazar—the con of all con artists—had been royally conned. All this time he'd been played by D.

Balthazar refused to panic. He'd make it in time and this would be settled one way or the other. If he had to slice down the Redeemer to get what he wanted, he had no problem with that. He'd take over the Crossroads, and Zakariel would have to return to Haven Redeemer-light. Then Arianne's face flashed before Balthazar's eyes. In his fit of rage, he'd forgotten about the chit. She wouldn't stand for Carrie's death—again. Then he'd just have to go over her dead body. Balthazar pushed the option away as soon as it entered his head. His bargain with her prevented him from inflicting bodily harm—and how was he to protect her from himself? Damn it!

Fury bubbled up his throat by the time he'd made it to the wall. He barely saw straight from it. One leap later, he landed in the calm courtyard. Where chaos once reigned, now only order remained. Shadow Guards—those not at their posts—surrounded him. Balthazar licked his chops and cut his way through the swath of them. They stood no chance against him. The minions moved out of his way. They only attacked if their master Reapers asked them to, and right now, the Reapers were too stunned to order anyone to do anything. They'd finally made it into the Crossroads. The lockdown had ended. Which meant they didn't know the whole story. Balthazar took advantage of their ignorance. The less resistance he went up against the better.

His heart sped up faster than his feet carrying him toward the main building. He crashed through the entrance, reducing the wooden door to the size of toothpicks like he'd done at the Voyeur's mansion. The whisps no longer littered the hallway wailing their tiny lungs out. Instead, they scattered at the sight of him, finally having learned their lesson the last time he'd stomped through these halls.

Order at every turn. The Crossroads had returned to its normal well-oiled machine status. Zakariel had been right, no matter how much he refused to believe the Heavenly Host's claim before he had actual proof.

A figure materialized in front of him. "Whoa! Where're you headed off to in such a hurry, Balty?"

Balthazar skidded to a stop in time to keep from colliding with the considerable bulk of the Reaper of Texas and his silly cowboy hat. "Get out of my way, Travis."

The Texan frowned. "Well, if that isn't rude."

Impatient, Balthazar lifted the blade of his scythe against Travis's neck. The Reaper of Texas shifted his stance, his face losing its good-natured expression in favor of a murderous one.

"I suggest you remove that blade from my throat, Balthazar."

"Or what?" Balthazar bared his fangs, unwilling to be intimidated by the second most powerful Reaper in the Crossroads. Hell, he'd been angling for a fight. He'd been played and he didn't appreciate it. Heads would roll before he finished with the Crossroads. Fighting Travis would weaken him, but he estimated he'd have enough juice against a weakened D if he dispatched Travis fast enough.

Travis pinched the tip of the black blade and pulled it away from his throat. Then he stepped back and stuffed his hands into the back pockets of his jeans. The mischievous smile returned to his lips, softening his features. He shrugged.

"Look, on account of being busy, I'll let you pass for now." The Reaper of Texas raised a finger pistol at Balthazar and winked at him. "But the next time you dare raise your weapon at me, Balty, it'll be a different story. You understand me, partner?"

The cowboy disappeared at the exact second Balthazar's scythe sliced through where his body had been. The blade cut air instead. Balthazar cursed like a drunken sailor fresh from the sea. He even used some of the more colorful language he'd learned from his stint in the Nethers.

His anger still had no outlet, so Balthazar leaped back into action. Each turn he took from the entrance of the main building toward D's office pissed him off more. He wasn't officially a member of the Crossroads so he didn't have the power to teleport from one place to another — something he'd take care off once he resolved this shit with D. Damn his mother for putting a kink in his plans. Dead and still meddling in his life.

Seething by the time he reached D's office, Balthazar yanked open both doors, tearing them off their hinges. He stormed in, scythe ready to murder anyone inside.

He froze.

The chair at the center of the room sat empty in the midst of all the dried blood. A note with Balthazar's name scrolled in D's girly handwriting was waiting on the seat.

Balthazar stomped to the chair and picked up the note and unfolded it. At the center of the white paper a line had been written in the same curly script. It said:

Gone Fishing

Chapter 42

FUBAR

Arianne's short life flashed like a movie in front of her eyes, unlike the time she'd actually died. Now the reality of everything crashed into her like unforgiving waves, pulling her out then pushing her back in. She couldn't breathe. Death had gotten what he'd wanted from the beginning: her soul. She should have known he wouldn't let having a Certificate signed against her go, and he'd gotten Ben's soul as a bonus. She hated herself for what she'd put Ben through. Because of her he'd been put up for auction and had almost become a Wraith.

All the hurt and the pain came flooding back now. She hugged herself tighter. The floor bruised her knees. She'd never see her parents again. She'd never go back to school. And she'd probably never be with Niko. Death had played her. Bargaining with him wouldn't matter much anymore. What else could she give?

Gentle hands touched her shoulders. "Get up, Ari," Carrie whispered, tears in her words.

Arianne looked up at her sister's dry face. Carrie had always been the stronger of the two of them. Arianne guessed that must be why she'd become the Redeemer.

"Everything's gone, Carrie," Arianne whispered back. "I have nothing left to give." Her fingers dug into her arms. She preferred any pain other than the loss she felt inside. When she started this journey, she had thought mourning Ben and Carrie her main concern. Little did she know that she'd be mourning herself by the end. Whoever said the journey mattered more than the destination lied. Arianne hated that person. The destination — death — mattered. Why would people be scared of dying if it didn't?

"I'm tired, Carrie." Arianne bowed her head until her chin touched her chest. "I'm so tired."

"Then rest."

"You don't understand. No amount of rest will save me."

"It doesn't mean you should give up."

Anger pinged inside Arianne's chest. She didn't think twice about pushing Carrie away from her. She couldn't stand the pep talk right now. She heard Carrie stumble back, but she didn't fall. Either she grabbed on to something or Tomas caught her before she hit the ground. Why should she care? Then guilt replaced Arianne's anger. Of course she should care. Carrie was still her sister.

"I'm sorry," Arianne said through the bitterness in her mouth. "I just don't know what to do from here."

"Let me talk to the Master," Tomas offered.

Arianne lifted her head again. Tomas had his hands on Carrie's shoulders. He'd caught her after all.

"And what good will that do?" Arianne snarled. "What else will he ask of me if I bargain with him again?"

Tomas's face softened. "You brought the Redeemer here. You saved him. I believe that's more than enough."

"But what about Niko? That was the bargain. I bring back the Redeemer and he gives Niko his humanity without taking my eyesight and my memories. Reattaching me to my body — or whatever he's gonna do — that's another bargain."

"You don't know that."

But Arianne saw the doubt in Tomas's eyes. Even he couldn't guarantee what Death would say or do. She might as well accept her death now and get on with the next step. Processing maybe? She didn't have to be escorted to the Crossroads anymore. And who would reap her?

"Tomas!"

All heads turned to Travis. He'd popped into the room, a panicked expression in his well-tanned face.

"Not right now, Travis," Tomas said, gesturing for the Reaper of Texas to leave.

"Oh, I think you'll want to hear this," Travis drawled, his accent getting thicker with each word out of his mouth.

"Fine." Tomas sighed. "What now?"

"The Master's gone."

"What do you mean the Master's gone?" Tomas cocked his head, expression unbelieving.

"Check for yourself."

Travis touched Tomas on the shoulder and they both disappeared. Carrie and Arianne looked at each other, mirroring each other's confusion. A second later, Tomas returned, his face ashen.

"He's gone," he said.

"What do you mean 'he's gone'?" Arianne repeated his earlier question to Travis.

Tomas swallowed. "He's nowhere in the Crossroads. The lockdown is over, which means anyone can come and go."

"But what about—"

The door to the room slammed open like a bomb had detonated. Arianne and Carrie flinched at the same time. Tomas widened his stance, like he expected something terrible to walk into the room. And he was right.

Balthazar, face blank but eyes blazing, entered the room. White flames covered his body like a wild aura. The flames touched his scythe, giving it an even deadlier edge. The hairs on the back of Arianne's neck stood while goose bumps covered every part of her body. In their travels together, never had she seen Balthazar this way. He brought scary to a whole new level. The Boogeyman had nothing on him right now.

"Balthazar?" Arianne said after she ripped her tongue from the roof of her mouth.

He kept his gaze on Carrie for some reason when he threw a crumpled piece of paper her way. Arianne reached for the ball and unfurled the note, her face clearly showing confusion.

"Gone fishing?" She looked at Tomas, but the Reaper of California only shook his head at her, the same confusion on his face.

Then Balthazar laughed. The sound should have broken the tension in the room. Instead, it sent a chill up Arianne's spine. Laughter may be leaving Balthazar's mouth, but his face remained cold and emotionless. If she'd ever imagined seeing anyone snap, Balthazar painted a perfect picture of what it would look like.

When his laugher died, he pointed his scythe at Tomas. "Your bastard of a Master played me, Tomas. And you know how much I hate being played."

"I don't understand."

Arianne didn't even see what happened. Balthazar moved too fast. First he stood by the door then a gaping cut ran across the Reaper of California's chest. Carrie screamed. She ran from Tomas to Arianne and they huddled on the floor together in each other's arms. Tomas fell to his knees like he couldn't quite understand what had actually happened. Blood quickly soaked the front of his expensive suit. He touched his chest before staring at his bloody hand. Then he collapsed into a pool of his own blood.

"Wrong answer," Balthazar growled at Tomas and kicked his prone body for good measure. Then he turned toward Arianne and Carrie. The tips of his fangs touched his lower lip. He tilted his head as if he'd forgotten they were in the room with him. Arianne held on to her sister tighter.

"Balthazar, what happened?" Arianne forced herself to ask. Maybe if she got him to calm down, he'd stop looking at them like fresh meat ready for slicing. No matter how much she wanted to blink, Arianne didn't dare.

"What happened?" Balthazar parroted back like he didn't recognize her. Then he pointed at the note.

"I don't understand." Arianne lifted the piece of paper. "What does this mean?"

"The one who pulls out the blade replaces whoever the blade has stabbed."

"You mean Carrie's the new Death? Is that why Death is gone?"

"What?" Carrie asked in panic. "I can't be the new Death. I'm just getting used to being the Redeemer. This can't be happening. Ow!"

Arianne squeezed Carrie's arm until her sister stopped babbling. "Carrie," she said without looking away from Balthazar, "I love you, but I really need you to shut up right now."

Carrie whimpered, but she clamped her lips shut, which Arianne thanked the heavens for. Fear trumped babbling every time.

"Give me the Redeemer, little girl." Balthazar fully faced them now.

Arianne hated it when he reverted to calling her anything other than her name. It said reasoning with him wouldn't work. But she had to try anyway.

"No," she said bravely. Arianne pushed Carrie back until her sister positioned herself behind her. Then she reached back and wrapped her arms around Carrie's waist. Carrie gripped Arianne's shoulders until they hurt.

"Oh come now." Balthazar took a step forward. "The bargain was that I got to challenge Death for ruling the Crossroads when Brianne's Bitterness had been pulled out. Since the Redeemer is the new Death, she doesn't need healing. Let's get on with this." He positioned his scythe across his front, ready to slash at them like he'd done with Tomas.

"Balthazar—" Arianne licked her lower lip, her breathing shallow "—let's talk about this." Her head spun from the lack of air. "I'm sure there's been a mistake."

"Zakariel told me about the blade. There's no mistake."

Arianne instinctively reached for the belt on her thigh.

"Are you looking for this?" Balthazar reached into his coat side pocket and pulled out the knife Tomas had given her. "You think I wouldn't take this away from you the first chance I got?"

"Don't be a jerk, Balthazar. Carrie's my sister."

"And I should care because?"

"After everything we've been through?"

Balthazar snorted. "Just because we shared some meaningless trip doesn't make us friends, little girl. I'm here for one thing."

"The Crossroads, I get it."

"Then hand over the Redeemer."

Arianne's eyes widened at the barely leashed insanity in Balthazar. Then she said the words she'd never thought she'd have to say, "Over my dead body."

A corner of Balthazar's lips quirked up. "Suit yourself." He raised his scythe and pushed off from where he stood over Tomas's body.

Never taking her eyes away from Balthazar—who'd become a black blur—Arianne prepared to die for the second time since she'd gotten to the Underverse. If it meant saving Carrie, even just for a second, she'd gladly do it.

Why did everything slow down when you were about to die?

The question popped into Arianne's head without her really thinking about it. She watched Balthazar lift the black blade above his head, his face showing no remorse for his actions. All of Arianne's hopes shattered. Whatever good she thought Balthazar possessed vanished the second he decided she needed to die for the sake of getting what he wanted. He'd been right all along. He was the bad guy in all of this.

A shadow ran in front of Arianne. Something wet splashed on her face, followed by blades grinding against each other. She wiped away the wetness on her cheek and blinked to focus her vision. The first thing her eyes latched on to was a striking blue blade with circle cut-outs preventing the black blade of Balthazar's scythe from coming down. Then — just as she gasped — her gaze moved from the wet black hair plastered against the back of a head she'd recognize anywhere. She'd spent most of her high school life staring at it. She realized the whole body standing in front of her was dripping wet. Only then did his being naked register. Arianne flicked her eyes up to the dueling blades again.

"Get out of my way, Nikolas!" Balthazar said through the wall of his teeth, fangs bared.

The words confirmed what Arianne already knew. Her heart soared. Somehow Niko had gotten out of that crystal coffin to save her from Balthazar. She'd never loved him more than in that moment. She should have never doubted her feelings for him. Balthazar only said all those things about not really knowing Niko to mess with her head. She shouldn't have trusted anything that came out of Balthazar's mouth.

"Niko." She said his name like a prayer.

Without losing his footing against Balthazar's push to bring the blade of his scythe down, Niko glanced over his shoulder at Arianne. She smiled up at him, expecting he'd grin back at her the way he always did.

Instead he frowned and said, "Do I know you?"

Acknowledgments

This novel took me a long time to write. I lost the story for a while. Then, when all hope seemed to be lost, Balthazar came along and brought the story back to life for me. He's the bad guy who saved the day. I love him to bits, even if he hates that I do.

As always, I first have to thank my family. We are a small group. Some even say a core group, and I'm fine with that. When someone's at the hospital, the house really feels empty. I thank the universe every day for having a father who forgives my shortcomings and bursts of temper and continues to be proud of me. I'm thankful for the constant presence of the Momager in my life. She's my guiding light. My trusted advisor. My Emily Gilmore. And my brother, the guy who tolerates me…and that says a lot. You don't know.

I want to thank Elizabeth for continuing to believe. This story wouldn't have been told without your gracious acceptance and awesomeness. Thank you for Omnific. You're on my People to Meet in the Future list.

Thank you, Lisa, for asking me when I would be submitting the next book. I started my 2013 right because of that email. As for the next book? It's getting there. I promise. ;-)

A hundred thank yous go to Colleen. You guide the way. I wouldn't have seen the holes in need of plugging without your excellent notes. You make the process so much fun. Looking forward to your notes for the next book…that is, after I finish writing it.

A meteor shower of gratitude rains on Kathy for batch after batch of comment bubbles. You totally helped me clarify images and avoid choppy sentences. You shined the light on the right spot at the right second.

A champagne bottle goes to my critique partner, Angie, for falling in love with this story. She is the first person who reads any of my stuff. She sees the raw and the ugly and never hesitates to help me clean shit up. I love you, Sis!

Baskets of chocolates go to Traci, publicist extraordinaire. Thank you for helping me think up ways to get people to pay attention to my books. Your support is priceless. I look forward to actually giving you a tackle hug in real life.

Bouquets of carnations go to everyone else behind the scenes. I may not know all of you by name, but please know that you are in my heart. I would be lost without your talents. All the mistakes found in this novel are my fault alone and no one else's.

Hugs and kisses go to you, dear reader. Thank you for accepting Balthazar into your life. Do you believe in the good in him? He won't ever admit it, but I think he can be a sweetheart when he wants to. Thank you for joining me in this journey through the Underverse. Know that the Voyeur is watching you.

About the Author

When Kate Evangelista was told she had a knack for writing stories, she did the next best thing: entered medical school. After realizing she wasn't going to be the next Doogie Howser, M.D., Kate wandered into the Literature department of her university and never looked back. Today, she is in possession of a piece of paper that says to the world she owns a Literature degree. To make matters worse, she took Master's courses in creative writing. In the end, she realized to be a writer, none of what she had mattered. What really mattered? Writing. Plain and simple, honest to God, sitting in front of her computer, writing. Today, she has six completed young adult novels.

✦ ⟶ Romantic Suspense ⟵ ✦

Whirlwind by Robin DeJarnett
The CONduct Series: With Good Behavior & Bad Behavior by Jennifer Lane
Indivisible by Jessica McQuinn
Between the Lies by Alison Oburia

✦ ⟶ New Adult ⟵ ✦

Three Daves by Nicki Elson
Streamline by Jennifer Lane
Shades of Atlantis by Carol Oates
Beside Your Heart by Mary Whitney
Romancing the Bookworm by Kate Evangelista
Fighting Fate by Linda Kage

✦ ⟶ Young Adult ⟵ ✦

The Ember Series: Ember and *Iridescent* by Carol Oates
Breaking Point by Jess Bowen
Life, Liberty, and Pursuit by Susan Kaye Quinn
Embrace & *Hold Tight* by Cherie Colyer
Destiny's Fire by Trisha Wolfe
The Reaper Series: Reaping Me Softly & *UnReap My Heart* by Kate Evangelista

✦ ⟶ Historical Romance ⟵ ✦

Cat O' Nine Tails by Patricia Leever
Burning Embers by Hannah Fielding
Good Ground by Tracy Winegar

✦ ⟶ Erotic Romance ⟵ ✦

The Keyhole Series: Becoming sage (book one) by Kasi Alexander
The Keyhole Series: Saving sunni (book two) by Kasi & Reggie Alexander
The Winemaker's Dinner: Appetizers & *Entrée* by Dr. Ivan Rusilko & Everly Drummond
The Winemaker's Dinner: Dessert by Dr. Ivan Rusilko

＊—•Anthologies•—＊

A Valentine Anthology including short stories by Alice Clayton,
Jennifer DeLucy, Nicki Elson, Jessica McQuinn, Victoria Michaels,
and Alison Oburia

＊—•Singles•—＊

It's Only Kinky the First Time by Kasi Alexander
Learning the Ropes by Kasi & Reggie Alexander
The Winemaker's Dinner: RSVP by Dr. Ivan Rusilko
The Winemaker's Dinner: No Reservations by Everly Drummond
Big Guns by Jessica McQuinn
Concessions by Robin DeJarnett
Starstruck by Lisa Sanchez
New Flame by BJ Thornton
Shackled by Debra Anastasia
Swim Recruit by Jennifer Lane
Sway by Nicki Elson
Full Speed Ahead by Susan Kaye Quinn
The Second Sunrise by Hannah Downing
The Summer Prince by Carol Oates
Whatever it Takes by Sarah M. Glover
Clarity by Patricia Leever
A Christmas Wish by Autumn Markus